IN THE WAVES OF TRISTWICK

IN THE WAVES OF TRISTWICK

A CORNISH ROMANCE, BOOK FOUR

DEBORAH M. HATHAWAY

DRAFT HORSE
PUBLISHING

BOOKS BY DEBORAH M. HATHAWAY

For Joanna—

My role model, my sister, my supporter,
my friend.

PRONUNCIATION GUIDE

Morvoren – more-VOR-in
Trevik – TREH-vik
Tristwick – TRIST-wik
Golowduyn – goal-oh-DEW-in
Tregalwen – treh-GAWL-when
Edern - ED-ern
Enyon - EN-yun
ye – ee

CHAPTER ONE

Cornwall, September 1815
   Tucked away in a secluded cove in Cornwall, a small fishing port by the name of Tristwick rested in the dim, grey light of dawn. By land, the residents' stone houses could not be seen, hidden by undulating hills and towering cliffsides. By sea, however, aboard his own three-masted fishing lugger, Trevik Honeysett had the perfect view of the quaint hamlet he called home.

Most of the land was silent, though candles glowed in the modest windows of the cottages dotting the cove. The soft lights amplified the sleepy atmosphere, flickering in rhythm with the gentle raindrops that fell from above.

The residents of Tristwick still in their homes would be stirring now, rising to make ready for the return of the fishermen, but at sea, Trevik and his men had been working since dusk the night before.

The low hum of their voices sailed over the sea and disappeared into the wind. "It may be a maid who holds me hand in the light, but the sea be the one that holds me heart through the night."

He'd always loved this song. Father used to tease Mother

by singing it, claiming he loved the sea more than he loved her, but everyone knew who truly held Father's heart. Just as everyone knew who—rather, *what*—truly held Trevik's heart.

He swept his eyes around him, breathing in the cool, autumn air, made crisper by the sea surrounding them. Rain clicked against the boat's deck, and gentle waves licked at the hull of the *Pilferer*, leaving behind bubbles against the dark wood.

The calm sea was a godsend that morning, especially after the storms they'd experienced the last few days. A tranquil sea made their task far easier than tumultuous waves.

"The nets be full, Trevik. Ought we bring 'em in now?"

Trevik joined his crew member, eighteen-year-old Jowan Cardy, at the starboard side. They both peered over the edge into the water. The cork buoys and buffs bobbed up and down in the lilting waves, revealing where the long net drifted behind the boat, four fathoms beneath the water's surface. From Trevik's vantage point, the reddish-brown hue of the pilchards could not be seen, but as their side of the boat dipped closer to the water, the weight of the fish in the nets was all too apparent.

"Pull 'em up," he finally agreed. "We ought to try to catch another load 'fore the sun rises. Closer to shore, I be thinkin'."

He glanced to Tristwick once more, the grey outline of the hovels a shade brighter. He and his men wouldn't be able to capture a full load before the pilchards went back down to the seabed at dawn, but any extra fish would be worth the effort of shooting the nets once more.

He secured his cap over his dark hair and pulled the collar of his coat closer to his neck, hoping for a small respite from the droplets of rain sliding down his spine. "Pull 'er up, lads!" he directed.

The two largest and strongest men on his crew—Jowan and Gryffyn Bosanko—worked together to roll the net back into the boat. As the fish were brought forth from the water,

2

two additional men stood on hauling boards, untangling the fish from the net and allowing them to fall into the fish room below deck.

The briny scent of pilchards and unsettled sea water permeated the air as the men worked without a hitch. Trevik oversaw the process, pitching in his help when needed, watching for loose pilchards, and ensuring they brought the net in slow enough to avoid tearing the intricate mesh.

"Nearly there," he called out as the last of the buoys inched closer to the ship.

As the older men worked, the youngest of their crew, twelve-year-old Charlie Bosanko, ran about the ship with his long-handled net, catching any spare fish that had managed to untangle themselves from the drift net. His ruddy cheeks shone with rainwater as he leaned over the bulwark, eager to prove his worth aboard the *Pilferer*.

"Well done, lads!" Trevik called out to his men, signaling for the skipper to move on. "We'll shoot 'er out once more, closer to shore."

As the men worked to set about the sails, Trevik approached young Charlie, clapping him against the back of his sodden jacket. "Ye be doin' well, Charlie. Your father must be proud."

"'Course I be," Gryffyn touted as he stood beside his son. Gryffyn was ten years older than Trevik's twenty-seven, but the two had been friends for years. "'E be comin' to take over me own task soon enough. If 'e e'er grows bigger 'an a mimsey, that is."

He tipped Charlie's cap to the side lightheartedly, and Charlie righted it straightaway. "Mother says it be only a matter of time, Father. Ye best be ready for it."

Gryffyn's chest and arms measured nearly wider than the barrels they stored the fish in. If Charlie was to take over his father's task of heaving up the heaviest side of the nets, the boy certainly had a long way to go.

3

The father and son playfully pushed one another about, and Trevik looked away with a twist in his heart. Six years had passed since his own father's death, and still, his steady presence aboard the *Pilferer* was sorely missed.

"Trev?"

Trevik blinked, his thoughts mercifully fleeing. "Did ye say somethin', Gryff?"

Charlie had since moved off to the side with his net, but Gryffyn still stood before Trevik. Rain clung to his unshaven face and gathered in the folds of the wrinkles shooting forth from the corners of his eyes.

"I just be askin'," Gryffyn lowered his voice with a glance around, arms folded across his chest, "do ye think it be wise to shoot the net so close to shore?"

Trevik paused. "We been doin' this for months now, Gryff. What be the 'arm now?"

"Only that, well, I did see a few men from them seinin' companies pokin' their pointed noses round St. Just last week."

"They be back from St. Ives?"

"Yes. And it only be a matter of time 'fore they come 'round to Tristwick."

Trevik released a heavy sigh. Those seining men were trouble—just like all large companies were. They thought they were God's gift to earth, with their fleets of boats and larger nets and thicker pocketbooks, appealing to poorer fishermen with fanciful promises of more money.

Well, they may have each of those things far and above what Trevik had, but he had something they would never possess—a loyal crew.

Still, their presence was concerning. His experience with seiners in the past—one seiner in particular—had been anything but pleasant. "Do ye know what they be after? Askin' for our fish or tryin' to take our men?"

"I don't know," Gryffyn responded. "All I know is that if

4

they catch ye fishin' closer to shore, they'll be sure to report ye."

Trevik ran his tongue over his teeth in frustration, shaking his head. Even though the nearest seining company was miles away in St. Ives, the law still held strong. Seiners could fish closer to shore, and drifters could not.

"Cursed law," he mumbled. "This'll be the last we do it, then. Least 'til they return where they belong."

Trevik was usually a proud, law-abiding Cornishman. But when the laws were set forth due to the influence of seining companies to benefit *solely* the seining companies, the rules were a greater struggle to swallow.

After the rest of the crew agreed with Trevik's advisement, Enyon Penna directed the lugger toward the shoreline. Trevik didn't waste a moment pulling out his spyglass to evaluate the cliffside and surrounding seas for any sign of the leeching seiners.

Satisfied that they were still alone and unseen, Trevik signaled for the skipper to turn the boat before the wind. Nearer to the shore, the sails were lowered to ensure the boat remained as still as possible.

Gryffyn and Jowan moved to the net room, a lowered area on the main deck, and Jowan hefted the cork rope side of the net up while Gryffyn lifted the heavier opposite end. Little by little, the net was shot into the water, the waves taking out the drift net with the current and pulling the mesh deeper and deeper into the water.

Trevik watched the buoys once again bobbing in the sea, willing the seining companies from his mind. Truthfully, he needn't worry about them. There were more than enough pilchards to go around this autumn, and the price they were fetching was far better than in years past. The approaching winter was sure to be a happy one with so many fish preserved.

Not only that, the waves were calm, the dark clouds

allowed them another shooting of the nets, and he had a crew of men who would be at his side until the very end. Nothing could go wrong, nothing could diminish his good mood. Nothing could—

A flash of white and shimmering blue caught his eye in the water. A passing fish, no doubt, feeding off the pilchards they'd caught. But then, there were no fish that size and that white in these waters.

He narrowed his eyes, leaning closer and peering through the waves. As the white rippled again in the water, his mouth parted. Was that a fish's tail? No, fabric. It was fabric. A torn sail from a shipwreck, perhaps?

"Lads," he called out, motioning to the water. "Be that…?"

His stomach tightened. Footsteps pattered close to him as he pulled out his spyglass again and peered into the water nearly forty feet away, the waves flashing past the small funnel of sight. Only when the water settled could Trevik finally see the truth—arms floating lifelessly in the water just below the surface and long hair swaying back and forth in the current.

A numbing sensation rattled his bones and pressed the breath from his lungs. "Haul up the net, now!"

CHAPTER TWO

a moment of confusion settled on the crew. Trevik lowered his spyglass and turned with an urgent look. "There be someone caught in the net!"

Without hesitating another moment, Gryffyn jammed the net roller back into the curved wooden chock and worked with Jowan to heave the net back in.

Jowan's grandfather, Edern Cardy, ran forward to pull up the buoys. Tufts of thick, white hair flipped out from the sides of his low cap. "Be slow, boys, or ye'll lose the fish," he warned.

Trevik immediately shook his head. "Hang the fish, Edern!"

"Ye be gawky, boy?" Edern returned, grunting as he hoisted the buoys forward. "An 'undred an' eight shillin's per hogshead. That be the rate now. We keep losin' pilchards, and it'll add up quick."

Trevik groaned. Were they really going to argue over such trivialities with this woman's life hanging in the balance? "I be well aware, Edern, but there be a woman who needs our 'elp down there."

"A woman?" He didn't pause in his work, though his small eyes peered over the edge, his lips set in a hard and fast line.

Trevik had an inkling what Edern was thinking of, but he didn't have time for such nonsense. The two disagreed often enough about matters ranging from when to set sail to what fish to catch and when. Trevik was not one to take on his authoritative role often, but when it became a matter of life and death, he had no problem assuming his duties.

And fortunately for Trevik, he was the one who owned the boat.

He faced Gryffyn and Jowan. "Pull swiftly, lads."

He wiped the end of his spyglass off with a section of his shirt that seemed the driest, then he peered through the lens once again, shifting slightly to see past the streaks his wet clothing had left behind against the glass.

After a quick search, he spotted the woman in the water again.

"Be she alive?" Gryffyn called out with a grunt as he hauled in the nets.

"I can't be sure," Trevik returned. "'Appen she is, she'll not last much longer down there."

More of the crew shuffled to his side, and the boat leaned closer to the water.

Trevik didn't lose his careful watch of the woman. His chest tightened as her limp body drew closer, floating like a ghost in the night, the frontside of her clothing eerily warped by the water.

With how tangled she'd become, the mesh wrapped multiple times around her limbs, he knew the *Pilferer* had not simply picked her up with her already unconscious. The woman had clearly struggled to break free. She must have been swimming deep to have been caught in the mesh, but then...would this have happened had he not made the poor decision to fish closer to shore?

The weight of culpability pressed against him, and he

fought the urge to jump in and rescue her himself. But what good would he be to the woman and his crew if he became entangled in the net, too?

"She be nearly 'ere, boys!" he called out, praying silently for her wellbeing. If she'd been under for much longer than a few moments…

Fish plopped back down into the water from the swiftly moving net, and the waves shifted back and forth, slapping against the boat until finally, the woman's body was pulled from the sea.

Her foot was twisted around the net multiple times, her arm tangled in the opposite side as her head lolled back, long hair dripping with water.

"She be dead!" Charlie called out as he saw the state of her, and a few men mumbled in agreement.

"Help me haul 'er up!" Trevik cried out, thrusting his spyglass into Charlie's hands and reaching for the woman so she wouldn't slam against the bulwark. He would not believe she was already gone. He couldn't.

Another of his mates reached over to help, and they heaved her over the edge, gripping her arms just beneath her shoulders as the net was brought up with her.

Gingerly, they untangled the shredded netting that wound tightly around her ankle and arm, then laid her across the deck as the net was set aside. Trevik ensured her head rested softly against the wood before assessing the length of her, searching for any apparent injuries. Wet strands of hair striped across her face, and she wore no gown, though her petticoat and undergarments ensured her ample coverage.

Voices whispered from behind as he moved to kneel beside her.

"She ain't breathin'," Charlie murmured.

"What she be doin' in the water?" said another. "Did someone put 'er out 'ere?"

Trevik leaned close to the deck to peer at the woman's

chest from a different angle, brushing aside a flapping pilchard that had managed to escape the nets but not the boat. He held his breath, willing the woman to use hers, but there was not even the faintest movement shifting her sopping petticoat.

"She be a danger to us all, mark me words," Edern whispered.

"Hush your 'alf-baked notions, Edern," Gryffyn growled, moving up from the net room to join the other men. He pulled a sail over her head to prevent the rain from falling on her further.

Trevik straightened, ignoring the words of those around him as he hovered over the woman, resting a few fingers against her neck. His crew fell silent again, standing in a half-circle around them as Trevik closed his eyes, focusing intently on the feel of the woman's cold, grey skin against his fingertips.

Almost indiscernibly, the feeble thump of her heartbeat tapped against him, sending his own pulse racing.

"She be alive!" he called out.

With swift movements driven by hope, Trevik swiped the strands of sopping hair away from her face and mouth, tipping her head back until her blue lips parted. He placed his mouth fully over her own and sent a great puff of air to purge the water from her lungs.

Her eyes shot open in an instant, and Trevik pulled back as her body roiled. She launched to the side, coughing the water out and spitting it across the deck as the men close to her jumped back.

Trevik leaned back on the heels of his boots, resting his hands on his thighs with heavy breaths. "Ye be safe now," he said, almost for his own sake as much as for hers.

The rush of relief rattled his bones. He hadn't killed her after all.

She sat forward, rolling to her side and propping herself

up on a hand as her whole body convulsed. Her petticoat slipped up in the process, revealing one bare leg up to her knee, but he quickly averted his gaze.

Rain splattered against the deck, the peaceful tapping broken up only by the sound of her coughing as she continued to rid her lungs of sea water.

"Are ye all right?" he questioned as she gave one final, ragged cough.

The woman cast startled eyes toward him, confusion flickering within their depths, though he couldn't decipher the color despite the rising sun. She raised a cautious hand to her lips and frowned.

Trevik pulled back, unsettled with her lowering brow. Did she think that he had—

The loud slap of her hand across his cheek echoed about the lugger. Trevik reared back as a collective gasp sounded from his men.

"What the devil did ye do that for?" he exclaimed, holding a hand to his cheek and staring at the woman as if she was mad.

If? No, she was most definitely mad. For what sane woman would slap her rescuer?

He stood, backing up to position himself by the rest of his crew. With fire in her eyes, the woman crossed her arm over her body and pulled her petticoat down to cover her legs once more. She took in the sight of the men aboard the lugger practically surrounding her, and fear flashed across her features.

Clearly, she'd assumed Trevik had kissed her instead of saved her—and clearly, she worried the others on the boat would take advantage of her in another way.

Lowering his pride, Trevik raised a tepid hand to ease her concerns, but it was too late. Her breaths came out in ragged spurts, as if she was no longer in control of her own body, then her eyes rolled back in her head, and she collapsed across the deck.

No one moved for a moment, Trevik hesitating more than anyone. Was she feigning the fainting spell? Or had she truly lost consciousness? And more importantly—was it worth the risk of another sound slap across his cheek?

"Be she dead *now*?" Charlie asked.

"No, I think 'tis only a fit, son," Gryffyn responded. He nudged Trevik with his elbow. "Go on, Trev. See 'ow she fares."

Trevik never should have taken his authoritative stance.

With his face still stinging, he inched toward the woman and reached down to check the strength of her heartbeat. It was far greater than before, to no surprise of his. Any woman who could strike as severely as she had done was not weak by any stretch of the imagination.

"She be alive, then?" Jowan asked after a moment.

Trevik straightened her head against the wooden deck, ensuring the angle of her neck was no longer cricked, then he backed away. "Yes, she be alive. Charlie, fetch a blanket for 'er, will ye?"

Charlie's quick footsteps skittered across the deck as he brought forth a blanket. Trevik and Gryffyn worked together to bring the woman off to the side, flattening the cover over her and willing her to stay warm enough until they could get her under proper shelter.

"'Tis a bad thing that's 'appened, mark me words."

Those aboard the lugger looked to Edern, one of his eyes wincing more than the other. The wrinkles across his face marred his weathered skin, evidence of years at sea.

"What be bad, Grandfar?" Jowan asked, standing a full head taller than him.

Edern narrowed his eyes further as he stared down at the woman, his lips pulled in so tightly, they fully disappeared. "Bringin' a sea-maid 'board the boat."

Jowan's eyes rounded, Charlie gasped, and glances scattered between the men, but Trevik shook his head at once. There was no chance he would allow Edern's superstitions to wreak destruction upon his men. Not again.

"She ain't be no sea-maid," Trevik said.

"What other reason do she 'ave for bein' in the sea?" Edern countered.

Trevik paused. He'd been trying to concoct an answer to that very question for the last quarter of an hour. Had she been thrown in the sea by some wayward man? Had she been on a boat that wrecked?

"Maybe she be takin' a mornin' swim," Charlie offered up.

Yes, because *that* was a logical suggestion. What woman would be swimming alone in the darkness? At least the boy was attempting to help Trevik, though. No one else had said a word. He glanced to Gryffyn for support, but the man merely shook his head with impatience and moved to straighten the netting in the net room.

So Trevik was on his own, then. He motioned to the woman's exposed feet. One ankle sported a large, purple bruise visible in the growing light. "Whether she be takin' a leisurely swim or not, she 'as two legs, just like the rest o' we."

"It be a siren's trick," Edern grumbled, rain spitting from his lip as he spoke. "'Fore she be pulled up, I did see 'er fins with me own eyes."

Trevik repressed the fact that he'd thought he'd seen a tailfin in the water, as well. Such an admission would hardly be for their benefit.

To some outsiders of Tristwick, the notion of actually believing in mermaids was laughable. But to Trevik, the very suggestion was more than troubling. Edern had once convinced Jowan and half the crew that if they participated in a game of hurling on Sunday, they'd be turned to stone. It had taken years for them to even set foot on a field on the sabbath.

If the elderly man could do that, Trevik could only imagine what damage could be done with myths about mermaids aboard a lugger.

"She be wounded 'cause o' we," Edern continued, raising his chin as he peered down at the woman. "It be only a matter o' time 'fore she seeks 'er revenge."

"Revenge?" his grandson asked, swallowing. Jowan was far too old to believe such stories, but with his father's death and only a superstitious mother and grandfar as guardians, the young man's rationality had no chance of survival.

"Yes, revenge," Edern repeated. "She ain't—"

"We oughtn't worry 'bout such things now, lads," Trevik interrupted, anxious to end any chance of filling his mates' minds with fanciful ideas. "We've a lugger full o' pilchards and a week o' fishin' ahead o' we." He motioned to the mer—to the woman. "And whether she be a sea-maid or not, we can't leave 'er 'ere all wounded. She'll be grateful when she sees we be takin' care of 'er."

"Like she be grateful for ye makin' 'er breathe again?" Charlie chirped up from the side of the boat.

Gryffyn nudged his son to keep quiet, but a few snickers rustled around the men. Trevik cleared his throat, fighting the urge to stroke his still-throbbing cheek. "Enyon?" He faced the skipper and motioned to the shore. "Time we be gettin' 'ome."

Enyon nodded, and the orders were called out for the men to ready the lugger for sailing once again. As they set forth toward the cove, Trevik glanced to the woman still lying on the deck. Gryffyn had placed a rolled-up blanket beneath her head and rigged a semi-shelter with a few crates around her to protect her from most of the rain.

Dark lashes rested against the pale skin over her cheekbones, and her lips were as delicately arched as her eyebrows. Heavens, but she was beautiful. Especially now, for in her unconscious state, her harried look had been replaced with one of pleasant delirium.

She had taken all of Trevik's peace and left him with her distress. Maybe Edern was right. Maybe Trevik *had* pulled a mermaid from the sea.

CHAPTER THREE

*M*uffled voices disturbed the deep sleep that Morvoren Hollow refused to leave. She stirred, moving her head against the hard ground she lay upon.

"Be still, miss. We be nearly there."

The deep words rumbled at her side, and she paused. Uncle Truscott? No. The words had been spoken far too gently to be he. But then, whose was that voice? And why did it speak so closely to her ear?

Before she could decipher if it was one to fear or not, the pull of her unconscious state drew her back in, and she was once more swallowed up in the peaceful surroundings of her dreams. She welcomed back the sound of the gulls sailing over the sea, the warmth of the sunshine kissing her face, and the feel of the sand tickling her toes. Uncle didn't like her walking in the sand without her boots.

But Uncle wasn't here.

Here. Where was *here*? And why were cold raindrops falling on her cheeks when the sun was shining?

She tried to open her eyes, rouse from her sleep, but they wouldn't budge, and she was once again transported to the beach. This time, more voices sounded on the wind, one male, one female, and the rain was gone. Had it truly poured down so greatly to have made her clothing drenched through?

No, that wasn't right. She'd been swimming. Uncle didn't like her swimming either, and Uncle always had his own way.

"What 'appened?"

"Ready a bed, Mother."

Mother? Mother was there? Morvoren's eyes fluttered open, but she swiftly closed them with a silent rebuke. Mother couldn't be there. She'd died more than five years ago. Father, too.

"Poppy, fetch us your extra chemise. Trevik, 'ave ye sent for Dr. Kent?"

"Gryff's already on 'is way to 'im."

Morvoren tried to tell the voices to quiet down. After all, she didn't have long to enjoy herself upon the beach. She needed to get to Sennen. Why was she going there again?

The disruption around her continued as the rough sand beneath her gave way to a bed. But why was there a bed on the beach?

"…get 'er into dry clothes…Trevik, out for a moment…"

The sleep pulled her in again, causing her lucidity to falter further as she wondered if she imagined her wet clothing being exchanged for dry ones and her body being covered by a thick blanket.

"Will she be well, Mother?" the younger female voice asked.

"I 'ope so. We do need Dr. Kent's 'elp, to be sure."

Morvoren didn't recognize that name. She was usually visited by Uncle's physician and his ever-trusty exercises of bleeding and sweating.

She winced. She oughtn't be thinking of such terrible things. Not while she was by the sea with a fire crackling nearby to keep her warm.

Snap. Snap. Pop.

She shifted her head toward the sound. Mother used to

love warm fires on the beach. Yet another thing Uncle disapproved of.

Yet another reason Morvoren loved it, too.

"Ought we to allow Trev back in?" the younger voice asked.

"No, 'e be waitin' for Dr. Kent."

"Do we try to speak with 'er 'til then?"

"I s'pose we ought to. Miss, can ye 'ear we?"

Morvoren shifted again, opening her mouth to express her desire for whoever these women were to leave her be, but nothing but a groan escaped. Only then did she recognize the burning in her throat and the ache in her chest, as if the weight of the sea pressed down upon her.

"Miss?"

The blue skies faded away, and the herring gulls vanished, but the sound of the rushing waves and the crackling fire remained.

"What has happened?" she mumbled in a haggard voice she didn't recognize. A throbbing at the back of her head thrummed like a drum against her skull.

She tried to roll over, but as she did so, blinding, white pain shot through her leg from her ankle, and she gasped.

Her eyes flew open, her vision blurred with bewildered tears. She blinked furiously to see where she was, looking back and forth at the unfamiliar surroundings—rain dotting the windows at either side of her bed, a small hearth playing host to an even smaller fire, a minute table holding a vase of white wildflowers, and the figure of a woman hovering over her bed.

"Where am I?" she asked. Her throat felt coated with sand.

"Fetch 'er a glass o' brandy, Poppy," the woman said, standing beside her as footsteps tapped away. Her Cornish accent was thick and rich as she addressed Morvoren again. "Worry not, miss. I be Mabyn 'Oneysett. Ye were caught in me son's net when 'e pulled ye from the sea and saved ye. 'E carried ye 'ere 'fore me daugh'er and I changed ye into dry clothes."

In the sea? A net? Dry clothes?

All at once, Morvoren's memory flooded her mind like a wave breaking on the sand. Attempting to take the coach to Sennen. Swimming in the sea. Diving deep to avoid the approaching fishing lugger, then becoming entangled in their net below the surface, and knowing, just knowing, she was about to die. Then that man—that, that *fisherman*—had brought her back to life.

Of course a fisherman would be the one to save her.

She groaned as the ache in her head pulsed harder. She'd only meant to swim for a moment, to allow the cold sea to rejuvenate her weakened spirits to help her finish with her task. Now she didn't even know where she was.

She cleared her throat, attempting to speak again as her hand still covered her brow and eyes. "Where am I in relation to the nearest city?" She cringed. That proper tongue had no place in this humble home. She could only imagine the woman's surprise at hearing it.

Curse Uncle Truscott for forcing her to hide her own accent, her mother's accent. He'd threaten Morvoren constantly, locking her away in her room until she would speak in the way he approved of.

But then, she needn't use Uncle's words any longer. She'd never see him again.

"Ye be in Tristwick now, miss," Mrs. Honeysett responded. "Right close to St. Just, we be."

Morvoren nodded against the pillow she still lay upon. After the stagecoach route had ended in St. Just the night before, she'd determined to spend the night at the inn, then walk the few miles that remained to Sennen after a brief swim. Now, with an ankle that still screamed in pain and lungs that felt as shriveled as a weeks-old apple, how was she to make the journey on foot?

Unless, of course, she hadn't yet missed the coach from St. Just to Sennen. "And…can you…can ye tell me what day it is?"

The woman paused before responding, no doubt noting Morvoren's change in accent. "It be Monday, the eighteenth o' September, miss."

Thank heavens. The coach only traveled to Sennen on Monday evenings. But then, if she didn't reach St. Just by nightfall, she'd have to wait an entire week to make it to her friend's home. How would she survive in the wilds of Cornwall without a home for seven whole days?

Her thoughts blurred as the ache in her head obscured her ability to think clearly.

Mrs. Honeysett's soft voice reached her ears again. "I know ye must 'ave many questions, and ye seem to be 'avin' an 'ard time rememberin' things, but…'ave ye a name we can call ye by?"

"'Tis Morvoren." She cleared her throat, every word a struggle to move past the burning in her lungs. "Morvoren Hollow."

"That be a lovely name."

The blood drained from Morvoren's face, her head spinning. How could she have been so stupid as to give her name? She and Uncle had differing surnames, but should someone connect the two somehow, or if Uncle eventually heard word of where she'd escaped to, her life—her freedom—would surely be stripped from her again.

"And can ye tell me where your 'ome be, Miss 'Ollow?" Mrs. Honeysett asked next.

Morvoren clamped her mouth shut. Saying nothing would surely raise their suspicions, but the risk was too great to say anything more. Besides, she had no home. She hadn't in years, despite living with her uncle since her parents had died.

Footsteps sounded across the floor, and Morvoren uncovered her eyes as a young woman no more than sixteen years old entered with brandy in hand. She and Mrs. Honeysett were clearly related, with the same dark hair and warm expression.

"This be me daugh'er, Poppy," Mrs. Honeysett explained, taking the glass from her and helping Morvoren to drink.

Poppy. That name had been said when Morvoren was sleeping. Morvoren pulled back from the glass with a nod of gratitude and settled back in the bed with a wince.

"Where ye be in pain, Miss 'Ollow?" Mrs. Honeysett asked next. Had the woman forgotten her question from before? Would that Morvoren could be so fortunate.

"Ye can call me Morvoren," she said. She hadn't ever minded 'Miss Hollow' until Uncle had forced it upon her, saying her first name was an "*utter abomination.*"

Mrs. Honeysett nodded. "Very well, Morvoren. Where be ye hurt?"

"My…me head and me ankle." How comfortable the accent felt on her tongue again. How natural.

Uncle had never been able to force it out of Morvoren altogether. She used to lie awake in bed at night, reading her books aloud the way Mama used to. When she really wished to irritate Uncle, she'd slip in her accent every now and again during balls and parties. Heads would always turn, but Uncle could say nothing until they returned to his townhome.

Mrs. Honeysett adjusted Morvoren's pillow. "Me son said your foot was tangled terribly in 'is net. Then ye fainted again and 'it your 'ead against 'is lugger."

Her son. Of course. Mrs. Honeysett had mentioned that before—her fisherman son. Heaven must be playing some cruel joke on Morvoren. Why else would she be thrown right back into the world she was trying so desperately to escape?

"Do ye remember 'im savin' ye?" Mrs. Honeysett asked gingerly.

"A little."

"Ye weren't breathin' when 'e pulled ye up. 'Tis a miracle ye survived."

Oh, yes, a miracle, indeed. A miracle that could have been avoided altogether had the drift net not been in her way.

At the thought of the man who'd apparently saved her life, Morvoren's lips tingled. She brought her hand up to her mouth and inwardly groaned. She distinctly remembered the moment she'd been awakened by the man's lips on hers, his face utterly too close to her own.

Of course, she hadn't realized then, amidst all the turmoil, that he'd merely been resuscitating her. She'd thought that he'd...Well, never mind that. What was done was done. And she didn't regret for a minute striking...Trevik, was it? He'd deserved it. The blasted fool had been shooting his net too close to the shoreline.

Typical drifter, breaking laws. They only ever thought about themselves. Not a lick of consideration for others, not even their wives and children. How she felt for Mrs. Honeysett and her daughter to be trapped in such a life.

"Morvoren..."

She looked up to Mrs. Honeysett opening and closing her mouth, as if she hesitated saying anything further.

But Morvoren knew what was coming—the constant barrage of questions that could no longer be avoided.

How unfortunate her mind refused to cooperate. Otherwise she might have been able to concoct a response that would not risk her one chance for freedom.

CHAPTER FOUR

"*C*an ye tell us where ye come from, Morvoren?" came Mrs. Honeysett's next question. "Or what ye were doin' in the sea?"

St. Ives. Morvoren had come from St. Ives by stagecoach. And she'd been in the sea because, frankly, she *could* be in the sea. Uncle disapproved of the pastime, but she'd always found ways around his and Society's censure.

This morning, though, she'd merely been swimming because the frigid waves had sounded far more appealing than remaining a moment longer in that forsaken room she'd been attempting to sleep in at the Golden Arms. The swim was supposed to have been brief, just long enough for the sun to rise so she could begin her walk to Sennen. Then that net had appeared.

Revealing all of that would lead to other questions, though —where was her family? And where was she headed to alone?

Tears flooded her eyes, but she forced them away with annoyance. Now was not the time to wither away like the dormant grass of winter. And yet, what could she say?

"I...I don't..." She stopped, unable to lie yet unable to speak the truth.

Mrs. Honeysett rested a gentle hand on her arm. "Ye can stop now, dear," she cooed. "I know it be 'ard for ye to remember."

Morvoren froze, the pathway before her illuminated by the woman's bright words. Slowly, she nodded, allowing Mrs. Honeysett's explanation to be her own.

"Yes, 'tis difficult to remember," she mumbled.

Morvoren should have corrected Mrs. Honeysett, should have told her that she remembered everything perfectly. But she would not snub the lifeline thrown toward her.

"That be more 'an fine," Mrs. Honeysett continued. "Ye've been through a terrible thing. Rest now. Dr. Kent'll be 'ere soon."

As the ache in Morvoren's head steadily spread to her temples and splayed out across her forehead, the physician finally arrived, and he and Mrs. Honeysett whispered quietly in the corner of the room.

Morvoren could only guess what the two of them were speaking about, but with exhaustion, cold, and aches spreading throughout her person, she was beginning to care less and less about anything but going to sleep again.

No, she couldn't sleep. She needed to stay awake. She needed to get back to St. Just. She'd sit in the inn for the next twelve hours if she needed to, so long as she boarded that stagecoach.

After another moment, Mrs. Honeysett led the physician forward. "This be Dr. Benjamin Kent. Dr. Kent, Morvoren 'Ollow."

Morvoren nodded, and the man greeted her with a kind smile. "Good day," he said in an accent even more proper than Uncle's—or rather, what Uncle had changed his to be. "My name is Dr. Benjamin Kent. I understand you've had quite the morning, Miss Hollow."

Morvoren nodded in silence, clearing her throat and trying to sit upright. How could the Honeysetts afford such a fine physician? Surely they didn't expect Morvoren to be able to afford him.

Dr. Kent raised a hand, signaling for her to remain still. "I should like to conduct a quick examination of your wounds, Miss Hollow, just to ensure all is well. Will that be all right with you?"

Morvoren glanced to Mrs. Honeysett with a wary eye. "I...I can't pay for a physician."

"Ye needn't worry 'bout that, dear," Mrs. Honeysett responded.

Morvoren lowered a brow. Not worry about payment? This could not be simple charity work for the physician. And surely such fine care could not be afforded by a fisherman's mother—and a fisherman's wife, perhaps? Where was the man of the house?

Dr. Kent placed the vase of white flowers at the back of the table to allow room for his medical bag. "Mrs. Honeysett and I have an agreement," he explained. "I'm quite partial to her stargazey pies, and since my lovely wife cannot make them —she can't stomach the smell, right now, you see—Mrs. Honeysett delivers me a lovely warm pie every time I see to one of her family members or friends." He leaned forward, pretending to lower his voice. "Just between you and me, I receive the better end of the bargain."

"Oh, I think not," Mrs. Honeysett piped in with a soft laugh.

Dr. Kent went about his examination, checking Morvoren's pulse, listening to her breathing, feeling the bump on her head, then requesting to see her ankle. All the while, Mrs. Honeysett and Poppy remained in the corner of the room, silent, as the doctor asked a few clarifying questions about Morvoren's injuries and jotted a few notes down on a piece of paper.

After his assessment, he stood, rinsing his hands off in the bowl of water Poppy had brought in earlier.

"Well, Miss Hollow, I'm pleased to tell you that I have no concerns with your current state. I expect you to make a full recovery, despite all you have been through this morning."

Finally, some good news.

"However…"

Her stomach tightened.

"Since we are unaware of where your family is at the moment, I feel it is important for you to remain under Mrs. Honeysett's care until that knowledge returns. I should also like to ensure the rest of the water has been fully expelled from your lungs, so I would advise that you remain abed at least until tomorrow."

"Tomorrow?" Morvoren asked, unable to hide her distressed tone.

Dr. Kent studied her, drying his hands on a rag. "I'm afraid so. Your head wound is minimal and should not bother you for long if you receive plenty of sleep and rest. As for your ankle, fortunately, there is no sign of anything but a small sprain. I recommend elevating the foot and remaining off of it for a full day. Wrapping it with a cool compress or salve ought to help, as well. When the swelling dissipates, you may begin to take small walks, but I would recommend that you avoid long distances for a week, at the very least."

Dr. Kent had given his recommendation easily, as if remaining off of one's foot was the simplest task in the world. To some people, perhaps it was. But to Morvoren, his orders were practically a sentence to the gallows.

Never mind the water in her lungs. Never mind the ache in her foot. She had not escaped Uncle to be caught a few towns over—or to be stuck for a week with *fishermen*.

"A week?" she asked. "Are ye certain?"

Dr. Kent tucked his paper and pencil into his bag with an apologetic look. "Unfortunately, yes. I fear that if you risk using your ankle before it mends, the damage will take even longer to heal—even possibly causing permanent impairment."

Morvoren pressed her lips together. There was nothing she could say further. Dr. Kent had his opinions, and she had hers. She would not risk Uncle bringing her back to the life he'd chosen for her, to force her into complying with his latest unthinkable demand—all for the sake of expanding his company.

"Thank ye, Dr. Kent," she said, hoping that was dismissal enough for him to leave. She needed to make ready to hobble her way back to St. Just, hurt ankle or not.

Now, where were her clothes?

Dr. Kent, however, did not leave. Instead, he fastened the clasps on his bag, then faced Morvoren again. "There's one more item I'd like to discuss with you before I leave. Mrs. Honeysett has informed me that you are having difficulty remembering a few things."

Morvoren glanced to the side where Mrs. Honeysett gave her an encouraging nod, then Morvoren pushed her eyebrows together and feigned concern. "Yes, that be right."

"It can be quite disconcerting, to be sure," Dr. Kent said, "and not entirely abnormal after one undergoes significant trauma. That being said, I should like to ask you another question or two, just in the event that you *do* remember something. Have you any objections?"

How Morvoren longed to say yes. "No, sir."

He paused, his eyes delving a little too deeply into Morvoren's. Was he suspecting her of dishonesty already, willing her to tell the truth?

Perhaps she ought to drop the façade, be honest with Mrs. Honeysett, and beg for a wagon ride to St. Just. But then, why would the woman do such a thing for a perfect stranger who'd already lied directly to her face? The woman would no doubt think she was doing what was best by finding Uncle for Morvoren.

"Do you remember your mother or father's names?" asked the physician, tugging her attention back to him. "Or another guardian perhaps charged to watch over you?"

Morvoren squinted her eyes, feigning deep thought before shaking her head with the best worried expression she could manage. "No, I don't."

Please forgive me, Mama, she thought.

She glanced behind Mrs. Honeysett to where sodden underclothing hung near the hearth. She'd stashed her portmanteau filled with extra clothing and gowns between some rocks situated near a secluded section of the beach. Of course, she'd fully expected to return to shore and be dressed before anyone might discover the hiding place.

Now she'd have to walk through all of Tristwick in only her stays and petticoat to retrieve her belongings. Assuming a fisherman hadn't already thieved them.

"And do you remember how you came to Tristwick?" followed Dr. Kent's next question. "On foot or by stagecoach perhaps?"

Morvoren shook her head. Disconcerted. She was supposed to be showing that she was disconcerted.

"Any memory of a traveling companion or friends in the area?"

She closed her eyes instead and furrowed her brow. Where were her tears now? "No, sir."

"Do you recall where you were headed, perhaps? Or anything of the sort?"

She blew out a slow breath. "No."

Silence followed.

She opened her eyes a fraction. Dr. Kent rubbed a hand to his chin with a studious look. He exchanged glances with Mrs. Honeysett, their expressions unreadable.

They didn't believe her, did they? Would Mrs. Honeysett toss her from her home that minute?

A very real and very discouraging worry rushed over

Morvoren, and she pressed a hand to her head with a wince, no longer needing to pretend to be upset.

Finally, Dr. Kent spoke in a softened tone. "That is enough questions for now. You are clearly…distressed."

The pause made her believe that he didn't trust her an ounce. Still, as his boots moved across the wooden floor in departure, relief encompassed her. He wouldn't press her, then.

"I have every confidence that your memory will return in its entirety within a matter of days, Miss Hollow. But for now, I think you will agree that it would be wise to remain in Tristwick where you can be closely watched over."

She nodded, feigning contrition. She certainly couldn't ask Mrs. Honeysett to help her get to Sennen now. By revealing where she needed to go, she'd also be revealing that her faulty memory had merely been a lie—a lie she was fairly certain the woman might have already caught onto.

"I know your family is quite busy with the pilchards, Mrs. Honeysett," Dr. Kent said in a low voice, "so I will gladly offer the use of my home to allow Miss Hollow to recover. My Lucy would be more than happy to have a companion."

But Mrs. Honeysett shook her head. "With a new babe on the way? I 'ardly think she'd appreciate your offer. 'Sides, ye've already done enough for we. We can care for the miss well enough."

Dr. Kent nodded. "I suspect your recovery will be even swifter with the help of the Honeysetts, Miss Hollow."

Morvoren returned a weakened smile.

Dr. Kent retrieved his bag and replaced the vase of flowers to the center of the table. "Until your memory does return, I will ask around St. Just to discover if anyone there might know more as to your identity. Perhaps someone might have seen you before or know where you came from."

Morvoren's heart dropped. Having a physician asking around St. Just for her, spreading her name for everyone to hear, making it easier for Uncle to find her? Could matters worsen further? "Oh, ye needn't bother."

Dr. Kent's brow twitched, so she rushed to explain.

"I-I'd just hate to inconvenience ye further," she lied.

Dr. Kent glanced sidelong at Mrs. Honeysett. Was he fully aware of her subterfuge?

To her relief, he nodded. "Very well. Why do we not wait a day or two to see if your memory returns. If it doesn't by then, we will discuss matters again, yes?"

"Yes, sir."

"Very good. Now rest, Miss Hollow. Your body needs it."

She nodded, pushing a yawn from her mouth and covering her eyes with her arm. "Thank ye, Dr. Kent."

"I'll see ye out," Mrs. Honeysett said softly to the physician. "Poppy, will ye join me for a moment?" Her voice raised a fraction. "I'll be in with a plate o' food in just a moment, Morvoren."

Morvoren hummed her acknowledgement of Mrs. Honeysett's words, forcing her breathing to become steady until the door closed and footsteps retreated down the corridor.

In an instant, she threw the cover away from her legs. The chill in the room attacked her limbs, but she warded off the desire to wrap back up in the warm blanket. She couldn't waste but a single moment.

Gingerly, she raised her foot from the bed, pushing through the pain that instantly seared through her limb. When she tried to stand, however, placing more pressure on her ankle, the world went black, and she crumbled back onto the bed, fighting the urge to scream out in pain.

Twice more she attempted to stand, beads of sweat forming on her brow despite her chill. And twice more, she fell back onto the bed. Tears of frustration billowed in her eyes, and she buried her face in her hands.

She couldn't do it. St. Just was a mere two miles away, but

she'd never be able to reach the town if she couldn't even get out of that blasted bed.

With a heavy sigh and wet cheeks, she grimaced and winced again as she pulled her throbbing foot back under the covers.

This was not how things were supposed to be. She was supposed to have traveled straight to Sennen, to have met with the Prouts and been helped to find a place for her away from the fishing trade.

But now? Now Uncle would find her and force her into the life she so desperately wished to escape—a lonely, empty life married to a fisherman.

CHAPTER FIVE

*T*revik closed the door behind Dr. Kent, then turned to face his mother as she disappeared into the kitchen. He followed after her, entering the small room adjoining the sitting room as she reached into the hutch and retrieved a plate.

"Fetch us the cheese from the cellar, Poppy," she said as she pulled out the barley bread. "Poor dear must be starvin'."

"Yes, Mother."

Poppy scampered away as Trevik watched Mother ready a tray full of food for the girl. "So ye be fine with that woman stayin' 'ere?"

"'Er name be Morvoren 'Ollow, son," Mother said without a glance in his direction. "And yes, I be more 'an fine with it."

"Are ye certain? Ye know 'ow busy we be with all 'em pilchards. Ought we really be takin' somethin' like this on?"

"It be the least we can do for 'er, Trevik."

He looked away, residual guilt pecking at his conscience. He hadn't meant to ensnare the woman, but perhaps Mother was right. They ought to ensure she was healthy before sending her on her way.

"'Ow long 'til she be well?'"

Poppy returned from the cellar with a slab of cheese, and Mother thanked her before responding. "Dr. Kent said it'd only be a few days. She be weak, ye know."

Weak? That woman was hardly weak, and his jaw could attest to that. He rubbed at his cheek as Mother continued.

"I'd like to keep 'er 'ere 'til we be certain she remembers what she needs to."

He paused, narrowing his eyes. "Remembers?"

"Fetch a glass, Poppy," she said as she cut into the cheese. Poppy dutifully obeyed as Mother continued. "The poor dear appears to be a bit…confused. Didn't know the day or where she be from." She paused. "She even seemed to forget 'er accent at one point."

Her accent? Trevik's suspicion grew. "'Ow be that possible, then? She can't remember any o' that, yet she remembers 'er name?"

"'Tis more 'an possible," Poppy piped up. "Dr. Kent said so 'imself."

He faced Mother. "So Dr. Kent believes she lost 'er memory?"

Mother hesitated, glancing to Poppy. "It be 'ard to say."

Trevik understood her reluctance at once. She and Dr. Kent were both hesitant to call the woman a liar, especially in front of Poppy. But Trevik didn't understand why the truth couldn't be known. After all, didn't they deserve as much with the woman living under their roof?

Finally, Mother paused in her frittering about and focused on Trevik with a warning look. "Don't be doin' that already, Trev."

"Doin' what?"

"Castin' all sorts o' suspicions 'bout 'er. She 'as 'er reasons for what she be doin'."

He scoffed. "'Cause she clearly be 'idin' somethin'?"

She shook her head, layering the cheese onto the plate.

"Ye best be careful, or ye'll start soundin' like Edern Cardy. No doubt that man's already been spreadin' lies 'bout the girl bein' a mermaid."

Trevik wasn't surprised at all with Mother's intuition. She'd been dealing with the Cardys since before Trevik was born. Of course she'd know what they were thinking.

But Poppy's eyes rounded with excitement. She looked down the corridor to where Miss Hollow slept in her room. "A mermaid? Wouldn't that be the most excitin' thing?"

Only Poppy could think the presence of a dangerous, mythical creature exciting.

"Well, she ain't one," Mother said. "She simply be a lost *woman*, and that be all." She turned to Trevik. "A woman ye ought not be suspicious of for wishin' to keep to 'er own."

"I ain't be suspicious of 'er," he lied. Truthfully, he'd never be so daft as to think the woman was a mermaid. But he had every right to be wary of a woman found in the middle of the sea before dawn, human or not. "I just be curious, is all."

Poppy placed a glass of brandy on the tray they'd filled for Miss Hollow. "Dr. Kent said it be perfectly normal to lose one's memory when one experiences such trauma as being nearly drowned by a fishin' net." She raised a condemning brow at him, but he ignored it.

"Don't fret, son," Mother said. "I'm sure she'll be feelin' better soon. 'Til then, we'll make 'er as comfortable as we can. Poppy, ye be fine stayin' in my room for the time bein'?"

"'Course, Mother," Poppy responded with an innocent look. "I be more 'an 'appy to 'elp by offerin' me room to 'er. Unlike *some* members of our family."

She cast a look at Trevik, and he struggled to ignore her again. Some days, his sister was far too successful at teasing him.

"Thank ye, Poppy, dear," Mother said, then she picked up the tray of bread, cheese, and brandy and moved to the door.

"I'll just be givin' these to 'er now." She looked between her children. "Behave, ye two."

"Ye know *I* will, Mother," Poppy said.

Trevik left the kitchen with his mother, intending to follow her into the room so he could ask Miss Hollow questions of his own. But the moment Mother opened Poppy's door, she paused, then slowly backed out of it, securing the door behind her.

"She be sleepin' already," she said in an undertone, taking the tray back to the kitchen.

Trevik followed Mother to where she removed her apron to don a thicker, darker one. "I'm off to the cellars, then," she said, buttoning the apron at the back. "Poppy, will ye be all right to stay 'ere and ensure Morvoren be well? Ye can keep an eye on 'er and bring 'er food when she awakens."

"'Course, Mother."

"Thank ye, dear." Mother faced Trevik next. "Are ye comin'?"

He hesitated. Typically, he'd go with both his mother and sister to the fish processing cellars in the early hours to oversee the work, but today…

"Soon. I need a bite first."

Mother stilled, staring up at him with an impassive expression.

"What?" he asked, shifting his feet.

"Trevik, don't ye even consider it."

He pulled back. "What?" he repeated.

"Ye know what. That look in your eye can't ne'er be 'idden when ye be up to somethin'."

"What look?" he questioned, hoping to blink away any culpability that might've lingered.

"I know what look," Poppy piped in. "It be the same one 'e 'ad when 'e stole Father's pipe and made 'imself sick breathin' it in all night."

"That was more 'an ten years ago, that," he defended

himself. "And what do ye know 'bout it, Poppy? Ye were only a pinnack when it 'appened."

His sister continued. "It also be the same look when ye went poachin' on Farmer Angwin's land."

"Poachin'? I wasn't poachin'. I was—"

Mother stepped in between them, stopping their argument. "I be in earnest, Trev. Don't go in there and wake up the poor girl."

He pulled an innocent expression. "As if I'd ever."

Mother simply pursed her lips and shook her head. "I'll be back shortly, and when I return, she best still be sleepin'."

"'Tain't up to I. I'll be at the cellars 'fore ye at this rate."

Mother sniffed in disbelief, then finally left the house behind with a wave.

Trevik didn't wait a moment, heading straight for Poppy's room.

"Trevik, ye can't!" Poppy cried out in a harried whisper, racing after him. "Mother told ye to let 'er rest!"

"She can rest after she answers me questions."

They reached the door, but Poppy jumped in front of it, her hands on her hips. Ever since she was old enough to speak, Poppy had been telling Trevik what to do, despite their eleven-year age gap. He'd always said that he had two mothers instead of just the one.

"I'll not let ye in there, Trevik," she whispered with a firm shake of her head.

He looked over his shoulder down the corridor with impatience, ensuring Mother did not appear again. "I 'aven't time for this, Popp. Stand aside."

"Never." She shook her head, then her eye caught onto his cheek. "What be that?"

He brought his fingers to his face in confusion. "What?"

"That red mark on your face." She ran a finger down his cheek.

Blast. He'd thought the woman's slap would surely have faded from his cheek by then.

He turned his face and shook his head. "I'll tell ye where it came from if ye move out o' the way."

"Not a chance."

He sighed, then easily reached his hand above her head and knocked on the door.

"Trevik!" Poppy scolded.

No response came. Poppy gave him a satisfied look. "There, she be sleepin' still. Will ye leave 'er alone now?"

He knocked again, despite Poppy hanging onto his arm to prevent him.

Finally, a muffled response came from behind the door. "Come in."

Trevik smiled. "There, ye see? She be awake."

Poppy's lips thinned, her brow furrowing. "Mother'll be furious with ye, Trevik."

"I be used to her scoldin' by now." He gently brushed Poppy aside, then opened the door wide enough to see the woman lying on Poppy's bed.

Her skin was pale, grey shadows hanging beneath her eyes in heavy half-circles, and her blonde hair—now dry—was splayed about in snarls on the pillow. She blinked as if in a daze, Trevik having clearly woken her up from a deep sleep.

He winced at his poor decision to awaken her when she clearly needed her sleep, but he didn't leave. He'd let her be just as soon as he received some answers.

CHAPTER SIX

The woman continued staring at them, her red eyes narrowing slightly as she peered at Trevik. "May I help you?"

His brow raised at her proper tongue. She most certainly wasn't from Tristwick.

Poppy nudged him over to stand beside him in the doorway. "We just be comin' to ask 'ow ye be doin', miss," she said when Trevik remained silent.

Miss Hollow shifted her head against the pillow. "I'm well enough, thank you." She paused, seeming to think for a moment. "I just be tryin' to rest."

Trevik could have laughed at the noticeable shift in her accent. Just what was this woman doing?

"'Course ye be," Poppy said with a reproachful look at Trevik. "Me brother 'ere only wished to ensure ye were well after pullin' ye from the sea."

Trevik didn't know what he'd been expecting from Miss Hollow after Poppy's words. A smile, perhaps? An expression of gratitude?

Instead, Miss Hollow's gaze hardened. "So," she said after a measured silence, "ye be Trevik Honeysett, the *fisherman*."

Had she spoken the word with derision? He folded his arms. "That be me."

Her gaze didn't flinch. "I s'pose I ought to be thankin' ye then for savin' me life."

Ought to be? She *absolutely* should be thanking him. Of course, had it not been for his net, she wouldn't have needed saving at all, but that was beyond the point.

"It be no trouble," he responded, shifting under her continued stare.

"I s'pose I ought to apologize to ye, too," she said.

He tipped his head to the side in question, and she motioned to his cheek. "For slappin' ye and leavin' that mark."

Heat bled across Trevik's face, made all the worse by Poppy's guttural laugh.

He scowled down at her growing smile.

"She slapped ye?" she whispered.

"I barely felt it," he whispered back.

"Well, she did leave a mark…"

A knock sounded at the front door, and he and Poppy both peered down the short corridor leading to the sitting room.

"Answer the door, will ye?" he asked.

Poppy hesitated, glancing from him to Miss Hollow before another knock occurred. With a sigh, she gave Trevik a look of warning that rivaled Mother's. "Don't be harrassin' 'er, Trevik," she said under her breath, then she scurried down the corridor.

Trevik took advantage of her absence the moment she was gone, facing Miss Hollow from the doorway again. "I be sorry for wakin' ye, but I 'ad a few questions."

A shadow crossed over Miss Hollow's face. "I already told your mother I don't remember much."

"Yes, she did mention that." He paused, her stare warning him off. But who was she to prevent him from ensuring those who stayed in his home wouldn't harm his family? "So ye can't remember where ye came from, then?"

She shook her head with a wince.

"But ye remember your name?"

Her upper lip twitched, and she responded with a flat, "Yes."

He was upsetting her, that much was clear. But was it due to his questioning, or the fact that he'd caught on to her lies? "I s'pose ye don't remember *why* ye were in the sea in the first place?"

She gave him a passive look. "Not at all."

Her response was far too scripted. She was lying. Again.

"Trevik!"

He looked to his side, still standing in the doorway of Poppy's room. Poppy motioned him closer from where she stood down the corridor, a portmanteau in her hands.

He glanced at Miss Hollow. "Excuse me," he mumbled, then he moved toward Poppy.

"Gryffyn dropped this off," she whispered, raising the portmanteau higher. Raindrops speckled the brown, faded leather. "Young Charlie found it 'tween a few rocks on the beach while 'e be lookin' for crabs. 'E thinks it might belong to the mermaid."

"She ain't be no mermaid." He reached for the portmanteau, setting about to remove the clasps that secured it closed, but Poppy reached forward to stop him.

"What ye be doin'?" she whispered, horrified.

"I be lookin' inside to see if it be 'ers."

"Why don't ye just ask 'er?"

"Well surely Gryff already looked through it."

She propped her hands on her hips with pursed lips. "Then *ye* oughtn't need to."

He paused. Perhaps she had a point. Miss Hollow could either lie about the bag belonging to her or admit that she remembered more than she was letting on. Either way, it would save him from rummaging through someone else's belongings.

43

He carried the sturdy portmanteau back down the corridor, Poppy close at his heels. With a tap against the open door, he stopped in the doorway once more.

Miss Hollow's eyes connected with his before dropping down to the bag in his hands. Her lips parted, and her soft intake of breath told him all he needed to know.

"Ye recognize this, then?" he asked. "A friend of ours found it by the beach."

He could almost see her mind racing to formulate a reason strong enough to claim her belongings.

"If ye don't, I guess I'll just put it back—"

"Wait," she interrupted, reaching out. She winced, no doubt having hurt herself by moving so swiftly. "I…I think I do recognize it."

She was a terrible liar. With knowing eyes, he took a step into her room. "Are ye certain? After all, I know your memory ain't reliable."

Her brow lowered. "It be reliable enough, I assure ye."

"Reliable enough to know that this be yours?" He raised the portmanteau.

Before Miss Hollow could respond, Poppy cleared her throat behind him. He glanced back to see her shaking her head, and he sighed. Fine, he'd stop teasing the woman. If only so Poppy wouldn't feed more of this to Mother when she saw her again. He was sure to be scolded fiercely already.

"If ye be sure then, I'll just leave it 'ere for ye." He walked the rest of the way to the table beside the bed. Miss Hollow's eyes focused on the portmanteau as carefully as a feral cat watched a floundering pilchard on land.

He set the bag on the table, moving to walk away, but his hand caught the edge of the portmanteau, and it tumbled to the floor.

The clasp popped open, and a few items fell forth across the wood—a brown glove, a bonnet pin, and a spare piece of paper.

"Forgive I," he mumbled, hurriedly picking up the items and setting them inside the portmanteau. As he was doing so, however, his eyes caught sight of a scrap of paper that appeared to have been folded and refolded a great number of times with writing scribbled across it.

He hadn't meant to pry too greatly, but in the brief moment that he glanced at the crumpled paper and put it in her bag, he saw the writing as clear as day.

Prout's Apothecary
No. 4
Sennen

Sennen. Was that where she was from?

Not wanting to be accused of snooping—by Poppy or Miss Hollow—he slipped the paper back into the portmanteau, secured the clasps, then placed the bag more carefully upon the table.

"We'll let ye sleep now," he said over his shoulder as he walked away. "Sorry for disturbin' ye."

"Wait."

Miss Hollow's soft voice made him pause in the doorway, and he turned to face her once again.

"Do ye have a carriage, per'aps?" she asked. "Or a wagon?"

He nearly laughed. "No, we ain't got the funds to keep one o' them."

She nodded, as if she'd expected his reply.

"Why, do ye remember where ye be from?" he tested. Had she seen him find the address?

She stared for a moment, then cast her gaze down again. "No, just wonderin'."

Another lie. Instead of accusing her of such, however, Trevik merely nodded, then left the room with Poppy. As he closed the door behind them, he stole one final glance at Miss Hollow.

She had brought an arm to rest over her eyes and appeared to be sleeping straightaway, but he paused when a trail of moisture glistened down her pale cheek.

His stomach knotted. Had he been the cause of her tears? Or was she merely crying due to physical pain? But then, he was responsible for that, too.

He tried to justify his actions—after all, she was withholding the truth from them—but regret still folded over him in an endless wave. Whether she was lying or not, the woman was clearly in turmoil. And he'd no doubt just made it worse.

Curse his stubborn pride. He never should have gone into that room.

CHAPTER SEVEN

$\mathcal{M}$orvoren winced as bright sunshine crept across her closed eyes. Surely morning could not have arrived already.

With a drawn-out yawn and a stretch of her back, she slowly opened her eyes. A brief moment of confusion clouded her mind, then she caught sight of the small hearth before her, her underclothing still hanging before the fire.

That was right. She was in the fisherman's home.

She yawned again, the ache in her chest and burning in her throat having eased only slightly from the morning before. She glanced out of the window beside her bed, blinking away the moisture brought to her eyes as the sun filed past the threadbare curtains in sharp rays of light.

It was sure to be a beautiful day. If she were north in St. Ives, she would be forced to accompany Uncle Truscott to watch his fleet of boats casting their seine nets into the seas. Here in Tristwick, she was condemned to remain in her bed due to an aching foot.

She didn't know which was worse.

The night before, after attempting and failing to leave her bed again, she'd finally resigned herself to the fact that she couldn't walk to St. Just, so she would be missing the coach to Sennen. She would catch the next one in a week—or perhaps her ankle would heal sooner than Dr. Kent expected, and she could make the journey to Sennen on foot.

Either way, each moment she spent in Tristwick was a moment closer to Uncle potentially finding her, and with the Honeysetts having no mode of transportation, she knew she was out of luck. Apparently, she'd used it all up yesterday, being rescued from the sea.

As the frightful memory flashed before her mind's eye once again, Morvoren flinched. She'd never been more terrified than when that water had trickled into her lungs, no amount of struggling being able to free her from the net's hold.

That same darkness that had crept over her in the sea now returned from the mere memory, but Morvoren forced her fears away, filling her lungs with the air around her. She was finished dwelling on what might have happened.

Instead, she was going to focus on what *needed* to happen— namely spending an entire week in Tristwick while feigning memory loss. Mrs. Honeysett had generously offered to house Morvoren until she was well. All things considered, such a stay wouldn't be too terrible. After all, the Honeysett *women* weren't the ones who caused Morvoren concern.

She shook her head to be rid of any thought of her supposed rescuer. Trevik Honeysett didn't trust her, even though he had no reason not to. Except, of course, that she was lying. But there was no way for him to know that. He was no doubt suspicious of her merely because she'd slapped him. And now she was trapped with another selfish fisherman who forced his workers to labor for a pittance and stunk of fish.

She wrinkled her nose. Uncle always smelled of codfish and oysters. She was not so naïve as to believe that all fishermen were terrible people. But after seeing what the trade had done to Father and Uncle and after meeting the man Uncle intended for her—that…that incorrigible seiner, Mr. Foss—she knew she'd never be happy living a life so close to the industry.

If the last two days had proven anything, it was that she was determined to escape that life once and for all.

With a sigh, she turned her head to the other side of the room. There, her eye caught sight of the portmanteau on the table beside her.

Relief flooded through her again, just as it had when Mr. Honeysett had first brought the bag to her. She really had convinced herself that her belongings had been stolen, so to see them returned to her had been a godsend.

Struggling to sit up, her ankle still pulsing in protest, Morvoren reached for the portmanteau, anxious to see if all was intact.

She unfastened the latches, peering at the items within the leather carrier. A few dresses, her underclothing, a coin purse —thank heavens her money was still accounted for—one pair of traveling gloves, hairpins, a soft bonnet, boots, a coat. But where was—ah, there it was.

Carefully, she pulled out the turquoise shawl that had once belonged to her mother, wrapping it around her shoulders. She drew in a deep breath of the fabric, the musty smell calming her nerves.

She moved the portmanteau back to the table, leaning against the bed before she caught sight of a scrap of paper that had fallen onto her lap.

How had that escaped? She'd read the piece of paper over and over again, the address ingrained in her memory forever, but still, she'd brought it with her as a symbol of the control she had finally taken over her life.

Tap, tap, tap.

Morvoren looked to the door. "Come in," she said, pulling the shawl tighter around her shoulders and hiding the address beneath the turquoise fabric. Would it be Mr. Honeysett, come to interrogate her further?

Instead of the fisherman, Mrs. Honeysett appeared with a bright smile and a cane in hand. "Good mornin', Morvoren. Feelin' better, are ye?"

"Much better, thank ye," Morvoren said, her shoulders relaxing. Her accent was still not as thick as the Honeysetts', but it came much more fluidly now, as if her tongue had found its place in this lower-class home.

"I be that glad. And 'ow be your foot?"

"Still sore, I fear. But the swellin' be down."

Much to Mrs. Honeysett's aid. The woman had come in multiple times throughout the night, ensuring Morvoren was still breathing well and that her foot was elevated and wrapped in a cold cloth.

Mrs. Honeysett raised the cane. "This ought to 'elp ye when ye be ready to walk about. Borrowed it from a neighbor."

Morvoren smiled her gratitude as Mrs. Honeysett rested it on the table near the bed, then moved to stoke the fire next. "Are ye 'ungry?"

Only then did Morvoren become acutely aware of the empty chasm that was her stomach. "Yes, ma'am."

"We'll be eatin' soon, if ye can wait." She straightened from the hearth, a few flames slipping up around the remaining logs. "And 'ow be your memory?"

Morvoren drew in a steadying breath. How she hated lying to this woman. "I still be strugglin', but…" She pulled out the paper from her shawl. "I recognized the bag your son brought in yesterday as mine. I was lookin' through it just now and found this." She lifted the paper. "It be an address in Sennen."

Mrs. Honeysett's brow rose, accepting the paper Morvoren offered. "So that be where you're from, then?"

"I be thinkin' so." Better to have them believe Sennen was

her home than to ever make a connection to St. Ives. "I do know that be where me friends live, the Prouts."

Mrs. Honeysett's eyes remained on the paper, her lips remaining in a straight line. Surely if she believed Morvoren's tale, she'd be more thrilled. "They must know ye be missin', then," she said softly.

Morvoren nodded, unable to say anything else to earn the woman's trust, for she'd already forfeited such a luxury. Now she could only pray the woman would play along.

"Ye be certain?" Mrs. Honeysett pressed. She extended the scrap of paper back to Morvoren. "I want to be sure ye'll be taken care of."

Morvoren pulled her shawl closer to her person, Mrs. Honeysett's words chipping away at her conscience. "Yes, we be the dearest of friends, see. They'll take care of I, to be certain."

In truth, Morvoren hadn't heard a word from Zennor Prout since she'd married Mr. Prout more than a year before in St. Ives. Zennor was the daughter of a seining gentleman, and she and Morvoren had bonded over their shared dislike of the whole trade.

On the day of her wedding, Zennor had offered Morvoren a way out of her life with Uncle. "Come and stay with us in Sennen," Zennor had said, scribbling the address on a piece of paper before thrusting it in Morvoren's hands. "My Mr. Prout has a lovely apothecary shop. You can work there with us, earn a fine enough income, perhaps find a man of your own to marry. Anything to escape that uncle of yours."

The offer had been in the back of Morvoren's mind for months, and she'd kept the paper as a symbol—a reminder of her one chance for freedom. Only when Uncle presented his latest plans for Morvoren did she finally attempt to flee to the one friend she'd ever had. Sennen wouldn't be her final destination, rather a stopping point for her to find another life in a place she could be free from her memories and free from Uncle.

Now she could only hope Zennor still considered Morvoren a friend.

"Well," Mrs. Honeysett said, interrupting her thoughts, "they must be worried sick. Ye must wish to send a letter to 'em. Let 'em know ye be safe."

Morvoren nodded. "I think that'd be for the best." If only to provide Zennor with a bit of notice. Morvoren had been in too great a rush to have sent a letter to her before leaving Uncle's. "And I'll take the coach to Sennen when me foot be better." She paused, tipping her head to the side to appear curious. "If ye can just tell me when the coach departs."

Mrs. Honeysett grimaced, taking Morvoren's bait. "I fear the coach only travels to Sennen on Mondays."

Morvoren did her best to appear disappointed, though she didn't have to try too hard, her frustration still lingering from the day before.

"But ne'er mind, dear. Ye know I already offered for ye to stay with us 'til ye be well."

"Ye be certain I'm not puttin' ye out?"

"Not at all. It be the least we can do." Mrs. Honeysett patted Morvoren's leg softly. "I just be glad ye remembered where ye were goin'. 'Twill 'elp folks 'round 'ere end their talkin'."

She gave a small laugh, but Morvoren narrowed her eyes. "What do ye mean?"

"Oh, they just be sayin' ye be from the sea," Mrs. Honeysett clarified with another flippant laugh.

Morvoren gave a half-smile. Would that she *could* be a mermaid. She wouldn't mind living in the sea, away from the troubles of this world.

"Now," Mrs. Honeysett said, heading toward the door, "Poppy and I'll be back soon from the cellars, then we can eat luncheon together. I've made a bit o' cherry tarts for after, too."

Morvoren nodded. "Thank ye, Mrs. Honeysett. For everythin'."

Mrs. Honeysett nodded, sending a warm wink to Morvoren before leaving her alone once more.

Morvoren released a satisfied sigh. That had turned out better than she could have hoped. Now all she needed to do was survive a week in the Honeysetts' home, pray no one connected her name to Uncle's, and attempt to dodge Mr. Honeysett's questionings.

That should be easy enough.

For now, however, she simply wanted to remove whoever's chemise she'd been wearing and dress in her own clothing.

Moving slowly, Morvoren managed to stand with the help of the cane Mrs. Honeysett had given her. Her ankle still protested dully in pain with each step, but soon enough, she managed to don her own underclothing and dark blue day dress before untangling the days' worth of knots her hair had accumulated. After pinning up her tresses and pinching her cheeks to hopefully detract from the exhaustion she still felt, she walked step-by-slow-step out of the room.

If only Uncle could see her now, tottering about a drifter's home with a cane, boasting lopsided hair, a faded dress, and grey circles under her eyes.

Uncle had always refused her departure from her room unless she looked *"a more presentable member of Society."*

Only recently, he'd hired a lady's maid to see to Morvoren's dress and hair and had given her jewelry and fine clothing to impress the upper societies with whom they mingled. At the end of every dinner party and ball, it was the very same. She'd be stripped of all jewels and silk gowns and left alone to her simple, dark clothing, ignored until the next party she'd be called on to flaunt for.

She didn't need silk gowns or ruby earrings. All she

needed was the sea. That was what had hurt her the most—when Uncle had stripped her of the waves as well.

The familiar pinching in Morvoren's chest brought her back to the present, and she squeezed her eyes to rid herself of the feeling. She didn't need to dwell on such memories any longer. Uncle was not there, nor could he ever take the sea away from her again.

With a raised chin she hoped would help her feel more confident than she was, Morvoren limped down the corridor, intent on exploring the modest home while its inhabitants were gone. Fortunately, the house was not very large, for after walking down the short corridor, peeking into the humble kitchen, and ending with the simple sitting room, she breathed heavily with exhaustion.

Curse this wretched foot. Would it never heal?

Leaning ever more on the cane, she moved to the wooden bench positioned at the side of the hearth. From there, her eyes roved over the simple decorations of the room. Rather than the dark walls giving off an overbearing, suffocating sensation, they wrapped the space up in a warm embrace. The friendly feel was enhanced only by the tan-colored curtains and a nearby vase of orange and yellow wildflowers with red berries as an accent.

A rudimentary painting of a family of four—no doubt the Honeysetts—was positioned near the vase, and a conglomeration of blue and white seashells decorated the frame.

How this differed from the imperious décor of Uncle's townhouse, with its tapestries, marble flooring, and green, velvet curtains. She'd always despised the large, arrogant paintings he'd purchased to give the appearance that he'd been wealthy forever—rather than having made his fortune in his early twenties.

Morvoren far preferred the Honeysetts' comfortable home, even if it belonged to a fisherman.

She thought back to Mrs. Honeysett's words, about those

in Tristwick believing Morvoren to be a mermaid. It didn't really surprise her. After all, Cornish lore and suspicions ran deep through fishing communities.

Besides, it was only fitting. Mother had always called Morvoren something similar. "Come along, my little sea-maid," she'd say as she tried to pry Morvoren from the sea. They used to spend hours in the water together, but Morvoren never grew tired of the rolling waves.

When Morvoren reached Sennen next week, she would spend every waking moment in the water again. When she wasn't helping at the apothecary shop, that is. Or dodging luggers near the busy fishing port.

But that was neither here nor there. Zennor would surely help Morvoren find a home near enough to the sea, but far enough from the fishing trade. Such a place had to exist whether in or outside of Sennen…hadn't it?

She pressed a hand to her temples, hoping to ward off the beginnings of a headache. She only needed to survive a week living under the Honeysetts' roof, then she'd be free to never, *never* be near a drifter or seiner again.

For now, she'd just be grateful that Mr. Honeysett wasn't home and that she—

The door creaked open behind her, and she swiveled her head to discover, much to her dismay, that Trevik Honeysett strode straight through the doorway.

Apparently, Heaven was not yet done playing cruel tricks on her.

CHAPTER EIGHT

"*Y*e be movin' about, then," Mr. Honeysett said, closing the door behind him.

Morvoren nodded. Had her foot not been so sore, she would have stood right back up and returned to her room. Such would be easier than attempting to keep her secrets around this suspicious man.

He removed his cap and jacket, hanging them on a hook near the door as the silence between them grew louder.

Uncle would surely die if he knew she was with a single man unchaperoned. He was always about keeping up appearances, forcing Morvoren to play the part of obedient niece. She could only imagine how furious he must have been upon discovering her escape. If she wasn't trying so hard to avoid him, it might have been enjoyable to see that vein pulsing once again in his brow.

Her eyes wandered across Mr. Honeysett's shoulders before he faced forward, drawing her attention away from any thought of Uncle.

"'Ow fares your foot?" he asked, walking past the back of the bench she sat upon as he stepped toward the kitchen.

She followed his movements with her ears alone. "It be a little better."

He didn't respond.

She looked to her left just in time to see him enter the kitchen. There, he stood with his hands propped on his hips, looking back and forth as if in search of something.

"I remembered somethin'," she said, raising her voice a fraction to be heard from the next room. "I was on me way to Sennen yesterday, to meet with me friends. I'll be takin' the coach come Monday."

"Mother told I only just now."

He offered nothing further. Had Mrs. Honeysett warned him of her lies? Or was he simply maintaining his suspicions from before?

He faced sideways so she could see his profile, though his eyes continued to rove about the kitchen.

Morvoren was not so proud that she could not admit that he was one of the more attractive fishermen she'd seen, what with his angled jaw and strong brow. Certainly nothing like Mr. Foss with his weak chin and overly shaped hair.

Then again, she hardly knew Mr. Foss enough to make such an observation. She'd only met with him a handful of times and had spoken to him even less. He was handsome enough, in spite of the chin, but his behavior—especially at the ball the night before she'd left—had been swift to secure him as last place in a veritably nonexistent list of men Morvoren would ever consider marrying.

Unfortunately, Uncle didn't think her opinion on the issue mattered.

She watched in silence as Mr. Honeysett's eyes settled on the table, where a plate of pastries sat. Those must have been the cherry tarts Mrs. Honeysett had mentioned earlier. He wasn't planning on eating them, was he?

Sure enough, he reached for the plate, removing one of the tarts.

Morvoren should remain silent. After all, as strangely as Mr. Honeysett was behaving, this *wasn't* her home. And yet, Mrs. Honeysett must have slaved over those tarts all morning. Surely she would not wish for her son to eat them before she was ready to serve them.

"I believe those were meant for after luncheon."

Mr. Honeysett paused, the tart halfway to his mouth. "Pardon?"

She motioned to the tart. "Your mother said those were for after luncheon."

He blinked. "She won't mind."

He moved to take a bite, and her mouth dropped open in disbelief.

She shouldn't have been surprised. She'd seen this thoughtless behavior before. Uncle was always disrespecting his cook, leaving plates of food untouched to go to waste and more often than not sending his meals away because it did not meet his impossibly high standards.

But to see Mr. Honeysett treat his own mother's efforts in such a way? She couldn't stand for it. Indignation boiled within her. "I be certain she *would* mind."

The pastry still hovered near his mouth as he turned to face her more fully. "Are ye now?"

She nodded with a single jerk of her head. "If I had a son, I wouldn't wish for him to eat what he wasn't s'pposed to."

"'Ave ye a son?"

She frowned. "No."

"Then I think I'll defer to me own opinion o' me mother's wishes, 'stead of a stranger's."

With that, he sunk his teeth into the pastry and chewed a hearty bite.

Morvoren pulled her lips into a frown. She had a mind to scold the man further, but when the door opened, she knew she didn't need to.

Mrs. Honeysett and Poppy entered the house, and Mr.

Honeysett promptly shoved the rest of the pastry into his mouth, swiftly turning away.

Morvoren would have laughed at the sight had she not been so irritated.

"Morvoren," Mrs. Honeysett greeted with a smile, "don't ye look lovely this mornin'. 'Ow did ye manage to dress? I…" She paused, turning to her son standing in the kitchen. "Trevik 'Oneysett, I know what ye be doin'!"

"Hmm?" came his muffled reply. His jaw worked as he chewed ferociously, but Mrs. Honeysett was already upon him, followed closely by Poppy, who gave a friendly smile to Morvoren in greeting.

"I should've known," Mrs. Honeysett said, covering the pastries with a cloth and setting them farther back on the table. "I told meself to put these away." She turned back to her son with a pointed look. "Ye know how rare it be when we can actually afford to make pastries li'e these. They be for *after* we eat."

"Ah, it be only one, Mother." Mr. Honeysett glanced to Morvoren with a look of annoyance, no doubt because of the grin she wore from ear to ear. How nice it felt to be right.

"Yes, but 'ad I not returned, ye would've eaten the lot of 'em." Mrs. Honeysett skirted about the kitchen, Morvoren only catching a glimpse of her now and again as the woman moved from the hutch to the table with plates and cutlery.

"I be sorry, Mrs. Honeysett," Morvoren piped up. "I did try to stop him."

Mrs. Honeysett popped her head in the doorway to smile at Morvoren. "'Tain't your fault, dear. No one could e'er stop me son from eatin' a pastry."

She disappeared back into the kitchen, Mr. Honeysett scowling at Morvoren before turning his back on her once again. She watched with interest as he glanced at his mother then back to the plate of pastries.

Slowly, he reached out to swipe another tart. Morvoren

opened her mouth, ready to defend poor Mrs. Honeysett's food, but Poppy jumped in first.

"Mother! Trevik be thievin' another!"

Mrs. Honeysett gasped as he snatched another cherry tart, sliding the entire pastry into his mouth once again. "Trevik, ye little pisky." She took a spoon from the table, swatting at him lightly, but he jumped out of the way with a chuckle.

"I won't eat another, I swear it," he said with a mouth full of food, still laughing as he dodged another swat from his mother. "I be starvin', see."

"Ye'll be starvin' when I be finished with ye," Mrs. Honeysett said, though she'd lowered her spoon and continued setting the table with a smile.

She'd not truly been upset, then? Poppy either? Morvoren studied the family, their smiles spreading warmth about the house like rays of autumn sunshine. She couldn't deny the happiness the family exuded, nor the effect such joy had on her, drawing her closer like a beacon of light to a lost ship.

But she closed her heart to such a temptation. She could appreciate their love for one another, but the fishing trade had destroyed everything she'd ever loved. Surely it was only a matter of time before it wounded the Honeysetts, as well—if it hadn't already.

Mr. Honeysett's dark eyes met hers then, and she started. She hadn't realized she'd been staring. His focus remained on her for a moment, then he shifted to stand behind the kitchen wall.

Wooden plates and bowls thudded mutely against the table as the places were set for the meal, and Morvoren ignored the unsettling feeling Mr. Honeysett's gaze had left her with.

"Can I help ye in there?" she asked.

Mrs. Honeysett's voice sounded from the other room. "No, no, dear. Ye just rest. Ain't nothin' ye can do with your foot. 'Sides, we be nearly done."

Morvoren waited in silence for the Honeysetts to finish,

then Mrs. Honeysett helped her into the kitchen to sit down opposite from Mr. Honeysett at the small table.

Morvoren settled down and eyed the herring soup in the bowl before her, onions, pepper, and pieces of fish floating about in a watery mixture. She'd never had a taste for fish, far preferring to watch them in the water than to see them looking up at her from a plate. But she would never wish to offend Mrs. Honeysett.

At least the herring's eyes weren't staring up at her like the pilchards in a stargazey pie.

She made for the spoon, only to pause when Mrs. Honeysett and Poppy both reached for her hands on either side of her. Morvoren hesitated just a moment before allowing them to take her hands in theirs.

Mrs. Honeysett spoke first. "Lord, make us able to eat what's on the table."

The family bowed their heads for a moment, then released hands and tucked into their meal.

Morvoren hesitated another moment before taking a spoonful of the watery concoction herself. To her surprise—and relief—the meal wasn't as repulsive as she had imagined. In fact, it tasted rather nice. Of course, that could simply be due to the fact that she was quite starved. Either way, she would take it.

"We 'ad a fine catch today," Mr. Honeysett said in between bites of his food, his jaw working as he chewed. Not that Morvoren noticed.

"We'll be blessed if it continues," Mrs. Honeysett agreed. "Though we do be drownin' in the cellars."

Mr. Honeysett lowered his spoon. "I've been meanin' to fix that. I think it be time to ask the miners for 'elp. It be early still, but some o' them won't mind 'elpin' now, I be sure of it. What do ye think?"

Morvoren paused. Uncle had always ignored the advice of

others, even when they very clearly knew better than he did. Was Mr. Honeysett truly asking his mother her opinion?

"I think the sooner we ask 'em, the better." Mrs. Honeysett chewed another spoonful. "Mrs. Merrick'll be wantin' to come. Though, we'll not 'ave the 'elp of 'er daugh'er this year."

Poppy gave an airy sigh. "Fortunate woman that she be."

Morvoren glanced between them, and Mrs. Honeysett explained. "Gwynna Merrick worked as a bal maiden over at Wheal Favour 'fore she married the owner's son. She be busy runnin' a household 'stead o' spallin' or processin' fish now."

Morvoren's brow raised, but she was hardly able to process what she'd heard before Poppy continued speaking.

"Yes, and 'twas the most romantic weddin' we ever saw, wasn't it, Mother? Both classes present and teary eyes aboundin'. Though, mind, not from 'em upper folks. But still, 'twas perfect." Poppy sighed. "Would that such a thing'd 'appen to I as to marry a wealthy gent." Then she dropped her gaze. "Oh, speakin' of 'elp in the cellars. I was thinkin'. Per'aps ye ought to 'ire Lieutenant 'Arris, Trevik."

Morvoren caught the look shared between Mrs. Honeysett and her son.

"Ye know the lieutenant already works at Golowduyn, Poppy. We see 'im there every week." Mrs. Honeysett turned to Morvoren. "The lieutenant's been on reserve from the navy and supplementin' 'is income while 'e nurses a wound, see." She turned again to her daughter. "Why'd 'e need more work than 'e already does?"

Poppy shrugged far too flippantly. "Per'aps 'e wishes to."

Mrs. Honeysett smiled knowingly, and Morvoren paused. Did Poppy fancy this Lieutenant Harris?

Before another word could be said, Poppy shifted the conversation again. Mrs. Honeysett did her best to fill in details for Morvoren, but soon enough, Morvoren kept her head down, not wishing to impose on their family meal and discussions any longer.

Would she feel like an imposition when she joined the Prouts? Or would Zennor be in no position to help Morvoren at all?

Her worried thoughts continued to spiral as she thought back to living with Uncle. Rather than a simple feeling, Morvoren *knew* she had been a burden on him. He could hardly stand to be near her, Morvoren rarely eating with him beyond dinner parties. Otherwise, she was forced to take her meals in her room alone, which was admittedly preferable to having Uncle's watchful, condemning gaze on her.

His condemnation had been the worst the night she'd left. *"Mr. Foss will make you a fine husband, Miss Hollow,"* he'd said. *"And his father will make me a fine business partner."*

A fine husband, indeed. That was the last word she would ever use to describe Mr. Foss. That gentleman seiner was rumored to have a mistress in nearly every town in the southwest of Cornwall.

She shuddered to think of suffering through life with such a husband. Living with Uncle had been unbearable—how would it have been living with an openly debased spouse?

"At any rate, the men won't be 'appy for long. I've 'eard talk…"

Mr. Honeysett's words pulled Morvoren back from her thoughts, and her ears perked at the instant dimming of the mood around the table.

Mrs. Honeysett lowered her spoon. "What news 'ave ye?"

Mr. Honeysett lowered his voice with a glance toward the door, as if someone might overhear their conversation. "Ye've 'eard o' who be in St. Just. They asked Gryffyn if 'e wanted to work for 'em."

"No."

Mr. Honeysett nodded. "Fortunately, it be 'im they asked. 'E won't be leavin' we. But the Cardys…"

Morvoren did her best to focus on her stew instead of their conversation. After all, why should she take any interest in what they were discussing?

"Ye ought to give 'em more credit, son," Mrs. Honeysett said. "Edern Cardy was friends with your father 'fore ye were even born."

His father. Morvoren had yet to have heard a single mention of the man until that point. Had he died? Is that why Mr. Honeysett owned the lugger?

"Yes, but we know 'e ain't be as devoted. And them seiners be awful sweet talkers."

Shock jolted through Morvoren's body at the mention of seiners, and a sudden numbness weakened her limbs. She tried to regain the feeling in her hands, but it was too late. Her fingers lost their grip on the spoon, and it clattered loudly against the table.

Instantly, the eyes of the Honeysetts were upon her.

CHAPTER NINE

$\mathcal{M}$orvoren mumbled an apology, retrieving her spoon and stirring her soup around for a moment. Her appetite had entirely vanished.

The conversation continued despite Mr. Honeysett's gaze in her direction, and she shifted against the dark wood of her chair.

Seiners. In St. Just. Morvoren shouldn't have been surprised. She'd heard of Uncle sending out representatives to various drifters before, luring them to join his company. Were those in St. Just sent by him? Had he been alerted of her presence already, or would the men not recognize her if they saw her?

"Sweet talkers or not," Mrs. Honeysett said, "it'd take an awful lot for Edern to leave ye, son."

Trevik's eyes were still on Morvoren when he responded. "I do 'ope ye be right, Mother."

Silence centered around the table, but Morvoren's mind hummed with concern. She had to know. She had to know if they were Uncle's men. If they were, she'd leave that very evening. She'd crawl to Sennen if she had to. Never mind that her foot still pulsed or that it might be a risk to walk alone. Waiting around for Uncle was even more of a risk.

"Do ye…" Her voice cracked, and she cleared her throat, beginning again with more confidence. "Do ye know the seinin' companies who be in St. Just?"

She was met with curious glances from each of the Honeysetts, so she rushed to explain. "It's just that, the word seinin' sounds familiar."

"Indeed." Mr. Honeysett's dubious expression matched his misbelieving tone. "They be Trenary and Verran of Port Isaac."

She nodded in silence, attempting to appear unruffled, though relief sailed through her limbs, leaving a numbing shock in its wake.

No Truscott. And she'd not heard of either of the other names. Thank heavens.

"Do they sound familiar to ye, Morvoren?" Mrs. Honeysett questioned.

"Afraid not," she said, twisting a disappointed frown on her lips.

She went back to her soup, avoiding Mr. Honeysett's watchful gaze as he drank a sip of his brandy.

He swallowed, then placed his glass near his empty bowl, leaning forward with his elbows on the table. "I s'pose that can only be a good thing," he said. "We'd 'ate to 'ave ye connected to those sorts o' people."

Morvoren met his gaze, and something within the depths of his eyes laced ice through her stomach. Did he know?

"They ain't all terrible, son," Mrs. Honeysett said, shaking her head as she swallowed her food.

Mr. Honeysett sniffed in disbelief. "All the seiners we've e'er known 'ave been terrible. And they'll keep comin' back over an' over to poach our men. 'Tis 'cause they ain't be good enough to keep their own."

For so long, Morvoren had endured Uncle's endless criticisms over drifters. *"They are as simple and stubborn as mules,"* he'd say.

Now, hearing the perspective of seiners from the drifters was rather humorous.

"'Tain't a lick of honor in 'em neither," Mr. Honeysett continued. He faced his mother. "Ye've 'eard 'bout the drifters in Mounts Bay?"

Mrs. Honeysett shook her head.

He glanced to Morvoren, but she pretended to stifle a yawn. She didn't want him to think he'd captured her attention.

"The men were served writs by Sir Percival St. John for fishin' too close to the shore. But the only ones who were served 'em were those who didn't vote for the man in the county election."

Mrs. Honeysett shook her head. "Terrible shame, that."

"Travesty, more like," Mr. Honeysett followed. "Them drifters ain't doin' nothin' wrong."

Morvoren blew out a disbelieving breath, only to realize too late that she'd done it loud enough for the others around the table to hear. She tried to disguise it by clearing her throat, but Mr. Honeysett's eyes hardened.

What was wrong with her? She had an opinion stronger than anyone on more matters than she cared to admit, even though Uncle had tried to stamp it out of her. Revealing her opinion, however, would bring more trouble than she cared for.

"Ye 'ave something to say, Miss 'Ollow?" he asked.

She opened her mouth to say exactly what was at the tip of her tongue, but she pulled back. She had very little care for the man seated in front of her, but she didn't wish to offend his mother and sister.

"Go on," Mr. Honeysett challenged. "Ye obviously be thinkin' somethin'. Though I can't decipher yet if it be 'bout seiners or drifters."

She pressed her lips together all the firmer.

"Ye be free to speak your mind 'ere, Morvoren," Mrs. Honeysett said with an encouraging nod. "We don't always agree on matters, but we still be family. While ye live under our roof, the same goes for ye."

Morvoren chewed the inside of her lip. Had the woman just said Morvoren was a part of their family? A flame sparked in her center, and she furrowed her brow, unsure of how to respond to such a statement.

"I was only thinkin'," she began, "that if the drifters didn't wish to be served writs, they oughtn't fish so close to the shore."

She looked pointedly at Mr. Honeysett, but he merely gave her a half-smile, obviously not picking up on her slight.

"I do wonder 'ow ye can 'ave such an opinion when ye 'ave no memory," he said.

"Trevik," Mrs. Honeysett softly warned.

Morvoren's cheeks warmed. "Per'aps one ne'er loses one's memory about what be breakin' the law and what ain't."

"Exactly right, dear," Mrs. Honeysett said, patting Morvoren's hand.

Mr. Honeysett shifted his gaze from his mother back to Morvoren. "So it be drifters you're against, then."

She needed to tread softly moving forward. Mrs. Honeysett may have encouraged her to speak her mind, but these people were still drifters.

"I be against anyone who ignores the needs of others and only focuses on their own gain," she said.

"And ye think the drifters be more like that than the seiners?" He scoffed. "That sea water must've addled your brain more than we thought."

Morvoren scowled at the man's audacity.

"That be enough, Trevik," Mrs. Honeysett stated firmly.

Mr. Honeysett lowered his eyes, seeming to take a calming breath. Morvoren should've done the same, but instead, she took the opportunity to speak again. "All I be sayin' is that laws be set up for a reason."

Mr. Honeysett shook his head, downing another gulp of his brandy before his voice lowered. "The law was set forth for the sake o' seiners, so they catch their fish 'fore we drifters can. But tell me this, Miss 'Ollow." He faced her, his brown eyes focused intently. "Do it make sense for us to follow that law when seiners don't even fish in Tristwick?"

Morvoren clamped her mouth shut, Uncle's words floating through her mind.

"The drifters always disrupt the shoals," he'd grumbled every autumn. *"They're the worst sort of men."*

But she wouldn't repeat them. She wasn't on his side, nor was she on Mr. Honeysett's. In her opinion, they both had inexcusable flaws.

Mr. Honeysett, however, took her silence as victory and leaned back in his chair with a raise of his chin. "One day, the men o' this country'll see that we drifters bring far more benefit to society as a whole than seiners e'er could."

Her blood boiled at his confidence, his pride mirroring Uncle's so greatly, she could no longer hold her tongue. "I can think of one very clear reason for ye not to fish near the shore." He watched her expectantly. "And it be the very reason I be sittin' here at your table with an injured foot."

His look of pride vanished, his eyes clouding over, and satisfaction swelled within Morvoren's chest. Oh, but she did enjoy winning an argument.

"Well," Mrs. Honeysett said, standing from the table, "I think it be time for 'em cherry tarts."

Morvoren glanced up at the woman, only then noting the look of discomfort on her brow.

All too swiftly, Morvoren's own pride disappeared. She'd allowed herself to become wrapped up too greatly in the argu-ment—an argument she shouldn't even really care enough about to win.

"Would ye like a tart, Morvoren?" Mrs. Honeysett asked.

Overcome with a sudden exhaustion, Morvoren pushed herself away from the table. "Would ye mind very much if I return to me room? I feel a bit palchy."

Mrs. Honeysett was at her side at once. "'Course, dear. Let me 'elp ye."

Together, the two inched down the short corridor, Mrs. Honeysett depositing Morvoren on her bed before leaving the room with the door closed behind her.

Morvoren bowed her head, rubbing her palms against her eyes before hushed voices found their way toward her room.

"I don't like when ye talk o' them seinin' companies, Trevik," Mrs. Honeysett said. "They make ye all riled up."

"'Course they do, Mother," he returned. "'Ow could they not after what 'appened to Father."

Morvoren looked toward the door, as if doing so might allow her to better hear their words. What had happened to his father? And in what way were the seiners involved?

"I know. But ye oughtn't allow that to affect 'ow ye treat that poor woman."

Silence followed Mrs. Honeysett's words, and Morvoren held her breath until Mr. Honeysett spoke again.

"Even if she be lyin'?"

"Yes, even if she be lyin'," Mrs. Honeysett returned.

Morvoren blanched. They all suspected her?

"We don't know 'er reasons for doin' so, nor what she even be lyin' 'bout," Mrs. Honeysett continued. "But to I, it 'ardly matters. 'Twas your nets that drowned 'er, so we'll be 'elpin' 'er 'til she be fitty."

"I didn't drown 'er, for Heaven's——"

"Stop, Trevik. She'll 'ear ye."

Their voices continued, though too softly for Morvoren to decipher another word. It was just as well. She knew Mr. Honeysett would continue to accuse her of lies and Mrs.

Honeysett would defend her further—even though Morvoren had, in fact, lied to her from the very start.

That knowledge alone was enough to shake the foundations of Morvoren's decisions, but she reminded herself once again what—and *whom*—she'd left behind.

She would continue with her lies, if only because she could not go back to her uncle, nor the man he intended for her to wed.

CHAPTER TEN

*A*fter being thoroughly scolded by Mother *again,* Trevik had spent the rest of the day catching up on his sleep and helping in the cellars, doing anything to avoid being near Miss Hollow.

How the woman had managed to dupe his own family to be on her side instead of his was beyond him. Clearly, she was lying about her memory. Her accent had strengthened, though not as greatly as theirs, and she had far too strong an opinion about fishermen—seiners and drifters alike—to have no recollection of either.

After their argument during luncheon, Miss Hollow hadn't joined them for dinner that evening. She was simply evading his family to avoid being caught in her lies, but Mother had blamed Trevik instead.

"She'd be out 'ere with us if she didn't fear she'd be questioned by ye all the time, Trevik," she'd said in a whisper as they cleaned up the meal. "I do think she be in trouble, son. Whether with the law or something else, I don't know. But she was adamant that 'er name wasn't to be spread about St. Just. Poppy and I 'ave decided to honor that. Dr. Kent, too. Will ye?"

Trevik had reluctantly agreed, if only to end his mother's arguments in the woman's defense.

He regretted being the cause of Miss Hollow's injury more than anything. He hated knowing that he'd truly wounded someone. But now more than ever, he was beginning to regret the accident if only because of how much trouble Miss Hollow was proving to be for him.

Bidding farewell to his mother and sister, Trevik closed the door behind him, setting off across the footpath that led from his home at the south curve of the cove down to the small harbor at the center.

He was eager to sail that evening, to clear his mind on the waves. Hard work always did a man's mind good. And hard work at sea was worth double.

"Evenin', Trevik."

Trevik glanced up as Gryffyn stepped out of his own home and joined him on the pathway. "Evenin', Gryff."

"Ye ready for another night?"

"As always."

They fell in step beside each other, a few other men filtering from their cottages farther down the pathway.

"Your mother and sister all right?"

Trevik nodded.

"And the mermaid?"

He glanced at Gryffyn sidelong. Humor was laced in his friend's words, but Trevik wasn't in the mood for such teasing after the scoldings he'd received. "Don't ye be startin' with that belief now."

Gryffyn chuckled. "'Tain't in the mood, are ye?"

Trevik rubbed the back of his neck. "Not after findin' out that the woman'll be 'ere 'til Monday next."

"Did 'er memory return, then?"

Trevik hesitated, lowering his voice. "Can I 'ave your word not to repeat this, Gryff?"

"'Course." His brow furrowed.

Trevik glanced around them. Revealing his anxiousness over the situation to anyone other than Gryffyn would prove to increase all of Tristwick's nerves. Allowing them to believe that Trevik had the situation under control would be far wiser. Father had always known just what to say to ease others' concerns, but Trevik's patience always wore thin when superstitions were believed over logic.

"I think she be lyin'," he whispered. "'Bout everythin'."

Gryffyn blew out a slow breath. "Why do ye say that?"

As they carried on down the pathway, Trevik briefly explained his reasoning. Her accent shifting, her memory coming and going. Her defensiveness over her bag and her knowledge of the law.

"What reason 'as she to lie, though?" Gryffyn asked after Trevik's explanation.

Trevik raised his hands in a helpless gesture. He'd gone through every option, from her being a spy of seiners to her being on the run from the law. "I can't say for sure. All I know is that if others find out, there'll be the devil to pay."

Gryffyn was silent for a moment as they rounded the ridge toward the center of the cove. From their vantage point, they could see the men already boarding the lugger, white sails and dark wood against a shimmering sea and orange sky.

Trevik tried to allow the sight to soothe his concerns, but Gryffyn's worried expression unsettled him further. "Don't tell me. Edern's already been talkin' to others 'bout 'er?" Trevik asked.

"'Fraid so. 'E's been tellin' everyone that ye brought a mermaid aboard the *Pilferer* and now ye be 'oldin' 'er against 'er will. 'E believes it be only a matter o' time 'fore she wreaks 'avoc on we. And Jowan be more afeared than 'is grandfar."

Trevik blew out an impatient breath. How was Trevik to keep Jowan and Edern silent so they could all focus on what was really important—staying alive that winter by fishing *now*?

"T'only good thing that's 'appened in all this is that Miss

'Ollow can't walk," he grumbled. "If she came out and all o' Tristwick saw 'er, they'd be certain she be from the sea."

"Why be that?"

"For one thing, she be a stranger. For another, she claims to not know where 'er 'ome be. Edern'd say at once that she wishes to 'ide the fact that she be from the sea. Then o' course, there be the matter of 'er looks."

Gryffyn didn't respond.

Trevik glanced over to see if he'd heard him, then pulled back when he was met with Gryffyn's sly smile.

"What ye be smilin' for?"

"Ye think she 'as the look of a sea-maid then, do ye?"

Heavens above. "Ye've seen 'er, Gryff. I'd be lyin' if I said she ain't be a docy maid."

And she was even more beautiful now. When he'd first pulled her from the sea, she'd been as blue as a mackerel with eyes that bulged like a flounder.

This afternoon, however, her cheeks glowed pink and that blue dress of hers had accentuated the green of her eyes. He'd thought her hair had been a shade darker, no doubt from all the sea water. But with it dry and piled at the back of her head, the color was as golden as a…well, a siren. All put together, she appeared rather elegant—which made him wonder yet again where she was from. The proper accent she'd first exhibited and her apparent grace both pointed to her home being far finer than Tristwick.

Noting the continued silence from Gryffyn, Trevik glanced up at him, catching another knowing grin.

Trevik shook his head. "I know what ye be thinkin', but she ain't me taste."

"Be that so?"

"Yes. Beautiful women be like wild roses, see. They be fine enough to look at, but when ye draw close to 'em, the thorns get ye."

Gryffyn chuckled, but Trevik was serious. In his admittedly limited experience, fine women were far more interested in wealth than anything else. That was fine by him. He didn't have time to waste on women who couldn't pull their own weight in a marriage.

"I will say this," Gryffyn finally said. "Ye can keep 'er tucked away in your 'ome if ye wish. But keepin' 'er 'idden will only rouse suspicions more."

Blast, if that wasn't a valid argument.

They reached the deck, their conversation pausing as they nodded in greeting to Enyon Penna, who walked past them toward the lugger.

"Then what do ye suggest I do?" Trevik asked softly once they were alone again.

"Bring 'er to the gatherin' on the beach tomorrow," Gryffyn suggested. "Show 'em 'ow 'armless she be so they forget all about the Cardys' gossip."

Trevik hesitated. "I don't know, Gryff. Bringin' 'er 'round so many folks, givin' 'er the chance to lie…Don't seem smart."

Gryffyn took a step toward the lugger. "Ye've got to make the decision yourself, Trevik. But sometimes, placin' the truth directly in front o' people be better than allowin' their minds to run free with all manner o' lies."

Trevik gave a defeated sigh. The man's logic could not be contested. "Ye be right, I s'pose."

Gryffyn clasped Trevik's shoulder with a strong hand. "I always be."

Trevik shook his head amusedly as Gryffyn laughed at himself, then they walked together to join the others on the *Pilferer*.

Gryffyn was right. Bringing Miss Hollow before the others would be for the best. Besides, having her in front of a large group would give Trevik just the opportunity to observe her behavior unhindered. Perhaps then he'd be able to discover just what she was up to.

Because no one told lies for no reason, and he was determined to find out hers.

CHAPTER ELEVEN

*M*orvoren clutched onto the cane with her right hand, her knuckles white as Mrs. Honeysett held her other arm.

"We can go as slowly as ye need," Mrs. Honeysett said, leading her down the pathway to the beach. Poppy walked at Morvoren's other side. "Just keep to the pace ye wish."

Morvoren nodded, unable to form a response as she held her breath with each step of her injured foot against the dirt path. The swelling had fully dissipated, but her ankle was still too weak to hold much of her weight.

Mrs. Honeysett continued. "And if the journey be too much for ye, we can bring ye right back 'ome. Ye just say the word."

As if Morvoren would dare suggest such a thing. The Honeysetts had all been adamant that she attend the evening's bonfire, though Morvoren had heartily protested. Going out in public with a group of fishermen, all while risking a possible sighting of seiners, could hardly be wise. Even now, she scanned the cliffsides, fearing Uncle watched her from above.

And yet, Mrs. Honeysett had gone so above and beyond in

her attempts to ensure Morvoren's comfort that Morvoren couldn't refuse. Not only had the woman reassured her that the guest list was small and controlled, but she'd even brought Dr. Kent back to ensure Morvoren's foot wouldn't regress because of the short walk to the beach.

"I see no reason for concern if you use the cane and remain off of your foot while upon the beach," he'd said, then Mrs. Honeysett had sent him off with another pie.

The scent of salt and fish wafted toward Morvoren on the breeze, signaling their approach to the processing cellars. She couldn't see beyond the towering, stone walls, but she knew what the courtyard within held—hundreds upon hundreds of pilchards.

She'd been forced to tour Uncle's pilchard palace every year, and the stench exuding from the dead fish was unbearable. So much waste was had from the pilchards they didn't cure, and the women and children were forced to work atrocious hours. Were Mrs. Honeysett and Poppy forced to do the same?

Being brought up in the lower class herself, Morvoren was not a stranger to the labor required of entire families, no matter the age or trade. She herself had strained alongside Mother and Father as they'd gardened, farmed, and spearfished daily.

But everything she'd seen with fishermen proved the trade took matters one step too far, especially in regard to her own family.

When Uncle moved from Mevagissey to St. Ives, drawing closer to Morvoren and her parents, he'd come with the promise of an easy fortune for Father. In the beginning, Father had maintained his growing wealth with humility, but soon enough, he'd become obsessed with the trade, investing in more seining companies and ignoring his own family. But what had that obsession given him apart from an early grave, a wife dead from sorrow, and a daughter in the hands of a despotic uncle?

With an embittered heart, Morvoren passed the cellars and walked down the cobbled pathway that led straight to the beach. It wasn't a large stretch of sand, but with the departing tide, there was finally enough space for the gathering.

"Thank 'eavens," Poppy breathed. "That seaweed's finally gone out with the tide." She turned to Morvoren. "There be so much of it 'fore that we couldn't even reach the water."

"And the smell was awful," Mrs. Honeysett added.

Slowly, they progressed until the cobblestone merged with sand, and the beach became fully visible. To the north, the edge of the cliff piled out in a gradual layering of thick, brown stones stacked atop each other like dark, rich pound cakes. A group of people gathered on the sand nearby, circling round a modest fire with smiles and greetings for those slowly converging on the beach.

Morvoren swiftly searched the faces of those in attendance. She didn't recognize any of them, and the humble dress on each of the fishermen and their families told her just what she needed to know—there were no seiners present.

Poppy ran forward to join a few girls her age, but Mrs. Honeysett remained by Morvoren's side, leading her forward through the sand until they reached the group.

"Evenin', Mabyn," the first woman greeted. Her curious gaze fell instantly on Morvoren.

"Evenin'," Mrs. Honeysett said as more eyes fell on them. She wrapped a supportive arm around Morvoren's waist and continued. "This be Morvoren 'Ollow, the lovely *woman* our boys pulled from the sea."

Morvoren didn't miss the subtle emphasis on the word 'woman.'

A few responded with easy smiles and kind words as they expressed their hopes for Morvoren's injuries to improve, but a hearty handful of men and women remained silent, only offering a single, stiff nod in greeting.

"Come," Mrs. Honeysett said softly as the rest of the group went about mingling with others, "we'll find ye a place to rest your foot." Then she added in a whisper, "And a place where ye won't be gawped at so greatly."

Morvoren was led forward to a large tree trunk laid flat near the fire, and she settled down with a stifled sigh, the pressure on her foot instantly lessening.

"Now rest 'ere," Mrs. Honeysett instructed. "I'll return shortly with a plate o' food for ye."

As Mrs. Honeysett left her alone, a rush of nerves clambered over Morvoren. More stares were sent her way, including a scowl by one woman with a thick set of shoulders and a grim stretch of her lips.

They were suspicious of her, afraid she truly was a mermaid. And though Morvoren couldn't blame them for making such an assumption, she also didn't appreciate being watched as if she would call upon the powers of the sea to destroy Tristwick in a heartbeat.

Then again, did they simply mistrust her because of their superstitions, or had Mr. Honeysett spoken to them about her lies?

With leveling breaths, she faced the sea's waves gently lapping at the sand. The clouds had finally given way that evening, allowing the sun a final peek at the earth as it began its descent toward the sea. The water reflected the sunshine in a blinding, white light that lingered behind her eyelids each time she blinked.

Morvoren lived for moments like these. Too long had passed since she'd experienced one. The fire crackling nearby, the gentle waves of an outgoing tide rumbling before her, the soft hum of pleasant conversation.

If she closed her eyes, she could imagine she was a child again. The condemning stares from others were actually smiles from Mother and Father as they sat around their fire, oysters roasting over the warm flames.

Those had been special moments. Memorable, perfect moments. Before Father had been seduced by Uncle's promises and Mother had gotten sick.

Morvoren opened her eyes, staring more intently at the water as it slid up the darkened sand. She forced aside the unpleasant memories that always invaded her warm thoughts like a band of ruthless fiends.

How she wished her memories could only be happy ones.

"You must be Morvoren Hollow."

Morvoren drew her attention away from the sea and glanced up to see who'd spoken to her. A man with an easy smile approached, accompanied by a woman with red hair.

"Yes, I…I am," she stammered, unease rising in her chest like a burgeoning weed. The man had spoken with a proper tongue. He couldn't be a fisherman, could he? "And ye are…"

"Gavin Kendricks," he said. Then he motioned to the woman beside him, a spattering of freckles across her nose. "And this is my wife, Mrs. Abigail Kendricks. The Honeysetts occasionally work for us at Golowduyn Lighthouse."

Just like that, relief plucked the weed of worry straight from her heart. She smiled up at the couple, remembering their names from the Honeysetts at dinner the night before. "Pleasure to meet ye both."

"And you," Mrs. Kendricks said softly, averting her gaze in a shy manner. "Mrs. Honeysett has told Captain Kendricks and I what you've had to endure. I do hope you are feeling better."

"Yes, I be much better, thank…ye." Morvoren's words faltered, her eye catching Mr. Honeysett's as he crossed the beach toward the gathering.

She had been more than shocked when he'd been the one to invite her to the party that evening, and she still hadn't guessed his angle.

Instantly, Mr. Honeysett looked away from her, turning his attention to the woman who walked beside him. She didn't look much older than Morvoren's twenty years, her brown hair tied in a loose bun at the back of her head. The woman smiled up at Mr. Honeysett with a coy expression, the admiration clear in her eyes. So Trevik had a sweetheart, did he?

"Mrs. Honeysett also told us that you wish to get to Sennen."

Morvoren blinked, redirecting her attention back to Captain Kendricks. "Yes, that be right."

The captain shared a glance with his wife. "Well, Mrs. Kendricks and I have been thinking about your circumstances and would love to help you in any way we can. That being said, we'd like to offer you and the Honeysetts the use of our wagon so that you may return to Sennen sooner."

Morvoren's lips parted, her heart rising as if with the tide. "Truly?"

Mrs. Kendricks nodded. "We won't be able to lend you use of it until Saturday. We know that isn't a great deal closer than Monday, but…"

Her words trailed off as Morvoren shook her head. "No, that be wonderful. How can I ever thank ye?"

"It isn't a problem," she replied. "The Honeysetts have been wonderful friends to us and have sacrificed much to help us at Golowduyn these last few months. We are more than happy to help them and you."

"Indeed," Captain Kendricks agreed. "We've only now just discussed the matter with Mrs. Honeysett. I'm certain she and Mr. Honeysett will be more than happy to take you."

Morvoren's shoulders dipped forward, disappointment dampening her rising spirits. She glanced toward Mr. Honeysett, his attention arrested by the same woman from before. He folded his arms as he listened to her, the fabric of his coat tight around his upper arms and shoulders. She supposed having him take her to Sennen was a small price to pay to be rid of the man's suspicions two days early.

Two days early. That meant two days fewer of lying to the Honeysetts—and two days fewer of glancing over her shoulder to ensure Uncle and Mr. Foss hadn't discovered her.

"I can't thank ye both enough," she said to the Kendrickses. "Your kindness will not be forgotten."

The Kendrickses spoke only a moment more, excusing themselves just as Mrs. Honeysett returned with a plate of roasted hake and potatoes for them each. Together, they enjoyed their meal, discussing Morvoren's upcoming departure before loud giggling drifted toward them. They followed the sound to where Poppy laughed with a handsome man who stood a full head taller than the girl.

"That be Lieutenant 'Arris," Mrs. Honeysett explained with a nod in their direction. "Our Poppy 'as fallen 'ard for 'im."

"I can see that," Morvoren said. The girl had veritable stars in her eyes as she peered up at the man. Whatever he was saying must have been very comical, indeed, for how hard Poppy still laughed at him.

"Does he like her in return?" she asked.

Mrs. Honeysett's face fell slightly. "I believe so, but 'ow greatly, we can't be sure."

Before any more could be said on the subject, another couple approached, and Mrs. Honeysett introduced them to Morvoren as the Bosankos. They were kind and generous, which almost made up for the fact that the broad-shouldered woman still cast daggers of suspicion toward Morvoren across the fire.

Beside the woman sat a young man with a thick head of blond hair and the same broad shoulders. Brother and sister, perhaps? Or did their ages allow them to be mother and son? Either way, the young man was also watching her, though with a far less condemning gaze. Instead of scowling, he merely skirted his eyes away in an instant, as if afraid making eye contact would upset the woman they believed to be a mermaid.

The Bosankos departed, and Morvoren bade farewell to the kind couple before catching the young man's eyes on her once more. She attempted an easy smile, but he pulled swiftly away, watching her from the corner of his eye.

Morvoren was not blind to the fact that she was considered an attractive individual. Uncle had always said it was the only reason he'd kept her all these years.

"Your features will fetch you a fine husband one day, niece," he'd said. *"I will choose that husband for you, if only to pay myself back for the grief you've caused me all these years."*

At least this broad-shouldered young man wasn't leering at her as some men did. He seemed more frightened than anything, which couldn't be too far-fetched, seeing as how he thought her to be a sea-maid.

After everyone in attendance had had the opportunity to eat, Mrs. Honeysett and a few other women moved to clean up the food, and Morvoren—once again seated alone—watched with measured interest as the younger members of the group organized a few games off to the side of the gathering.

"Will you be joining in, miss?"

Morvoren glanced up from her spot on the log, taken aback as Lieutenant Harris himself smiled down at her. "Thank ye," she said before motioning to her wrapped foot. "But I won't be able to do much with a sore foot. I be happy to watch from the side, though."

He nodded with understanding. "You are Morvoren Hollow, yes?"

His ease and confidence exuded a natural charisma that was difficult for a person to remain humble about. This man, however, had seemed to conquer the feat. It was no wonder Poppy had fallen so hard for him.

"Yes, I am."

"It's a pleasure to meet you. Lieutenant Edmund Harris at your service. Poppy Honeysett was just telling me that you're staying with her."

"Yes, she's been gracious enough to allow me the use of her room." She paused, attempting nonchalance. "That Poppy be a very generous girl."

The lieutenant looked beyond Morvoren, and she followed his line of sight to where Poppy bounced lightly up and down on the balls of her feet, no doubt excited for the games to begin.

"Indeed," Lieutenant Harris agreed somewhat distractedly. He blinked, then looked back to Morvoren. "You are certain you cannot join?"

"More than certain, sir. Thank ye. But I be enjoyin' the fun from afar, I assure ye."

He tipped his head in departure, then walked away, moving at once to stand beside Poppy, who beamed up at him as brightly as the sun.

Morvoren didn't know either the lieutenant or Poppy very well, but she was fairly convinced that the two were meant for each other. She'd never seen a sweeter couple, the two of them constantly stealing glances at one another when the other remained unaware.

Better yet, if they did marry, Poppy could escape the fishing trade as a whole and be the wife of a naval officer. That was far more admirable.

She watched the younger group gather into a circle near the water—Mr. Honeysett standing beside the same young woman from before—but the unsettling feeling of someone watching her prickled down her neck. She first looked to the cliffsides, but when she came up empty, she dropped her gaze to the fire. Sure enough, the broad-shouldered boy, who now sat alone, watched her unabashedly.

Ready to be done feeling like a caged animal to be gawked

at, Morvoren faced him directly and motioned a finger toward him, signaling for him to join her.

He looked away, startled, but she continued the movement until he finally acknowledged her.

"I?" he mouthed out across the fire, pointing to himself.

She nodded, and with a whitened face, he stood and made his way toward her.

Finally. Now she would see what the real reason was for why he—and the rest of those at the gathering—felt the need to stare at her.

CHAPTER TWELVE

*M*orvoren waited to speak until his stocky figure approached, his blond hair splayed out across his brow.

"Evenin'," she greeted when he stopped before her.

He nodded in response.

"Ye may have a seat if ye'd like." She motioned to the log beside her.

Carefully, as if afraid he'd tip them both over, he sat down at the far end of the log.

"I be Morvoren Hollow."

"I know."

She waited for more.

Nothing.

"Have ye a name?"

He glanced around him before replying. "Jowan Cardy."

Cardy. Was he another one the Honeysetts had spoken about over dinner?

"Do ye not want to join in with the others?" she asked, motioning with a toss of her head toward the games being played.

He shrugged. "Ne'er been one to enjoy games much."

"Why be that?" she asked, watching the others as they laughed together. Mr. Honeysett nudged Poppy with his elbow, and she playfully pushed him back in response. Had his sweetheart finally been stripped from his side?

Jowan shrugged nearby again, his bulky shoulders rising and dropping like a large boat in the water—as if the action was made with great effort on his part. "Can't run fast enough."

She looked back to the group. One young man raced toward the sea with a stick in hand, lunging it into the wet sand before running back to the shore while attempting to escape the returning waves. "I can understand that. I ain't fast neither. 'Specially with this sore foot."

He didn't look at her, nor did he respond. Was he truly so frightened of her? It seemed as though a sudden sneeze from her would send him running for the hovels beyond the cove.

Perhaps speaking about something he was comfortable with would ease the tension between them, then she could ask the questions she really wanted the answers to.

"Are ye a fisherman, Jowan?"

He nodded, his chest puffing out like a robin's on a cold winter morn.

"And were ye on the boat when I was pulled from the sea?"

Another nod, another skirted glance.

"I s'pose I have ye to thank for savin' me, then," she said.

The tips of his ears beamed red. "No, 'twas Trevik who did that."

She huffed internally. Mr. Honeysett was right—he *did* have a loyal crew.

"But ye must've helped him," she pressed.

He dug the tips of his boots into the sand. "I s'pose I did pull up the net."

"Ah, see? I do have ye to thank, then."

A twitch of his lip hinted at a future smile, and she shifted closer to him, careful to hold her ankle in a way she could keep the weight off of it.

"Do ye like bein' a fisherman, Jowan?" She tipped her head to put on a playful air, if only to let him know she wouldn't hurt him.

"I do."

"And what do ye like about it?"

He cleared his throat. "Many things, I s'pose."

He said nothing further.

"Do ye like the wages that ye receive?"

He gave her an odd look, then turned his attention to the waves. "I s'pose. But more 'an anythin', I like bein' on the sea."

She smiled genuinely this time. "We have somethin' in common with that."

He gave her a knowing look, the first shred of confidence she'd seen in him all evening. "Ain't much of a surprise there."

"What do ye mean?" she questioned.

"That ye like the sea."

She waited for a moment, feigning innocence until he leaned slightly closer to her and whispered, "Seein' as 'ow ye *be* from the sea."

So it was true. They really did think she was a mermaid.

He straightened. "That's what me grandfar's been sayin', at least."

"And what do ye think about it all?" she asked, the humor of the conversation slipping away as swiftly as the lowering sun.

He drew a deep breath, seeming to take courage as he shifted toward her. "It be 'ard to say, miss. But ye do 'ave the look of a sea-maid."

"Ye be too kind." Her voice fell flatter than she'd intended, but she couldn't help it. She never should have brought the young man to speak with her. Just knowing that he and the others thought her capable of the very things mermaids were known to do—lure men to their deaths and wreak havoc on towns—hurt more than she thought it would.

Truthfully, how had she ever wronged anyone? She'd done everything Uncle had ever asked her to do, and still he despised her. Now, she'd merely kept her identity a secret to maintain her safety, and most of Tristwick believed her to be capable of such heinous acts as befitting a siren. How was such treatment fair?

Laughter brought her attention back to the game on the beach, but instead of turning to see smiles and good-natured fun, she found Mr. Honeysett watching her.

His dark eyes studied her with that same suspicion that was always present, and her chest pinched tightly in the center. Had he been watching her the entire time simply to ensure she stayed in line while speaking with one of his own?

Irritation scratched at her patience. All she wanted was freedom. All she wanted was to find a place to live out her life in peace in the way she chose. But no matter what she did, suspicions would still be had, assumptions would still be made, and *she* would still be the one injured.

Very well. If Mr. Honeysett and Tristwick expected her to behave as a sea-maid, then she would behave as a sea-maid.

Pulling her eyes from Mr. Honeysett ceremoniously, she shifted her body so he could see her more clearly, then faced Jowan with a demure smile.

"Do ye really think I could be a…a mermaid, Jowan?" she asked with a little laugh. "Seems to I that be a bit too fanciful."

"Not accordin' to Grandfar."

"Well what reasons does your grandfar have to believe such a thing?" She flashed another grin, glancing at Mr. Honeysett. His brow furrowed, and he'd turned to face her more fully.

"'E be suspicious that ye don't 'ave no 'ome," Jowan began. "And o' the fact that ye were found in the sea. 'E says that no self-respectin' woman would be caught dead swimmin' in her underclothes."

Morvoren forced her smile to remain. She didn't like this grandfar of Jowan's. Not one bit. What did it matter if she enjoyed the occasional swim? At least she was clothed at all.

"'E says no mermaid can be trusted. And no woman, for that matter."

Morvoren stared dully at him. He was beginning to sound just like Uncle.

"Women are meant to be indoors and silent," he'd say. *"Not galli-vanting through waves. You are not wise enough to make your own deci-sions, Miss Hollow. That is why I am here."*

All fishermen were the same, wishing to control women in every aspect of their lives. That was the real reason a man was afraid of sea-maids—not because of their power but because they were *women* with power.

She sent another furtive glance at Mr. Honeysett, pleased to see him still watching her with disapproval. He was no doubt dying to know what she was up to.

Let him wonder and assume the worst of her. She was used to such a thing by now. "Your grandfar, Jowan. Be he a fisherman, too?"

Jowan nodded proudly. "And me grandfar before that. Fishin' be in our blood."

Morvoren smiled, though she longed to curse the man's very words. Being a part of such a trade was nothing to be proud of—not when it so consistently destroyed the lives of others.

Uncle's obsession had caused him to neglect his poor wife long before Morvoren might have had the chance to meet her. And Father? He not only forgot himself but his wife and daughter, too. What was admirable about any of that?

She leaned closer to Jowan and from the corner of her eye, she saw Mr. Honeysett take a step toward them, as if ready to run to Jowan's aid at a moment's notice.

"Can I share somethin' with ye then, Jowan?"

"I s'pose."

"I would listen to your grandfar."

"Why?" he breathed.

Her smile disappeared, and her words iced over greater than any frost. "He is very wise to be on his guard…for he seems to be the only one who knows a sea-maid when he sees one."

His eyes rounded, and he pulled away from her.

"Jowan?"

The young man jumped, and Morvoren turned to face Mr. Honeysett, who'd approached them both in the last moment unnoticed.

"Your grandfar be lookin' for ye," he said.

Jowan nodded, glancing at Morvoren as he scrambled to stand.

She allowed a slow smile to spread across her lips, and with a smooth voice, she said, "Thank ye for talkin', Jowan. I hope to see ye again soon." Then she turned with fluid movements to watch the sea.

Jowan didn't respond, scurrying away as quickly as his legs would allow.

Mr. Honeysett remained behind, and Morvoren braced herself for the storm of words that was inevitably on its way.

CHAPTER THIRTEEN

"What were ye talkin' about with 'im?"

The condemnation in Mr. Honeysett's voice rankled Morvoren's pride. It was only natural that she'd want to rankle his right back.

She kept her eyes on the waves rolling in, replying with a simple, "Nothin'."

He moved around her, stepping in front of her view of the sea and casting a large shadow across half of her. "What were ye talkin' about?" he repeated more slowly.

She scowled up at his towering figure, but the sun right to the side of his chest burned her eyes. She looked away with a wince. "We were only havin' a friendly conversation. A friendly conversation that ye rudely interrupted."

Mr. Honeysett stared down at her, remaining silent. Since Morvoren could no longer see the sea, she looked to the group instead as they began a new game. Poppy stood next to Lieutenant Harris, her gaze continually flashing toward him.

"I know ye be up to somethin', Miss 'Ollow," Mr. Honeysett stated, making it impossible for her to ignore him further.

She craned her neck to see his face, this time shading the sun with the palm of her hand. It was rather rude of him to continue standing there so close to her, blocking her view of the sea but not of the sun.

"Do ye, now?" she asked. "What be that, then?"

His lips twitched, as if he wished to speak but wasn't allowing himself to.

"I see," she said with an amused expression. "Well, it do seem to I that ye know a great deal."

She made to look away, but he spoke again.

"I know more 'an ye think I do."

She raised her brow in a challenge. "Then prove it, sir."

He hesitated a moment longer, glancing around him before lowering his voice so only she could hear his words. "I know ye be lyin' 'bout your memory. I know ye remembered Sennen long 'fore seein' that note o' yours in your belongin's. And I know ye know exactly where ye came from 'fore swim-min' in Tristwick's waves."

Morvoren tried to remain unaffected. After all, she'd known he'd suspected her of lying the entire time. And at least she knew now that he'd kept his suspicions to only his family, otherwise he would not have spoken so quietly.

With a raised chin and a dismissive smile, she responded. "Are ye always this skeptical, Mr. Honeysett? Or do ye merely act this way 'cause I slapped ye for takin' advantage of I?"

A line formed between his eyebrows as he frowned. He glanced around him again, as if to ensure no one else had heard her words. "I didn't take advantage of ye. I was savin' ye."

She knew that as well as he did, but there was something so satisfying about getting under this man's skin.

He closed his eyes in a clear attempt to calm down. "Ye can believe whate'er ye want to. So long as ye stop spreadin' lies to young Jowan there."

"Lies? Ye don't know what I be sayin' was—"

"Ye were tellin' 'im ye be a mermaid."

Oh. So he had heard. She gave a lift of her shoulder. "What do it matter what he thinks? 'Tain't no harm done."

"No 'arm? Ye be intimidatin' me crew so greatly they be afeared of ye callin' a great storm down upon we."

She sniffed out a laugh. "Would that I could do such."

"I be serious, Miss 'Ollow." Though frustration still lingered with his frown, he spoke more earnestly. "Our liveli'ood be at stake."

Morvoren wanted to accuse him of exaggerating, of thinking of only himself and his own plight. But the concern in his eyes was apparent, and it made Morvoren pause. It made her *feel*.

But she didn't want to feel, especially for a fisherman. She wanted to remain indifferent, to maintain her lack of interest in the trade. But every time she spoke with the Honeysetts—especially this Honeysett—she found herself considering their perspective more than…

No. She wouldn't allow her mind to stray further. She was finished with this conversation.

With an impatient huff, she took her cane in hand and placed it in front of her to help her stand. Gripping the handle, she heaved herself up on one foot, certain she was secure enough. But when the end of the cane sank farther into the sand with her weight pressed upon it, she tipped to the side, instantly using her injured foot to catch herself.

With a sharp intake of breath, she crumpled toward the ground, wincing in pain and bracing for the impact of her fall. Instead of the sand catching her, however, Mr. Honeysett's strong hands wrapped around her upper arms and steadied her in an instant.

"Are ye well?" His deep voice rumbled at her side—just like it had when he'd carried her in from the sea.

She peered up at him, chutes of warmth sailing up her arms where he held her, as if the sun itself heated her limbs. Their eyes met, and she expected to see more annoyance. But when concern rose in their brown depths instead, she paused. Was he concerned...for her?

No, it was more likely that she'd imagined the look.

Instantly, she shrugged free of his hold, steadying herself with the cane for good this time. Her limbs shook, and she gave a little shudder to rid herself of the feeling.

Mr. Honeysett stared down at her. Hurt flashed in his eyes, and only then did she realize her shudder may have been taken in a way she had not intended.

Before she could decide whether to correct him or not, disbelief inched across his features, and he rubbed the back of his neck with a shake of his head. "What *do* ye 'ave against fishermen, Miss 'Ollow?" he asked.

The question might have been asked rhetorically, but the concern he'd shown her had shaken the very foundation of her beliefs.

As if to reassure herself that her feelings for fishermen remained the same, she hardened her tone. "Where do I begin? They be greedy, selfish..." She paused, raising her lips so her nose wrinkled. "And they all stink of fish."

Regret encompassed her the moment the words left her mouth. Not only for her cruelty, but also because it brought something to mind she didn't wish to acknowledge—the fact that she'd been very near Mr. Honeysett twice now and she had yet to smell even the faintest hint of a fish on his person.

"Thank ye for explainin'," he muttered. Then he motioned to the log she'd been seated upon. "Sit back down 'fore ye fall again. I'll be the one to leave."

Then with a tip of his head, he walked away and Morvoren was left alone with a regret that tore apart her insides for reasons she couldn't begin to explain.

CHAPTER FOURTEEN

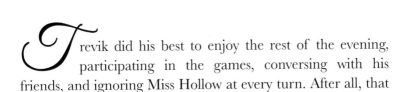

*T*revik did his best to enjoy the rest of the evening, participating in the games, conversing with his friends, and ignoring Miss Hollow at every turn. After all, that was clearly what she wanted—to keep her distance from the stench-ridden fisherman.

When the sun edged closer to the sea, and the time was nearly upon them for the men to depart aboard the *Pilferer*, the group joined together, circling the fire with shared smiles and conversation.

"Anyone sittin' 'ere, Trevik?" asked Mary Penna—the skipper's daughter—sitting down before he could respond.

He smiled all the same, despite having had enough of the woman's presence that evening. She'd been lingering beside him for far longer than he'd wished. Matters could be worse, though. Miss Hollow could be the one pasted to his side, instead.

He glanced across the fire to where she sat beside Mother, Miss Hollow's eyes downcast, lips unmoving.

He'd never understand the woman. Why she wished people to believe she was a mermaid was beyond him, other than perhaps to keep people at arm's length.

"Will ye be leavin' to fish soon, then?" Mary asked him.

"After the songs, I reckon."

"That be a shame. I'd 'ave liked to spend more time with ye."

He shifted, uncomfortable against the log and with the conversation. Mary was a lovely woman—pretty, kind, and sweet-tempered. But there was no spark between them, at least from his side.

Fortunately, before Trevik had to either lie or injure the woman's pride, Gryffyn spoke from the top of the circle. "We don't 'ave much time for songs this evenin', but we can surely squeeze in a few. 'Ow 'bout *Come 'Ome* first? Anyone like to take the female lead?"

This was one of Trevik's favorite songs, the lines sung by the group of men while the chorus was carried by a single woman.

A few women raised their hands, Mary included, but when Trevik's gaze caught Miss Hollow's, he paused. Was she…

Sure enough, her hand slowly raised among the others. Trevik swiftly shook his head at her, which only proved to make her raise her hand all the higher.

Collectively, the group's eyes turned toward her, and Trevik stifled a sigh.

"Miss 'Ollow?" Gryffyn asked. "Ye know the song?"

She nodded in silence.

Gryffyn smiled kindly, which was more than Trevik could do. He was fairly certain he was scowling again, trying to decipher the woman's desire to sing in front of a group of strangers.

"All right. Clemo, will ye start us off?"

The middle-aged man sitting near Mother hummed the starting note, then the men began to sing, Trevik included.

The sun has departed, the stars are alight.
The rigging is set. I sail tonight.

The sea, she's calling, and I must depart.
Though, how can I leave ye—
my maiden, my life, my heart?

As the men ended, the attention was once again directed at Miss Hollow. Her eyes remained focused on the fire, as if she was unaware that all of Tristwick watched her. The wind softly blew her blonde whisps of hair against her cheeks as she sang the chorus.

And she says, "I'll watch for ye, darling,
I'll keep me eye on the sea.
I'll do what it takes, and I'll wait for ye.
My love is fast, my heart will not roam,
'twill wait, steadfast, for ye to come home."

The haunting lyrics had always affected Trevik, stirring respect for the men at sea who'd left behind their loved ones, but when Miss Hollow sang the words, the purity of her voice coupled with the emotion with which she sang, his chest tightened.

"She sings beautifully," Mary whispered beside him.

He could only nod.

The chorus ended, and Miss Hollow sat in silence, the fire-light flickering in her eyes. Most of the men missed the beginning of the next verse, apparently captured by her voice, as well.

Trevik, though, if only to prove to himself that he could, continued with the lyrics without a glance in her direction.

The days pass slowly, and me memories remain
of the maiden I left for the sea and the strain.
I hear her words now, her voice on a wave,
a gentle whisper I cannot help but crave.

When Miss Hollow's turn to sing the chorus came back again, Trevik was determined to look elsewhere. After all, he had the inkling that her decision to sing was yet another tool in her arsenal to convince all those of Tristwick that she was, in fact, a mermaid. But why? Was she simply wishing to seek revenge on him for capturing her in his net?

He glanced around the group, wary expressions— including from the Cardys—contrasting with the beauty of her voice.

Finally, the last verse was sung by the men.

Well, I did me best, maiden. I kept safe for so long.
But the blast of the cannon was simply too strong.
'Tis time for ye to find a new love,
though I'll remember ye always, watching ye from above.

If Trevik didn't know any better, he would have been on the Cardys' side, believing that Miss Hollow *was* a mermaid. Everything pointed to the fact that she was different than the others. Her smooth skin, her blonde locks shining golden in the waning light of the sun. Her soft voice not overly done with trills and lilts. Simply…pure.

And then there was the matter of her eyes—green with flecks of gold that shimmered in the sunlight.

Now, however, something else shone within their depths, something sorrowful. But why?

She sang the final chorus as the men joined in, her voice harmonizing perfectly with the low hum of the others.

Now she says, "I watched for ye, darling,
I kept me eye on the sea.
I did what it took, now ye can't come back to me.
But me love is still fast, me heart will ne'er roam,
'twill wait, steadfast, 'til I come home."

As the song ended, silence settled around the group. The waves rushed on the sand, and the fire snapped in its heat until finally, the spell Miss Hollow had weaved around the group was broken.

A few people around the fire clapped, though most of them whispered to their neighbors beside them—about what, Trevik could only fear.

"What we be singin' next?" Gryffyn asked, finally breaking the silence.

A few songs were suggested, and Trevik tried to appear interested in what was being said, but when he took another glance at Miss Hollow, her eyes, still reflecting the fire, now shimmered with tears. Their gazes caught, but she swiftly pulled away, focusing on the sea instead.

Trevik's heart contorted, though it shouldn't have. He didn't need to feel anything for the woman who'd expressed nothing but animosity toward him.

The next song was chosen, and Trevik did his best to keep his eyes from Miss Hollow, but blast it all, if he didn't want to hear her singing again.

Did the others, as well? He cast his eyes around the group, only to stop a moment later when he caught onto Poppy whispering something to Lieutenant Harris, their shoulders pressed together.

The lieutenant smiled in response to her words, nudging her with his elbow. When he looked up, catching Trevik's eye, the smile slipped from Lieutenant Harris's lips, and his gaze dropped as he shifted farther away from Poppy.

Trevik grimaced. He'd hoped that Poppy's admiration of the lieutenant would have faded away, but he could see now that it had only grown. Such feelings would do neither her nor the lieutenant any good.

The man had been injured in a shipwreck only a few months before, but with his arm now fully healed, it was only a matter of time before he set sail again. Was Poppy aware of such a thing? Or was she choosing to remain blissfully ignorant?

Either way, she would be heartbroken when the lieutenant's departure inevitably came, and unfortunately, having one's heart broken at the vulnerable age of sixteen was, in some ways, more painful than at any other period in one's life.

Unless, of course, Trevik could stop the wound from even occurring.

"'Ave we time for another?" Gryffyn asked, the song having ended without Trevik even realizing.

"No, Gryffyn," Edern Cardy responded. "'Tis time for a story, instead." The man waved his wrinkled hands toward the children present. "Gather round. Methinks it be time for a cautionary tale."

The children moved to sit before him, encouraged by their parents' soft nods. Typically, Trevik enjoyed the tales the man would share, but for some reason that evening, he had the distinct feeling that Edern had something less than pleasant up his sleeve.

He exchanged worried glances with Gryffyn, who gave a commiserating shake of his head before Edern began.

"Many years ago," Edern said, his sagging neck jiggling as he spoke, "a fisherman was out huntin' for seals."

Trevik winced. Of course Edern would choose this story. He glanced to Miss Hollow, catching her staring at him before she hurriedly looked away.

"With no luck on 'is 'unt," Edern continued, "the fisherman was just about ready to give up when 'e came across a beautiful woman combin' 'er 'air on a rock near the shore. She 'ad long locks, see, as golden as the sunshine, and 'er green eyes were as clear as the Cornish sea."

Trevik rubbed a hand over his eyes. He was fairly certain the mermaid from the story had blue eyes and red hair. Had Edern changed it specifically for Miss Hollow's benefit?

"The very moment 'is eyes fell on that woman, 'earin' 'er

pure singin', the fisherman fell in love. So 'e asked 'er to marry 'im dreckly."

Gryffyn's youngest daughter, seven-year-old Ruby Bosanko, clasped her hands together in an airy sigh. She clearly did not remember the ending of this particular tale.

"Now," Edern said, "the woman might've accepted 'is 'and, but she told 'im that she couldn't, for she be..." He paused, raising his brow and lowering his voice to a guttural whisper, "a mermaid."

The children's eyes widened, but Trevik was no longer paying attention to their reactions. He was captured instead by Miss Hollow, who watched Edern with an unamused expression.

"The fisherman was upset with 'er refusal," Edern continued. "So upset that 'e tried to capture 'er and *force* 'er to wed 'im. But she refused again." He lowered his voice. "So the man took revenge by takin' the woman's life."

A few of the children gasped, and Ruby looked back at her father with wide eyes. Gryffyn grimaced, waving her forward and embracing her as he whispered what had to be words of comfort in her ear.

Miss Hollow must have seen the girl's reaction to the story, as well, for her scowl increased.

Edern seemed none the wiser to the poor reactions around him, simply continuing with his tale. "While the sea-maid lay dyin', she used 'er final breath to cast a curse on the town's 'arbor. After 'er death, a terrible storm came, one the likes o' which no one 'ad e'er seen. Durin' that storm, a sandbar formed before the town of Padstow, ne'er to be removed. Still to this day, it lingers, wreckin' sailors' ships and endangerin' people's lives."

He paused, his eyes wide with warning. "That be why ye don't trust strangers. And that be why ye always be on the lookout...for *mermaids*."

As he said the final word, his focus shifted to Miss Hollow.

His accusation was clear, and a palpable silence followed around the group, as if they waited for her to refute Edern's claims.

Instead, her eyes hardened further, and she leveled her gaze at Edern until *he* was the one to look away.

"Well," Gryffyn said, "at least we know that sea-maids be better than seiners."

Finally, the tension dissipated, and laughter broke out among them. Miss Hollow, however, merely dropped her gaze to her hands in her lap.

As the evening finally drew to a close, the group dispersed, allowing a wide berth around Miss Hollow, though Mother and Poppy stood at her side.

Trevik moved to join his own family, but he stopped when Edern reached for his arm, clutching it tightly.

"Now she does know we be on to 'er," he grumbled with a triumphant smile.

Trevik gave an awkward nod, then excused himself, glancing around to see if anyone else had heard, but most of the group had already reached the cobblestones.

Mother's expression was tight as Trevik approached, standing at her opposite side away from Miss Hollow. "What tales that man can weave," Mother said under her breath as they moved together across the sand. "I do 'ope ye can talk sense to 'im, Trevik."

Trevik didn't bother responding that he had not the smallest hope that Edern would ever believe Miss Hollow was anything but a sea-maid.

Instead, he turned to something he could control. "Where be Poppy?"

He glanced around, only to find her back at the fire with Lieutenant Harris, and frustration bubbled inside his already boiling stomach.

He liked Lieutenant Harris. The two had become quick friends over the few months they'd known each other. But

Trevik couldn't stomach seeing Poppy injured, even if it was unintentional. He'd allowed their friendship to progress for far too long. Poppy should have seen sense by this point, but it was now up to Trevik to find it for her and the lieutenant both.

"Poppy?" he called.

She met his gaze, giving him a covert shake of her head before turning back to the lieutenant.

"Poppy, we're goin' 'ome now," he called out again.

Mother and Miss Hollow's eyes were both on him, but he ignored them, focusing intently on Poppy until she gave a bob of her head to Lieutenant Harris, then stormed toward Trevik.

"Why'd ye do that?" she seethed, fists clenched at her sides.

"Do what?"

"Ye know what, ye 'ateful man," she said, then she stomped past him.

Her reddened cheeks seared into Trevik's conscience. He should have found a way to bring her home without embarrassing her.

"Poppy, don't be angry with I," he said, catching up to her and trying not to be too keenly aware that Miss Hollow still watched him. "Ye just need to be careful, that be all. Come now. We can talk about it when we get 'ome."

When Miss Hollow would be tucked away in another room and out of earshot.

"There ain't nothin' to talk about," Poppy said, then she picked up her pace and left him behind.

Trevik slowed, staring after her with disappointment.

"Ye need to be softer with 'er, Trev," Mother said, finally catching up to him after he and Poppy had scurried ahead.

He glanced toward her, catching Miss Hollow's judgmental scowl in the process. In what world did *she* have the right to be upset with him?

The sun silhouetted her golden hair, causing it to appear

as a halo around her head, and he could have laughed at the
irony. Angel, indeed. The woman was more of an imp,
creating more trouble by the moment.

"I'll see the girls 'ome, Trev," Mother said with a soft pat
to his cheek. "Then I'll bring ye down your food and satchel
for the lugger."

Without awaiting a response, she moved forward with
Miss Hollow at a slow pace. Mother didn't look back, but Miss
Hollow did, and the superior look she cast him was enough to
curdle his insides.

So much for helping Poppy, and so much for easing Tristwick's suspicions over the woman.

What an absolute disaster of an evening that night had
turned out to be.

CHAPTER FIFTEEN

N ow that Morvoren had experienced the beauty that Tristwick boasted, she could not be kept from returning out of doors, even with her sore foot and the possible threat of a seiner catching her.

Poppy and Mrs. Honeysett were occupied with the cellars that morning, so instead of being cooped up in her room all day—or risking the chance of happening upon Mr. Honeysett in his home—Morvoren had taken the first opportunity to enjoy a walk out of doors.

Unfortunately, she'd overestimated the wellness of her ankle, and by the time she was halfway up the pathway on the northern side of the cove, the swelling in her foot had returned as it pressed angrily against the side of her boot.

"Just take one step at a time," she muttered to herself, leaning heavily on the cane and taking her time to traverse up the steep incline.

She didn't think she'd make it all the way back to the Honeysetts' home if she turned around now. But if she kept moving forward, she was sure to find a bit of respite at the top. There, she could spend the entire day recuperating if she needed to. After all, she didn't have anything else to do.

By the time she reached level ground with the view of Tristwick behind her, the throbbing in her ankle had caused her stomach to turn.

Rest. She needed to rest.

Before her, the pathway diverged into an upper route that overlooked the other, lower path. Desperate to not step another foot onto an incline, she limped toward the lower path and settled down onto a large boulder that protruded from the cliffside in a makeshift seat.

Her ankle moaned up at her, so she scooted back on the rock just enough to swing her leg up, gingerly propping the injured ankle on the boulder beside her.

Blood still pulsed in heavy heartbeats through the appendage but being off of the foot was a blessed relief. Perhaps she shouldn't have walked so far. If she wished to be fighting fit for Zennor and the Prouts' apothecary shop, she really needed to behave more wisely.

She leaned back against the side of the cliff, drawing in soothing breaths as she took in the sight before her. From her vantage point, the hamlet of Tristwick was no longer visible, but the entirety of the vast sea was.

Far on the horizon, dark clouds gathered once more, a sure sign that autumn had arrived, bringing with it its usual storms. But closer to Tristwick, the whole sea was lit in bright shades of blue. Directly below the sun, the light hit the shifting water like stars scattering the night's sky, shimmering and twinkling by the hundreds.

St. Ives—at least what she had seen of it—was beautiful of its own accord. But Tristwick...she'd not seen such beauty offered in years. It reminded her of where she'd grown up farther north, near St. Agnes. She and her parents would take nightly walks on the beach, searching for seashells or hopping over incoming waves.

Then Uncle had moved his seining company closer to them. Mother had warned Father not to become too entangled with her sister's husband. But Father never did learn to heed his wife's admonitions.

A hint of voices on the wind caught her attention, and she turned her head to the sound in a panic. Was it seiners? That awful Mr. Cardy coming to end her life because she was a sea-maid?

She looked around for a place to hide, but if those approaching chose to take the lower pathway, there was no way she would not be seen.

She leaned closer against the cliffside, holding her breath, waiting, listening, for any recognition of the voices. One was female, the other was…was that Mr. Honeysett?

Her pulse slowed, the tightness around her chest easing.

"Last evenin' was nice, wasn't it?" the female voice said, growing louder. "I do wish we could've spent more time together, though."

"'Tis difficult when we 'ave to fish at dusk."

That was most definitely Mr. Honeysett. Did that mean that the woman speaking was the same as the one at his side the evening before, his sweetheart?

"I enjoyed listenin' to ye sing," the woman continued.

Morvoren raised a brow with an amused smile, her worries easing. Their voices were right upon her, yet there was no sight of Mr. Honeysett or the woman. They must have taken the upper pathway.

"Thank ye, Mary," Trevik responded.

"Ye 'ave such a fine voice," Mary continued.

"Ah, ye be flatterin' I."

"No, I be in earnest, Trevik. One o' the best I've e'er 'eard."

Did he truly have a nice singing voice, or was the woman flirting? Morvoren hadn't heard him amidst all the others last night.

Mr. Honeysett didn't respond for a moment. "Well, y-your voice be fine and fitty, too."

Morvoren pressed a hand over her mouth to stop her laughter. Was that the best he could do at mustering a compliment? It was so forced, so rigid.

"Per'aps we might sing together, then," Mary suggested. "Me father wishes to invite ye for a meal at our 'ome soon. Would ye like that?"

The voices didn't fade away. Had they stopped directly above Morvoren? Slowly, she peered forward, the inclined cliffside above her revealing Mr. Honeysett's white sleeve billowing from the breeze.

She pulled back to avoid being seen and continued listening to their conversation, feeling only slight remorse for imposing.

"Thank ye," Mr. Honeysett responded. "That'd be nice to spend more time with your family. And…and yourself."

His voice sounded as if ready to snap. Was this because he didn't wish for the woman's attention, or because he didn't know how to give her attention in return?

"I'll speak with Father, then," Mary said. "I best be off, though. Thank ye for walkin' with I. I know ye be a busy man. I don't know 'ow ye do it all."

Morvoren blew out a puff of air at the woman's exhausting flattery.

"'Tis no trouble walkin' with ye, 'course," Mr. Honeysett responded, his words dripping with discomfort. "I enjoy the time we spend together…'course."

"Ain't ye sweet, Trevik."

Silence followed, and Morvoren leaned her head against the cliffside in sheer anguish. Just say goodbye to the girl. End the agony already.

"I look forward to seein' ye again," he finally said.

Then footsteps shifted above.

Thank heavens.

Morvoren leaned forward, spotting a glimpse of the

woman's skirts as she descended the pathway. Was Mr. Honeysett watching Mary depart, as well?

With a curious gaze, she shifted farther along the boulder until she spotted Mr. Honeysett staring out at the sea instead of Mary. He ran a hand through his hair with an agitated expression.

Morvoren remained where she was until his surprised gaze met hers, and his hand dropped to his side.

"Mornin'," she greeted in a chipper tone.

His gaze narrowed, his cheeks shifting to a shade of red. "'Ow long 'ave *ye* been there?"

Morvoren grinned. "Long enough."

CHAPTER SIXTEEN

 $\mathcal{M}$ orvoren could not help but delight in Mr. Honeysett's squirming.

"What are ye doin' up 'ere?" he questioned, still speaking from above. "'Sides spyin' on I."

"Spyin'?" she asked in mock horror. "How dare ye accuse me o' such. I was merely sittin' here, enjoyin' me view o' the sea when ye and your sweet'eart there stopped right above me so I could hear every…last…word." She emphasized her final words with deliberate pauses, forcing her look of innocence to remain.

His frown increased. With swift steps he disappeared from her view, and she wondered if, perhaps, he'd had enough of their conversation and was now returning home.

In a few short moments, however, he appeared on the lower pathway before her.

"Mary Penna and I ain't sweet'earts," he stated.

"I must say, that be more logical," she said. "I've been wonderin' just 'ow ye were able to capture that woman with your, well, your *remarkable* flirtin' up there."

His jaw twitched. This was just too delightful.

He studied her for a moment, his eyes dropping to her elevated ankle. "Ye've 'urt yourself again, 'aven't ye?"

She ignored the heartbeat in her ankle. "No."

He shook his head in disbelief. "I do wish ye'd rest so your foot would 'eal."

"That be kind of ye."

"Then I might not be beholdin' to 'elpin' ye walk every day."

She raised a satirical brow. "And here I was thinkin' ye enjoyed helpin' I. But worry not. Come this Saturday, I'll be out o' your hair for good."

He narrowed his eyes. "The coach only travels to Sennen on Mondays."

She paused. "Did your mother not tell ye?"

His silence answered her question. Oh, but she would enjoy breaking the news to him.

"The Kendrickses were kind enough to offer the use of their wagon to me on Saturday. Your mother has agreed to come along and promised that ye'd drive the wagon."

"Oh, did she now?" He looked away, muttering. "As if I don't 'ave anythin' better to do with me time."

Morvoren sniffed. "Don't pretend like ye ain't been dyin' to get rid of I." She paused, then raised her lips in a smile. "'Sides, with me gone, ye'll be able to get back to your flirtin' with Mary."

He looked over his shoulder at the sea. "I wasn't flirtin'."

"What be that?" she asked in a louder voice, though she'd heard him clear as day.

"I said I wasn't flirtin'."

"Oh!" She blew out an exaggerated sigh of relief. "I be 'appy to 'ear that. I thought ye be worse at flirtin' than ye be at fishin'."

"And what be the matter with me fishin'?"

"Well, ye did mistake I for a fish, did ye not?"

The muscles in his jaw worked once again as he clearly struggled to not retort.

Uncle had always said Morvoren had too sharp of a tongue. She'd gone without meals after telling Uncle just exactly how she felt about him and that lecher Mr. Foss.

"What do ye know 'bout flirtin', anyway?" Mr. Honeysett asked with a toss of his chin toward her.

"Enough to realize that ye ain't s'posed to sound as rigid as a frozen mackerel."

His brows knit together. "'Twasn't so bad. I just ain't comfortable with 'er. She ain't…" He blew out a pent-up breath, seeming to think better than to finish his sentence.

"She ain't, what?" she pressed, if only to see his ears turn as red as his cheeks.

"'Tis none o' your business."

"Ah, I see. I s'pose that it also ain't me business to wonder why ye be allowed to flirt with Mary—"

"I wasn't flirtin'."

"—when Poppy ain't allowed to flirt with Lieutenant Harris."

In a flash, his eyes hardened, indignation replacing the discomfort in his expression.

She wasn't surprised by his reaction. After all, any man would be defiant when the attention was being drawn toward the poor decisions he'd made.

But poor Poppy deserved vindication. She had looked absolutely mortified when Mr. Honeysett had interrupted her time with the lieutenant. How would the girl feel now, knowing she wasn't allowed to flirt with whomever she pleased when her brother was?

Morvoren looked away, watching the water's movements before them, the subtle shifting of the waves changing the color from dark blue to light. "I do wonder what Poppy'd say if she discovered what be goin' on 'tween ye and Mary."

"Ain't nothin' goin' on with…" He paused again, letting

out another exasperated breath. "Ye really be a wicked sea-maid, ain't ye?"

A genuine smile spread across her lips. "Did ye ever doubt it, sir?"

For a single, brief moment, she thought she saw a flicker of amusement in his eyes, but he turned away before she could be sure.

"Ye can tell Poppy whate'er ye like," he said. "It won't change the fact that she oughtn't be fallin' for that sailor."

Morvoren tipped her head. "Why? Be there somethin' wrong with sailors? 'Tain't as if they be fishermen."

He raised a brow. "I be well aware of 'ow ye feel 'bout fishermen, thank ye very much."

She shrugged. Her feelings could not be helped.

"What I don't know," he continued, "is if ye feel that way only 'bout drifters, or if your dislike do extend to seiners, as well."

She tipped her head back and forth, as if she didn't know her answer already. "Ain't they the same?"

He scoffed, turning to stare out at the sea, the wind tugging playfully at his shirtsleeves. "'Ow be your memory, Miss 'Ollow?"

"Same as before. Why?"

"Only wonderin' 'ow ye seem to remember a great deal 'bout some matters, while in others, ye forget the simplest o' things, like where your 'ome be."

She didn't like the direction the conversation was going. She didn't like it one bit. "Dr. Kent said selective memory be more than normal," she said.

"Selective. In that, ye *choose* what ye remember and what ye forget?"

Her shoulders tensed. "His words, not mine."

He fell silent, his dark eyes boring into hers as if willing her to admit the truth. But she wouldn't. There was too much at stake. Nor would she ever allow him to receive the upper hand with her.

After a moment, he sighed. "Well, I ought to be gettin' back to me work. I'll leave ye now to get back to yours— singin' and callin' ships to their deaths."

"Thank ye," she stated, unruffled by his teasing.

He walked away, and the tension in her neck eased just a moment before he turned back toward her. He opened his mouth, only to close it again, as if hesitating to speak. Was he debating whether or not to pursue further questions?

"Did ye really injure your foot again?" he eventually asked.

That was the last thing she'd expected him to say. "No, it still be injured from your net."

She wasn't sure if he hadn't picked up on her pointed words, or if he'd simply chosen to ignore them. "If 'tain't worse, why don't ye prove it to I by standin'?"

"'Cause I ain't done watchin' the waves yet."

"Do ye know 'ow to speak without lyin', Miss 'Ollow?"

"Do ye know how to speak to others without expectin' the worse of them, Mr. Honeysett?"

He released a heavy sigh, rubbing his eyes with his fingers. "This arguin' be pointless." He dropped his hand and faced her head-on. "I'll be frank with ye, Miss 'Ollow. I know ye've injured your foot again. So, to avoid another lashin' from me mother, I'll 'elp ye back. Will ye accept me offer? Or are ye willin' to risk further 'arm to your foot?"

Morvoren mulled the options over in her mind. Uncle told her she was too stubborn for her own good. But Mother had always admired Morvoren's tenacity.

"Ye don't let anyone push ye anywhere ye don't wish to, Morvoren," she'd said. *"'Specially no fisherman."*

But then, Mr. Honeysett was giving her the options as her own. Should she really snub his offer of help when she wasn't entirely certain she'd be able to make it down the cliffside again without resorting to crawling or shuffling down on her backside?

Swallowing her pride as best she could, she gave a single nod. "Very well, Mr. Honeysett. I'll accept your help."

Surprise flickered in his eyes, but he nodded it away, reaching his hand toward her.

She moved her leg from its place on the boulder, clenching her teeth to avoid showing any sign of weakness at her still-throbbing ankle. Then she scooted forward across the boulder until she was close enough to accept Mr. Honeysett's hand.

She eyed his fingers for a moment—callused, tanned, masculine—and she hesitated. How unfortunate she'd left most of her gloves in St. Ives. A pair would certainly be convenient in such a matter as this.

"Come on, then," Mr. Honeysett pressed, wiggling his fingers toward her.

Well, best to get this over with.

She pressed her hand to the man's palm, his fingers encircling hers, then instantly, a pleasant numbness spread across her flesh, and a heat as potent and wild as any fire ignited in her heart.

Her eyes snapped to Mr. Honeysett's, and her breath was snatched away from her lungs.

What the devil was happening to her?

CHAPTER SEVENTEEN

*I*n an instant, Morvoren pulled her hand away from Mr. Honeysett's, clutching the cane instead and willing her breathing to remain steady.

His touch. Why had his touch felt as if it was…nothing. It was absolutely nothing. The man was attractive—she couldn't deny him that, what with his wind-tossed hair and eyes the color of darkened sand. But the numbness that had taken over her was no doubt due to her lack of physical closeness with anyone for years. She would be wise to not invest in any other explanation but that.

She mumbled a quick expression of gratitude for his help, then tore her gaze away from his, only to draw it straight back to him when she caught sight of his fisted hand shifting to stretch his fingers outright.

She paused. Had he felt the same thing she had?

No, that wasn't possible. Because what she had felt had been nothing.

"Shall we?" he asked with a gesture for her to lead the way.

She nodded, taking a single step forward, but even with

the help of the cane, she could not hide the great limp she had to adopt to walk at all.

"It be 'urtin' that badly?" he asked from her side.

What was the use in pretending any longer? It was not as if she was doing a superb act of hiding her injury in the first place.

"'Tis," she said.

Mr. Honeysett reached out his arm toward her, and she accepted it, careful to hold onto the fabric of his sleeve instead of his bare forearm.

They managed a few steps forward before she stopped again with a breathless shake of her head. "'Tis no use. I'll just wait 'ere and watch the waves a bit longer. I'll make me way back when 'tisn't hurtin' so much."

He gave her a dubious look. "And if 'tain't ne'er better?"

She gave a shrug. "I'll live out me life on the boulders, then."

"Mmm, that be a fine plan." He studied her for a moment, unnerving her under his stalwart gaze, then in a fell swoop, he scooped her in his arms.

Morvoren gasped, wrapping her arms around his neck instinctively, somehow managing to maintain hold of the cane, which rested against his back.

"What are ye doin', Trevik Honeysett?" she questioned at once, gripping him all the tighter.

"I be returnin' ye to Tristwick 'fore nightfall." He readjusted his hands to hold her more securely around her back and beneath the crook of her legs.

Then, as if nothing out of the ordinary was occurring, he strode across the cliffside.

"I-I can walk, ye know."

"I believe we've already established that ye most certainly cannot."

She eyed the swift-moving ground beneath them as they began their descent toward Tristwick. His footing was secure, but she still gasped when he landed hard stepping over a rock.

"I'll not let ye fall," he said.

She'd expected such words to be said in a defensive manner, but they were spoken so calmly, so certainly, she had a difficult time *not* believing them.

As they continued, Mr. Honeysett's breathing grew labored, but he carried on, and a droplet of humility dribbled over into her vast sea of pride.

"I s'pose I ought to be thankin' ye," she said, "for helpin' me back."

"It be no trouble."

She glanced toward him, eying the sweat beading on his brow. "The strain ye be under might beg to differ."

"Well, if ye weren't so 'eavy…"

She scowled over at him, only to find the corners of his lips curved up into a little smile. Heavens, but that smile was charming. Charming and insufferable.

She looked away, catching a sharp, sweet scent on the wind. What was that—lemons? She cast her eyes about, attempting to decipher from what direction the scent had originated, but as she turned back to Trevik, the smell increased.

The fisherman? That wasn't right. He wasn't supposed to smell of citrusy soap, he was supposed to smell of pilchards and hake.

"Are ye certain ye be fine walkin' like this the entire way back?" she asked. Perhaps if he put her down now, she wouldn't have to smell him so closely.

"It be the least I can do after I nearly drowned ye."

Another glance back at him, another whiff of lemons. Such a fruit was common enough in soap, but for some reason, she wanted to breathe it in, to allow the clean, sharp smell to permeate her senses.

"I can only hope ye weren't tryin' to drown me on purpose," she returned.

"'Course not. But 'twas me fault for fishin' too close to the shore." He glanced at her sidelong. "As ye mentioned 'fore."

She had lectured him on that a time or two, hadn't she? "Ye can't be all to blame, I s'pose. I be the fool choosin' to swim in the sea at dark."

He was silent for a moment, and she wondered if he would focus on walking for the remainder of the journey. They passed the first house on the north side of the cove, just beginning to enter the hamlet.

"So that be what ye were doin'," he said after another moment, "swimmin'?"

Blast. How had she been so distracted as to have allowed that piece of information to escape her?

Lemons.

"I s'pose there ain't no other explanation for me bein' in the sea, be there?"

"I s'pose not." This time, he made no move to speak again.

A strange disappointment took hold of Morvoren's spirits at his silence. She despised the man and his pretentious ways. And yet, speaking with him—verbally sparring with him—had been the most excitement she'd experienced in years.

Before long, they passed by the stench-ridden cellars, then moved to the south cottages. Mr. Honeysett shifted his hold on her, tightening his grip around her legs as his fingers pressed against her ribcage. If she didn't know any better, she would have believed the heat from his touch could have very well melted through her dress.

Thank goodness they were nearly there.

Just short of the Honeysetts' home, they reached another cottage where an older man stood outside the door, leaning against the grey stone wall with a pipe in his mouth.

Morvoren recognized him in an instant. He'd been the one who'd shared that awful tale of the mermaid last night. If she hadn't distinguished his face from that, she surely would have recognized the sheer animosity seeping from his eyes.

"Trevik," the older man greeted.

Trevik nodded. "Edern."

Thankfully, Trevik didn't stop their progress, simply walking past the man without another word.

When they were out of earshot, Morvoren released a heavy breath. "Heavens, but that man doesn't trust me."

"Can ye blame 'im after what ye told 'is grandson yesterday?"

She dared a glance at Mr. Honeysett, his angled jaw boasting a brushing of facial hair she hadn't noticed before then. "Grandson?"

"Jowan, the young man ye were talkin' to yesterday, convincin' 'im ye was a mermaid."

Her lips parted. Oh, dear. No wonder Jowan was so convinced with a grandfar like Edern.

"I was only havin' a bit of fun with him," she grumbled. "I didn't mean any real harm."

He sniffed in derision. "Then what be all that singin' 'bout?"

"What do ye mean?"

"Ye were singin' like a sea-maid." He paused. "Speakin' o' which, 'ow *did* ye remember all 'em words? I thought your memory be in jowds?"

Her instinct was to concoct another lie, but at the memory of the song, her heart tightened. How could she tell a false-hood and dishonor her mother's memory in such a way?

"It be me mother's favorite song," she said softly. "Rather, it was."

His eyes settled upon her, but she couldn't allow him to ask another question, nor allow him more insight into the truth about her background—how she'd sung the very song to Mother as she lay dying.

Instead, she sent a sly smile up at Mr. Honeysett. "Now,

was I imaginin' it, or did ye not just say I have the voice of a sea-maid?"

He blinked, seemingly unaware of his own words until then. "I only meant to say that some people might think that."

"*Some* people? Oh, I be fairly certain ye were speakin' of yourself."

He frowned, apparently unable to come up with a rebuttal.

They rounded a small ridge and finally reached the Honeysetts' home. Mr. Honeysett gently lowered her to her feet, his arm remaining around her back until she was secure in her footing.

She mumbled her gratitude, then leaned against the cane, her back to the front door. "So…"

He looked at her expectantly, waiting for her to continue.

"Ye don't think my singin' be beautiful, then?"

He watched her with an unreadable expression, then slowly, a half-smile tugged at his lips. "Ye know what I think, Miss 'Ollow?"

"What be that, then?" she asked, delighted that he was playing along.

But when he took a slow, deliberate step toward her, her smile vanished. Why did he suddenly appear like a fox watching its prey?

She tried to move back, but the door prevented her departure.

His eyes captured hers as he took another step, his gaze flickering down to her lips. Was he…

Her thoughts ceased altogether as he reached toward her, about to slide his hand round her back. What was he doing? Better yet, what was *she* doing? Why was she not stopping him? And why did her heart race so?

He drew ever closer, though his hand had yet to make contact with her back. The smell of those lemons, however, had already wrapped her up in a soothing embrace.

"I think…" he whispered, pausing right before her, "that I be better at flirtin' than ye think I be."

Before she could register what was happening, a click sounded behind her, and the door opened.

She blinked. He hadn't been reaching for her, he'd been reaching for the door. And he hadn't been about to kiss her. He'd been teasing her.

With a smile that revealed just how pleased he was for having gotten the better of her for once, Mr. Honeysett finally pulled away. He gestured for her to enter his home, then with a tip of his head, he bade her farewell and made his way back toward the cellars.

Morvoren stared after him, her heart skipping a beat when he took one final glance back at her before disappearing around the ridge.

Blast, if he wasn't right. He *was* better at flirting than she'd given him credit for. Now how else was that fisherman going to surprise her?

CHAPTER EIGHTEEN

*T*revik left Miss Hollow, intent on heading straight for the cellars, but he was only a few steps around the first ridge when he spotted Edern still standing outside of his home.

He gave a pleasant nod. "'Ow ye doin', Edern?"

He continued walking, hoping the man would let him pass without grief, but he should've known better.

"A word, Trevik?"

Trevik's shoulders tensed. He should have known he wouldn't have made it back home without being spotted carrying Miss Hollow. What would it look like to all of Tristwick, especially the Cardys? But what was he supposed to have done, force the woman to crawl back to his house?

"I was on me way to the cellars, Edern. Can it wait?"

"'Twill only take a moment."

Trevik finally stopped with an innocent look. "All right. What be the matter, then?"

Edern pulled the pipe from his mouth, his lips instantly twisting. "I just be wonderin' what ye were doin' with that seamaid in your arms."

Well, at least the man was forthright with his issues. "Miss

'Ollow aggravated 'er ankle a bit more, so I 'ad to carry 'er 'ome. And as I said 'fore, she ain't be no sea-maid."

"Are ye certain that be all ye was doin'?" Edern asked, skirting right past Trevik's words.

Heavens, what did the man think Trevik was doing? And why did Edern feel he had the right to interrogate him anyway?

"I only be askin' 'cause I 'eard rumors about the two of ye," Edern clarified. "'Bout the two of ye fancyin' each other."

Trevik barked out a laugh. "Miss 'Ollow and I, fancy each other? Well, ye needn't worry 'bout that."

Of course, there was that strange reaction Trevik had had when he'd helped her down from the boulder and the way his heart had stuttered as he'd carried her home. And, of course, when he'd teased her at the door about flirting…His heart quickened, but he readily set it aside. The woman was attractive, yes. But that didn't mean he fancied her.

Edern narrowed his eyes.

"Really," Trevik continued. "I like that woman less than she likes I." Not that that was difficult. Miss Hollow had made it very clear how she felt about fishermen and their way of life —just as he'd made it clear how he felt about deceivers.

The woman was trouble, her beauty and her talent for singing notwithstanding.

"We've the right to worry, Trevik," Edern said. "I be concerned not only for the sake o' we men, but also for ye."

Trevik lowered his guard, attempting to accept the man's kindness. As a fellow fisherman, Edern *did* have the right to worry, and doing so only proved his devotion to their crew.

"I know that, sir," Trevik began, "and I be grateful for it. But I assure ye, I've everythin' under control."

Edern nodded, his frown subsiding only slightly. "So what's to be done with 'er, then?"

Trevik wasn't sure he liked the way Edern spoke about Miss Hollow like she was some common codfish one could simply toss back into the water. "I'll be takin' 'er to Sennen on Saturday."

He'd have to remember to thank Mother for so conveniently keeping such knowledge from him.

"Sennen?"

Trevik nodded. "She 'as friends there."

Edern seemed to consider the information, rolling the pipe around his tongue. "I've 'eard of many mermaids sighted round Sennen Cove," he said with an extended nod. "And ye said Saturday?"

"Yes, Saturday."

Edern sucked on his pipe, then released the white smoke into the air around them. "Two days still a long while to 'ave one of 'er types 'ere. Ye see 'ow easily she captured all o' we durin' 'er singin'. The longer she be 'ere, the 'arder it'll be to withstand 'er wiles."

Trevik couldn't deny that. But surely it was the beauty of her singing—and the emotion with which she sang—that had captured their attention, not because she was a sea-maid.

He paused, recalling the revelation she'd made, that the song had been her mother's favorite. Was that why she'd had tears in her eyes while singing? Because her mother had died?

"I know ye think I be mad, Trev."

Edern's voice pulled Trevik from his musings.

"But I ain't be," the man continued. "I saw a mermaid once meself. Gorgeous, she was. And dangerous. She sang and brought in a storm so strong that three men died from the waves. I don't want the same to 'appen again."

Trevik lowered his gaze. He'd heard the story from Edern so often, he could recount the tale himself. But that was just it. It was a tale. Still, he knew how deeply superstitions ran through some people, and though he couldn't agree with Edern's, Trevik would do his best to accept the man's reasoning to be as valid to Edern as Trevik's reasoning was to himself.

"I understand, Edern. Really, I do. And ye 'ave every right to be concerned. But I assure ye, if ye can wait 'til Saturday, all will be well."

"'Ow can ye be sure?"

"'Cause I'd ne'er do anythin' to risk the safety o' me men."

Edern studied him, as if to gauge the truthfulness of Trevik's words. "And she'll be gone by Saturday?"

Trevik gave a firm nod, clasping the man on his shoulder. "Ye 'ave me word."

Edern puffed on his pipe twice more before nodding. "Very well. 'Til Saturday."

The words should have eased Trevik's concerns, but he knew Edern was not so easily mollified. With a tip of his cap, he left the man and headed for the cellars.

Saturday could not come swiftly enough.

CHAPTER NINETEEN

*A*fter the evening meal the following night, Morvoren was instructed under no uncertain terms to remain on the bench in the sitting room until bedtime—the same direction she'd received the day before.

"Your foot'll ne'er be 'ealed otherwise, dear," Mrs. Honeysett said.

"That be what I told 'er," Mr. Honeysett added.

From her place on the bench, Morvoren could still see him in the kitchen, conversing with his mother about the cellars and the best way to utilize the new miners and maidens who'd agreed to work for them that winter.

He leaned against the table, his feet crossed at the end and arms folded with his shirtsleeves rolled up. She traced the ridges in his forearms, their presence coming as no surprise to her after he'd carried her across the entirety of the cove just a couple days before.

Since then, the two of them had had no opportunity to speak, but that could only be for the better. Morvoren had no wish to draw any closer to the Honeysetts than she already had.

She peered down at Poppy, who sat on the floor near the

fire in the sitting room, a slab of wood and a pile of seashells before her.

"What are ye doin' with those, Poppy?" she asked.

Poppy didn't look up as she responded. "Just a bit o' shell-work." She ran her finger across the various shapes, sizes, and colors of shells spread out before her, ultimately selecting a small, white scallop shell. "I be tryin' to create a wave's crest."

She replaced the scallop shell she'd chosen with an even smaller option, then moved it to the piece of wood. Rearranging the shells a bit more, she soon formulated the beginnings of a wave across the bottom of the slab.

"That'll be beautiful," Morvoren said. "Have ye done others of the like?"

"A bit. But I mostly paste 'em on frames and such." She placed another shell onto the wood. "I've sold a few in town 'fore."

"Have ye?"

She nodded matter-of-factly. "Most fine folk visitin' from other counties and London buy 'em and bring 'em 'ome. I think they like feelin' close to the sea when they leave. It don't account for much money, but it be a nice way to pass the time."

Morvoren watched her work in silence for a moment, impressed with her attention to detail with the design. "Ye be quite talented, Poppy."

Poppy smiled, her freckled cheeks blushing. After a moment, she straightened her hunched-over back and faced Morvoren. "Are ye ready to leave tomorrow, then?"

Morvoren drew a deep breath, responding as she exhaled. "I am. 'Twill be good to see me friend again."

Although, it had been so long since she'd seen Zennor, Morvoren was beginning to think she was better friends with Mrs. Honeysett and Poppy now.

The thought startled her, bringing a storm of confusion to cloud her mind. She had grown closer to the Honeysetts, but that didn't mean she wasn't longing for Sennen. The cove was only a stopping place, of course, just like Tristwick. But reaching there would mean it was one step closer to having the life she wanted.

"We'll miss ye 'ere," Poppy continued, moving back to place another shell near the others.

The sentiment was kind and much appreciated, but surely the girl didn't mean it. "I be certain ye won't miss me takin' o'er your room for so long."

"Oh, I don't mind sharin' a room with me mother, though I be certain she be finished with my stayin' with 'er. I keep 'er awake 'til all hours talkin'."

"'Tis a shame we didn't share a room, then. I don't mind speakin' through the night."

Poppy looked up, her brow furrowed with disappointment. "I wish I would 'ave known such a thing. I spent most nights talkin' to Mother without realizin' she already be asleep."

Morvoren smiled. She didn't know a great deal about Poppy, but she couldn't help but admire the girl's spirited humor and ability to stand up to Mr. Honeysett.

She stole a glance toward the kitchen again, catching Mr. Honeysett's eyes on her before he swiftly pulled away and responded to his mother.

Morvoren hid another smile, then glanced about the room with a contented sigh. She certainly would miss the charming nature of the Honeysetts' home. It always felt warm within the walls, despite the bitter, autumn wind whistling against the cold glass of the windows.

She allowed her eyes to continue to travel about the room before they settled on the framed painting of the family she'd seen on her first day out of her room.

"Poppy," she said softly, "can I ask what happened to your father?"

"'E died," she responded, her voice lowering just a fraction. "Six years ago now."

Morvoren had expected as much. But the knowledge that they, too, had lost their father made her heart ache. She could only hope he'd departed in better circumstances than her own father had.

"I be sorry," she said softly.

Poppy glanced up at Morvoren then, tipping her head to the side curiously. "Do ye remember anythin' 'bout your parents yet?"

Morvoren swallowed, shifting against the thin cushion Mrs. Honeysett had laid down for her atop the bench. "A little," she responded, not wishing to lie to the girl any more than she already had. "I do remember that they've passed on, too."

Poppy's brow rose. "Both of 'em?"

She nodded. She'd kept such knowledge away from the family on purpose, but what with her leaving tomorrow morning, what was the harm in allowing the girl such information?

"Did ye 'ave any brothers or sisters?"

"No, 'fraid not."

Poppy looked away in a sort of daze. "No brothers or sisters. That be a tragedy, that."

Morvoren gave a half-smile. "Well, ye only have the one."

"Yes, but I could've 'ad more. Mother lost three babes 'tween 'avin' I and Trevik."

"Oh. Oh, I be sorry to hear that." She'd had no idea the woman had suffered so great a loss three times over. Such heartbreaks were not unheard of—though it didn't make them any less excruciating to suffer through.

"I s'pose that be why she be so grateful for Trevik and I," Poppy continued, pulling off the lid of her jar of paste set beside the wood and shells. "And why I be grateful for Trevik, as intolerable as 'e can be at times."

Morvoren gave a short laugh. Intolerable was putting it politely. "Like when he won't let ye speak with whom ye wish to speak?"

Poppy's smile faded away, her voice falling to a whisper. "Trevik be a good man. 'E be a fierce protector over I and Mother. But…'e can be daft, as well. 'E still thinks I be a child, too young for an 'usband."

Morvoren had a great deal to say in regard to Mr. Honeysett, but criticizing the man Poppy held in such high regard would not be wise—nor kind. Instead, she held her tongue and broached another subject. "Tell me 'bout Lieutenant Harris. When did ye first meet him?"

Instantly, Poppy's expression lightened, an airy smile stretching across her lips. "I met 'im a few months back, when 'e was shipwrecked near Golowduyn. Mother and I began work there last May, same time as 'im. That be when I first saw 'im." Her cheeks glowed pink. "'E do be the most kind, most 'umorous, most 'andsome man I ever saw."

Morvoren's smile grew at the admiration in Poppy's words. "And he loves ye, too, then?"

"Love?" Poppy pulled back, her blush deepening. "Oh, I could ne'er 'ope as much. I only wish 'e'd stay in St. Just for longer, rather than goin' back to sea."

"He has plans, then, of goin' back?"

Poppy shrugged. "I s'pose. I can't ask 'im, too afeared o' the answer, see."

She fell silent, her eyes taking on a distant look and appearing much older than her sixteen years of age. After another moment, she sighed, shaking her head and staring back at her shellwork. "Anyway, they just be fanciful ideas. It'd be only a dream, for no man such as 'e would e'er wish to be with I."

Her dejected words pierced Morvoren's heart. Mr. Honeysett clearly did not believe Poppy was old enough to have a suitor, but was his reluctance on the matter causing Poppy's confidence to falter?

Unwilling to allow such a thing to occur, Morvoren leaned forward, focusing intently on Poppy as she spoke. "No woman, no matter the age, should e'er believe she ain't worthy of receivin' all she desires." She paused. "'Sides, I noticed your Lieutenant Harris watchin' ye, and I saw more than simple admiration in his eyes."

Poppy pulled her lips together to hide her smile. "Ye must've mistaken 'im for lookin' at ye. I don't 'ave your looks. And I sure as anythin' can't flirt."

Morvoren didn't believe that for a second. After all, she'd thought Mr. Honeysett had been unable to flirt, and she'd been proven wrong tenfold. But then, why had he been able to flirt with Morvoren and not Mary?

She shook the thought from her mind, convincing herself she didn't need to know the answer. "Sure ye can flirt, Poppy. All it takes is practice."

But Poppy shook her head. "I s'pose if I did learn, Trevik'd just disapprove."

Morvoren leaned closer. "All the more reason to do it, then."

The girls stifled their laughter when Mr. Honeysett glanced at them from the kitchen. Morvoren knew she was skirting around an open flame by teaching Poppy to pursue the lieutenant. But if Morvoren left the girl happier and with more control over her own life, then she would not stop her encouraging.

Besides, what with her leaving tomorrow, she didn't have to deal with any of the repercussions anyway.

She waited until Mr. Honeysett looked away again, then she waved Poppy closer. "Come. Let us try it together. All ye have to do is look at a man like this"—she eased a demure smile across her lips and batted her eyes—"and he'll fall for ye like anythin'. Then ye just comment 'bout his hair or his smile. Anythin' to make him strut about like a pheasant."

Poppy laughed behind her fingers.

"Now ye try," Morvoren said.

Poppy lowered her hand and straightened her back, still

on the floor. "All right. 'Ow 'bout…Oh, Lieutenant 'Arris, ye 'ave such fine shoulders. As wide as a bull's."

Their laughter joined together again. "Well done, Poppy. Ye be better at this than I be. Per'aps I'll take that and use it for meself one day."

"Feel free to use it on me brother, if ye wish."

Morvoren stilled, the smile slipping from her lips. "Your brother? Why would I use it on him?"

Poppy batted innocent eyes. "'Cause 'e 'as broad shoulders. And well, ye do find 'im attractive, don't ye?"

Morvoren was suddenly regretting ever getting herself into such a conversation. "Well, I-I s'pose…" She glanced in his direction, and his eyes pulled away again. Heavens above. Had he heard them?

She looked back to Poppy, desperate to change the subject. "But enough about I. Are ye now convinced to say such things to Lieutenant Harris?"

Poppy's grin returned. "I be gettin' closer, I think." She looked away, delivering a heavy sigh. "I just wish all o' this be easier."

Morvoren gave a soft smile. "Don't we all. But anythin' worth havin' be worth the struggle to achieve it."

Poppy seemed deep in thought for a moment, then turned searching eyes on Morvoren. "'Ave ye e'er been in love?"

A sadness twinged Morvoren's heart. "No, I haven't. But I know what it be like to *not* be in love." She hesitated, unsure of how much to share, but Poppy's stalwart gaze shook the grounds of her reticence. "I was supposed to, well, I was asked to…" She paused, beginning again. "I was *expected* by me caretaker to accept the hand of a man I didn't love."

Poppy's eyes widened. "Ye were engaged?"

Morvoren glanced to the kitchen, but Mr. Honeysett's eyes remained focused on his mother.

"Not officially, no," she responded. "But there was an understandin' 'tween our families."

An understanding forced upon them both by the man's father and her uncle. Legally, Uncle Truscott couldn't force Morvoren into anything, but then, he had never been one to behave with absolute morality. Either way, she was fairly certain Mr. Foss didn't care whether he married her or not. After all, his riotous living would continue either way. She'd said as much to Uncle, but he'd merely shrugged the notion aside.

"What 'appened?" Poppy asked in a whisper.

"Nothin'. Other than the engagement ne'er comin' to fruition. I realized I couldn't give up the life I had planned for meself for a man I didn't love—a man who clearly didn't love me in return." She reached for Poppy's hand, and the girl shuffled closer to accept it, still kneeling on the ground before her. "I hope ye'll have the courage to do the same, Poppy. To fight for what ye want in life. Ye deserve the world for your generosity. And a generous heart deserves a generous heart in return."

Poppy stared up at her, moisture glistening in her eyes before she lunged forward, embracing Morvoren around the middle from where she still knelt upon the hard floor. "Thank ye, Morvoren," she whispered.

Morvoren didn't know what she'd said to elicit such a reaction, but she returned the embrace in an instant.

Though the feeling was odd, holding a near-stranger, she felt a curious sense of familiarity, of familial love for this girl. But all too swiftly, that love shifted to a heaviness that pressed upon her heart as heavy and thick as saturated sand.

Despite the belief of her being a devious mermaid, despite Mr. Honeysett's continuous suspicions…she was going to miss Tristwick. The incomparable view, the comfortable home, Mrs. Honeysett's kindness, Poppy's goodness. She'd been welcomed by them, treated as an equal, as if she had been wanted. Morvoren had not felt such a way in years, since before Mother died and Father changed.

Would she be welcomed in the same manner by the Prouts? Or would she be a burden on them as she had been to Uncle?

As Poppy's embrace continued, Morvoren glanced to the kitchen with a heavy heart, feeling Mr. Honeysett's stare on her before she met his eyes. Instead of looking away, he merely observed her with a steady gaze.

No doubt he disapproved of her embracing his sister, assuming Morvoren was up to no good.

Perhaps she was. Or at least, her heart was. Why else would it play such a cruel trick on her, learning to love a family she was never supposed to, the night before she would leave them forever?

CHAPTER TWENTY

$\mathcal{F}$reedom was within Morvoren's grasp. She was so close, she could taste it. She was so close, she could *feel* it.

And yet, as she looked back at the cliffsides surrounding Tristwick, the quaint hamlet no longer in view, a fraction of her heart tore away from the whole and lingered along the cliffs. This place would always hold that sole piece of her heart, but she was ready to move on. She was ready to find a home of her own, a place in this world where she would finally know she belonged.

But then, if she was ready, why did her stomach toss like a ship lost at sea? She glanced to Poppy, who was seated across from her in the back of the Kendricks's wagon, noting a hint of sadness in the girl's eyes. Was she feeling the weight of Morvoren leaving, too?

No. No, there was no weight. There was only excitement and the rest of Morvoren's future to look forward to.

"Are ye all right back there?" Mrs. Honeysett asked. Her voice raised to be heard above the wagon rustling across the dirt road and the horse's tack jingling against her dapple-grey coat.

Morvoren nodded. "Thank ye again for takin' me all this way."

"Oh, it be no problem. We be 'appy to 'elp, ain't we be, Trev?"

Mr. Honeysett nodded from where he sat next to his mother. With their placement in the wagon, Morvoren could only see the back of his dark green fisherman's cap, but she could imagine the delight written across his face at the mention of Morvoren leaving.

She still wasn't sure if he'd heard her conversation with Poppy the night before, but did it matter? Either way, with Morvoren gone, his life was surely about to become exponentially easier.

She tore her gaze away from him, determined to no longer dwell on how much he disliked her. The journey to Sennen would be more than an hour, and she would not be brought lower by thoughts of the fisherman.

After all, today was a glorious day. Every moment that passed brought her farther and farther away from her past. She would find her place in the world, and it would not be with a fisherman and his family—drifters or seiners.

Clutching the handles of her portmanteau, the sound of coins jingling within her coin purse reached her ears. She knew Mrs. Honeysett would never accept payment for the trouble of taking her to Sennen, but she would empty the purse into the Honeysetts' possession before they left, no matter who she had to give the money to. The inconvenience was too great to allow them to go unpaid.

"Be your foot troublin' ye, Morvoren?" Mrs. Honeysett asked, turning round in her seat again.

"No, 'tis better than ever."

"I be glad to 'ear that."

Morvoren was, too. Remaining off her foot after her excursion days before had finally allowed her ankle enough time to begin to heal, though the ache was still there to a degree with each step. At least she could walk on her own with only a limp to mar her stride. Surely she would be a better help to the Prouts now she could stand on her own two feet.

"Do ye think your memory will come back once ye see your friends?" Poppy asked, the upper half of her body swaying back and forth with the unsettling movement of the wagon.

"I hope so," she responded.

She looked forward to a great deal about Sennen, but nothing more than the fact that she would no longer have to lie.

Poppy nodded in response and turned to watch the passing view. Morvoren did the same, silence falling over their traveling party as they progressed across the countryside.

Morvoren would dip her head low each time a carriage would pass by, fearing Uncle would spot her moments before she was guaranteed her freedom. But then, being in Sennen would guarantee nothing, only a few extra miles between her and Uncle Truscott.

Still, a place with the Prouts would do just fine until Zennor could help Morvoren find a more permanent residence—somewhere Uncle would never think to find her. Or at least, so she hoped.

As her worried thoughts intensified, the journey dragged on. Poppy eventually fell asleep, and Mrs. Honeysett and her son were quiet at the front of the wagon, which only allowed Morvoren's descending spirits to pull her down farther.

She just couldn't make sense of it. This was what she'd been wanting for so long, to reach Sennen, to be with someone who could help her, someone with whom she could be honest, someone she could trust. Perhaps she simply needed to be positive. To believe that she would lead a happy life and that one day, she would find a place of her own, and perhaps even have a non-fisherman husband who promised to never tear her apart like the fishing trade had done to her family.

"Nearly there," Mrs. Honeysett said, interrupting her thoughts.

Morvoren looked ahead, spotting a wooden sign sticking up from the grass at the side of the road. In simple carving, the sign read,

SENNEN COVE,
ONE MILE

Instead of feeling excitement or relief as she ought to have, Morvoren's nerves jumbled so violently, she thought she might relieve her stomach over the side of the wagon.

Would Zennor welcome her still? Would Mr. Prout? After all, he had not been the one to invite her to stay with them. Would he help find a place for Morvoren, or would he turn her away without a second glance?

Poppy stirred soon, rising from the blanket she'd rolled up to form a pillow and looking around her. Morvoren gave her a little smile, but the two remained silent as the cove loomed ever closer.

"Any o' this lookin' familiar, Morvoren?" Mrs. Honeysett asked.

Unease eddied in Morvoren's chest. The view was beautiful—turquoise seas, sapphire skies, grey stones covered in patches of grass—but it glared with unfamiliarity to Morvoren.

"No," she replied truthfully. She'd never been to Sennen before, so why did it upset her that it didn't feel like…home?

Perhaps this was a good thing, though. She'd only ever planned for Sennen to be a temporary home, so maybe leaving here would be easier for her to do than it had been for her to leave Tristwick.

"I'm sure the moment ye step foot in the apothecary shop,

ye'll remember everythin'," Mrs. Honeysett said with a reassuring nod.

Morvoren cringed. Would it be far too obvious if that was exactly what happened to her?

"Do we know where the shop might be?" Mr. Honeysett asked, his voice gruff. Was that from frustration or simply lack of speaking?

"'Ere be someone we can ask." Mrs. Honeysett pointed to the side of the road where a man in a weathered jacket walked along the path.

They pulled up alongside him, and he stopped with a curious gaze. "Can I 'elp ye?"

Mr. Honeysett leaned forward. "We be lookin' for the apothecary."

The man nodded, pointing down the road. "Carry on down 'ere and ye'll reach the shop on't left side o' the street."

Mr. Honeysett expressed his gratitude, and the man tipped his cap before the wagon rode past him.

Morvoren leaned her head back over the side of the wagon to see farther down the road. Sennen was sprawled out across the cove that was nearly double the size of Tristwick, the houses, cottages, and shops far larger and far more concentrated than Morvoren had expected.

At least she'd be able to blend in more easily with the crowds here. But then, with more people in Sennen, there would be more seiners to hide from.

With her eyes darting from face to face of the inhabitants of the town, Morvoren didn't notice the apothecary shop until Mr. Honeysett stopped just outside of it.

She drew in a shaky breath. The shop was quaint, with bottles displayed in the windows and a wooden sign sticking forth from the two-story building.

SKEWES'S APOTHECARY
No. 4

She narrowed her eyes. *Skewes's* Apothecary? Wasn't it…

As the Honeysetts readied themselves to leave the wagon, Morvoren pulled open her portmanteau. She'd hoped to enter the building alone, but at the moment, she had something else on her mind.

She rooted around for a moment, finally finding the piece of paper Zennor had given her over a year ago. As clear as day, *Prout's Apothecary* was written across the paper.

She eyed the wooden sign again. Perhaps they were at the wrong shop. Perhaps the *Prouts'* Apothecary was farther down the road. But then, why would there be two apothecary shops in one location—and why would it have the same address as the one on the paper?

Her heart dropped, and panic flapped in her hollow chest.

"Miss 'Ollow?"

She glanced down at Mr. Honeysett, who stood just at the back of the wagon. He'd helped his mother and sister down already and now stood by Morvoren with an outstretched hand.

Only vaguely aware of how relieved she was to have been wearing her traveling gloves, Morvoren allowed Mr. Honeysett to help her from the wagon, then she stepped away from him in an instant and stared at the shop as if its dark brick and brown paint was part of a great, looming mountain.

It very well might have been, for the very thought of summiting that mountain, of entering through the door was far too daunting. What would she find inside? And more importantly—whom?

"Shall we?" Mrs. Honeysett asked at her side with an encouraging smile.

Morvoren opened her mouth, but no words followed until Mr. Honeysett spoke instead.

"Excuse I," he mumbled, backing away. "I've a job to see to. I'll return in just a moment."

"Now?" Mrs. Honeysett asked in a tight voice.

He nodded, still departing. "I'll return soon," he repeated, then he turned on his heel and strode away.

"Men," Mrs. Honeysett muttered, then she turned toward Morvoren with another smile. "Are ye ready, me dear?"

No, Morvoren was not ready in the slightest. But concerned glances from the Honeysetts broke through her stupor, and she limped forward, her head swirling like the waves of the ocean she could hear from the shop but not see.

She opened the door, the bell jingling above them as they entered the apothecary. The pungent smell of spices, herbs, and tinctures greeted them. Glass jars of the extracts and mixtures lined multiple shelves behind an empty, front counter.

The dark walls added a squalid quality to the room, but the rectangular-paned windows provided just enough light to improve the overall atmosphere of the shop.

"Do ye recognize it?" Mrs. Honeysett asked, her whisper carrying about the room like a draft of wind.

"Not exactly."

Oh, how she wished she could be honest. How she wished Zennor would round the corner and ease all of her concerns.

As if on cue, footsteps padded from the backroom, but it was not Zennor nor Mr. Prout who appeared.

Instead, a large man with greying hair greeted them with a smile as he smoothed the front of his apron. "Sorry to keep ye waitin'. Mr. Skewes, at your service. 'Ow can I 'elp ye?"

Morvoren froze. Mr. Skewes. As in, *Skewes's Apothecary*.

Her mind raced to place the shattered pieces of her plans back together. The Prouts must have sold the shop. Did that mean they hadn't any money to keep it running? Surely… surely they had enough to take her in for a time.

Mrs. Honeysett's gentle hand on her arm brought Morvoren back to the present.

Mr. Skewe was glancing between all three women, his smile faltering at their prolonged silence.

"I..." Morvoren squeaked out, clearing her throat and beginning again. "I be lookin' for Mrs. Zennor Prout."

The man paused, his brow raising in surprise. "Zennor Prout?"

Morvoren's palms began to sweat within her gloves as she wrung them together. "Yes, sir."

Slowly, he shook his head. "I be sorry, miss, but I ain't seen 'er in o'er six months."

CHAPTER TWENTY-ONE

*M*orvoren reached for the counter, clasping on as her legs threatened to give out. She became acutely aware of the Honeysetts behind her. Though neither of them said a word she could only imagine their thoughts.

Didn't Morvoren say she'd been in contact with the Prouts?

If she was untruthful about that, what else has she been lying about?

"Can ye tell I where she be?" she asked, leaning closer to the counter in the faint hope that the man would only share such news with her and not Mrs. Honeysett or Poppy.

The clerk blew out a slow breath. "Oh, bound for Scotland, last I 'eard. They sold the apothecary to meself, see, 'fore they packed up and left."

Scotland? The air rushed from Morvoren's lungs as the last of her hope fled her heart. *Gone. Scotland. Left.*

The overpowering spices from the room clouded her mind, and she couldn't draw a breath, as if she was once again drowning in the sea. Only this time, she was caught in the net of her own lies and mistakes.

She couldn't go back to Uncle. She couldn't marry Mr. Foss. But then, what other choice did she have? Remain in

Sennen and knock from door-to-door, begging for food and shelter?

"Morvoren?" Mrs. Honeysett's concerned voice slipped into her thoughts, and Morvoren blinked.

Concerned? How could the woman be concerned? Surely she had already pieced together the situation and was now aware of Morvoren's deception. Why was she not angry?

"Are ye well, miss?" Mr. Skewes asked. "Might I offer some very fine smellin' salts I 'ave in stock 'ere—"

"No, no," Mrs. Honeysett interrupted, her words echoing in Morvoren's ears, as if spoken from a great distance. "We'll see to 'er now, thank ye." Then she wrapped her arms around Morvoren's shoulders and led her from the shop.

The bright sunshine pierced into Morvoren's eyes, and she winced, turning away. In the next moment, however, she wished she'd kept her eyes closed, for Mr. Honeysett stood before her, confusion pressed against his brow.

"What 'appened?" he asked, his gaze shifting to his mother's.

Morvoren didn't miss the subtle shake of Mrs. Honeysett's head.

Mr. Honeysett looked back at Morvoren, as did the rest of his family as they searched for an explanation, but she only ducked her head, blinking back tears of fear and humiliation. Why had she not been honest with them from the start? She'd used them ill, had treated them in a manner no one ought to be treated. But now, it was her responsibility to right the situation. After all, they deserved the truth after everything they'd done for her.

She straightened her back and faced them, pulling away from Mrs. Honeysett's comforting arm. She didn't deserve such kindness, not after the lies she'd told them.

Swallowing against the growing lump in her throat, she began. "I…I have some things I'd like to say to ye all. If ye care to listen."

At once, Mrs. Honeysett nodded, and she led the four of them to the inn down the road. The dining area was mostly empty, one man seated at the bar and a couple near the front door, so the Honeysetts and Morvoren chose a table at the back of the room. After the plates of food had been given to the women and a drink to Trevik, Morvoren began her confession.

"I first need to say how sorry I be for all of this. I can't imagine what ye be thinkin' of I now, and ye really have no reason to trust what I be sayin', but I'd like to be honest with ye now."

Poppy's eyes were rounded with worry, though Mrs. Honeysett gave Morvoren an encouraging nod. Mr. Honeysett merely focused on his drink.

Morvoren winced. He would be the most difficult to speak with about all of this. After all, he'd given her multiple chances to tell the truth, and she'd only lied all the greater.

With a burning conscience, she continued, focusing hard on the smooth, knotted wood of the table they sat around. "I have no memory loss from me near drownin'. I admit that I was confused in the beginnin', but soon after, things were quite clear." She took another breath. "Five years ago, when I was fifteen, me parents died one after the other, leavin' I to be looked after by me only livin' relative. Uncle took me in, but… he didn't care for I. He changed me accent, forced me to do as he wished, and threatened to take away everythin' I loved if I didn't. His last command was to help him with a business venture."

Humiliation branded across her cheeks in a heated blush. For so long, she'd refused to blame herself for Uncle's lack of care. But admitting his animosity toward her made it difficult to not to blame herself for his behavior. After all, had she done more, had she been a different person, could Uncle have ever loved her?

"He made an arrangement with another gentleman," she

explained, "a joinin' of their two companies—and a weddin' 'tween me and the gentleman's son."

She grimaced, picturing Mr. Foss's ceremonious bow to Morvoren when his father and Uncle had let them both know of the arrangement. They'd been at a ball the night before she'd left, and after Mr. Foss's expression of pleasure over their arrangement—and Morvoren's stunned silence—he'd promptly helped himself to half the drinks at the refreshment table.

"I couldn't agree to the marriage," she said, her voice as small as she felt, "so I...I left."

Memories of her and Uncle's last argument flooded her mind. He'd shouted at her, far louder than he ever had before. And though he didn't strike her, he had always found different ways to cause her suffering.

"You shall marry Mr. Richard Foss," he'd threatened, *"or I'll send you to a workhouse in London where you'll never see your beloved sea again."*

She shook her head. "I took the earliest coach I could, stoppin' in St. Just. From there, I swam in the sea to clear me head, though I was intendin' to only be a moment."

"And then ye were caught in the net," Mrs. Honeysett finished.

Morvoren nodded. "I hadn't been allowed near the sea in weeks, so I took the first chance I could."

Poppy frowned. "Ye weren't allowed to see the sea?"

Morvoren shook her head.

"Your uncle *do* be a tyrant."

"Poppy," Mrs. Honeysett said in a soft rebuke.

But Morvoren shook her head. "'Tis an accurate description." She moved to tell them that he was a seiner, as well, but then, wouldn't that sully their opinion of her more fully?

She drew a deep breath and continued with more important truths. "I would've told ye all this 'fore, but I didn't want no chance of Uncle findin' I and forcin' I to go back to St.

Ives with him. Feignin' forgetfulness seemed the easiest option."

Mrs. Honeysett nodded, understanding filling her eyes. "I can see why ye kept most o' this to yourself. Must've been harrowin' to make such an escape, then to end up with a family ye didn't know if ye could trust or not."

Morvoren swallowed hard, blinking furiously to keep her tears at bay. Was there no end to this woman's generosity? Poppy, too, seemed more than willing to forgive Morvoren's trespasses, her eyes as soft as her mother's.

Mr. Honeysett, however, maintained his stoic expression, swirling his drink back and forth in his glass, having yet to take a single sip.

"Did ye…" Mrs. Honeysett hesitated before Morvoren urged her to continue. "Did ye really 'ave a friend 'ere in Sennen?"

Morvoren pumped her head up and down, anxious for them to know she wasn't a total wretch. "Yes, I truly thought she'd be here. After I swam, I was fully intendin' on walkin' to Sennen. I had no idea she wouldn't be here. Although, I…" She hung her head. "I hadn't corresponded with her like I said. I didn't have the time 'fore I left. I realize now, had I waited for a response from her, all o' this could've been avoided, and for that, I be sorry." She paused, shaking her head. "For *everythin'*, I be sorry. I ne'er meant to hurt any of ye."

She paused, reaching into her portmanteau at her feet and retrieving the coin purse. She withdrew a few coins—enough for a night at the inn and perhaps a bit of food—then dropped the purse on the table before Mrs. Honeysett. "I hope what be left will suffice for the trouble I've caused ye all in bringin' I down here for no reason."

Finally, Morvoren stopped, staring down at her plate of untouched food and wallowing in her shame. If she didn't wish to allow the Honeysetts an opportunity to share their true feelings about her, she would've left right then. But she owed them that much.

Mrs. Honeysett leaned back in her seat, the wood creaking out across the room. "Well, what an ordeal ye've been through, even before ye were near-drowned." She eyed the coin purse, then glanced between her son and daughter. "But ordeal or not, 'course we forgive ye for actin' in a way ye only deemed fit for survivin'. Don't we?"

Poppy instantly nodded, but Mr. Honeysett's silence remained. Mrs. Honeysett either chose to ignore her son or simply didn't see his lack of response, for she leaned forward and pushed the coin purse toward Morvoren. "And we'll not be takin' that."

Morvoren shook her head. "Please. I have to give ye some-thin' for all your troubles. I'd not wish to be indebted to ye more than I already be."

Mrs. Honeysett paused, looking thoughtful for a moment. "What do ye plan to do now, with the Prouts not 'ere?"

"I'll still stay in Sennen," Morvoren said, attempting to come up with the plan she'd been asking herself for the better part of an hour. All she knew was that she couldn't ask the Honeysetts for more help than she'd already been given. "I'll ask 'round if anyone be needin' any help, or who might be willin' to take me on." She shrugged. "And if that don't work out, then I'll…I'll find a workhouse, I s'pose."

The very thought struck fear throughout her person. Working there would be nearly the complete opposite of obtaining freedom.

Mrs. Honeysett's brow lowered. She glanced once more to her son, then faced Morvoren with a smile. "I tell ye what. S'pose ye return with we to Tristwick?"

Mr. Honeysett's head remained in place, though his eyes instantly flicked to his mother's, who again gave no notion that she'd seen her son's actions.

"I don't wish for no charity," Morvoren said at once. "I already was a burden to ye all."

But Mrs. Honeysett shook her head. "Ye won't be no burden if ye work with we."

Morvoren listened, attempting to understand, though she felt as if she was swimming against the tide.

"If ye return with we and work in the cellars, ye can pay your keep and save any extra wages ye earn 'til ye can become self-sufficient. Or 'til ye decide what it is ye want to do next. Ye'll not need to worry 'bout your uncle either, as now that we're aware of 'is actions, we can keep an eye out for 'im, as well." She ended with a hopeful smile. "What do ye think?"

Morvoren couldn't believe such a generous offer had been made after all she'd put this family through. But there was no possible way she could accept it, no matter the appeal of being tucked safely away in Tristwick with the Honeysetts as a beautiful buffer between her and Uncle.

Not only would she be a burden, but she would also be going straight back to living with a fisherman. And not just any fisherman, a fisherman who'd made her heart jump like a fish out of the sea with his flirting. A fisherman who had warmed her skin with his mere touch and had caused her blush with his stares.

She sent a furtive glance in Mr. Honeysett's direction, though he'd returned to staring at his drink again. Living with him would only bring about more opportunities for the two of them to be together, to draw closer. But such a thing was dangerous if she wished to keep a hearty distance from the trade.

"Thank ye so much for the offer, but I couldn't inconvenience ye any longer."

"Nonsense," Mrs. Honeysett said. "'Twouldn't be an inconvenience at all. Ye'd be 'elpin' we to get the fish in faster and joinin' in cookin' meals and cleanin' 'round the 'ouse. Not to mention the fact that we'd love to 'ave your company for longer."

Poppy sat forward in her chair, the legs creating a high moan against the wood floor. "And we could share a room then!" she said with excitement.

Morvoren couldn't help but smile at the girl's enthusiasm, nor could she deny the appeal of the portrait these two were painting for her.

Perhaps Tristwick, instead of Sennen, could be her next steppingstone for where she wanted to end up in her life. Surely she could stomach living with fishermen for a while longer without risking becoming tainted by them as Father and Uncle were.

But then, living with the Honeysetts did not solve everything.

She cast her eyes down. "I'd love to stay with ye. Really, I would. But I know what my bein' in Tristwick has done to some folk. I'd hate to upset 'em more than I already have."

Mrs. Honeysett huffed out an impatient breath. "If ye be referrin' to Edern and 'is superstitious ways, ye oughtn't give 'im another thought. That old goat'll be onto the next thing that worries 'im 'fore long."

The weight around Morvoren's shoulders began to lessen, but she pulled it straight back into place. She needed to think rationally about this. She needed to ensure she wasn't behaving selfishly again.

Yes, she could work for them and solve the issue of being a burden. She could reassure all those in the hamlet that she wasn't a mermaid. And the Honeysetts would help protect her if Uncle ever *did* find her.

Heavens, she would even be humble enough to live with a fisherman in exchange for living on the streets of Sennen.

But there was one thing she couldn't look past. "I just…I can't put ye out again." Her gaze found Mr. Honeysett. "Any of ye."

A beat of silence followed her words.

"Ye won't be puttin' we out," Mrs. Honeysett reassured her, then she turned to face her son. "Will she, Trevik?"

Mr. Honeysett finally glanced up from his drink, staring at his mother for a moment before finally meeting Morvoren's gaze. With a smile that looked as strained as her shoulders felt, he nodded. "No, ye won't be no trouble at all."

"There, ye see?" Mrs. Honeysett said with a satisfied smile. "We'll not take no for an answer. Ye'll stay in Tristwick with us for as long as ye need."

Morvoren hesitated, but with Mrs. Honeysett's expectant stare and Poppy's grin, she found herself nodding. "If ye insist."

Poppy grinned from ear to ear. "Oh, I be so 'appy ye be comin' back!"

Morvoren attempted a smile, but uncertainty still tightened in her stomach. Mrs. Honeysett and Poppy may have been more than pleased, but Morvoren knew at once that Mr. Honeysett's approval hadn't been genuine. His words had been too stoic, too rehearsed.

As his sister and mother celebrated, he averted his gaze from Morvoren's, jerking away from the table as if he'd spotted a rat crawling toward him. "I'll ready the wagon for our return," he mumbled, replacing his cap on his head. "The three of ye ought to eat 'fore we leave."

Mrs. Honeysett and Poppy nodded in agreement, but Morvoren merely watched his back as he departed, wondering who would regret her return to Tristwick more—she or Mr. Honeysett.

CHAPTER TWENTY-TWO

$\mathcal{O}$n the journey home, Mother attempted to involve Trevik in their conversation numerous times, but he could only manage a few grunts and nods in response. He didn't trust himself to speak, afraid his irritation would manifest itself and he'd say what he really thought of Morvoren Hollow.

Of course, his frustration was merely a mask to disguise the hurt and embarrassment she'd caused him. He'd known she'd been lying. Well, he hadn't *known*. But he'd suspected it of her since the beginning. In truth, he rather admired the humility she'd exhibited in admitting to her falsehoods, but after all she'd put them through, her deceit, riling up the Cardys, then making them go to the trouble of borrowing a wagon and traveling to Sennen, he was ready to part ways with the woman.

He felt for her plight and had compassion for her past. But what person in this forsaken world did not have his or her own struggles? At some point, one had to accept life the way it was or rise above it—without exploiting another's charity.

More than anything, Trevik was concerned for the well-being of his family and for Tristwick. For what in heaven's name was he going to say to Edern and his crew when they discovered Miss Hollow would be staying with them indefinitely?

At least Mother and Poppy seemed more than happy with the situation, though he believed them to be entirely too forgiving. Mother was smiling a great deal more, and Poppy chatted away in endless streams of jolly musings until they stopped to stretch their legs midway through their travels.

Trevik checked the horse's tack—if only to avoid being near the others—but just before their departure, Mother approached with Miss Hollow limping along beside her, the woman's cheeks a charming pink, green eyes averted.

"Me legs keep seizin' up sittin' in the front," Mother said. "I need to stretch 'em in the back o' the wagon, so Morvoren'll be takin' me place beside ye."

He narrowed his eyes, glancing to Miss Hollow, who shook her head. "I told ye, Mrs. Honeysett, I don't need to—"

"Nonsense," Mother interrupted. "'Twill be nice for ye to 'ave the view o' the sea from the front o' the wagon. When we round that ridge, you'll be glad to see it."

She walked away without giving either of them a chance to contest, though she took the time to turn around behind Morvoren, mouthing out, "Be nice," to Trevik before she clambered into the back of the wagon with Poppy.

Trevik stood there with Morvoren, who shifted her footing with another limp. "Your mother insisted," she mumbled.

"I've no doubt," he returned, then he offered his hand to help her into the wagon.

She hesitated a moment, finally resting her bare hand in his, having forgotten to replace her traveling gloves after the meal at the inn.

He ignored how small her hand felt in his—and how smooth her skin was—waiting until she was settled securely in the seat before releasing his hold of her and walking around to the other side.

The wagon's seat shifted back and forth as he climbed up, taking the reins in hand and tapping the leads against the horse's back. "Move on, Glastaish."

The horse moved forward, and he focused his gaze straight ahead, grateful the width of the seat allowed him ample room to avoid any accidental touch.

Poppy and Mother chatted behind them, discussing their plans to find a mattress or cot for Miss Hollow to bring into Poppy's room, and the situation again hit him with full force. Miss Hollow really was going to be living with them, and he could only begin to imagine all that would entail for him, his family, and his men.

Before long, they rounded the ridge blocking their view of the sea, and the water came into full view. The green countryside was accentuated with tufts of burnt orange bracken and tall, yellow grass, set up nicely against the backdrop of the clear, blue skies and the creamy turquoise of the sea.

At the edge of the cliffs, vibrant gorse bloomed brightly amidst the mounds of purple and pink-hued heather, and the autumnal wind blew the flowers, mimicking the waves of the sea below.

Even with his soured mood, Trevik couldn't deny how stunning the view was. Miss Hollow must be simply beside herself.

He struggled for a moment, fighting the urge to see her expression, but when he heard a sigh escape her lips, he glanced sidelong at her.

Moisture glistened in her eyes as her gaze focused intently on the landscape before them, and Trevik's chest seized.

He thought back to her words at the inn in Sennen, and a question popped in his mind. He didn't need to know the answer. But then, Mother would surely scold him if he didn't at least make some attempt to speak with Miss Hollow on the journey home.

With a deep breath, he asked, "Did 'e really not allow ye to see the sea?"

She looked away, swiping at her eyes before facing him. "Uncle?" she clarified. After he nodded, she continued. "Yes, he kept me away whene'er he could."

"Why? What would possess 'im to do such a thing?"

He waited, her brows furrowed across her smooth forehead. Was she contemplating lying again? Or would she finally tell him the truth?

"It be a complicated story," she finally responded.

"Well, we still 'ave half the journey left," he pressed. Really, he was testing her, wanting to know if she was serious about being honest with him and his family.

He released a pent-up breath when she finally began.

"I didn't meet me uncle 'til I was fourteen. 'Fore that, I'd only heard stories from me mother 'bout him losin' all 'is virtues when he gained his wealth through various investments. Mother didn't like him for stealin' away her sister and marryin' her, and he didn't like me mother in return 'cause she was too common for his dignified tastes."

She shook her head. "After me parents died—and 'is own wife, too—'e took me in, and I'd stupidly thought he'd done so out o' the goodness of 'is heart. I was brought to balls and parties, and 'e purchased gowns and fine jewelry. But I quickly realized, the only reason 'e took me in was to use me as a bargainin' chip—a way to increase 'is wealth."

Trevik grimaced. He couldn't understand the behavior of some people. How could any man treat a woman so despicably, especially his own niece?

"Once I realized I wasn't goin' to receive anythin' from him, I didn't bother doin' what he said. Every social gatherin' was like a death sentence. Every gown, a noose. When he saw me resistin', he responded in a way he knew would hurt the most. He knew I be like me mother, that I loved the sea more than anythin'. So he'd forbid me from goin' to the shore, then lock me in me room when I didn't obey." A small smile tugged at her lips. "He didn't know, but I could still see a sliver of the sea from me room. I'd stand atop the window seat for hours—the only place I could glimpse it—and just watch that slight section o' the water shimmer as the sun moved across the sky."

She paused, her eyes taking on a faraway look as she no doubt remembered her past life.

Trevik rolled his neck, attempting to dispel the tension that had steadily crept in with her words. The image she'd evoked, a lonely young woman standing atop her chair just to catch a glimpse of the thing she loved most, the thing she'd been stripped of...he couldn't bear it.

Regret filled him with a dark emptiness. No wonder she'd escaped her uncle. No wonder she couldn't trust the truth to anyone—for the only person she should have been able to trust had betrayed her.

She cleared her throat after a moment and continued. "So there ye have it," she ended, shifting against the wooden seat. "I know ye have no reason to believe I, but I swear it be the truth."

He stared down at her, the words at the tip of his tongue. He couldn't believe he was actually going to say this. "I do believe ye."

Her eyes jerked to his. "Ye do?"

He glanced at her sidelong. "What other reason would ye 'ave for keepin' the truth to yourself now?"

She gave a half-smile. "Ye be right about that."

Their eyes met, but he looked away in an instant. He still didn't know a great deal about this woman who'd lived with them for nearly a week now. Would she continue to answer any questions he asked? "So ye were raised to be a fine lady, then, to attend balls and parties and such?"

To his surprise, she once again replied. "By Uncle, yes. But he couldn't remove what I'd already been taught by me own parents. I didn't care for balls and finery. 'Tis not the way of life that suits I."

He could understand that. Trevik had passed by the odd assembly in town, and though it looked like everyone involved heartily enjoyed themselves, he far preferred the simple parties they held on the beach. Singing and conversing over an open fire on a beach with friends was to be far preferred over a formal dinner in a stuffy dining room with mere acquaintances.

Give a man a lugger, a sunset at sea, and a meal of salted fish, and he would be content.

Was Miss Hollow the same? Or was she upset deep down about having to give up such a life *and* such a husband? "And it be true that he tried to force ye into a marriage ye didn't agree to?"

She nodded grimly. "Yes."

A strange burning occurred in his chest. "I'm certain ye left your poor betrothed distraught. 'E must be nursin' 'is wounds for bein' jilted."

She barked out a laugh. "I'm sure he'll recover."

He paused, eying her. "Did 'e not want the marriage to occur?"

"Oh, I think he hardly cares one way or another."

She certainly seemed to feel the same way. Why did that knowledge lighten the load across his shoulders? "What makes ye say that? The man agreed to marry ye, didn't 'e?"

"Only 'cause he be forced to do as his father said or he'd lose his own fortune." She glanced behind her, as if to ensure the others weren't listening, then she faced forward with a lowered tone. He had to lean slightly closer to hear her. "He's not the type of man to commit to just one woman. Even in marriage."

Trevik's brow lowered, and his jaw tightened as she continued.

"The day we were told that we'd marry, we attended a

ball. We were supposed to share the supper dance together, but when he didn't appear, I sought him out, catchin' him headed toward the gardens with a woman with a painted face." She sniffed with derision. "'Fore that, I'd almost managed to convince meself to go through with the weddin'. After, though, I knew I couldn't."

The horse tossed her head before them, and only then did Trevik realize his grasp on the reins had tightened. He loosened them, drawing a steadying breath. "Surely your uncle would've stopped the marriage 'ad 'e known…"

She cast him a sidelong glance. "Surely, he wouldn't. I spoke to Uncle that evenin', sayin' I wouldn't marry a man who couldn't be true 'fore we were married. Do ye know what his response was?"

He waited, afraid he already knew the answer.

She tucked in her chin, lowering her voice and putting on an accent as fine as the one he'd first heard her speak in, though now he knew why it had changed.

"'That will be in your future no matter the man you marry, Miss Hollow. You must simply learn to accept it.'" She shook her head. "That was the moment I made up me mind to leave."

Trevik didn't know what to say. He couldn't understand men who chose not to remain true to their wives. He, himself, had been raised by a morally chaste father and mother. How he longed to tell Miss Hollow that not all men behaved in such a debased manner. But how could he share such a thing without her assuming that he was saying he would make a better husband?

Instead of risking saying something that could be misconstrued as an utterly ridiculous invitation, he held his tongue.

"Trevik," Mother called from behind, "can ye 'and me the bag at your side, please?"

"'Course." Trevik shifted the reins to one hand, reaching down with his left to the side of the wagon. He struggled for a moment with a grunt, the bag not budging with only one hand to tug it free.

He straightened, shifting the reins to Miss Hollow. "Will ye 'old this for a moment?"

Miss Hollow lifted her hands in a gesture of retreat and leaned back. "Oh, ye best not put me in charge o' the beast."

He paused. "'Twill only be for a moment."

"Per'aps, but I ne'er controlled a horse in me life. Best not leave your fate in me hands."

"Ye be so afeared ye won't even *hold* the reins?"

"Afeard?" She looked affronted. "I ain't afeared. I just… She be so large."

He fought another smile.

"Ye find this humorous, do ye?"

"Frankly, I do."

She waited for him to explain.

"Ye be a woman who can swim in the darkness o' the sea without battin' an eye and sing in front of a crowd full of strangers who thought ye be a mermaid. Yet, ye be nervous to 'old the reins of a tacked up 'orse?"

A slow warmth slid across her eyes as she peered up at him. "I s'pose ye have a point."

"'Ere," he said, reaching for her hands himself. Gently, he placed the reins in one of her palms.

At the touch of her skin on his, their eyes caught, and a pleasant prickling slid across his hand, just as it had when he'd helped her home from the cliffside.

But such a feeling did not bode well. The woman was going to be living with his family, for heaven's sake. He would be wise to rid his system of any reaction to the woman's touch.

Pulling away, he cleared his throat. "Just 'old the reins steady and she'll remain calm."

He leaned over the side of the bench, bending over to unhook the satchel that had become stuck beside him. Only a moment later, he pulled up the bag and delivered it to his mother, gingerly taking the reins from Miss Hollow without a touch.

Mother and Poppy's soft chatter reached Trevik's ears as he sat beside Miss Hollow in silence. He ought to say something else, but his questions for her had fled from his mind the moment he'd touched her.

He didn't have to worry for too long, however, when Miss Hollow spoke instead, her voice soft. "I be sorry for all the trouble I've caused ye, Mr. Honeysett. I'll not stay with your family for long, as I don't wish to be a burden. And I…I know ye must despise me, but…I really do be sorry."

Shame rose up behind Trevik in a dark shadow. The woman had gone through enough. She shouldn't be made to feel worse because Trevik's pride had been wounded by her secrecy. "I don't despise ye, Miss 'Ollow."

"Well, ye certainly don't like me."

"Do ye like *me*?"

"I think I'd like ye a lot more if ye'd stop scowlin'." That playful lilt to her voice had finally made its way back to her tone, and he found his spirits brightening at the knowledge.

"Per'aps I'd stop scowlin' if ye'd stop criticizin' me fishin' ability," he returned.

She opened her mouth then paused, a smile spreading across her lips. "Very well. Per'aps I will stop, now that ye didn't leave me in Sennen."

"I wouldn't 'ave been able to if I'd tried. Mother and Poppy wouldn't 'ave allowed it." His lip twitched as he fought his smile.

"Do ye regret bringin' me back, then?" Her playful tone continued, though he knew the question held a heavy weight.

He straightened, facing forward as he struggled to maintain the balance between them, though his desire to share the truth outweighed everything else. "I did regret it 'fore. But now I can see why ye kept the past to yourself." He turned to face her. "My family and I really do wish to 'elp ye."

She didn't respond for a moment, her brows tipped up. "I don't deserve your family's kindness. Ye all be too good to me."

"Ain't that the truth."

Finally, a genuine smile spread across her lips, lighting her eyes as small lines stretched out to the side of them. "I ne'er thought I'd see the day that we'd agree upon somethin'," she said. "What next, admittin' that we might become friends?"

She'd meant her words as a joke, of course. But his smile vanished and the light mood around them departed.

Friends. How could they be friends when he was supposed to have left her in Sennen? He'd given Edern his word that she'd be gone. What would happen now that he had, essentially, broken his trust with the man?

The rest of the journey was met mostly in silence, Miss Hollow watching the sea as Trevik worried over how he'd defend his actions to his crew.

When they reached Tristwick, he helped the women down from the wagon on the cliffside just above their home, dropping them off before climbing back into the wagon himself, intent on taking it back to the Kendrickses without the others.

"Mr. Honeysett?"

He paused, looking down from the wagon. Miss Hollow stood nearby, Poppy and Mother already crossing the cliffside. "Yes?"

"I just…I wanted to thank ye again. For everythin'."

He dipped his head. "It be no trouble, Miss 'Ollow."

She made to leave, though she turned back to him with a hesitant expression. "Ye…ye may call me Morvoren, if ye like. We will be livin' with each other, after all."

Trevik stared, his throat tightening. He couldn't call her by her given name. Doing so would only prove to bring the two of them closer together.

Still, her expectant look pulled the next words from his

mouth before he had time to stop them. "Trevik to ye, then," he returned.

A small smile tipped up the corner of her lips, and the sight nearly pushed him to offer his room to her next, or perhaps his place at the dinner table—anything to bring forth another smile.

Instead, he tipped his cap in silence and faced forward, urging the horse on. He fought his desire to look back at her for as long as he could, but when he did finally glance over his shoulder, Miss Hollow—not Morvoren—had finally disappeared over the ridge, taking the remainder of his peace with her.

CHAPTER TWENTY-THREE

A creaking bed beside her roused Morvoren from her slumber, and she blinked sleepily with a groaning stretch of her arms. The darkness from the night before had alleviated only a shade, and dull light from the still-sleeping sun slipped through the windows.

"Are ye ready, Morvoren?" whispered Poppy nearby.

Morvoren opened her eyes more fully, spotting Poppy near the small wardrobe as she tightened her stays from the front.

Was it time to rise already?

"I can let ye sleep a bit longer," Poppy offered, "or ye can always come to the cellars later."

But Morvoren shook her head. "No, I be awake."

She threw back her covers from the cot the Bosankos had lent her and stepped onto the frigid floor. Together, she and Poppy dressed, though Morvoren's limbs refused to move as quickly as she wished them to. She had the sneaking suspicion that her sluggishness was due to the two late nights she'd shared in conversation with Poppy. The girl hadn't been lying when she'd expressed how greatly she loved to talk. Fortunately, Morvoren was more than happy to listen to her.

Once dressed, they joined Mrs. Honeysett in the kitchen,

who greeted them with cheerful smiles. "Bit o' pillas for ye this mornin', girls," she said. "Give ye some strength for the long day ahead."

The porridge sat like thick mud in Morvoren's stomach, though she willed herself to eat every last bite. She wasn't used to eating so early—or rising so early, for that matter—but she was determined to earn her keep. Even if that meant joining the women in the cellars she so despised.

After the meal, their small party left the Honeysetts' home and made their way toward the dock. Morvoren still walked with her ever-present limp, but Mrs. Honeysett and Poppy no longer had to slow their pace in order for her to keep up.

"Did ye sleep better last night, Morvoren?" Mrs. Honeysett asked as they neared the mouth of the cove. "That old cot suitin' ye?"

Morvoren nodded. "Yes, thank ye."

"And I trust ye didn't keep 'er up too late with your chatterin', Poppy," Mrs. Honeysett asked with a condemning brow.

Poppy gave a quick shake of her head, then slipped Morvoren a knowing grin.

Mrs. Honeysett watched them with amusement before facing the shore. "Ye'll be regrettin' these late nights if ye continue on so."

"Who could e'er regret speakin'?" Poppy said with a bewildered look.

The three of them reached the dock then, standing back with the growing group of women, children, and a handful of men. Soft greetings around them were delivered amid yawns and bleary eyes. Even the sea seemed hesitant to rise that morning with only its gentle lapping at the dock.

The wind, however, didn't hesitate to slide its cold draft around Morvoren's shoulders and nip at her uncovered nose.

"Mornin', Mabyn, Poppy," Mrs. Bosanko greeted, coming to stand beside them near the back of the group. Next, she faced Morvoren with a warm smile. "Come to 'elp us with the pilchards, 'ave ye?"

Morvoren nodded. "Yes, ma'am."

"We do be glad to 'ave ye join us."

Morvoren wanted to believe Mrs. Bosanko's words were true and that she spoke for all the fishermen's wives, but the steady stream of heavy glances sent her way—some with mere curiosity, others sheer disapproval—made her believe that she might have been wiser to remain tucked away in the Honeysetts' home.

A voice rose out above the others, clearly intending to be heard. "What she be doin'? She don't belong 'ere."

Morvoren's cheeks burned, despite the frigid sea air. She sought the owner of the voice, finally meeting the gaze of the stocky, middle-aged woman she recognized from the gathering on the beach the week before.

The woman scowled unabashedly at Morvoren, then looked away with a turned-up nose. Most of the group ignored her words, though Mrs. Bosanko and Mrs. Honeysett exchanged worried glances.

"That be Katherine Cardy," Poppy whispered under her breath.

"Related to Jowan Cardy?"

"'Is mother."

Of course. Morvoren should have recognized the thickset shoulders.

"The whole family be mad," Poppy continued. "She ne'er married, see, raised Jowan on 'er own. 'Is father died at sea durin' a storm 'fore she even discovered she be with child. 'Course 'er father, ol' Edern, believed the storm to be brought on by a sea-maid." She huffed out her cheeks. "Ridiculous, the lot of 'em. I'd love to believe in mermaids as much as they, but I'd ne'er condemn an innocent woman like they be doin'."

A rustle of excitement moved at the front of the group,

and the girls faced forward as they heard the call. "They be comin'!"

Morvoren strained her neck back and forth, searching for any sign of the lugger, but the mist hung heavily atop the sea, the grey water disappearing into the endless, impenetrable fog.

"It be straight ahead," Poppy said.

Morvoren narrowed her eyes, focusing where she was told, then finally, the lugger's sails crawled through the mist, emerging past the white clouds like a creature in the night.

Her heart thrummed at the sight, though she knew it wasn't the lugger but *who* was on the lugger that caused such a reaction.

She had only seen Mr. Honey—Trevik a few times since they'd returned from Sennen two days before. She'd thought they'd parted that night on good terms, but since then, he'd fallen silent, and she couldn't help but feel like her presence was the reason why. After all, she recalled his hesitance when sharing their given names. Did he not wish to be friends with her, then?

Surely seeing her there that morning, working at the cellars alongside his mother and sister, he'd be pleased. Surely then he would know she truly meant to earn her stay.

A few of the children cheered nearby, and Morvoren returned her attention to the present, watching the young boys and girls jumping up and down with excitement.

How could they be so cheerful so early in the morning, especially with the day they had before them? They certainly weren't as thin as the children who'd worked in Uncle's pilchard palace, but their happiness would not last through the day. No one's good spirits could under such strain.

She focused again on the lugger drawing ever closer to the land, the men aboard the *Pilferer* just now beginning to stand out over the dark bulwark. Their shadowy figures roved across the deck, a few of the men raising their arms in greeting to those awaiting their arrival near the small harbor.

As they approached, Morvoren heard cheers from above, and she glanced up to the hovels on the cliffside as families gathered outside their doors, raising their hands to the lugger. Did they do this every morning?

She made to face the sea again, but a movement at the highest cliffside caught her eye. A man with a top hat and walking stick perched just above the Honeysetts' home, standing as still as the statues in Uncle's gardens. She couldn't make out his features from the distance, but his clothing told her he was no fisherman.

She nudged Poppy softly with her elbow, her stomach churning. "Do ye know that man?"

Poppy glanced up, then shrugged. "Don't believe so. 'E could be a seiner 'ere to observe the drifters' work."

A seiner, perhaps one who worked for Uncle?

Poppy didn't seem concerned at all as she turned back to watch the lugger drawing ever closer, but Morvoren's apprehension did not ease, especially when she looked back to the cliffside to find the man had seemingly vanished into thin air.

Would he come down to meet the drifters, spying Morvoren in the process?

She pulled her shawl over her thin bonnet to further shield her face, then forced herself to think logically. There was no possibility the man could have spotted Morvoren in the size of the crowd brimming near the harbor. More than likely, he was an unrelated seiner, just as Poppy had suggested.

Drawing in a deep, calming breath, she waited as the lugger made its final stretch into the cove. The Honeysetts would protect her. They'd promised, after all. But then, would Trevik help her despite his obvious reticence with her presence in his home?

When the lugger finally docked, a few men left the ship, greeting their wives and children with smiles and kisses before jumping straight back to work.

"Those be the gurries," Poppy explained to Morvoren,

pointing out the large, two-handled boxes the men carried back to the lugger. "They can 'old more than a thousand pilchards in each."

Morvoren's brow rose, watching as the gurries were deposited on the deck of the lugger, then filled with piles and piles of fish. Herring gulls landed on the bulwark, calling out their squeaking cries, anxious to partake in the fishermen's haul.

Morvoren had expected Trevik to oversee the job, but he was right in the center, working alongside his men, his cap low over his head. The shoulders of his jacket were a darker brown than the rest of the fabric, no doubt due to the rain that had fallen the night before.

She stood a little taller, hoping to catch his eye, but he was too focused on his task.

As the first gurry was filled, two men held the long handles at either side, toting the box toward the land as the gulls took to circling right above them.

As much as Morvoren disapproved of the trade, she couldn't help but admire the work ethic of these men, shooting nets all through the night and still having the energy to lug their catch to shore. At least they worked as hard as their wives and children. Did they ever take a moment to rest?

"Are ye comin', Morvoren?"

Morvoren started at Poppy's voice from somewhere behind her, only then realizing that the crowd now migrated toward the cellars.

She hurried to catch up, sending a fleeting glance back at the lugger—and Trevik. Her heart lurched when she found him looking her way.

CHAPTER TWENTY-FOUR

*T*revik turned swiftly away when he caught Miss Hollow's eye, willing himself to not look back at her. He'd done a fine job at avoiding her since Saturday, although it had made it exponentially more difficult to not stare at her now as her limp made the swish of her skirts to flourish all the more.

He blinked the image away from his mind, focusing on his work instead as he climbed down to the fish room, reaching in with his oversized wicker basket and filling it full of pilchards.

"'Ere be another," Trevik said, grunting as he heaved the basket to Jowan, who would then deposit the fish into the awaiting gurry.

Instead of Jowan standing alone above the fish room, however, his grandfar accompanied him, as well as two more members of their crew, brothers Hedrek and Kenver Roskelley.

Trevik struggled with the weight of the fish, lowering the basket a fraction as he took in the solemn lips of the brothers and the scowls from the Cardys, each of them staring down at him with stoic eyes.

"We need to talk, Trevik," Edern said, his thick jacket buttoned to just below his neck.

"And now be a convenient time?" Trevik asked, motioning to the basket of fish still in his hands.

"Yes."

Trevik hesitated. He'd attempted to speak with his men about Miss Hollow the moment they'd set sail the evening before, but half of them had been so upset, they'd refused to listen. Were they ready to be reasoned with now, or was Edern simply going to say his piece without allowing Trevik to say his?

Either way, the words needed to be spoken by them both.

He raised the basket onto the deck himself, then climbed out of the fish room before dumping the pilchards into the gurry and facing his men.

"So, what be your issue?" he asked, planting his feet apart and folding his arms.

"What she be doin' workin' at the cellars?" Edern questioned.

"I reckon the same as the other women, processin' the fish."

Edern hardly looked impressed. "Ye know what I mean, Trev. She don't belong in there. S'pose she injure the other women."

Trevik closed his eyes, willing himself to find the patience he needed to continue conversing with this man. "Look, lads. We be tired, cold, and 'ungry. Per'aps we ought to speak o' this later—"

"No, we be speakin' o' this now," Edern interrupted. "Ye 'ad no right bringin' a sea-maid back to our cove."

Trevik blew out a slow breath. Jowan stood behind his grandfar with a nod, but the Roskelley brothers remained silent.

"Are ye two in on this now?" he asked. "Ye believe Miss 'Ollow be a mermaid, too?"

The brothers exchanged glances, the elder, Hedrek, speaking first. "No, we don't."

Edern turned sharp eyes on them, and Trevik was filled with relief, though it didn't last long.

"But 'e 'as a point, Trevik," Hedrek continued. "Ye 'ad no right bringin' 'er back 'ere after ye promised she'd be gone."

Trevik had done his best to skirt around the issue, blaming Edern and his superstitions for the problems in his crew. But the truth of the matter was, he was also to blame. He had made a promise—a promise he'd broken.

He gave a seceding nod. "Ye be right. And I be sorry that I've broken your trust in I, but really, what would ye 'ave done if ye were put in the same situation?" He leaned forward, lowering his voice. "She 'as no 'ome, no family." That was the truth, for her uncle certainly didn't count as one. "She 'as nowhere else to go but Tristwick. Would ye really turn 'er out now?"

The brothers exchanged glances again, their frowns lessening, if only slightly.

But Edern's glower remained. "'Tain't be our responsibility to 'ouse a sea-maid. 'Tain't right what ye be doin', putting the safety o' that woman o'er your men."

Trevik's jaw tightened at such an accusation. "That ain't what I be doin'. I merely be 'elpin' a woman 'til she be ready to 'elp 'erself. I promise ye, I'll not allow any 'arm to come to Tristwick."

Edern's gaze hardened, his voice cool. "We've 'eard your promises 'fore, and now we know what they be worth. Nothin', compared to what ye be doin' for your new sweet'eart."

Trevik blanched. The very notion, the very idea… "I told ye already that she ain't be nothin' o' the sort to I."

But Edern had already turned away, leaving the lugger behind.

Trevik stared after him, shaking his head before he turned to the other three.

"Ain't nothin' I say 'is gonna change that man's mind," he said with a helpless shrug.

Jowan didn't respond, merely going back to work filling the gurries full of fish, but the Roskelleys remained.

"We don't like what this be doin' to the crew," Hedrek said. "We know Miss 'Ollow ain't no sea-maid, but ye be right. Edern won't be convinced otherwise."

"Then what can I do?" Trevik asked.

"Ain't nothin' ye can do except prove 'im wrong 'bout the two of ye, I s'pose."

Prove Edern wrong. That would be easy enough, as Trevik didn't have feelings for Morvoren anyway, beyond that of compassion for her past and an inconsequential racing of his heart whenever she smiled up at him.

But he could stamp out such reactions in a moment, for he would not risk his crew breaking apart over a supposed sea-maid.

The stench of pilchards had been sneaking past Morvoren's nose since they'd passed the cellars on their way to the docks, but she'd managed to ward off the smell by breathing mostly through her mouth.

Now, however, breathing through her mouth only seemed to make the smell worse as she entered the processing cellars of Tristwick. How was she to endure such a stink over the next few weeks, or even months?

But then, she knew how. She would simply dwell on the fact that smelling pilchards in the cellars here was better than smelling pilchards on Uncle or Mr. Foss.

"Ye'll get used to the stench soon," Poppy said with a reassuring smile.

Morvoren's cheeks warmed. She thought she'd been hiding her disgust better.

As the group poured into the cellars, filing to their respective locations, the area before her cleared, and Morvoren was provided with a better view.

The cellars, which were not set in the ground as the name suggested, were made up of a central, cobblestoned courtyard with no roof. At the back of the space, a set of rickety stairs led up to the lofts that surrounded the entire courtyard, the bottom of the lofts open to provide shelter for the workers when needed.

When Morvoren had toured Uncle's pilchard palace, she'd kept her gaze down and learned as little as possible, just to drive him mad. It had worked, as she'd been banned from his library for a fortnight. Of course, she'd just stolen the books anyway, hiding them in a loose board beneath her bed.

What she *had* remembered at his cellars were the piles of waste, the oil of fish running in streams down the cobblestones, and women comforting their crying children who begged to leave for home.

Tristwick's cellars, however, were nothing like she'd imagined, nothing like she was used to. The grounds weren't nearly as large as Uncle's, and the wooden walls of the lofts were splintered and faded.

But instead of piles of fish parts, near the center of the courtyard stood a wall of pilchards about waist-high and four feet wide. Layers of whole fish were stacked between more layers of thick salt, the wall remaining upright with a wider bottom and a smaller top layer.

The men with the gurries moved forward, depositing the fish near the women who were already working to extend the wall of pilchards.

"Me 'usband, rest 'is soul, spent years savin' to build this," Mrs. Honeysett said beside her. "Men 'round St. Just donated buildin' materials in exchange for fish in the winter. 'Tisn't much to look at, but we be proud o' the work we do 'ere." She gave Morvoren a smile, then turned to Poppy.

"Will ye show 'er 'round, Popp? Get 'er to work at the bulkin' first?"

"Yes, Mother."

Mrs. Honeysett joined a group of women near the back of the cellars where strung-up nets dripped with moisture, but Morvoren followed Poppy instead to the gurries being unloaded.

Poppy reached in and retrieved a large handful, carrying them to the bottom, salt-covered layer of the wall. When she noted Morvoren standing and staring, she coaxed her closer. "Do ye know what to do?" she asked.

Morvoren shook her head, standing to the side as another woman passed her with an impatient glance and a handful of fish. The process seemed fairly straightforward, but her stomach churned as the pilchards' ogling eyes stared up at her, wide and undaunted.

"Ye just reach in," Poppy said, doing the very same as she spoke, "take a big ol' 'andful, then put 'em in a single layer on the salt. That'll dry 'em of any extra moisture in just a few weeks' time."

"And…if some of them still be alive?"

Poppy gave a flippant shrug. "Put the creature out of its misery and move on, I s'pose."

Morvoren cringed, though she drew a deep breath. She'd skinned, gutted, and eaten fish long before living with Uncle. But somewhere along the way, she'd begun to associate fish with the breaking apart of her family. After all, blaming something tangible was easier to do than casting blame on Father's greed.

But many years had passed since then, and she'd eaten her fair share of fish over the years. Perhaps it was time to move on, to overcome such childhood fears.

Pushing all inhibitions aside, she plunged her hands into the pile of pilchards and pulled up a handful, their slippery scales and fins sliding along her fingertips. She held them out from her person, then walked toward the pile and gently lowered them upon the salt, releasing a slow breath as she arranged them more neatly across the layer of salt.

"There ye go," Poppy said with an encouraging smile.

Despite the cold, slimy feel between her fingers and the briny smell of the pilchards, Morvoren returned Poppy's smile.

As the morning progressed, rather than dwelling on the continuous looks from those around her—and the scowls from Katherine Cardy—Morvoren focused instead on how many pilchards she could grasp in a handful.

Before long, just as Poppy said, the smell around her also didn't seem as pungent, the salt taking the edge off, as well as the steady wind slipping over the walls around the courtyard.

There was something else she noticed as the morning wore on, as well. Something she'd not anticipated. In fact, it was the *last* thing she'd expected.

The women, even some of the children, seemed to be actually *enjoying* themselves as they worked together. At Uncle's cellars, they'd been miserable—red eyes, hollow cheekbones, sluggish movements, silent lips.

Here, however, though their faces were pink from exertion, the children giggled as they scared away the gulls from the fish, and the women watched on with amusement as they caught up with their neighbors and friends, occasionally breaking out in song together.

Morvoren couldn't understand it. They were working, after all, and for what—a pittance of money? Or was it enough for them to know they were preparing for the future, all while enjoying the time with their family and friends?

Her questions were answered soon enough, though, as Poppy's jolly nature and never-ending optimism brightened the time they spent together.

"Nearly there," she said as she and Morvoren reached into the final gurry brought in by the fishermen.

"What's to be done after the gurries be emptied?" Morvoren asked, stretching her aching back from side to side as she and Poppy piled the salt higher with the other women.

Poppy brushed her hands free of the salt, motioning to the upper end of the pilchard wall. "The fish that were bulked a few weeks ago'll move to processin'. First pressin', then preservin' in barrels."

"And do they go on to be sold, then? Abroad, per'aps?"

Poppy wiped a strand of hair from her brow with the back of her hand. "No. Father and Trevik did try that, but they received next to nothin' after hirin' a captain and a ship to deliver their catch."

A fisherman motivated by money? How insipid. Morvoren shifted her gaze so Poppy wouldn't see her knowing look. "So they sell them 'round St. Just instead?"

Poppy nodded. "They be sold for a fraction o' the price to those who be less fortunate—miners and the like. 'Fore that, though, most o' the barrels and the oil be shared amongst the fishermen and their families."

Morvoren paused. "Ye just…share the fish free of charge?"

Poppy gave her a funny look. "Well, yes. We all work for it, so 'tis only fair. 'Sides, we need somethin' to survive durin' the winter months. We'll be catchin' herrin' next, but January and February make for miserable months without no pilchards to feast on."

Morvoren's attention slipped. How could she not have considered that they simply shared their fish? Of course, she was conditioned to believe a fisherman's actions ran on greed. But here, something else drove them forward—their liveli-hood, their welfare, the fact that they all worked hard because they knew they'd be given what was fair. Was that why they all seemed more than happy to be there in the cellars, handling pilchards all day long?

But surely not all the money was spent so responsibly.

"What happens to the money earned from sellin' to those 'round St. Just? Does the rest go straight to the fishermen?"

"No, Trevik splits it 'tween those who work 'ere and the men on the lugger." She leaned closer to Morvoren, her voice lowered. "Though 'e gives more to them families who need a bit of 'elp, usually from 'is own pocket."

Morvoren stifled a groan. That was not what she'd wanted to hear. She scrambled to keep hold of her prejudice, to fight the truth breaking down the walls around her heart, but the more Poppy spoke, the more the earth crumbled to sand beneath her defenses.

"'E's always been generous, me brother," Poppy said. "Though, mind, 'e did 'ave a mischievous streak as a boy— sneakin' food, trespassin', findin' ways 'round deliverin' the fishin' tithes to the vicar."

Morvoren couldn't help but smile at the image her words evoked. "I s'pose no one can be perfect."

"Indeed," Poppy agreed, reaching for more fish. "But 'e more 'an made up for it all since. Do ye know, when me father died, Trevik could 'ave sold everythin'—the lugger, the nets, the cellars. We would've been set up nicely for years. But 'e chose to keep the business so the fishermen in Tristwick could work."

Morvoren didn't know what to say. She *had* nothing to say, for everything she thought would just reveal how unkind and ungenerous she had been in judging Trevik and his actions before she'd really come to know him.

The world here turned so differently, so confusingly, that she felt as if she were spinning out of control—everything she'd ever known, her beliefs about greedy fishermen, unraveling.

"Are ye certain he chose not to sell 'cause the purchasers were seiners?" she guessed, piling another handful of fish onto the salt.

Poppy frowned. "'Eavens, no. The seiners don't want no

small lugger or cellar. 'Sides, they can't fish 'ere since we don't 'ave a big enough shore for their great seinin' nets."

Morvoren chewed on her lower lip. "Well surely the men 'ere could've found work with seiners 'round about."

"They could 'ave," Poppy agreed. "Some folks be fine workin' for both drifters and seiners. But 'round Tristwick, 'specially after what me family 'as dealt with…" She wrinkled her nose. "'Tisn't worth sullyin' our souls workin' for the devil."

The breath rushed from Morvoren's chest, and her whole face burned. *Sullying their souls.* Would Poppy and her family be thinking the very same about working alongside a seiner's niece? What had caused *their* poor opinion of seiners, something in regard to the elder Mr. Honeysett?

She turned toward Poppy, wondering if she could ask the very question, but movement near the doorway of the cellars drew her attention away, and her heart jumped.

Gryffyn Bosanko walked across the courtyard first, carrying the front end of the large net rolled together in thick layers. Behind him, Jowan Cardy held up the middle, then finally, with the heavy netting propped up against his shoulder, Trevik entered the cellars.

CHAPTER TWENTY-FIVE

*T*he strain of the hemp weighing down upon the fishermen was evident to Morvoren by their focused gazes and red faces. Trevik no longer wore his jacket, his shirt-sleeves rolled up and his kerchief loosened from around his neck.

He kept his gaze ahead of him as the men maneuvered to the back of the cellars, toward the stairs leading up to the lofts. Morvoren kept her eyes on him until he disappeared up the steps.

She didn't need to make eye contact with the man to know in an instant that everything Poppy had said about him was true. How could Morvoren have been so foolish? Trevik was not greedy, nor was he selfish. He helped everyone around him every chance he received, his crew, his family—even Morvoren. And how had she repaid him? She'd tried to make trouble with those in Tristwick, criticized his fishing ability, coerced his family into taking a fruitless trek to Sennen.

And yet, even as remorse filled her, she could not forget her past.

Things were different in Tristwick. Trevik was different. But she couldn't forget what Father had done nor how Uncle had treated her. People changed and greed grew steadily, no matter a person's best intentions, but Morvoren would not be abandoned again. She could admire the Honeysetts and all of Tristwick for what they did, but this, life in the cellars, in Trist-wick…it wasn't for her. She wished for something more, something safer. Somewhere she didn't have to worry about ever being hurt again.

"Morvoren, did ye 'ear I?"

Morvoren started, facing Poppy, who watched her expectantly. "We be 'eaded to do the pressin' now," she explained.

Morvoren nodded, setting aside her worrisome thoughts and following Poppy to the opposite, far end of the wall of pilchards. Mrs. Honeysett met them there with a bottle of brandy, allowing a few nips from Morvoren before sending the bottle around to the other women.

For the next hour, Morvoren did her best to set aside her thoughts of Trevik by following Poppy's instructions. Carefully, she and Poppy packed the dried pilchards into the barrels in a tidy rose pattern, their tails facing the center. When the pilchards reached the brim, Poppy placed a buckler—a false lid smaller than the barrel—over the fish, then Morvoren helped her heave a heavy, granite boulder on top.

Moments later, a trickling of liquid sounded, and Morvoren shifted to the side to see the oil flowing slowly down makeshift, wooden gutters.

"That be the train pit," Poppy explained. "That oil'll be used for our lamps, though Trevik likes to use it for water-proofin' the deck o' the lugger. 'E claims it 'elps, but I just think it makes it stink."

This was yet another way these fishermen were unlike Uncle—using every bit of the fish they could.

At Poppy's mention of Trevik, Morvoren glanced once more to the stairs, though Trevik, again, did not appear. What was he doing up there in the lofts? And why was he taking so long to come down?

"Ready to fill the next barrel?" Poppy asked. "We'll come back to this one when all 'em fish are nice and pressed. Then we can fit more inside."

Morvoren nodded, shuffling to the side where a new barrel awaited its pilchards. As they worked, she did her best to listen to Poppy's chatter about the new shellwork she was piecing together, though Morvoren's eyes constantly strayed to the stairs.

She looked so frequently, in fact, that when brown boots finally did appear at the top step, her mind did not register the sight, and she looked back with an odd jolt of her stomach.

Trevik came down first, followed closely by the other men, who laughed about something Mr. Bosanko had said. Trevik's lips remained in a straight line, though, his brow pursed as if he was deep in thought.

"Trevik!"

Morvoren jolted as Poppy shouted his name and waved him closer. He swiveled, his lips curving when he caught sight of his sister, but his smile slipped again when his gaze turned to Morvoren.

He glanced to the door of the cellars, as if contemplating leaving, but he bade farewell to Gryffyn and Jowan instead and made for Morvoren.

No, he made for Poppy, not Morvoren.

Still, as he approached, her nerves got the better of her, and the pilchard she'd been handling fell to the floor. She rushed to pick it up, straightening just as Trevik reached his sister.

"'Ow ye doin', Trev?" Poppy asked.

Trevik picked up a pilchard from their barrel and tossed it at Poppy's head. "Better 'an ye."

"Trevik!" Poppy exclaimed, sounding more upset than she clearly was as she smiled at his teasing.

She picked up the pilchard that had fallen to the floor ,

throwing it back at him as hard as she could, whacking Trevik in the side of his head, despite his attempt to duck.

He chuckled, rubbing the side of his head. "Ow, Poppy!"

"Ye two stop it now," Mrs. Honeysett said, standing near her own barrel. She sent an apologetic grin to those around them, but the women merely smiled in amusement, as if this was an everyday occurrence.

Trevik backed away from his family, smiling once more at Poppy before glancing to Morvoren with a lingering, heavy look. He waited a moment, then tipped his cap and left the cellars behind.

Morvoren released a shaky breath. What on earth had such a look meant? And was he truly so displeased with her being in Tristwick that he couldn't utter a word to her?

She kept her gaze on the closed doors a moment after he left, facing forward only to be met with Poppy's sly smile.

Morvoren ignored her, filling the barrel instead. "Have ye spoken with Lieutenant Harris, Poppy?" she asked, anxious for the attention to be shifted.

Fortunately, Poppy took her bait. "Once more since the bonfire, at Golowduyn."

"And what happened?"

Poppy needed no further encouragement, launching into a detailed explanation of her time with the lieutenant. Morvoren didn't mind, for it helped to pass the time so greatly that when the break for the midday meal arrived, she was astonished that time had passed so swiftly.

The latter half of the day, however, dragged on for what felt like double the time. Though Morvoren enjoyed speaking with Poppy, Mrs. Honeysett, and even a few of the other women who seemed to be pleased with her efforts that day, she couldn't deny the toll the work had taken on her body. Her back was stiff, her arms weak, and her fingers had been rubbed raw from the amount of salt she'd handled.

"Your fine 'ands ain't be used to all that coarse salt," Mrs.

Honeysett said with a pat to Morvoren's arm. "We'll 'ave ye wear gloves tomorrow."

Tomorrow. Morvoren would have to do all of this again tomorrow.

When the final barrel had been filled with salted pilchards, the women filed from the cellars in droves and headed to their respective stone cottages.

"Do ye usually finish at this time?" Morvoren asked, wiping her hands free of the salt and slime on the apron Mrs. Honeysett had lent her.

"It depends on the fish and the amount caught," Mrs. Honeysett replied. "But the days do be shorter durin' the winter months."

As they neared the Honeysetts' home once again, Morvoren's legs protested with every step. She'd spent most of the day favoring her still-healing ankle, and the tightness in her limbs called out to her, begging her to give them respite.

"Will ye be comin' with us to Golowduyn now, Morvoren?" Poppy asked, springing up the cliffside at the south end of the cove, as if the last eight hours had been child's play.

"Golowduyn?"

Poppy nodded. "We 'elp Mrs. Kendricks on Mondays, Tuesdays, and Wednesdays."

Morvoren's shoulders sank. Now she was to work at the lighthouse?

But Mrs. Honeysett sent her a compassionate smile. "Per'aps we ought to go to Golowduyn alone today, Popp. Allow Morvoren to rest. The first week o' workin' always be the worst."

Relief flooded through Morvoren's limbs at the suggestion, though she still felt the need to protest. "Are ye certain?"

Mrs. Honeysett nodded as Poppy forged ahead. "Yes, ye've done enough." She wrapped her arm around Morvoren's shoulders in a tight embrace. "We'll see 'ow ye feel tomorrow."

Morvoren blinked, surprised at the sudden onset of tears flooding her eyes. She hadn't been treated with such under-standing since Mother had died, and she didn't realize until then how greatly she missed someone truly caring for her.

Once home, Mrs. Honeysett encouraged Morvoren to rest, so Morvoren swiftly changed out of her pilchard-stained clothing and fell fast asleep before Mrs. Honeysett and Poppy even departed. And finally, for the first time in far too long, her dreams were filled with nothing but peace.

CHAPTER TWENTY-SIX

*M*orvoren woke to a quiet house. With a yawn and a stretch of her arms, she sat upright, glancing to the window where the sun still blazed above. She must have only slept for an hour or two, which was all she'd needed. Besides, she didn't wish to waste any more time.

Rolling out of her cot, she rubbed the sleep from her eyes, loaded her portmanteau with a change of underclothing, donned her boots and shawl, then stepped out of the room with haste. She had great plans to accomplish that afternoon and very little time to do them.

With Mrs. Honeysett and Poppy still at Golowduyn and Trevik…She paused. All other thoughts scattered from her mind like a flock of warblers fleeing from an impending wave.

Where *was* Trevik? Working? At the cellars? On the ship? Or…was he sleeping in the room down the corridor?

Slowly, her eyes traveled the short distance to where his bedchamber was situated, the door securely closed. Was he finally taking some much-needed respite? Or would he arise as swiftly as Morvoren had?

The thought of facing him without Mrs. Honeysett or Poppy to take the edge of discomfort off was enough to pour common sense back into Morvoren's mind. She swiftly closed the door to her and Poppy's chamber, then escaped the house as quickly as she could manage.

Once outside, she drew a steadying breath. With no home she could stay within, no more work to complete, no friends to visit, and the Honeysetts occupied, there was only one thing left she could do.

Her eyes made their way to the sea, and a smile spread across her lips.

Without missing a beat, she set off north across the cliffside, taking the pathway that curved round the back of Tristwick, hoping to avoid any fishermen—or Cardys—on her way.

She would have loved to swim in Tristwick's waters again, but she'd been told by Poppy that a more secluded option lay to the north of the cove. Tregalwen was littered with great boulders and sea stacks at low tide that provided a great deal of privacy, and, according to Poppy, many of the fishermen and their families didn't bother with that beach when they had Tristwick to occupy instead.

With a skip in her step she hadn't known existed, Morvoren picked up her pace as much as her limp allowed. She enjoyed spending time with the Honeysetts, more so than any other family she'd ever known, but she was not used to such constant companionship.

A bit of privacy on Tregalwen Beach and a warm afternoon swim would be just the thing to buoy her spirits before she set about her next plan—making dinner for the Honeysetts before they returned from Golowduyn. After all, they deserved respite as much as Trevik did.

As she continued on the pathway, Morvoren fought the urge to check the cliffsides around her, pushing away any niggling fears of being spotted by Uncle or the seiner she'd seen that morning. The more time she spent in peace in the secluded cove, the more she realized that Uncle would have no reason to search for her in such an isolated place as a fishing hamlet. Besides, being down on the beach, she'd merely be a distant dot to any passerby who chanced to spot her.

With the blaring sun behind her, she lowered her paisley shawl until it hung between her arms, drooping low behind her back. The end of September very rarely brought warm days such as this, and October would hold them fewer and farther between, so she was grateful to be taking advantage of such warmth.

A few moments later, she finally took the pathway that veered toward Tregalwen. The moment she reached the sand, she plopped down and removed her boots and stockings, tucking them securely in her portmanteau before progressing across the vast beach.

Tregalwen was nearly four times as large as Tristwick, with its white sands and towering sea stacks. And fortunately, Poppy had been right—there wasn't a single person in sight.

With the warm sand pressed between her toes and the cool sea air caressing her face, Morvoren finally reached the shoreline, water sliding toward her in a lazy lap before slinking straight back to the sea. A large pillar of light shone down the center of the waves, reflecting the sun's blaze in a perfect white that gradually shifted to a vibrant turquoise. Each glimmering reflection called to Morvoren, beckoning her closer.

Come, sea-maid, the waves gently roared. *Do not leave me again.*

And she wouldn't.

With her eyes still trained on the waves, Morvoren headed straight for the large sea stack at the south of the beach, knowing the mound would allow her the most privacy. When she reached it, the cliffside no longer in view, she placed her portmanteau on a lowered section of the rock, admiring the blue and black mussels secured to the drying stone as she removed her shawl first. Then something dark behind the mollusks caught her eye.

She tipped her head, leaning closer to peer between a thick crevice in the rock. Shirtsleeves, boots, and other articles of clothing were shoved inside, and her heart dropped. Whose clothing was this?

Morvoren swiveled, ready to flee, but when she turned to the sea, her breath caught in her throat as a man rose up from the waves directly before her.

Trevik. Of course it would be Trevik.

At least she hadn't begun to undress yet. But had she known he was out here, she never would have left the house. She cursed her lack of vigilance. How had she not seen him before? He must have been below the water or just above its surface for her not to have noticed him until then.

Now, however, she couldn't look anywhere else.

He moved forward from the midst of the sea, only forty or fifty feet away as he strode through the low, rushing waves that raced him to the shoreline. He wore only his soaked-through trousers, light glimmering across every inch of his bare, wet torso, shoulders, and face. His hair hung in dripping strands, and his gaze was low to avoid the glare of the sun.

So he hadn't seen her yet. She snatched her portmanteau from the rock and took a step away, determined to leave before he spotted her. Perhaps she would hide behind the sea stack until he left.

Unless, of course, he changed nearby from his wet trousers into his dry ones.

She swallowed. She certainly couldn't be around for *that*. Better to just leave the beach entirely, even if he saw her departing.

She'd only taken a few steps away from the rock when she glanced back to the water, hoping to assure her presence had remained unnoticed. Unfortunately, Trevik decided to look up at that very moment, and their eyes locked.

She froze, and his pace slowed as surprise registered across his features.

Foolish girl. Why had she looked back at him? Now she didn't know what to do. Walk away without a word? Wait for him to reach her? Whatever she did, she needed to stop staring at the formed lines across his abdomen, chest, and shoulders.

Heavens, but all those years aboard that lugger had done him good.

His hand raised in greeting. "Afternoon," he said, his voice carrying across the wind only slightly above the rushing waves.

Now she'd have to stay. If she left after his greeting, he would surely know she was ruffled by his appearance— which, incidentally, she shouldn't be. She was living with the man, for heaven's sake. He could practically be seen as her brother.

And yet, as he continued his advancement toward her, his shoulders subtly shifting back and forth as he walked, she knew he was nothing like a brother. Not with the way her heart flapped wildly about her chest like a sparrow caught in a net.

"Afternoon," she finally returned, forcing a light tone. "Havin' a swim?"

He nodded, his chest rising and falling with heavy breaths, seawater dripping from his lower lip. With eyes averted, he responded. "I thought I might as well. The water won't be this warm for much longer."

He finally left the water's reach, standing between her and the sea with a glance behind her shoulder. "Are ye out 'ere to do the same?"

"Oh, no," she instantly replied. "I was simply walkin'."

His eyes dropped to her portmanteau then back to her. Silent, he awaited an explanation—an explanation she didn't have.

"Very well," she conceded, "I was out here for a swim."

Humor lit his eyes, though it vanished in a moment, and he took to fidgeting again. "Well, I'll leave ye to it."

He made to walk past her, but she shook her head. "Oh, I'll not be swimmin' now."

He paused, looking at her for another explanation. Why was he behaving so strangely? Had he no teasing word to say to her?

"I just...have things to do," she said.

He gave her an odd look, but she didn't say anything further. After all, how could she explain that there was no chance she was going to undress with Trevik nearby—or watching from the cliffside as he left Tregalwen?

Her eyes darted to the straight line his shoulders cut, sun glinting off the wet ridges. When she met his gaze once more, his lip twitched, as if to fight off a smile.

Heat rushed to her cheeks, setting them aflame. He had to have seen her admiring him, what other explanation was there for the confidence that now lit his eyes?

She blew out a breath. What was the world coming to, now that she, Morvoren Hollow, admired a fisherman?

CHAPTER TWENTY-SEVEN

*T*revik had planned to do as his crew suggested. He would never be near Miss Hollow unless Mother or Poppy was present. He would never be seen speaking with her in public. He would prevent their friendship from growing, would never admit to how he respected her standing up to her tyrannical uncle, and would never again admire her green eyes and golden hair.

Then she'd watched him come in from the sea, and his determination to remain far, far away from her had slipped through his fingers as swiftly as water filtered through a drift net.

Even now, he could see the fight within her to maintain her focus on his face, but her eyes continued to graze across his shoulders and dart down to his chest.

He would never wish to make a woman uncomfortable with his state of undress—which was why he always swam in seclusion. But that was just it. Miss Hollow was not uncomfortable. She was appreciating him. He could see it clear as day in her expression.

Such knowledge should have shaken sense into his mind and sent him straight home. Instead, pride swelled within him, raised his beaten down shoulders, and placed a long-overdue smile to his lips.

To have a woman as stunningly beautiful as Morvoren Hollow find something to esteem about him, a humble fisherman—a fisherman she critiqued and found constant flaws in—was more than satisfying. And he couldn't help but allow his pride to play along with the woman further.

Besides, none of his crew were present at the moment, so no harm could be done.

"So," he began, "ye didn't come out 'ere for a walk, then?"

She shook her head, blinking distractedly.

"But ye came out for a swim that ye aren't goin' to take now?"

"Yes," she murmured, glancing out to the sea then back at him.

"I s'pose that be one explanation for ye bein' out 'ere."

Her eyes snapped to his. "That be the truth."

He believed her. He also believed that the reason she wasn't swimming now was because she'd been rattled by his appearance and wouldn't chance having him see her swimming now. Still, it was far more fun to play otherwise.

"If ye say so." He walked past her, her eyes following him every step he took. "But I rather think ye were out 'ere to spy on I while I swam."

Her mouth dropped open, her smooth brow furrowed. "I beg your pardon."

He raised a shoulder, her eyes tracking the movement. "Ye've spied on I 'fore. What's to say ye aren't doin' it again?"

Her cheeks pinked, and he fought his desire to admire her own features then.

She raised her portmanteau ceremoniously. "Would I be carryin' this down here"—she waved it back and forth—"if I was just intent on spyin'?"

The wind slid over his wet body, and chills spread across

his skin. Despite the deceptive sun, the air was distinctly autumnal.

He turned his back to her, reaching across the rock to pull his clothing from the crevice. When he faced her again, her eyes pulled up from his torso. "So ye were plannin' on swimmin' with I then, rather than just spyin'?" he wickedly suggested. "I s'pose that would allow ye a better view."

Her eyes widened with indignation, and he fought the urge to laugh with delight at her reaction. It was far too easy to rile this woman.

Instead of rising to the occasion as he'd expected her to, Miss Hollow raised her chin. "Ye would be so lucky to swim with me."

His heart missed a beat at the image her words had conjured, but he swiftly blinked the vision away. Perhaps he'd taken his teasing a step too far.

He pulled his shirt out of his pile of clothing, bunching it together and swiping it down his wet arms and front before placing the damp garment over his head, acutely aware of Morvoren's watchful eyes as he moved.

"If ye wish to swim, ye still can," he offered, shaking out his sleeves. "I'll not spy on ye in return." He cast her a knowing glance, softening it with a smile.

She paused, narrowing her eyes a fraction before her lips pulled together as if to fight a grin of her own. "I wasn't spyin' on ye, but…" She returned her attention to the sea, then squinted up at the sun. "I s'pose I ought to be gettin' back already."

"Ye 'ave a pressin' engagement?" he teased, replacing his waistcoat next and leaving it unbuttoned.

Her eyes dropped to where his shirt dipped past his chest. "As a matter of fact, I do. I'll be makin' dinner for your family tonight."

His brows raised in surprise. "Ye can cook?"

"Does that surprise ye?"

"I thought ye'd 'ave a cook to do all that for ye. After all, ye were a fine lady 'fore comin' 'ere."

She sniffed a laugh. "Try to convince me uncle o' that fact," she muttered under her breath, raising her voice as she continued. "I cooked with me mother growin' up."

He nodded, still unable to picture a fine woman like Miss Hollow at home in a kitchen, flour swiped adorably across her brow, blonde tendrils loose from her chignon.

He shook the image away, leaning against the rock and using his stocking to dust off the sand from his feet. "Well, I be lookin' forward to seein' what ye can do, then."

He'd meant his comment in earnest, but she narrowed her eyes. "I *can* cook."

"I believe ye."

She still didn't look as if to believe him, though. "I've been doin' me best to convince ye that ye've done the right thing by bringin' me back to Tristwick, ye know."

He pulled back, surprised at the sudden change in topic. "I know."

"Then why have ye been avoidin' me?"

He winced. Of course she wouldn't beat around the bush. He longed to tell her the truth—that his crew was being pulled apart by her presence and that he was doing his best to straddle the line and keep them together—but how could he put such a burden on her shoulders after all she'd been through? "I ain't avoidin' ye. I've just been…busy."

She scoffed. "If ye say so."

He glanced up at her, noting the hurt behind her expression, and frustration suddenly surged throughout him. This time, however, it wasn't directed at Miss Hollow. She had proven time and time again that she was no mermaid, but Edern was still blinded by superstition.

So why should Trevik have to be the one to suffer when *Edern* had taken issue with the woman? Surely Trevik could find a balance between helping Miss Hollow feel at home and helping Edern overcome his fears.

Either way, he'd have to try, or he'd never survive under the stress of keeping both of his worlds aligned and happy.

He faced her directly, speaking carefully so she would know he spoke the truth. "I be sorry," he said. "I 'ave been avoidin' ye, but that doesn't mean I regret bringing ye back 'ere."

She studied him for a moment, her expression unchanging, then suddenly, a smile broke out across her lips. "Well, I still don't understand why ye be avoidin' I, but I'm glad ye don't regret me presence 'ere, Trevik."

His name on her lips was his undoing. It sounded far too lovely, far too natural.

She walked away from him then, taking a few steps back. "Now I'll leave ye to change your trousers." She arched her eyebrows. "And no, I'll not be spyin' on ye as ye do so."

He grinned despite himself.

She turned away and moved across the beach, her skirts raised to her calves as she limped across the sand.

Trevik blew out a breath, running his hand through his wet hair before shaking his fingers dry with a single flick. He could be friends with Miss Hollow while still maintaining that he didn't have feelings for her—couldn't he?

Or had he just made the biggest mistake of his life?

CHAPTER TWENTY-EIGHT

*T*revik was exhausted. Instead of returning to the house where he knew Miss Hollow would be cooking dinner alone, he'd found a quiet place in the lofts above the cellars and hunkered down for a few hours of sleep.

He usually managed to catch enough on the lugger between shifts of shooting the nets, and then a few more in the early to late afternoon after the midday meal. But since Miss Hollow's arrival in Tristwick, his schedule had been relentlessly interrupted.

He tossed restlessly aboard the *Pilferer* because of his unsettled crew, and he simply didn't feel comfortable sleeping in his room at home when only Miss Hollow was present and his family wasn't—especially because he knew what the crew would think of him.

Sleeping in the cellars upon a rolled-up fishing net would not pass for much longer, though. He'd simply have to discuss the matter with Mother so she might help them maintain propriety.

Knowing dinner was soon approaching, he emerged from the lofts, lumbered across the courtyard, exited the cellars, and sluggishly began the climb up the cliffside to his home.

Mother and Poppy would have returned from Golowduyn by now, otherwise he wouldn't have chanced seeing Miss Hollow alone.

He hadn't been able to help himself earlier, teasing and doing whatever it took to coax a smile upon her lips. But now he feared what else he'd do if left alone with the woman for too long.

That thought accompanied him as he finally reached home, opening the door and being greeted by the comfortable, earthy scent of Cornish pasties.

"There 'e be," Mother said, scurrying past the doorway to the kitchen as he closed the front door. "Wash up, Trev. The food be ready."

He nodded, making for his room as he removed his jacket. As he walked past the kitchen, he caught a glimpse of Miss Hollow bending low toward the oven, her back toward him.

Swiftly, he averted his gaze and forced his mind on the lugger, his men, the pilchards—anything to rid his mind of what he ought not be thinking about.

After splashing his face with the cool water from the basin and pitcher in his room, he ignored the beckoning call of his bed and returned to the kitchen.

He caught Miss Hollow's eye in an instant, and she took in the sight of him, a knowing look in those emerald depths before she resumed setting the table. Had she been thinking of the moments they'd spent together on the beach only a couple hours before?

Before he could figure out for certain, Poppy greeted him with a smile and Mother, with a kiss to his cheek. "Morvoren's made pasties for us," she said. "'Tis a lovely surprise"

"A lovely surprise indeed," he said. Miss Hollow's gaze skirted toward him again, this time accompanied with a smile.

He was fairly certain he shouldn't be enjoying these secret looks as much as he was, but he couldn't help himself.

"Can I 'elp with anythin?"

"I think we just about be done," Mother said, motioning for him to take his seat at the head of the table.

As he did so, Poppy sat to his left, Mother to his right, and Miss Hollow finally took her seat directly across from him. They said their usual prayer over the food, then dished themselves a helping of leeks, turnips, and a pasty each.

"Thank ye for this, Morvoren," Mother said, cutting into the pasty, the heat from the pocketed pastry bursting out in a plume of steam. "It be lovely to come 'ome and not 'ave to worry 'bout puttin' food on the table."

"It be the least I can do," Miss Hollow replied.

Silence followed as she and the Honeysetts cut into their food. Trevik could hardly wait. Pasties had always been a favorite dish of his, and while the pastry looked a little clumsy, the smell was perfection.

Perhaps the woman *could* cook then.

He delivered a single, cooling breath to the pasty before popping a forkful in his mouth, rolling it around until the heat subsided. The first few chews were divine, the flavor of the meat and potatoes spreading through his mouth with delicious warmth.

And then…he paused.

With puckering lips, he prevented an outright shudder. How much salt had she put in these? He peered down at the pastry, swallowing his mouthful hard to prevent it from coming straight back up.

Glancing at the others, he watched Mother and Poppy flinch after their first few chews, then they delivered the same hard swallow Trevik had.

Miss Hollow, however, had yet to take a single bite. She peered happily down at her creation as the three of them watched her, each of them at the edge of their seats, awaiting her reaction.

She cut into the pastry, then scooped a modest portion onto her fork before eating the concoction herself.

After three chews, she paused, pulling back with a look of repulsion. "What—" She stopped abruptly, looking at the others around the table with horror. "Stop. Don't eat the rest of 'em," she finished, her mouth still full.

Mother spoke first. "What do ye mean?" Her voice was weak as she feigned confusion.

"The pasties," Miss Hollow said, giving a shudder as she fought to swallow her own bite. "They be awful. Don't take another bite."

"Ye be too 'ard on yourself, dear," Mother cooed. "They be a difficult meal to perfect, after all. They really be fine."

"No, they be horrifyin'," Miss Hollow said. "How did I manage that? They be saltier than the sea."

Trevik's lips twitched in amusement. She wasn't exactly wrong.

Miss Hollow promptly stood, retrieving the tray the pasties had been on and popping hers back on in swift movements to avoid being burned. "I'll eat each of these to avoid 'em goin' to waste. But I'll not have any one of ye suffer through another bite."

"Oh, nonsense," Mother protested. "They might be a touch salty, but we can eat 'em just fine, can't we Poppy? Trevik?"

Poppy remained silent, staring at the unappetizing food with untrusting eyes. Mother, however, gave Trevik a look he understood at once.

He straightened, bringing the fork to his lips again. "No, 'tain't bad at all."

Miss Hollow shook her head. "No, stop!"

But it was too late. Trevik took another bite, attempting not to breathe so the taste of the pastry wasn't so overpowering. After swallowing, he cringed in a half-smile. "See? Not bad at all."

Miss Hollow shook her head all the more fiercely. "None of ye are foolin' me."

She went for Poppy's plate first, who didn't protest a lick as Miss Hollow swiped the pasty and placed it beside hers on the tray. "I do hate to think that ye'll have to cook after all, Mrs. Honeysett, but I fear that ye must. I'll not risk ruinin' another meal."

She took Mother's pasty next, and though Mother allowed her to, she shook her head. "'Tain't a total loss, Morvoren. The pastry be a tad salty, but the fillin' be quite nice. S'pose we eat that and warm up the leftover likky pie from last night, eh?"

Miss Hollow eyed her warily. "Then I can eat the pastry?"

Mother still hesitated. "The Bosankos be raisin' a right large pig. Per'aps we could give 'em the pastry for the pig to eat in exchange for a bit o' bacon when the time comes?"

Finally, Miss Hollow lowered her gaze. "That be well enough I s'pose."

Trevik had watched the entire exchange in silence, his plate still positioned before him. As humorous as the situation was, he could feel Miss Hollow's dismay. She really had been trying to help.

Mother moved toward her, raising her chin with her finger. "Cheer up, deary. 'Tain't all bad." With an encouraging smile, she motioned to Poppy. "Will ye 'elp me take this to the Bosankos?"

Poppy jumped up immediately, she and Miss Hollow helping Mother scoop out the insides of the pastries into a separate bowl.

"Don't forget Trevik's," Miss Hollow said.

Mother went for his plate, but after another glance at Miss Hollow's red cheeks, the sorrow pulling her lips down, he held up his hand. "I'll be finishin' mine, thank ye."

"Suit yourself," Mother said, then she waved Poppy forward. "We'll be back in just a moment."

Miss Hollow stared at Trevik in disbelief, the two of them

left alone in the kitchen as she stood before his seat at the table. "Ye can't be serious about eatin' that."

"'Course, I be." To prove his point, he took another bite.

"Ye'll make yourself sick with that much salt in ye."

He shrugged with a swallow, the salt coating his throat as it slid down at a snail's pace. He attempted to cough with his mouth closed, but a bit of the food sputtered out.

"Delicious," he muttered with an exaggerated wince.

Her green eyes danced as she fought a smile. "Ye be a cruel man."

She reached for his plate, but he slid it out of her grasp. "I ain't done," he protested, taking another bite.

After chewing, he smacked his tongue and reached for his glass of brandy. "Ye know, 'tis nearly edible with somethin' to wash it down."

She released a scoff, though a smile finally played about on her perfectly arched lips.

Not perfectly arched lips, just *lips*. Plain old lips that hadn't felt the least bit soft when he'd breathed the life back into her those many days ago.

"Just for that, I'll not allow ye to take another bite," she said. She leaned forward, attempting to take the plate again, but he shifted his body in front of it.

"Don't ye know you're not s'posed to take a man's plate o' food 'fore 'e finishes it?"

"Ye aren't goin' to finish it," she said.

"I don't know why ye be goin' on about 'ow awful they be. I've 'ad worse, I promise ye that."

"That may be so, but ye've certainly had better."

He glanced up at her with a feigned wince. "'Twouldn't be difficult now, would it?"

Surprise laughter erupted from her lips, as lilting and as calm as the sunshine at dusk.

He moved a forkful close to her lips, offering her another taste, but she held out her hand. "No, please! Stop!"

The food was beginning to hunker heavily in the pit of Trevik's stomach, but he wouldn't stop. Not if it meant he could see more of that dazzling smile.

He swallowed another mouthful, his nostrils flared with exaggeration. But when the salt triggered his gag reflex, he no longer had to pretend as the food nearly reappeared on his plate.

"That be a close one," he breathed, taking another sip of brandy.

She laughed again. "Ye be terrible, ye know? I tried to make 'em right. Ye just got in my head down there on the beach."

He raised his eyebrows. "Did I now?"

She shook her head, fighting another smile. "Not because of any other reason apart from your doubtin' my ability to cook. I did know how to once."

He swallowed again. "'Ow much salt did ye use exactly?" Then he waved a passive hand. "Ye know what? It 'ardly matters now. I just be glad the tax on salt ain't as bad as it 'as been durin' the war. We'd not be able to replenish the supply ye've clearly drained to make these pasties."

"All right," she said through her laughter, "ye be done now."

She reached forward, grasping the plate, but he speared another bite with his fork. "No!" she exclaimed, wrapping her hand around his wrist. "Ye'll make yourself sick!"

He could have wrestled away from her easily, but he allowed her to hold him back as laughter bubbled up within him, too. "No, I won't stop. I love it too much."

They struggled for a moment, but as the fork moved closer toward his mouth, she reached forward and clasped her fingers over his lips.

The moment he felt her warm touch, all sense was lost, and time stood still. His grip on the fork weakened, and it dropped from the table to the floor with a clatter.

But he wasn't looking at the fork. He was looking at Miss Hollow, staring into her eyes and becoming lost in their green depths as flecks of gold shimmered within them. Their chests still rose and fell from the laughter they'd shared during their struggle, and neither of them moved apart, though Trevik knew he ought to have.

His head spun as if he stood at the top of a dizzying cliff, teetering dangerously toward the edge. And yet, he couldn't step back, an invisible pull toward Miss Hollow keeping him in place.

After a moment, her focus dropped to her fingers at his lips. Her touch relaxed, but she didn't pull back. Instead, she tipped her head to the side with a softened expression and slid her fingers down his lips in small, calculated movements.

His breathing grew ragged, his heart pounding furiously against his chest and in his ears until he could no longer prevent himself from dropping his gaze to her lips, as well.

Those lips *were* perfect, just like the rest of her flawless face and figure. The woman was entirely, undeniably bewitching.

But when the door clicked open, the spell was broken, and Miss Hollow tore her fingers away from his lips, leaving a coldness in their wake he'd never experienced.

She swiftly turned her back to him, and Trevik bent down to retrieve the fork that had clattered to the floor, straightening just as Mother and Poppy joined them in the kitchen.

Poppy began speaking with Miss Hollow in an instant, but Mother's curious eyes flicked between Miss Hollow and Trevik.

He couldn't bear the questions he knew she longed to ask —questions he didn't know the answers to himself—so he pushed back from the table, pardoning himself with a mumbled excuse of needing to use the privy.

Once outside, he leaned against the side of the house with rattled breaths.

What was that? Why had he been so affected by the

woman, and why, *why* had she leaned forward, looking as if she wished very much to…?

He ran his fingers through his hair with both hands, taking a few steps beyond the house to view the sea from the cliff's edge. The water's rhythmic waves reverberated in his chest, though they did nothing but remind him all the greater of Miss Hollow.

He couldn't afford to lose his head in such a manner. Yes, he was attracted to her—what man wouldn't be? But he would not allow his thoughts to stray any farther than that. Falling for her would bring untold problems to Tristwick. Edern would stir up greater trouble, the Cardys would leave, the *Pilferer* wouldn't have enough men to bring in the fish for the winter, and Tristwick would not only be divided, but it would ultimately be at risk of starvation.

Trevik wouldn't do that to his family or to his community.

With his resolve back in place, he returned inside with a steely gaze and defenses at the ready.

And yet, as the evening progressed, he couldn't keep his eyes off of the woman. She moved about the kitchen with Mother and Poppy, as comfortable as if she'd been living there for years.

Dinner only made matters worse, for she quipped about her failed pasties, listened happily to Poppy and her endless chatter, and conversed about her time as a child, swimming with dolphins in the sea and spending every morning hunting for crabs with her mother.

All the while, like a gullible guppy, Trevik listened, intrigued and heartily captured by the woman and her charisma. And he couldn't help but wonder, when had he begun to think of Miss Hollow—of Morvoren—more as his friend and less as the desperately troublesome, self-proclaimed sea-maid?

When had she become…one of them?

CHAPTER TWENTY-NINE

$\mathcal{T}$he next week passed swiftly for Morvoren as she adapted to life in the fishing hamlet. Despite the backbreaking tasks in the cellars and the continued glares from the Cardys, she began to take pleasure in the work, for she knew that every pilchard she preserved, pressed, and packed away would help during that winter, as well as add a small fraction of payment to her coin purse for the future.

Each day, she looked forward to rising, Mrs. Honeysett's encouraging words buoying her spirits as Poppy's happy chattering propelled time forward even faster.

In between working at the cellars, helping at Golowduyn, and pitching in with the chores at the Honeysetts' home, Morvoren still found time to relax, sneaking in a few frigid swims with Poppy and taking walks along the cliffside at every opportunity.

Her freedom with the Honeysetts could not be contested, despite the work she was expected to do. No longer did she have to hide her accent, force a curtsy, or spend her days rotting away in a single room. In Tristwick, she could wear her hair in as simple a manner as she liked. She could walk across the cliffside unchaperoned. And she could admire the sunset every night, watching the fishing lugger float out to sea, white sails tinted purple, blue, or pink as the sun dozed off into the endless waves.

The only thing she wished she could do more of was spend time with the owner of the lugger. Trevik was busy—inordinately so. Fishing all evening, overseeing the processing, mending nets, holding meetings with his crew, taking trips to St. Just, paying the fishing tithe to the vicar, and countless other tasks.

Morvoren saw him throughout the day as he moved about the cellars, his eyes always finding hers across the courtyard. He'd send a small smile her way, then continue with his busy day. They were able to speak more over the evening meal, but as soon as he finished, he was off to board the *Pilferer*.

Spending so little time with him was really for the better. Leaving Mrs. Honeysett and Poppy would be difficult enough; having a relationship with Trevik would make it near impossible to leave.

One late afternoon, when most of the work had been completed, Poppy was with friends, and Trevik was meeting with Gryffyn about the sale of the extra oil, Morvoren darned stockings with Mrs. Honeysett in a comfortable silence in the sitting room.

She would miss moments like these, being productive but still relaxed, sharing moments with people she'd grown to love, hearing the ocean roaring just outside the door. Leaving would be difficult, but surely wherever she ended up would be just as wonderful—if not a little lonely.

She paused. Lonely? Before, she hadn't minded being alone, but that was in comparison to being with Uncle. Now, however, the thought of isolation, the thought of never seeing the Honeysetts again, brought an emptiness to her chest she couldn't begin to understand.

"Somethin' on your mind, dear?"

Morvoren glanced up from her darning, blinking as she

stared at Mrs. Honeysett. She hadn't realized she'd been scowling until then.

Pulling on a smile, she shook her head. "Just...thinkin' about the future."

Mrs. Honeysett looked back down at the brown stocking she mended. "What about it?"

If Morvoren had learned anything in the last couple of weeks, it was that Mrs. Honeysett had a knack for getting a person to speak, no matter the topic.

"Nothing excitin'," Morvoren responded. She shifted her stocking in her hands to focus on another hole. Standing on them all day long had swiftly worn out the soles and toes of the stocking. "I'm just wonderin' what I'll do when I leave." That familiar hollowness once again filled her chest, but she pushed it aside. "I don't 'ave much to offer anyone in the way of skills."

"Ye ought to 'ave more faith in your abilities. Ye can do whate'er ye put your mind to. 'Sides, ye've found your talent for cookin' again, 'aven't ye?"

Morvoren nodded. Thank heavens for that. After the debacle of the pasties, she was just grateful Mrs. Honeysett had allowed her usage of her kitchen again—though Trevik had teased Morvoren by removing the salt from the kitchen altogether.

She smiled at the thought.

"Ye also know 'ow to sew, read, and write," Mrs. Honeysett continued. Then she paused, thoughtful. "Ye know, Mrs. Kendricks'll need more 'elp come winter. Poppy and I 'ave only been workin' there since May, but 'twill be 'arder for us to travel there so often in poor weather. I do wonder if she might wish to pay for someone to stay there and work a few days at a time instead."

Morvoren couldn't deny the appeal of having a steady job at a lighthouse. She'd still have the view of the sea, still be close to the Honeysetts, and best of all, she'd be away from the trade that was so volatile, so uncertain, so…so close to everything that had ruined her life. Working at Golowduyn would be a temporary fix. A way to transition from spending all of her time with the Honeysetts to eventually having no attachment at all. That's what she wanted, was it not?

"'Appen she does need ye," Mrs. Honeysett continued, "ye could stay there, earn a better wage, be away from the smell o' pilchards." A somber smile stretched across her lips. "Though, we'd miss ye 'ere fiercely."

The woman's words were doing nothing to ease the sorrow that was now beginning to fill in the void in Morvoren's chest. "I could visit," she offered weakly.

Mrs. Honeysett reached forward, squeezing Morvoren's hand. "Ye be exactly right. And I'd prefer ye live there than somewhere we'd ne'er see ye again."

So Mrs. Honeysett thought she'd stay at Golowduyn indefinitely? Morvoren swallowed, squeezing her hand right back, for she couldn't utter a word.

Mrs. Honeysett smiled. "I'll speak with Mrs. Kendricks next we go to Golowduyn, then."

The news should have brought relief to Morvoren, but all it did was weigh heavily on her mind and heart. If the mere thought of leaving made her feel this way—what would the actual departure do to her?

She glanced up as Mrs. Honeysett lowered the stocking she worked on, glancing back and forth around her feet.

"Did ye misplace somethin'?" Morvoren asked.

"I can't find me sewin' basket…" She paused, realization dawning in her eyes. "Oh, I left it back at the cellars."

Morvoren nodded, only remembering then the women sitting together during one of the few breaks they were allotted, sharing a bottle of brandy as they mended spare bits of clothing.

"I'll fetch it for ye," she offered, jumping from her seat and setting her own supplies to the side of her.

"Oh, ne'er ye mind. I need to start with dinner soon anyway."

But Morvoren was already moving toward the door, snatching her shawl from the stand near the doorway. She needed a bit of fresh air to clear her mind. "I don't mind at all."

Without waiting for Mrs. Honeysett to protest again, Morvoren slipped from the house and closed the door behind her, breathing in the cold, salty air.

October had finally arrived, bringing with it her brisk, stormy winds. Many people despised the sea during the colder months, but that was when Morvoren thrived. A colder sea meant fewer people dotting the beaches. Furthermore, one could never go wrong with the gorgeous scenery—tempestuous, gray skies, crushing, thunderous waves, and faded cliffsides in muted shades of yellows and browns.

Meandering slowly down the cliffside, Morvoren tried not to focus on what her future held. After all, in Tristwick or away from it, with or without the Honeysetts, she was going to be desperately happier without Uncle and Mr. Foss involved.

"Afternoon, Miss 'Ollow."

She pulled her focus away from the sea and spotted Gryffyn Bosanko walking toward her, no doubt headed for his home.

She nodded her head in greeting. "Lovely day out," she said, motioning toward the swelling sea that promised of a storm that evening.

He gave her a look of amusement, tipped his cap, then continued on.

Morvoren had always liked Mr. Bosanko. He seemed a genuinely good man. Trevik seemed to like him, too. In fact, the two of them were more often than not seen together. So where was Trevik?

She reached the cellars shortly after, grateful for the shelter the walls provided as the cold began to slip through her shawl and dress.

She entered the empty courtyard, scanning past the barrels and the wall of pilchards to where a few benches were situated beneath the lofts. There, she finally spotted Mrs. Honeysett's small basket.

As she walked, her boots thudded against the cobblestone, echoing softly around the space until she retrieved the basket from its spot and turned to leave.

When she heard a soft humming coming from up in the lofts, she paused, enjoying the deep, soothing lullaby.

"'I brought 'er with me, to flowers so sweet. I 'ad 'er trust. I would ne'er mistreat.'"

Her heart stuttered. She'd never heard Trevik sing before —the group had been too loud that evening on the beach— but there was no mistaking his rich, smooth tone.

"'But a strong wind blew and pulled 'er away, so I watched and waited as the sky grew grey.'"

Glancing back to the courtyard doors, she hesitated. She really ought to be getting back to Mrs. Honeysett, to deliver the sewing basket and to help with dinner. Besides, part of Morvoren wondered if Trevik was avoiding her again—especially after she'd so brazenly caressed his lips.

Her cheeks warmed. He'd been so kind that evening a week ago, forcing himself to eat the awful pasty she'd cooked, then making her find humor in a situation she had been horrified with only moments before.

She'd been so wrapped up in the joy of his attention that she hadn't been able to pull her fingers away from his lips. Even now, the rush that had come from being so near to him filled her limbs.

Surely that was another reason to remain away from him. And yet, a simple greeting could hardly draw them closer. A short conversation either.

Needing no further convincing, she advanced up the stairs.

She'd had the notion to soundlessly ascend them, but the rickety wood was a lost cause, and she creaked and cracked her way up them.

Trevik, curiously enough, did not stop his singing, though there was no possible way he hadn't heard her.

"'Grow strong, *tykki duw*. Fly far, *tykki duw*. Leave me 'ere, as we know ye must do.'"

When she reached the top step, she peered around the corner in silence. Trevik faced her, though his head was down as he hunched over a net stretched out before him, no one else in the room.

"That ye, Gryff?" he asked, pausing in his singing though he didn't straighten. "Did ye forget somethin'?"

She smiled. "Do ye really think I look like Gryffyn?"

CHAPTER THIRTY

$\mathcal{T}$revik's head darted up in surprise, Morvoren's smile only growing. "Miss 'Ollow?"

Morvoren hesitated, just as she always did with his proper usage of her name. She'd given him permission again this week to use her first name, and still, he resorted to the formal option.

Brushing aside any lingering concerns as to why, she continued. "I be highly offended if ye think I do look like Gryffyn."

His lips tipped upward. "Ye do be a touch smaller 'round the shoulders and middle."

"A touch?" she asked in mock offense.

He gave a small laugh, peering back down again at the netting he worked on. "Come to spy again?"

She smiled. She'd come to know Trevik's mood with his teasing. He never seemed to do so when overwhelmed with work—which was more often than not—but whenever that mischievous sparkle in his dark eyes appeared, it never failed to pull a smile from Morvoren, especially with the attention that accompanied it.

He only ever seemed to tease Poppy in the same manner,

and Morvoren couldn't decide if it was because he was as comfortable with Morvoren as he was with Poppy...or if he considered Morvoren a sister, too.

She wasn't sure she liked the sound of the latter.

"As much as I know ye'd like me to be spyin' on ye," she responded, "I only came to fetch your mother's sewin' basket."

She raised the basket, but he didn't look up at her. "Shame that."

He focused his attention on the short piece of hemp he wound through a hole in the net, his lips pulled in slightly as he concentrated.

"What ye be doin'?" she asked.

"Just mendin' these 'oles *someone* managed to tear in me net." He gave her an accusatory look, but his brown eyes squinted slightly, as if hiding his smile.

She eyed the three spaces torn into the mesh. "How long 'til ye finish?"

"Not long. An 'alf hour or so."

She watched him work for a moment, the cool light from outside shining through the cracks in the walls. Wind whistled through the spaces, and she tightened the shawl around her shoulders.

Trevik, however, wore no jacket, his shirtsleeves rolled up and kerchief loosened. As he leaned closer to the net, his shoulders raised, and the braces over them caused the width to appear even broader.

"Ain't ye cold up here?"

He shook his head. "Ye get used to it after a while."

He said nothing further, and Morvoren hesitated. She knew she had to be disturbing his work. But if she spoke *about* his work, she wouldn't be a distraction then. Right?

"Are ye the only one who mends the nets?"

"No, Gryff was up 'ere a moment ago, but I sent 'im 'ome to be with 'is family. We all learn to do the task, though, since we all own a bit o' the fleet."

She paused. "Fleet? Ye have more than one boat?"

"Ah, no. I was referrin' to the sections o' nettin' all tied together. They be called a fleet."

"Oh, I see."

He moved down the line, tying up another section of the mesh.

"Can ye not hire out the work to a netmaker instead of doin' the work yourselves?" she asked.

"We can, and many towns do. But we do it 'ere to save us a bit o' money. 'Sides, we may as well do the work if we can."

She placed Mrs. Honeysett's sewing basket near the doorway and drew closer, watching his fingers tie the intricate pieces in a secure knot. The net was stretched out six feet across the room, held up by stands, while the rest of the material was rolled neatly together at the foot of the propped-up net.

"Are ye 'avin' terrible memories o' bein' tied up in these?"

For a moment, she wondered if he was teasing, but his expression was sober. "At times I do," she answered honestly. "In dreams, usually. And once when I swam with Poppy." Her lungs would burn at the memory, and panic would steal her breath away before she eventually calmed down. "But those moments are comin' fewer and further between."

He didn't respond for a moment, but he looked up at her with a contrite expression. "I be sorry."

His words were simple but heartfelt, and a warmth bloomed in her chest. For so long, he'd defended his fishing near the shoreline. She knew he felt remorse for entangling her, and truly, she knew he never meant to. But to hear his apology void of excuses or animosity meant more than she'd thought it would.

"Thank ye," she said.

Their eyes locked, but Trevik pulled away a moment later.

She should have taken the continued silence as a signal for

her to leave, but it had been so long since the two of them had had a minute alone together.

Every moment ye spend with him will make it harder to leave, she reminded herself.

And yet she couldn't pry herself away. She'd managed to part from Zennor Prout last year, hadn't she? And she had been her friend for months. Surely befriending Trevik couldn't be harder than leaving her.

She set aside the disbelief instantly pouring over her and peered down at the netting once again. "So tell me about this net of yours," she said. She wasn't particularly interested in a simple drift net, but she could be if it meant a moment longer with Trevik.

"What do ye wish to know?"

She drew a few steps closer to him, moving to stand on the same side of the net. "Do ye only have just the one?"

"One fleet, yes. But it 'as multiple sections tied to cork rope so we can remove and add on as needed." He motioned to the section he worked on. "We removed this to repair it, though there be another net aboard the *Pilferer* already."

She nodded her understanding, watching as he worked around the hole, left to right, then right to left, one row at a time, threading the hemp through the remaining mesh in a neat pattern.

"So ye don't have to replace the entire section?"

"If the 'ole was bigger I would've 'ad to." Then he looked up at her with twinkling eyes. "Fortunately ye were a small fish."

Morvoren pulled her lips in to hide her smile as Trevik continued with his work. She glanced again at the net, noting the small cords looped thickly just below the cork rope. "These can't be for the pilchards, can they?"

He glanced to where she stroked her hand across the hemp. "No, those just be orsels. They 'old the rest of the nettin', bringin' it lower to ensure it stays under the water."

"Ah, I see. But *these* are to catch the fish." She ran her fingers along the rest of the netting, the hemp rough against her fingertips.

He nodded. "The headin' be 'eavy at the top, the gaurdin' be at the bottom, and the sides be made up o' skilven."

Morvoren listened to the words, surprised that her interest was piqued. She'd seen the large, triangular seining nets Uncle owned, but obviously, she'd paid no attention to them. With Trevik, however, she couldn't help but hang onto every single word he said about the drifters' nets.

"Do they take much upkeep?" she asked next.

"A great deal," he responded, moving horizontally to tie the next strings. "When the fleet be tied together and it drifts in the water, the cork rope stretches 'bout sixty yards and the nettin' reaches more than an 'undred. Keeping that much nettin' fitty be difficult. We bring 'em in every Saturday so they don't heat up and catch fire 'board the lugger. It be then that we see to any repairs, barkin' every so often to preserve fibers and prevent rottin'."

"Barkin'?"

"That just be when the nets be dipped in boilin' bark."

"Oh, I see."

"The barkin' eventually shrinks the meshes and makes 'em less effective to fish with, though. So we 'ave to look at repairin' the nets then, too."

He straightened, stretching his back from side to side and unwittingly flexing his arms in the process.

Morvoren struggled to maintain her attention on the nets. "Are they very hard to tie?"

His finger held open another section of mesh, then twisted the free rope around to secure another knot. "Not a great deal." For the first time, he looked up at her with a long pause. "Would ye like to learn?"

She pulled back in surprise.

"They do be your own 'oles," he said.

She fought another smile. "I wouldn't wish to disturb your work."

"Ye ain't. 'Tis 'elpful to pass the time 'avin' someone to speak to." He waved her forward. "Ye can finish this smaller section while I mend the other. Then I'll be done for the day."

He motioned her closer again, and she bit the inside of her lip to keep her growing smile at bay, though she was thrilled at his desire to have her stay.

Cautiously, she walked toward him. "Ye be sure ye want me help after what I did to them pasties?"

She was delivered with the smile she'd been hoping for. "Ye can't add more salt than what already be coverin' this net, I assure ye."

He winked, and Morvoren's heart jumped like a pilchard attempting to escape the gurries.

Trevik reached for the torn section, creating another opening with his third finger, then looping the loose strand of hemp around the existing netting and securing it tightly. He released the string and motioned for her turn to begin.

On her first successful try, after a number of failed attempts and instructions from Trevik, he nodded with approval.

"Excellent. I'll make ye a fisherman yet."

Morvoren blanched, the mesh falling from her fingertips as the words jarred her. What was she doing? Working in the cellars with fishermen's wives, living with a fisherman's family, now she tied a net with a fisherman? Was this not the very thing she was trying to prevent—becoming so used to a fisherman's ways that they were second nature, that she didn't care to leave them?

Trevik must not have noticed her hands stilling as the worry filled her, for he continued speaking. "Now do that all the way across the torn section, then I'll show ye 'ow to go back along the bottom."

He took a step to the right, getting straight to work on the larger tear in the net.

Morvoren looked away from the y-shape of his braces and willed her nerves to settle. Just because she was tying a net didn't mean she was fully embracing the life of a fisherman. She was merely earning her keep before she could leave and find the life she wanted.

Slowly, she moved on with the knotting, paying close attention to where she lifted and lowered the hemp—instead of dwelling on the rock forming in her stomach.

"Are ye out o' questions, then?" Trevik asked.

"Just focusin'," she lied. Then she cast him a sly glance. "Was this your plan all along, to get me to quit speakin'?"

He laughed, the deep rich sound filling the space between them. Perhaps tying the net wasn't so bad with Trevik's laughter for company. After all, they were friends. Friends were always good to have.

More silence followed, and though Morvoren did her best to focus on mending the hole she'd created herself, she couldn't help but become distracted with her proximity to Trevik, the section of his net close to her own as he worked back along another row.

She needed something else to focus on instead of the fact that he stood a mere foot from her now. "So, if ye fish at night, carry in the catch in the mornin', mend nets in the afternoon, then head out to sea at dusk…when do ye ever sleep?"

"I find a few hours 'ere an' there," he answered simply. "Durin' the pilchard months, I sleep less with the amount o' work that needs doin'. But we take shifts at times on the lugger, and I always manage a few hours in the early afternoon."

"I can't imagine how ye still be standin'."

"I could say the same for ye. Processing 'em fish ain't easy. 'Specially when ye ain't be used to doin' it." He paused. "Can I ask ye somethin'?"

Morvoren's stomach tightened. When a person requested permission to ask a question, one could always expect a less than pleasant conversation to follow.

Still, she responded with a polite, "Of course."

He didn't look up from the netting as he continued. "I know your feelin's 'bout fishermen be less than favorable, but…what made 'em so?"

A thousand answers poured into Morvoren's mind, nearly escaping her lips, but she clamped her mouth shut. She couldn't burst the perfect atmosphere she'd created with the Honeysetts by letting them know she came from a seining family. She just wasn't ready—nor, she believed, were they.

She didn't think they would despise her or throw her out, but she was almost certain there would be some small degree of mistrust that would arise for her having two seiners in her family. And what would happen if the Cardys learned the truth? Would they treat her more poorly as a seiner's niece or a sea-maid?

If only Morvoren could leave Tristwick without ever having to tell them at all.

She wouldn't allow herself to lie again, but perhaps she could share just enough to satisfy his curiosity.

With a hard swallow, she began. "There be many reasons, but most of all, it was me Father. He was convinced to invest in the trade and little by little, he let it take over his life."

Trevik's brow rose in surprise, but she hardly noticed, unwanted memories sweeping over her like a rogue wave.

For so long, she'd pushed them aside, unwilling to relive the worst years of her life. Father's ever-present smile shifting to a constant, stress-filled frown. His attention on his family redirected to various contracts and money orders. He used to tell Morvoren stories every night before bed and walk on the beach with them every morning, but toward the last year of his life, he couldn't even be bothered to return home before she'd already fallen asleep.

"Bein' in the trade changed 'im," Morvoren said softly, "He became obsessed with havin' better catches and findin' more ways to make even more money." She shook her head. "He was told to invest in drifters first, but they'd make fun o' Father's lack of wealth and make distasteful comments about Mother and me. Father defended us for a time, but soon enough, he laughed along with 'em and did the same to others."

She continued looping the knots together, focusing more intently on her actions to not allow her feelings from the past to resurface alongside her memories. "He wasn't even there when Mother died, though he knew she'd taken ill."

It had been five years, and still, her grief sat at the edge of the door to her past, ready, waiting for her the moment she opened it just a crack.

"When did your father die?" Trevik asked, his voice soft.

"A few weeks after her. Died o' the same sickness. The night before, I'd discovered 'im comin' home, stinkin' o' drink and other women's perfume."

Bitterness threatened to rush over her as powerful as the sea's currents, but she swiftly quelled the desire. She'd lost a great deal of respect for her father over the last few years of his life—so had Mother. But Morvoren refused to forget the good times they'd shared, though the wall she'd built around her heart would never be lowered.

"I be sorry," Trevik said, his voice pushing away the darkness. "That…that shouldn't be somethin' a child should e'er 'ave to go through. Any of it."

She felt his compassion, his understanding in his few simple words, and she nodded with gratitude. "'Twas unfair of me, I know, to blame all me woes on fishermen in general. But I held that belief for years." She cast him a sidelong gaze. "Trust ye and your family to prove me wrong."

She reached the end of the row and straightened, arching her already smarting lower back. "Even still, what 'appened to

Father just made me realize that I'd ne'er willingly choose to entangle me future with that of a fisherman's again. That way o' life…'tisn't for me."

Silence followed, and she glanced at Trevik to see his head ducked down as he continued his work in silence.

Her stomach dropped, leaving her with regret that swirled in her chest as she realized the words she'd said aloud. How could she have stated such a thing? "I-I didn't mean…"

But it was too late. Trevik merely shrugged. "Ye don't 'ave to explain. I ain't be ignorant to your opinion o' we fishermen."

"'Tain't fishermen…" Her words trailed off when he raised his hand.

"Like I said, ye needn't explain further. What 'appened with your father gives ye ample reason to feel such a way."

He didn't seem heartbroken at her words, and though she should have been relieved, she couldn't help but feel… saddened. Did he not wish for her good opinion? Surely, as friends, he ought to.

With a sigh, she shook her head. "Mother always said I had a tongue as sharp as a hake's teeth, and Uncle said I had very little tact." She gave a wry smile. "I s'pose he be right about one thing."

Trevik didn't deny her words. Why had she expected him to? He'd been on the receiving end of her cruelty one too many times.

Desperate to be rid of the conversation and the turn it had taken, Morvoren motioned to the net. "I finished with that row. How do I get it back 'round the other way?"

Trevik dropped his eyes to her section of the net, and she stepped carefully off to the side as he showed her how to tie the mesh below the other row, continuing on in the opposite direction.

"It really be remarkable," she said, picking up the hemp and moving on to the next row. "How did ye learn to do it?"

Fortunately, Trevik allowed her to change the conversation. "Me father taught all of 'is crew when 'e hired 'em. But I learned when I was just a boy, spendin' hours up 'ere with 'im."

Morvoren eyed him. She didn't often hear about the elder Mr. Honeysett, but whenever he was mentioned, his memory was almost spoken with a sort of reverence by his wife and children.

"What was your father like?" she asked.

Trevik's features warmed, and his voice softened. "'E was the best o' men. Patient with everyone 'e knew. Demanded respect from 'is crew—not with fear, but with loyalty and fairness. 'E taught me everythin' I know."

She listened to his words, warmed by his sentiment.

"'E was the one to 'ave named the lugger the *Pilferer*," Trevik continued with a half-smile. "'E thought it fitty, as the seiners always called Father a thief of pilchards."

Morvoren smiled. She would have liked this man, she was certain. Still, something niggled at the back of her mind, the memory of Trevik and his mother speaking, something about his father's death being related to seining companies?

"Can I ask how he died?" she questioned gingerly.

"Illness."

The word was short and ended any hope she had to question him further about the topic. Clearly, he wished that part of his past to remain closed, so who was she to beg him to open the door?

"Did ye take over the lugger straightaway?" she asked instead, hoping to ease his discomfort.

Fortunately, he nodded. "Yes. When I be twenty-one."

"And the crew followed ye well enough?"

He tipped his head side to side, as if weighing his words as he began a new row of netting. "A few of 'em did. I 'ad to earn the respect o' the others."

"Well, it be clear that ye 'ave it now. I can tell just by lookin' at 'em, they'd follow ye to the ends o' the earth."

A shadow crossed over his features, and she wondered what she'd now said to offend him.

"They obviously think more of ye than of I," she said, hoping to alleviate the tension she didn't quite understand.

He cracked a smile, but it didn't reach his eyes. Was he truly offended by her words? Or was he still upset about her pretending to be a mermaid to Jowan Cardy?

Guilt swirled in the pit of her stomach. Katherine Cardy still eyed her with disdain each day in the cellars, and Jowan had taken to scowling at Morvoren instead of watching her with fearful admiration.

Would that she could take back all her foolish actions.

Desperate to recreate the pleasant atmosphere they'd had before, she peered at the section he mended, then at her own. "We be nearly finished."

He nodded. "Yes. Thank ye for your 'elp."

Still rigid.

She pulled in her lips. "Perhaps we ought to race to see who can finish their nettin' first."

Finally, he glanced up at her, his dark eyes lit with amusement. "Don't ye think that might be a bit unfair? I am more experienced, ye know."

"But I've only a single row left. Ye've got at least two that be double the size." He remained silent, and she shrugged. "Suit yourself. I just ne'er thought I'd see Trevik Honeysett back down from a simple challenge."

He raised a daring brow and finally took her bait. "Very well, then. We race."

Without a moment's hesitation, he ducked his head down and went straight to work. Morvoren laughed as she did the same.

Together, they worked alongside each other, but she didn't

realize how close they'd drawn together until her elbow grazed against his.

Forcing away the chutes of warmth sailing up her arm, she focused on the meshes she created. One, two, three. She glanced over at Trevik's. He was nearly finished with an entire row.

"How have ye done so many already?" she exclaimed in despair.

He merely laughed.

"Ye be right. 'Tisn't fair," she said. "I think I'd like to end the race now."

"Ye can't. This be more 'an fair, since ye were the one who extended the challenge."

She huffed, hunkering down in hopes of making her fingers move faster.

"Them 'oles need to be small enough for a pilchard to be caught," Trevik said, apparently catching a glimpse of her work. "Those be large enough to catch another fish your size."

She laughed. "Ye just focus on your own tyin', sir."

They worked swiftly, neither of them saying a word until Morvoren trapped her finger in one of the knots.

"Blast!" she grunted, tugging the finger free and retying the mesh.

Trevik chuckled beside her without looking up. "Flustered, are ye?"

She ignored him, unable to respond without losing out on another tie. With a glance at his work, her heart dropped, then picked up at twice the speed. He had five left—she had two.

"Come, Morvoren, work more quickly," she encouraged herself.

Her elbow brushed against his again, but this time, he didn't apologize. How the devil could she win with fire shooting up her arm each and every time they touched each other?

He only had four left. Three left. Two.

A giddy laugh escaped her lips as she moved the hemp around the existing mesh of her final knot, but when Trevik gently nudged her to the side, she lost hold of the string with a gasp.

"Ye cheated!" she cried out.

He laughed. "I didn't."

She nudged him back in retaliation, warmth blossoming in her heart and burgeoning through her limbs. "Yes, ye did."

Not willing to be outdone by a cheater—as charming and as handsome as he was—Morvoren reached over with her free hand and tugged the string away from his grip.

He scoffed in dismay, and she laughed, moving her body partially between him and the net, all while attempting to finish her mending.

Trevik tried to nudge her out of the way, but she held firm.

"Ye ought to give this last one to I for free," she said.

"Is that 'ow ye go about life, expectin' things for free?"

He reached around her with both arms over hers, preventing any tying at all, and she half-yelped, half-laughed in surprise as he lifted her into the air.

"This isn't fair!" she breathed, her laughter causing her eyes to blur with tears. She struggled to maintain hold of reality as his strong embrace infused warmth throughout her body.

His deep chuckles in her ear seemed to lift her higher from the ground than even his arms. "I'm just bein' resourceful, that be all."

She struggled to break free, though only because she was expected to. In truth, she could have remained for hours in his arms, enjoying the feel of his controlled strength, the scent of lemons rushing past her nose.

He shifted his footing, turning her around and depositing her on the opposite side of him before finally releasing her. Swiftly, he whirled around and returned to his section.

Her head spun with elation, and she scrambled toward her own area, but he shifted his body, preventing her progression.

"'Tisn't fair!" she laughed, still trying to reach past him, for she could hardly lift the man as he'd lifted her.

Finally, he finished his last knot and swung around with a triumphant laugh, arms raised high in the air. "Victory!"

"Victory? Ye can hardly call it that," she said, feigning disappointment. How could she feel the least bit disheartened when her heart trilled in such a way?

She stared up at him, his hands lowering to prop against his hips, his chest rising and falling with heavy breaths. In their tousle, his kerchief had loosened and hung limply round his neck, the top button of his shirt popping open.

Her eyes dropped to the top contours of his chest. She didn't have to wonder if they were as formed and firm as the rest of him.

The air thickened around them, as if a heavy fog had rolled in from the sea, drowning out all other distractions.

She felt his gaze on her. Slowly, she trailed her eyes up his throat, past the ridges of his neck, and over the shadow of facial hair spread across his jawline, until finally, she settled on his eyes.

His smile had faded away, just as hers had, leaving his lips parted as he breathed more smoothly.

After she had touched him in the kitchen last week, Morvoren had made it a point to keep her distance from the man, knowing if a simple hand across his mouth had tripped up her heart so fiercely, what would something else, something *more* do?

She couldn't afford to feel *more*, though. It would bring an attachment she didn't wish to accept, an attachment that meant more than friendship with a fisherman. *This* fisherman, who, at this very moment, was looking at her lips and rendering her lungs breathless and mind thoughtless.

The world stopped moving, though seagulls still cried

above the lofts and the waves still crashed on the shore just outside of the cellars, the sound of the thundering water slipping in through the cracks of the walls.

Trevik took a step toward her and raised his hand, hovering midway between them. She couldn't draw a single breath as she waited with anticipation. Would he finally touch her? Caress her as she'd caressed him?

Finally, he slid his fingers across the lower half of her cheek, settling at the hollow of her ear. His touch sent new waves of warmth rushing over every inch of her, sending her mind into a frenzy. Never mind that they were friends. Never mind the repercussions. She was overcome with a strong desire—stronger than she'd ever known—to have him kiss her.

He pulled in his bottom lip for a moment, hesitating, and she knew that he was thinking the same as her. They both wished for this affection, but they both knew how their lives would change if they gave in to their desires.

Really, Morvoren should have run out of the door that moment, pulled his hand away from her face and begged his forgiveness while apologizing for the fact that she simply couldn't kiss him.

But she couldn't run. She wanted him too fiercely.

Instead, she took a step toward him, his fingers sliding toward the nape of her neck in reaction. She closed her eyes for just a moment, relishing in his touch.

This was going to happen, friends or not, consequences be what they may. She couldn't hold back any longer.

She needed his kiss to be hers.

CHAPTER THIRTY-ONE

*W*hen Miss Hollow's eyes opened again, Trevik's breath once more slipped from his lungs. Those ocean-green depths stared up at him with a desire he couldn't deny—a desire that matched his own.

This woman, she truly was a siren from the sea. How else could he explain the way his heart heaved so heavily against his chest, like waves to the bulwark of the *Pilferer*?

It was an ache he welcomed, though, for it spoke measures to just how real this moment was. Her smooth hair in his fingertips, her body so near to his, he was just one step away from holding her, cradling her fully in his arms as he'd done only moments before.

Ever since that moment in the kitchen, he'd fought with his mind, refusing to believe just how badly he'd wished to draw closer to the woman, and yet, each day he spent in her company, he fell more and more for her siren's song. Only, it wasn't a song. It was her helping his mother with every task under the sun. It was her not only listening to Poppy but engaging in her conversations with similar excitement.

It was the way Miss Hollow looked at the sea during a

storm—breathless, thriving, in awe. And the way she tackled the tasks before her with dedication.

It was…it was the way her golden hair fell over her brow, and the way her sea-filled eyes looked up at him with the promise of a kiss he would never forget.

But he couldn't. He couldn't damage the friendship between them. And he couldn't damage the trust he'd only just begun to tentatively win back from some of his crew.

He'd promised them that nothing was going on between him and Miss Hollow—that nothing would keep her in Tristwick longer than necessary. And this was a promise he had to maintain.

Besides, what would kissing her do anyway? She'd made it perfectly clear that she wanted no future with him or any other fisherman. And who could blame her after what had happened to her father with other drifters? This kiss she so desired was no doubt all she wanted—no commitment, no future. No promise of something more between them.

Slowly, with more strength than he had known he'd possessed, Trevik dropped his hand from her face and took a step back. He never should have allowed himself to get this close to her, to even touch her. He was a fool, as simple as that.

Looking away, he noticed his mother's sewing basket Miss Hollow had placed beside the stairs. "I s'pose I ought to let ye get back to me mother with 'er sewin' supplies," he said, his voice more gruff than he'd intended.

He kept his gaze off of her, hoping to alleviate the embarrassment she must be feeling. He longed to explain to her his reasoning, but surely she should know already.

After a moment's hesitation, she stepped away from him, then scurried toward the door. "Yes, she'll be wonderin' what's kept me."

Trevik cringed. Would she tell Mother what had occurred? Or rather, what had almost occurred? He couldn't bear giving his mother false hope. He knew how much she and Poppy had grown to love Miss Hollow. If they even had the smallest inkling of a hope that he might feel something for Miss Hollow. That…that he might…

He shook his head, looking away. Entertaining such thoughts would lead to unhappiness for everyone involved.

"Will ye tell 'er I'll be 'ome soon?" he asked.

She nodded.

"And, Miss 'Ollow?"

She paused in the doorway, turning back to face him with rosy cheeks. "Yes?"

"Thank ye for your 'elp with the net."

A half-smile spread across her lips. "'Twas the least I could do after makin' the holes in the first place." A flicker of sorrow flashed across her features, then she turned on her heel and left down the stairs with Mother's basket in hand.

As her footsteps slowly retreated, Trevik blew out an unsteady breath. This was for the best. Not kissing her was for the best. Dismissing her was for the best.

Or so at least he tried to convince himself.

That night, Trevik was mostly silent during dinner, excusing himself early to arrive at the docks before dusk and the rest of his crew. He simply couldn't bear being in Miss Hollow's company any longer.

She'd behaved as if nothing untoward had occurred between them—smiling and laughing with his mother and sister and speaking with Trevik nonchalantly. But, he'd been unable to do the same, barely managing a single smile and sentence throughout the meal.

As his men began to arrive at the *Pilferer*, Trevik greeted them with tentativeness, as well. Edern and Jowan still weren't speaking with him, though the Roskelleys had appreciated

Trevik's efforts in convincing the others that Miss Hollow was not to be feared.

Unfortunately, Edern's superstitions and naysaying had slid their way into the skipper, Enyon Penna, and his daughter, Mary. Trevik had been asked to postpone the meal they were supposed to share together until further notice, no doubt because of Miss Hollow staying with the Honeysetts.

His friendship with Mary had strained, but it was no great loss to him. He and the girl had never had much in common anyway. But the burden it was putting on the other friendships throughout Tristwick was beginning to take its toll on Trevik and his nerves.

If the worst happened and Edern and Jowan left their work aboard the lugger, the loss would be devastating. Fortunately, most of the men seemed to be letting that sleeping dragon lie, for they knew they had to fill their bellies for winter, and getting along well enough aboard the lugger was the only way to do so.

Gryffyn, of course, had remained on Trevik's side. The man reached the lugger last, a grim expression to his face as he pulled Trevik back down to the dock to speak with him.

"Ye should know," he said in low tones, "Edern saw Miss 'Ollow go into the loft with ye this afternoon. 'E be tellin' others that ye've been lyin' to 'em."

Trevik groaned, his heart sinking. When would his crew believe him that nothing was between him and Miss Hollow? But then, could he truthfully say such a thing now when he'd almost kissed the woman?

Gryffyn's wary gaze shifted to curiosity at Trevik's sustained silence, but Trevik swiftly looked away. He wasn't about to give away any knowledge that would help Edern's case.

And yet, when he turned away from the lugger, he noticed that Gryffyn's eyes were not on Trevik at all. Instead, he focused on the very woman from their conversation heading toward them that moment.

"Blast," Trevik muttered under his breath. "This ain't goin' to 'elp."

Miss Hollow strode forward with a basket in her hands, a blue cloth draped over the top of it. Her skirts rippled against her legs from the soft, sea breeze, and tendrils of her blonde locks blew back from her face.

As she greeted those aboard the lugger and those still standing on the dock, a gentle smile played about her lips.

"Evenin'," she said softly. She lifted a tentative gaze toward Trevik, then faced the others.

Thankfully, she stopped on the dock and didn't attempt to move farther. Edern would have insisted they burn the lugger to a crisp, then send it to the bottom of the sea if she'd boarded the boat again.

"Ready for your night o' work?" she asked.

A few men aboard the lugger mumbled in response. Edern squinted his glare so tightly, his eyes nearly disappeared. Jowan merely folded his arms with an impassive look, though his eyes had yet to waver from Miss Hollow's.

Trevik knew he ought to say something, but memories of their near-kiss, of her flawless skin beneath his fingertips, rendered him speechless. How was he to behave with the woman in front of all of his men?

"I believe we do be ready, ma'am," Gryffyn responded kindly, glancing at Trevik. No doubt he wondered why Trevik wasn't saying a word.

Morvoren must have wondered the very same, for her uncertain look flicked to his once again.

Trevik could only muster a strained smile, worry plaguing his thoughts. No matter how he acted, his behavior would be judged. And if they asked Trevik if he truly did have feelings for the woman...he wasn't so sure how he would respond.

Matters would be far better if he urged her to leave. "What can we do for ye, Miss 'Ollow?" he finally forced out.

Uncertainty flashed across her features. How he wished to settle her nerves, to give her some indication that he would be happy to see her anywhere else but near the lugger and his crew. How he wished to tell her that he thought she looked perfectly lovely in the waning light of the sun, her hair glowing pure white at the ends.

Instead, he remained silent.

"Your mother sent me." She extended a satchel that he hadn't noticed slung over her shoulder. "Ye forgot this."

"Thank ye," he mumbled, accepting the satchel.

She lingered for a moment, then held out the basket. "And I thought…I thought your crew might like these."

He took the basket with a shift of his eyes to his crew.

"They be sugar biscuits," she said, motioning to the basket. With a quick glance around, she leaned close to him with a sly smile, whispering, "To win o'er their affection, see."

Trevik forced a smile, the eyes of his crewmates searing into the back of his head. Even with his nerves and the judgments being cast toward them, he should have smiled, graciously thanked her, invited her to distribute them to the men herself.

Instead, he took a step away from her, mumbling a quick word of gratitude, then made to leave without another word —but not before seeing her own grin faltering.

His departure was stopped, however, as Gryffyn moved forward. "These be for us, then?" he asked, taking the basket from Trevik's hands.

Miss Hollow nodded, eying those around her with a wary brow.

"Ah, bless ye," Gryffyn said, taking a long sniff from the basket. "They be me favorite. The men'll enjoy 'em greatly."

Finally, Miss Hollow's smile returned. Regret pinched at

Trevik's heart to know that smile could have been for him instead.

"I know it's but a small gesture," she said, "but I ne'er got to thank ye all for savin' me from the sea and for welcomin' me into your community. I hope to make myself as useful as I can throughout me stay here."

"Accordin' to me wife, ye already 'ave," Gryffyn said. "Ye be a great 'elp in the cellars, accordin' to 'er."

Trevik remained silent, still feeling the watchful eyes of his crew, as if they were just waiting for him to reveal his feelings for her—as if waiting for him to fail.

"When do ye intend to leave Tristwick, then?"

Trevik nearly jumped at Edern's voice directly behind him. When had the man left the lugger to stand with them on the dock?

"Oh," Miss Hollow began with a hesitant glance at Trevik, "I don't know yet exactly. I was perhaps goin' to see about workin' at Golowduyn or somewhere in St. Just, but the Honeysetts have allowed me stay at their home 'til I decide."

Edern's beady, untrusting eyes shifted to Trevik. "That be so, eh?"

Trevik knew he had to say something now to ease Edern's suspicions, to prevent him from spreading more lies to the rest of the crew. The man was volatile, like an impending storm cloud, overflowing with moisture, just waiting for the right moment to ruin someone's picnic or afternoon on the beach—or life.

"Ain't nothin' set in stone though," Trevik said. "Ain't that right, Miss 'Ollow? Ye could just as easily find work in Mousehole or Penzance. And ye said sooner rather than later, ain't that so?"

Trevik regretted his words instantly. The hurt in her eyes glared so brightly, he wished he could crawl into the fish room aboard the *Pilferer* and welcome the same fate as the rest of the pilchards they would catch that night.

He hadn't meant to offend her, but his insinuation for her to leave earlier and farther away was so obvious, silence fed through the crew. Even the gulls seemed hesitant, their calls distant from the muted shores.

Miss Hollow only missed a beat, blinking away her hurt and raising her chin with hardened eyes. "Yes, that be right. I think I'll make some inquiries in Mousehole or Bodmin. It be for the better. After all," she paused, waiting until Trevik finally met her gaze, "I wouldn't wish to be a burden on anyone any longer than I already have."

Warmth seeped into his cheeks.

She looked to Gryffyn then, placing a genuine smile on her lips. "Enjoy the biscuits, sir."

Then without another look at Trevik, she walked away.

A few moments passed by before anyone spoke again.

"See, Edern," Hedrek Roskelley said from over the bulwark of the lugger, "our Trevik be a man of 'is word. The sea-maid be leavin' shortly."

Trevik winced, and Edern snorted. "I'll believe it when she actually leaves."

Trevik didn't notice Edern boarding the boat, nor Gryffyn following shortly behind. He was far too focused on Miss Hollow's departing figure and the light she seemed to take with her.

Hedrek's words echoed continually through his mind.

"Our Trevik be a man of 'is word."

A man of his word. Trevik used to pride himself on his honesty, on his ability to be truthful with those around him. What had happened to make that stop? He wasn't being honest anymore with anyone. His crew, his family, Gryffyn, Miss Hollow. And mostly, himself.

Why couldn't he have simply said how pleased he was to help the woman? That he was happy to have her in his home for as long as she needed? Yes, he was scared of what her staying in Tristwick might mean for the future of his crew, but even when he'd turned his back on Miss Hollow to satisfy Edern's worries, the man still didn't believe him.

So what was the point of it all? Edern would be angry and crazed no matter what Trevik did or said. But would Edern ever be so daft as to leave the only security he had that winter by refusing to fish on the lugger? And was Trevik willing to no longer be a man of his word just to ease Edern's superstitions?

When he put it that simply, no. Trevik was not.

Swiftly, he strode forward, aware that most eyes focused directly on him. "Ready the boat, Gryff," he called over his shoulder. "I'll be back shortly."

"Trevik," Edern called after him, "let the girl go."

Trevik paused, his shoulders tensed, but not with his usual reticence. Instead, impatience slipped through his limbs. He turned to Edern, and with a firm shake of his head, he responded. "No, Edern. I'll be speakin' with 'er now."

Fire lit within the man's eyes, but Trevik hardly noticed, turning back around and sprinting off the dock.

"Miss 'Ollow?" he called out, reaching the pathway leading to the cellars.

She turned around, surprise only thinly veiling her caution. "Ye be wantin' somethin', Tr—Mr. Honeysett?"

He stopped a few steps away from her, his heart twisting at her correction. She hadn't called him 'Mr. Honeysett' since the ride home from Sennen. "I just wanted to speak with ye. I didn't want ye to think that I..." Why were the words not coming? Why could he not say what he wished to say?

She gave a shrug, backing away. "Ye don't have to worry. I know ye want me gone."

"Ye don't understand. I—"

"I do," she interrupted. "Ye be concerned with what your men be thinkin' with me stayin' here for longer, and rightly so, for some of them still be thinkin' I be a sea-maid."

Trevik stared. Her assumption had been stunningly accurate, which only made him feel all the worse.

"As I said," she continued, backing away again, "I understand. And ye don't need to worry. I'll be speakin' with your mother tonight about findin' work farther away from Tristwick and your crew."

"'Tain't that be what ye wanted all along? To be as far away as ye can from the fisherman's life?" He was trying to make himself feel better, pulling up facts from their conversations before and using it to pad a wall around his heart.

She sniffed, looking down at the pathway before gazing out at the sea. "You be right. I do want a life away from all this. Just as badly as ye want a life where your crew doesn't have to worry 'bout some washed up, wounded sea-maid callin' down a storm upon ye." She paused, turning back to look at him. "And where ye don't have to worry about her disruptin' your life."

Her words broke through his barrier with one swift sentence. "Miss 'Ollow…"

"They be waitin' on ye, Mr. Honeysett. Night."

Then she walked away from him, and he, like a fool, allowed her to go.

CHAPTER THIRTY-TWO

*T*hat evening, Morvoren stared into the fire in the sitting room of the Honeysetts' home, wondering how many more nights she'd be allowed such a luxury. If it were up to Trevik—or should she be calling him Mr. Honeysett now?—she would no doubt be gone within the week.

She sighed, watching the flames in the hearth flicker warmly before her. She'd seen the change come over him in the loft, the fear entering his eyes before he'd stepped away so abruptly.

Of course now she knew why. His crew wanted her gone, and Trevik? Well, he didn't want her to stay badly enough to say anything in her defense.

"Ye be troubled again this evening, Morvoren," Mrs. Honeysett whispered beside her. "What be on your mind now?"

Morvoren glanced to Mrs. Honeysett, the two of them seated together on the wooden bench. Poppy sat between them fast asleep, her head resting on her mother's shoulder.

"We don't 'ave to speak of it if ye don't wish to," Mrs. Honeysett said, taking Morvoren's silence as hesitance.

Morvoren shook her head. She didn't wish to speak of

anything at the moment, but she couldn't prolong the inevitable any longer. That much had become clear today.

"I...I think perhaps I need to find work outside of St. Just." She kept her head low as she spoke, not wishing to see Mrs. Honeysett's reaction. "Golowduyn might be fine for a time, but I do believe Bodmin might be the better option for I."

"Bodmin?" Surprise buoyed the woman's voice, though she quickly checked her tone, nodding to show her support. "And-and what will ye do in Bodmin?"

"I'm not certain yet." Actually, she wasn't sure if she'd ever be certain. Bodmin hardly sounded appealing, being nearly sixty miles away from Tristwick and landlocked in every direction.

"So ye don't wish to work at Golowduyn, then? Or remain in Tristwick for the winter?"

Morvoren didn't know what to say. "I was goin' to stay, but...well, I was only supposed to remain 'ere for a short time anyway. And there'll be more options for me future in a bigger city."

Mrs. Honeysett nodded, falling silent.

Desperate to ease her own conscience, as well as to convince herself that what she was doing was right, Morvoren scooted forward on the bench to face Mrs. Honeysett more directly.

"I'd like to stay. Really I would. But I think it be time I give your family some space. A few more months of me wouldn't do any of ye any good."

Mrs. Honeysett rested her cheek against her daughter's head, staring into the fire. "I know your stayin' 'ere would be for Poppy's and my benefit. So...might I safely assume ye be doin' this for me son?"

Morvoren shook her head, quick to protest. But then, what other reason had she but the truth? Her shaking head slowly shifted to a single nod. "I just know me livin' 'ere be upsettin' 'im."

"What makes ye say that?"

Because Morvoren had been nothing but a burden to him. A pebble in his boot. A windless night to his lugger. "I know his crew is havin' trouble with my bein' here still. He has enough to worry about without me stirrin' up trouble, even if it be unintentionally."

To her surprise, Mrs. Honeysett huffed out an impatient sigh. "It be them Cardys. Daft fools, they be." She rested her shaking head against the back of the bench. "Destroyin' other people's 'appiness to secure their own. 'Tain't right."

Morvoren couldn't agree more, but she couldn't blame her own misgivings on the Cardys, no matter how she wanted to.

"In truth, they aren't the only reason I'm leavin'," she said in a whisper. "I told Trevik about my father earlier today, but I…I'd like to share more about him with ye."

Mrs. Honeysett nodded, her eyes focusing on Morvoren.

After recounting what she'd told Trevik, Mrs. Honeysett listening to every word, Morvoren continued. "When his greed grew, it ruined my parent's marriage. Seein' that deteriorate, and me mother's health after that, I promised myself I'd ne'er settle for a future of bein' a fisherman's wife." She paused. "Your son is a wonderful man. And I don't presume to think that he e'er, that he feels…" She shook her head, beginning again. "My leavin' be for the best. The longer I spend here, the harder it'll be for me when I have to leave. And I…" Emotion stuck in her throat. "I have to leave 'fore I grow more attached."

Mrs. Honeysett was silent, her features downcast. "I understand. Truly, I do. 'Specially in regard to what 'appened with your father." She drew a deep breath. "But I…I've ne'er seen me son take to someone as much as 'e's taken to ye."

Morvoren looked away with a disbelieving sniff. Poppy

shifted at the noise, then settled deeper into her mother's shoulder.

"It be true," Mrs. Honeysett said more softly. "I've seen it. Things 'ave 'appened in Trevik's past to make it 'ard for 'im to trust others. Terrible experiences with seiners and 'is father."

Morvoren's ears perked up. She longed to know more about the connection, but if she said a word about seiners, Mrs. Honeysett would surely be able to deduce Morvoren's own connection to them.

"That was why 'e 'ad a difficult time with ye in the beginnin'," Mrs. Honeysett continued. "'Cause o' your need to 'ide the truth. But once ye were honest with 'im, once ye told 'im the truth 'bout where ye be from…" She paused, shaking her head. "Like I said, I've ne'er seen 'im take to someone more 'an with ye."

The words should have secured Morvoren's fate to remain in Tristwick for the rest of her life. After all, hearing that Trevik didn't think of her as a burden, that he was truly happy with her presence there, was comforting beyond words.

And yet, she couldn't set aside how he'd treated her in front of his crew that day, nor could she forget that she hadn't been entirely honest with Trevik. Whatever had happened between him and the seining companies had been traumatic. How could she ever admit to the Honeysetts now that they'd been harboring a seiner's niece under their very roof?

Her thoughts were interrupted as Mrs. Honeysett reached over, taking Morvoren's hand in hers. "I don't blame ye for your decision to keep away from the fishin' trade," she whispered. "And I'll support ye no matter what ye decide. But remember, ye can't control what others do, only what *ye* do. And sometimes, the risk o' fishin' in a storm be worth the rain that falls on ye, for the catch'll be all the better."

Mrs. Honeysett ended her words with a smile and another gentle squeeze to Morvoren's hand, then she released her and replaced her arm over Poppy's shoulder.

They sat together in silence then, listening to the fire snapping as the flames slowly died before them.

For so long, Morvoren had prayed for guidance from her mother, for the distance between heaven and earth to thin for just a moment so she might see Mother's encouraging smile again, to feel her embrace just one more time.

How had it taken Morvoren so long to see that Mrs. Honeysett was that answer to her prayers?

Tears blurred her view of the fire, the orange and yellow flames softening as the wood shifted lower into the hearth. Mrs. Honeysett's words had been exactly what Mother would have said—encouraging, uplifting, filled with sense.

But Morvoren could not disregard her fears so easily, and Trevik's feelings for her—if he, indeed, had them—would never be strong enough to guarantee he wouldn't change just as Father had.

She'd made the right decision. Leaving Tristwick would be best for all involved.

She could only hope that one day, she would be able to overcome the debilitating sense of loss that now consumed her soul at the mere thought of having to leave Tristwick and the Honeysetts—the one place she'd felt at home in years.

CHAPTER THIRTY-THREE

"What did ye say to 'er?"

Trevik blinked, coming out of a deep sleep —the sleep he only allowed himself on Saturdays when the lugger was docked through the night.

What time was it? He couldn't have been sleeping for that long.

"What did ye say to 'er, Trevik?"

Groggily, he rolled over in his bed, looking to his open doorway where Mother stood, fists propped against her hips.

"What?" he mumbled. He scrubbed a hand over his face and looked to the window. As he'd suspected, the sun was still shining, though not as brightly as before. Blast, he'd hoped to sleep through the night. "What time be it?"

"It be six in the evenin' and time to answer me question."

He looked back to his mother, surprised to see her lips pulled in a taut line, brow low over her dark eyes.

His insides twisted. "What question?"

"Don't ye play daft with I, Trevik Locryn 'Oneysett. Ye know I be speakin' o' Morvoren. Now tell me what ye said to 'er to make 'er want to leave Tristwick for good."

With a groan, he sat upright, an ache pulsing between his

brows. He pinched the bridge of his nose. At least he'd be able to sleep that evening. Thank heavens he wouldn't have to suffer with a headache all night aboard the lugger.

"Can't we speak o' this later?" he asked. Or never? He was already feeling terribly about his conversation with Morvoren, why did Mother have to make him feel worse about it?

"No, ye've avoided I for long enough. We'll speak o' this now, thank ye."

She had a point. Four days had passed since his time with Miss Hollow at the docks. He'd attempted to speak with her twice since then, but the woman was apparently determined to never forgive him, brushing aside any attempt he'd made to speak with her and finding Poppy or Mrs. Honeysett to converse with instead.

Naturally, Trevik had then kept away from his mother, Poppy, and Morvoren alike—eating while they were out of the house, taking naps aboard the lugger, and always running late so no one had time to say more than a word to him. But he'd known Mother would catch up to him at some point.

He only wished it hadn't been when he was trying to sleep for the first time in days. Apparently, his body was punishing him for what he'd done to Miss Hollow. He'd been unable to sleep soundly at all since Monday.

He motioned to the door. "Won't she 'ear?" he asked quietly.

Mother shook her head. "She and Popp are out findin' shells at Tregalwen. Now, out with it, son."

He blew out another heavy breath. Mother was as stubborn as Trevik when it came to having her way.

He tossed his cover aside and moved to the pitcher and basin of water nearby. "I be seven and twenty, Mother. Ye don't 'ave to scold I any longer."

"Apparently, I do need to scold ye, for ye still be actin' like that fool boy, gettin' into all sorts o' scrapes."

"I ain't gettin' in no scrapes. I just asked when she thought she'd be leavin' and suggested, per'aps, that she look beyond Tristwick for that work."

He washed the cold water over his face, then dried it with a towel. The cool moisture did nothing to ease his burning cheeks as he considered his cruelty once again.

Mother shook her head in silence.

"I was only askin' for the sake o' me crew," he defended weakly.

"Oh, your crew. Yes, they need to know such a thing."

He raised his shoulders in a helpless gesture. "I just…they be breathin' down me neck, Mother. What else was I s'posed to do? They s'pect a relationship 'tween we and fear she'll ne'er leave, so I needed 'em to believe that I wanted 'er gone as much as they."

After Trevik had followed Miss Hollow, matters had worsened. The Roskelleys, the Ederns, and Enyon Penna now believed Trevik to be lying—that he'd prevent Miss Hollow from leaving. After all, why else would he have run after her? He didn't regret attempting to fix things with the woman, but then, even that had been futile.

"And do ye?"

Mother's question brought him back to his room, and he blinked. "Do I what?"

"Do ye want Morvoren gone?"

Leave it to Mother to ask an impossible question.

"I…I don't know. I can't think beyond me crew."

"Don't be ridiculous, Trevik."

He nearly jumped at her snapping words. He hadn't heard her speak so harshly since he was sixteen and he'd been caught sneaking the tithes into his own pockets instead of the vicar's.

"The only one ye need to worry 'bout is that fool Edern Cardy and 'is family," she continued. "Anyone else'd follow ye to the ends o' the earth without that man stirrin' 'em up."

"Don't ye think I know that?" he asked, lifting his hands

out to the side of him in a gesture of his hopelessness. "I've spoken with 'em, told 'em that she ain't be nothin' to worry about, pointed out what she be doin' for Tristwick. Nothin' 'elps. Only Gryffyn believes I now."

Mother set her chin firmly. "Then it be time to do what your father taught ye. Put your foot down, Trevik. Be firm with your crew or lose 'em entirely. Be firm, or we'll lose Morvoren." She took a step forward, her brow low. "She's set to ask Captain Kendricks to see if 'e 'as any connections for work up in Bodmin. She be determined to leave as soon as she can 'cause she fears she be tearin' apart your crew and injurin' our livelihood."

Regret weighed down on his chest. So Miss Hollow was serious about leaving, then. And it was all because of the lie he continually told himself.

The truth was not that Miss Hollow was tearing apart his crew. Edern had had fears before of deceptive mermaids, devious Cornish piskies, and island-building giants long before Miss Hollow had been rescued. He no doubt would have them again.

But the man was merely a scapegoat, an easy way out, a person to blame for Trevik's own fears of trusting anyone. Because the truth of the matter was that he was perfectly frightened. Frightened of not being able to continue the rigors of his work and providing for his family and all of Tristwick. Frightened of trusting an outsider after what happened with father and the seiner.

And most of all, he was frightened of losing his heart to a woman who clearly despised him and his way of life. Trevik had never met anyone he'd fallen for so hard, so quickly as he had with Miss Hollow. It had only been a few weeks, for heaven's sake.

He didn't know if what he felt for her was, in actuality, love. But he knew *whatever* his feelings were, they ran deeply, warmly, throughout his veins and across every inch of his heart. No woman had ever left such an indelible mark upon him—no woman's siren song had ever captured his mind—until Miss Hollow.

And it was terrifying.

"Ye be a good man, Trev," Mother said softly, pulling him from his conflicting thoughts. She reached forward, a hand to his cheek. "I know there be pressure from all around ye to do what others want ye to do. But it be time now to decide what ye want for yourself. Ye can't straddle two longin's forever."

Then with a soft, motherly pat against his cheek, she gave a half-smile and left his room. A few moments later, the front door closed behind her, and Trevik was plunged into the silence of his home.

Mother was right. He could not live this way forever—welcoming Miss Hollow and her company one moment and pushing her out the door the next.

Whether he was terrified or not, it was time to make a decision. And it was time to make it right now.

CHAPTER THIRTY-FOUR

$\mathcal{M}$orvoren scoured the beach before her as she walked, spotting a shell sticking out of the cream-colored sand. She pulled it out, revealing a smooth, white shell in the shape of a fan.

"Found another, Poppy!" she called out, holding the shell up.

Poppy's face brightened, and she ran back to Morvoren, her steps sinking in the sand.

"Oh, that be perfect!" she exclaimed, taking the shell and turning it from back to front. "Thank ye."

She opened her reticule and gently lay the shell within, the bag sagging from the weight of all that they'd already discovered. She secured the top, and the shells softly clinked against each other.

"Ye keep lookin'," Poppy said, already peering at the sand once again. "I think Mother found a few nearer the waves that'll work."

She was off before Morvoren could even agree. With a smile, she went back to her duties, meandering across the beach with a careful step. She and Poppy had gone searching for seashells nearly every night since returning to Tristwick.

Morvoren was becoming very adept at finding the ones Poppy needed.

She would miss this when she left for Bodmin.

She squeezed her eyes shut at the thoughts, refusing to allow them to enter again. She couldn't stomach even the notion of living so far inland. But she was willing to do what it took to secure the future she wished for.

Neglecting her task for but a moment, Morvoren eyed the lazy waves lingering across Tregalwen Beach as the tide went out. A few managed to break forward with trickling crests, but mostly, the water simply slipped forward inch by inch before retreating, leaving behind broken, blue shells and popping, white bubbles.

The clouds had broken apart and scattered across the sky after the day's rain, and now, a golden orange light settled across the sea and the shoreline. They weren't alone on the beach, a few other families and couples taking advantage of the stunning evening outside of their homes.

Was she truly willing to give up such a paradise?

"Morvoren!"

She glanced up. Poppy was waving wildly back and forth. "I've found the master lode!" she cried out. Then she motioned to the sand with excitement.

Her mother stood beside her, shaking her head in amusement before reaching down to gather the shells Poppy had found.

Morvoren laughed to herself, moving to join the women at once. What surprised Morvoren more than anything since she'd arrived in Tristwick was how swiftly she'd bonded with Poppy. How she would miss that young woman. Sharing a room and working together had brought the two of them closer than Morvoren could have ever hoped for.

Would that she could bring Poppy with her to Bodmin. The two of them would have a right fun time exploring the city together, finding a shop to work in, living wildly from inn to inn. But she couldn't tear Poppy away from her home. She belonged in Tristwick as greatly as Morvoren didn't.

She reached the others as they picked up far more than ten shells—"Can't ne'er 'ave too many shells, Mother"—Poppy's reticule growing heavier and heavier.

While they rifled through the sand, a couple passed by whom Morvoren recognized from church.

"Mr. Causey, Mrs. Causey," Mrs. Honeysett greeted, straightening as she brushed off the sand from her hands. "Lovely night out."

"Indeed," Mr. Causey said, tipping his top hat toward her. "I trust you are well?"

The three of them nodded in unison.

"Adding to your collection, Poppy?" Mrs. Causey said, a hand to her swelling belly. Mrs. Honeysett had said the woman would enter her confinement in November, but she looked close to bursting that evening.

"As always, ma'am," Poppy said with a grin.

The Causeys then shifted their attention to Morvoren. "And how is the newest member of Tristwick's community faring?" Mr. Causey asked. "We've heard you have taken to the cellars with ease."

Morvoren nodded. "If so I can only give credit to the Honeysetts here, sir. They teach very well."

"I'm sure." Mr. Causey tipped his head to the side, still holding his wife's hand that was laced through his arm. "You'll be more than prepared to work through winter then, I trust?"

Morvoren hesitated, glancing to Poppy, then Mrs. Honeysett. Neither of them had told Poppy that Morvoren was planning to leave before winter set in, and now would certainly not be the right time to admit as much.

"I hope so," Morvoren said simply.

"I'm surprised to see ye walkin' about, Mrs. Causey," Mrs. Honeysett said, swiftly changing the subject. "Ought ye not be restin'?"

Mrs. Causey blew out a breath, though her smile remained. "I fear I would surely die if I had to rest any longer than I already am being made to do. Just yesterday, we held a party at Leighton House with the Hawkinses and the Trevethans. Not a moment went by without the four of them insisting I sit upon cushions and eat until I was fit for bursting. Of course, my old friend Mr. Frederick Hawkins also has his hands full with his own wife." She lowered her voice, leaning toward Mrs. Honeysett. "Who, I hear, is also in the motherly way. At any rate, I was exhausted by the end of the evening after the fuss that was made."

"It does sound terrible to be waited on hand and foot, my dear," Mr. Causey said with a twinkle in his eye.

Mrs. Causey patted her husband on the arm. "Oh, you are right. I really shouldn't complain. You all are taking such good care of me. Especially you, my dear." She turned to face Poppy and Morvoren. "When the two of you marry, you must find yourselves someone as dutiful as Mr. Causey here. You will want for nothing then."

"Wise words, Mrs. Causey," Mrs. Honeysett said.

Morvoren smiled, but not before catching Poppy's weakened expression. She narrowed her eyes. Why did she look so forlorn?

"Well," Mrs. Causey continued, "I do wish I could continue speaking with you, but I fear once I stop for long, I lose all desire to move at all. I'll have to have Mr. Causey carry me the rest of the way home if I prolong our departure further."

The group laughed, but Mrs. Honeysett stepped forward. "Would ye mind if I walk with ye for a moment?"

Mrs. Causey smiled. "Oh, please do."

"I'll be back soon," Mrs. Honeysett said, then she moved forward with the couple, their voices reaching Morvoren as she and Poppy remained behind with the shells. "So ye saw

Gwynna Merrick…Oh, I always do say 'er old name. Mrs. Trevethan. 'Ow she be, then?"

Mrs. Causey nodded. "She is doing wonderfully well. I do believe she is having a difficult time adjusting, but as we all could have guessed, Mr. Jack Trevethan is as patient with her as he always has been. The two of them are still as happy as a portrait. Just the other day, I saw them riding across…"

Her voice slowly trickled away, replaced with the rushing of waves.

Morvoren didn't waste a moment before turning to Poppy. "What be the matter?"

Poppy pulled on an innocent expression. "Pardon?"

"I saw your change back there. What 'appened?"

Poppy hesitated a moment, waving a passive hand through the air. "Oh, nothin', really. I just…I was thinkin' 'bout me talk with the lieutenant t'other day."

Morvoren paused. "Ye spoke with him?"

"At Golowduyn."

"Why didn't ye tell I?" Morvoren exclaimed.

Poppy shrugged. "Well, 'cause it didn't end well, really."

Morvoren waited impatiently for Poppy to continue.

"We were 'avin' a right nice conversation, I was bein' confident and flirtin', as ye taught I. I was 'appy as I thought 'e be flirtin' right back."

Morvoren smiled, nodding her head and lapping up the story like a kitten to spilt milk. "And?"

"And…nothin'. Our conversation ended when 'e spoke of 'is arm bein' right, enough for 'im to return to sea. 'E's been called to leave in a fortnight, maybe earlier."

The excitement fled from Morvoren's heart, and her stomach plummeted. "I…I didn't realize he'd be goin' back so soon."

"Neither did I." Poppy picked up a shell.

As far as Morvoren was aware, the smooth edges and white

glaze looked as perfect as the other shells they'd collected that evening, but instead of pocketing it in her reticule, Poppy took another look at it, then threw it fiercely toward the sea.

"I thought…it be silly, but I thought 'e'd retire early and continue work at Golowduyn. There ain't no reason for 'im to not. I know 'e be 'appy there. But I guess not enough."

She ended with a helpless shrug, and another piece of Morvoren's heart shattered. "I'm so sorry, Poppy," she whispered. "Had I known, I'd ne'er have encouraged…"

Her words trailed off as Poppy shook her head. "Oh, 'tain't your fault. It be me own stupidity. 'Course 'e'd return to sea. That be 'is life."

Morvoren hesitated. "Does he know how ye feel about him?"

"Oh, there can be no doubt that 'e does. I be that obvious."

"But ye've ne'er admitted the like to him aloud?"

She shook her head fiercely. "I couldn't bear it if 'e didn't return me feelin's."

Morvoren nodded in agreement. She wanted to encourage Poppy, to advise her to throw caution to the wind. But how could she say such a thing when she, herself, was far too fearful of the very same things?

She watched Poppy carefully before the girl straightened her shoulders and her smile returned. "At any rate, all will be well eventually. 'Til then, I'll just be glad to 'ave your company. I don't know what I'd do without ye, Morvoren."

Another knife to her chest, another twist of her heart, and Morvoren's smile was weaker than ever before.

Mrs. Honeysett soon returned from her short walk with the Causeys, then the three of them moved together as a family across the beach.

As a family.

Morvoren shook her head. She kept doing that, lumping

herself in with the Honeysetts, calling them a family when she'd not earned the right to do so.

Truth be told, she hadn't felt so close to having a real family again since Father had changed and Mother had died. Was she being a fool by trading her relationship with these women for a shop or workhouse in Bodmin?

"Trevik!" Poppy exclaimed. "I didn't think ye'd be joinin' us this evenin'."

CHAPTER THIRTY-FIVE

orvoren's heart skittered across her chest at Poppy's words. He wasn't supposed to join them that night. After all, he'd been avoiding Morvoren as much as she'd been avoiding him.

But as she glanced over her shoulder, the man strode toward them in the sand, his hair lazed across his brow from the wind, shirtsleeves billowing and jacket tossed easily over one arm.

She wanted to keep going, to pretend that she hadn't seen him, but when Mrs. Honeysett and Poppy stopped, she was obliged to do so as well.

His dark eyes settled on Morvoren as she watched him approach. He gave a simple nod in greeting, but she looked away without a response. She didn't want to speak with him. It was too painful, knowing he wanted her gone. And though she understood his reasoning why, that hardly made the matter any easier.

"Ain't ye tired, Trevik?" Poppy asked as he reached them. He stood beside Morvoren, and she shifted discreetly away from him. "Ye must not 'ave slept for long."

He glanced to his mother. "No, I…couldn't sleep. I thought to join ye all out 'ere this evenin' instead."

Mrs. Honeysett was watching her son with a knowing smile, but before Morvoren could decipher what her look meant, Poppy continued.

"We be that glad ye joined us," she said. "I bet ye be 'appy to not 'ave to fish tonight. Just look at that sunset."

"Ye forget I can see the sunset at sea, Popp."

Poppy scrunched up her nose, her freckles nearly disappearing in the slight folds of her skin. "Oh. Well, at least ye don't 'ave work to get in the way o' this one."

The scent of lemon drifted toward Morvoren as Trevik's gaze settled on her once again. She merely turned her head the opposite direction and watched the waves herself.

"Collectin' more shells?" he asked, motioning to Poppy's reticule.

Poppy nodded. "And we be nearly finished. Ye can 'elp, now ye be 'ere."

She described the shells she was still looking for, then continued along the beach, her family and Morvoren falling in step beside her.

To Morvoren's dismay, Trevik moved to walk at her side, and an irritating itch arose within her. She did her best to listen to Poppy's continual chatter, but Trevik's presence did nothing but ruin the peace she'd felt before.

Why was he even there that evening? And why, after spending so long avoiding her—and she avoiding him—did he choose to walk beside her?

Folding her arms and tugging her shawl closer to her person, she peered down at the sand, willing herself to look for shells instead of thinking anymore on the man.

But when his deep voice reached her ears, she cringed.

"Are ye cold?" he asked as Poppy continued speaking with Mrs. Honeysett.

Morvoren blinked. Was his question out of concern or was

he simply making conversation? "No," she responded simply, turning to listen to Poppy instead. She was infinitely more interested in what Poppy had to say than Trevik.

"That shawl won't keep ye warm once the sun lowers," he continued.

Why was he so concerned with her well-being now? Or were her actions alone a burden to him?

His words picked at her patience. Was this to be their relationship from now on—Trevik pushing her to leave Tristwick while in front of his crew, then being civil and conversational only when they were alone?

Well, she wouldn't stand for it. Not any longer.

She didn't bother to respond. Instead, she stopped in place as the others continued, bent down to retrieve a shell that wasn't there, then straightened.

Unfortunately, her plan backfired as Trevik stopped to wait for her and the others continued. Swiftly, she caught up to them, feigning infinite interest in Poppy's words until they reached the large sea stack toward the south of the beach— the same place Morvoren had observed Trevik emerging from the water like some sea god.

She closed her eyes to be rid of the image *and* the words. He was hardly a sea god, that fisherman.

When they reached the other side of the sea stack where the rocks were lower and piled out into the sea, the four of them climbed up the higher rock, Trevik helping his mother up the slippery sections as Morvoren and Poppy observed a few empty tidepools.

When Poppy straightened, she gasped, propping her hands on her hips. "Would ye just look at that sunset? Simply breathtakin'. We ought to take a moment to admire it."

She went to where the rock jutted forth, hanging her skirts over the edge just out of reach from the waves that occasionally lapped up. Morvoren followed suit, and soon enough,

Trevik and Mrs. Honeysett joined them, sitting on Poppy's other side.

Poppy hadn't been exaggerating—the sunset truly was something special that evening. The sky was lit with a creamy orange and soft pink that splashed across otherwise white clouds, causing the beach to feel warmer, despite the cold wind rushing in from the waves.

The sea took on a darker hue of pink closer to the horizon, but nearer to the shore, the gentle waves shone a soft blue. Every wave that broke upon the sand or tagged the rock they sat upon whispered up to Morvoren.

Are ye really willin' to give up all o' this? it asked.

And time and time again, she had no response.

"'Tis breathtakin'," Mrs. Honeysett murmured as silence fell upon their little group.

Even Poppy was quiet as she nodded in agreement.

Of course, her silence only lasted a moment. "Spendin' time out 'ere," she said, "it be the best. 'Specially with family."

There was that word again. *Family.* Poppy was beginning to make the same mistake as Morvoren.

"'Course, Trev doesn't understand that," Poppy said, leaning forward with a teasing smile at her brother. "'E be too busy to spend time with 'is own family."

"What ye be talkin' 'bout?" he questioned. "I be 'ere now, ain't I?"

Poppy huffed. "For the first time in months."

"That ain't true."

"Ye know it is. Just like we know the only reason ye be out 'ere now is 'cause Morvoren be with us."

The blood drained from Morvoren's cheeks before returning in droves. What the devil was Poppy thinking, saying such a thing? Trevik didn't say a word in response, and Morvoren could have sworn she'd seen Mrs. Honeysett hiding a smile before Poppy continued, apparently unaware of the discomfort she'd caused upon the others.

"Well," Poppy said, standing up, "that be enough rest for I. I need to find just a few more shells 'fore the sun disappears altogether."

"I'll join ye," Mrs. Honeysett mumbled. "'Elp your mother, Poppy."

Poppy helped her stand, as well, then took her arm as the two walked side-by-side across the rocks.

Morvoren moved to stand, desperate to not be left alone with Trevik, but when she saw him leave the rocks, too, she paused.

She needed a moment to recoup from Poppy's words. Her face still burned like she'd sat near a fire for too long, though the wind had become considerably colder with the sun sinking closer to the horizon.

Bringing her legs up to her chest, she ensured her skirts covered her, then she wrapped her arms around her legs and rested her chin against her knees.

"Are ye cold now?"

She started, whirling around to where Trevik stood on the lower ledge of the rock she still sat upon. She'd not known he'd stayed behind. Mrs. Honeysett and Poppy had continued on, now scouring the sand near the lapping water. Should she join them, make another escape?

"No," she replied, making to stand, but he held his hand up.

"I'll leave so ye don't 'ave to." He took a step back from her. "I just needed a moment away from Poppy's chatterin'."

Morvoren stared, unsure of how to respond. "I enjoy her conversation."

"Always?" He tipped a single brow up in disbelief. "Surely not."

Very well, he'd caught her out. Morvoren did prefer silence every so often. But she wasn't about to let him know that. "Growin' up without a brother or sister—and eventually without parents—makes one appreciate conversation as much as silence."

Trevik's smile faded. "Do ye wish me to leave?"

She shrugged, watching the lilting water further beyond the shore. "Ye can do what ye wish."

It was as indifferent a response as she could muster. But the truth of the matter was, she didn't know what she wanted him to do.

His sigh sounded above the waves. "Miss 'Ollow, please. I…" He broke off, and when he spoke again, his voice was strained, like the strings of an instrument pulled too tightly. "Listen, I know things 'ave been tense 'tween us, but if ye'd let me explain…"

She shook her head. "There isn't anythin' to explain. I took your suggestion and will leave. There isn't any reason to keep goin' on about it. Ye have your wish."

Bitterness hung on every word she spoke, and she cringed. She'd not meant to reveal so much of her feelings.

"Ye be wrong," Trevik said, his voice growing as he came to stand right beside her. "I ne'er asked ye to leave. I—"

"Ye didn't have to ask," she interrupted. "Your hint was as good as beggin'."

Another sigh, another moment of strained silence. "All right," he said, running his fingers through his hair. "All right. Ye be right. The truth is, I promised me crew ye wouldn't stay for long, so I was hopin' to prove to 'em that they could trust me words by gettin' ye to say when ye'd leave. That be all."

A weight raised just a fraction from Morvoren's shoulders.

"What be more," he continued, "I don't want ye to leave."

She scoffed, refusing to believe his words. They were too close to what she wanted to hear. "What a change of heart you've had. Did the Cardys' finally give ye their blessin' to have me stay?"

"No," he said, as if offended at the very idea. "I just

figured if ye leave, there'll be no one to stand between me and Poppy's chatterin'.'"

She snapped her eyes toward his to deliver another scolding, but she stopped when a smile played on his lips.

Despite her best efforts, a crack of light broke through her shell, and she bit her lip to keep her own smile at bay.

The tension between them eased, and Trevik moved forward, taking a seat beside her and resting his jacket between them. She fought the urge to shuffle away, though a hearty foot's length was already between them.

They sat in silence for a moment, both of them watching the sea's waves before he spoke again. "I was bein' truthful before. I really don't want ye to leave."

She glanced up at him, studying him for a moment but unable to find anything but the truth in their brown depths.

Instead of what she'd hoped to feel from hearing those words—peace and security—they only made the reality of her future even more dismal.

"Thank ye," she said softly, her anger and pettiness from before dissolving into the cool, evening air, "but I can't stay with ye and your family any longer."

"'Cause o' what I said?"

"Well, that certainly didn't help," she joked. "The truth of the matter be, though, that the longer I stay here, the more confused I become. As much as I like to pretend otherwise, I ain't a part of your family." She lowered her voice. "That be somethin' I shouldn't even want."

"Because we be fishermen?"

She nodded. "'Tis not what I want with me life." She said the words too forcefully, as if trying to convince herself she still believed them.

He shook his head in disbelief. "I'll ne'er understand ye, Miss 'Ollow."

"What?"

He waved a hand in a helpless gesture. "Ye've spent days

'ere in Tristwick with me family. Ye've worked in the cellars and 'ave eatin' pilchards for countless meals. Ye've sung with us and gone to church with us. I know ye 'ave your misgivin's based on what 'appened with your father, but…after all that ye've done 'ere, 'ow can ye not see the good we be doin'?" He picked up a spare stone beside him and tossed it into the water. "'Tain't like we be as bad as seiners or anythin'."

Slowly, she looked up to him. "Ye think ye be any better than seiners? Well, I 'ate to tell ye, but they feel the same about ye."

"And just 'ow do ye know what seiners be thinkin'?"

She bit her tongue. No good would come of her telling just how well she knew seiners.

"Miss 'Ollow?" His voice had changed from disbelief to suspicion.

Still, she remained silent. She'd fought so hard to keep this part of her past a secret from them all, fearing their judgements, their displeasure. And yet, in that moment, exhaustion overcame her. She was tired. Tired of the deception, tired of hiding moments from her past. After all, what did it matter now? She'd be gone soon, never to see the Honeysetts again. Perhaps if they truly despised her, it would be easier for her to leave them.

"Have ye ne'er wondered how I knew so much 'bout fishin' and seinin' companies before?" she asked.

Trevik narrowed his eyes. "I thought your father invested in drifters."

"He did at first. But that's only half of it." She looked out to the sea. "My uncle be a seiner."

CHAPTER THIRTY-SIX

*T*revik stared. He must not have heard Miss Hollow correctly.

"I...I don't understand," he stammered.

"My uncle owns a seinin' company," she repeated. "In St. Ives. That's how I know 'bout the laws and practices. The company my father invested in after the drifters? The man who led him astray? 'Twas Uncle."

Trevik blew out a slow breath, trying to comprehend what her revelation entailed. A seiner. She was related to a seiner. One he knew?

"In St. Ives?" he asked.

She nodded.

He knew of no seiners there. When he'd first pulled her from the sea, he'd thought of Miss Hollow as a potential spy from a rival seining company. Had his worries been accurate, then? No, that wasn't right. She despised her uncle and what seiners had done to her father. This hardly made any sense.

"Why did ye not tell me?" he asked, still processing her words.

"I was goin' to on the return journey from Sennen, but after the way ye went on and on 'bout seiners and how ye disliked them, I thought it best not to say anythin', fearin' ye'd really regret bringin' me back, even more than ye already did." She huffed a mirthless laugh. "'Sides, I know the fear of seiners be even stronger than Tristwick's fear o' sea-maids. I was afraid o' riskin' Edern Cardy *really* runnin' me out of town."

Trevik tipped his head to the side with a raised brow. He couldn't fault her for that. Still, the niece of a seiner, under his very roof for days without his knowledge.

Then another thought occurred. "The man ye were to marry…"

"Mr. Foss?"

He nodded. "'E be a seiner, too?"

"Yes. His father, more so. Uncle wanted to combine their companies to create a bigger seinin' business with more boats and nets."

"And your leavin' made that impossible."

"I s'pose." She looked off to the side. "But Uncle always gets what he wishes. He'll find some way to merge their companies. And Mr. Foss will go along with it if it suits him and his father."

Trevik blew out a heavy breath. The thought of Mr. Foss before had rankled Trevik's patience. Now, knowing he was a seiner, Trevik's insides burned.

"Are ye very angry?"

Angry? No, he wasn't angry. He was…he didn't know what he was. Frustrated, embarrassed, confused. Envious.

Envious? He frowned. How could he be envious of a man Miss Hollow despised? Was it merely because he'd recalled the fact that she'd given Mr. Foss a single possibility of her considering a marriage between them—and she hadn't given Trevik one?

"Ye have every right to be upset," she continued. "I'm sure you're wonderin' what else I be hidin', but I swear to ye, that be all."

He rubbed a hand down his face, ridding his mind of all thoughts of jealousy, of Mr. Foss, and of…of marriage. "Are ye certain?"

"Yes."

"Ye ain't hidin' the fact that ye really be a sea-maid?"

"Oh…'bout that…"

Their gazes caught, and the sparkling in her green eyes warmed him to his core. Finally, he smiled, shaking his head with a little laugh. "That would be the one thing that wouldn't surprise me if it be true."

They shared another smile before a heavy silence filled the air between them.

"I s'pose your despisal o' the trade be warranted, then," he said. "E'en more so than I thought."

She frowned, her voice soft as she replied. "Ye be a good man, Trevik. So be Gryffyn Bosanko and the other men I've met. I've no doubt your father was, too. But then, my own father was a good man 'fore he changed. I keep seein' my mother's face every time I imagine…" Her voice broke, and she shook her head, clearing away her emotion. "We were happy before. Mother begged Father to not go into business with Uncle, but he did so anyway. She ne'er wanted that life. She didn't ask for it."

Her eyes took on a faraway look, as if miles out to sea instead of seated right beside him. How he wished to bring her back, to soothe her worried brow and ease her concerns.

But then, was this not what he wanted? To have Miss Hollow leave so he could keep his promise to his men?

"I just…I can't be a part of it all any longer," she said. "There be too much greed. Too much heartache. Too much of men smellin' of fish. And I—"

She stopped abruptly, glancing at Trevik sidelong with regret. "I've done it again."

He waited for her to explain.

"My words gettin' me into trouble."

He sniffed, amused. "Worry not. I be used to ye tellin' me 'ow poorly I smell."

"That be the most frustratin' part of it all, though," she said. "Ye don't smell of fish."

Thoughts flooded his mind. Why was that frustrating for him not to smell? And if he didn't smell of fish, what exactly did he smell of?

He waited, but she didn't expound. "Do I smell o' sweat, then?"

She shook her head.

"Brine?"

"No."

"Hemp from the nets?"

"Not a great deal."

"Well, what, then?"

A smile played on her lips. "Wouldn't ye like to know."

Trevik would very much like to know, but clearly, the woman was simply stringing him along.

They sat in silence for a moment, Poppy's laughter with Mother drifting toward them from somewhere on the other side of the sea stack, his family no longer visible.

When had they wandered away so far? He really ought to join them, but he just couldn't get himself to leave.

"So…" Miss Hollow began. "Are ye goin' to run me out, now ye know the wicked truth 'bout me?"

"No." Then he leaned closer to her and bumped his shoulder against hers, warmth sparking in his chest. "But I'd run ye out for not tellin' I what I smell of."

She laughed. He could get used to such a lovely sound. He stared down at her, his eyes lingering on her golden wisps of hair, blowing across her brow in the wind.

She looked away quickly, and he did the same. Focusing on the woman's beauty wouldn't lead to anything satisfactory. She said herself that she'd never want his way of life.

"Really, though," she pressed. "Do ye think I be terrible now? I know how ye dislike your seiners."

He sobered, his heart thudding against his chest.

"What?" she asked, her voice softening.

She must have sensed the change that had come over him, his hesitance. He didn't like speaking of such things, but perhaps, since she had opened up, he could find the courage to do the same.

"I've ne'er told ye why I do dislike seiners as much as I do, 'ave I?"

She shook her head in silence.

He drew a deep breath, picking up another stone and rolling it between his fingers as the sun edged closer to the sea, ready to take its final plunge.

"Years ago, me father made an agreement with a man who owned a seinin' company. It was a fine year, and we didn't 'ave enough space at the cellars to store all the fish we caught, even after the excess we sold 'round Tristwick and elsewhere. So Father reached out to a few seinin' companies to sell 'is fish to 'em.

"One man agreed, but 'e ne'er specified the amount of fish 'e'd required. When the deadline came, the seiner asked for more, and when Father couldn't deliver 'em, the man threatened to break the contract unless Father could fill the order by the end o' the day."

Trevik grimaced, the memory at the forefront of his mind. He could see Father's frazzled expression perfectly, as if it had happened yesterday. "Desperate to not lose out on wages for 'is men, Father chose to work on a Sunday in the darkness. The seiner found out and rallied other towns to come to Tristwick. They made a barricade along the shore so the fish couldn't be brought from the gurries to the seinin' company—all 'cause they were displeased with Father fishin' on Sunday."

He shook his head, anger still riling within him. "We knew

'twas a risk, just as we knew we oughtn't be fishin' on Sunday, but Father was only doin' so for the good o' Tristwick."

"What happened?" Miss Hollow asked softly beside him.

"Father couldn't keep 'is end o' the bargain, and the seiner pressed charges. 'E was sent to debtor's prison for nigh on six months."

She released a dismayed sigh. "That be terrible."

"It was. Fortunately, the men 'round Tristwick rallied, and saved enough money to get 'im out. Still, Father's 'ealth was not the same after. And 'e died a few months later, still hurtin' from the environment he'd suffered while in gaol."

"I be so sorry," she said, her eyes not leaving his. "I…I see that it is no small reason for ye to mistrust seiners. And I wouldn't blame ye if ye don't trust me any longer, seein' as 'ow…"

"Seein' as 'ow ye be a seiner's niece?"

She nodded, and he gave a half-smile.

"'Tain't like ye be a seiner yourself. 'Sides, ye ain't givin' me no reason to mistrust ye."

How could he say such a thing? She'd given him ample reasons to not trust her. And yet, had she not told him the truth of everything? Even while fearing his disapproval?

Their eyes met, surprise lighting her face before a warmth as soothing as the sun melted across her features. He found himself powerless to look away, even when she did.

He followed the soft curve of her profile, the slight upturn of the end of her nose, the shadow of wrinkles beside her eyes as she winced, staring into the sunset. Her lips were arched up at the ends, as if she didn't know she smiled.

"Do ye e'er forget things 'bout your father?"

He started at her words. How long had he been staring at her? He looked away, clearing his throat. "There are certain things that 'ave faded from me memory. At times I think I be forgettin' what 'is face looked like. I s'pose that can't 'appen, though, as everyone says I look just like 'im."

She smiled. "That must be nice."

He watched her again. "What about ye? Do ye look like your mother?"

"She had green eyes like me, but Father was the fair one." She stretched her legs out before her, dangling them over the rock and leaning back on the palms of her hands. "It be the small things that I keep forgettin' that upset me. Like how Mother looked and what her voice sounded like."

His heart folded. He had the same issue with his father. And yet, he cared more about easing her burden than his own.

"The song ye sang that night on the beach," he said, "ye mentioned it bein' your mother's favorite?"

"Yes, she loved it. She had me sing it to 'er moments 'fore she died. Said it brought 'er some comfort with the aches. I can hear 'er voice each time I sing." She stopped, her eyes brightening as she turned to Trevik. "Oh. I hadn't realized 'til now. I *can* hear 'er."

The warmth in her eyes rushed over him again, and his chest swelled for the woman before him. Again, she looked away from him first. And again, he found it hard to follow.

"Did she' 'ave a voice like yours?"

"What, like a sea-maid's?"

He delivered an exaggerated, exhausted sigh. "If ye say so."

She laughed. "She had a voice better than one. She sang all manner o' songs to me when I was young."

The light from the sunset graced her smooth skin, painting it in subtle shades of rose pink, her lips a deeper red.

Trevik swallowed.

"What be your favorite song?" he asked. He wanted to— no, he *needed*—to know everything about her, the knowledge filling his empty soul, like water to a parched seaman.

She drew a deep breath. "Oh, there be so many. Obviously any that mention the sea. But…" She hesitated. "I think ye'll tease me for my favorite."

"Why?"

She raised a brow. "'Cause it be *Beware the Maid of the Sea.*"

He chuckled. "I should've known." He hummed a bit of the tune himself. "It do be a fine song."

"The very best."

"Ye ought to sing it, then."

She gave him a heavy look. "Are ye, Trevik Honeysett, askin' I, a mermaid, to sing right now? Happen I call on the waves to drown out Tristwick?"

"I s'pose that be a risk I be willin' to take."

She laughed, then faced the sea, her eyes shimmering as she drew a deep breath and began.

Trevik knew he shouldn't have asked her to sing. He remembered the trance that had come over him when he'd last heard her, and that had been when he'd despised the woman.

Now, as her smooth voice—as pure and clear as the Cornish waters in the summer—sailed out over the sea, Trevik was wrapped up in ribbons of warmth and light, and he was taken once again.

There's a mermaid I know who's as fine as can be.
She dwells at the far end of the deep, blue sea,
with her coral red hair, and her seaweed green eyes,
and a tail that stretches straight up to her thighs.

The melody was upbeat, no-doubt sung by ancient fishermen, keeping their eyes out for any sighting of the women who could destroy their boats.

"Are ye goin' to make me continue by myself?" she asked with a sidelong glance.

His heart skipped a beat, then raced to catch up. He shouldn't. He had no notion what would happen if he sang with this woman.

And yet, the sincerity in her eyes coaxed the song from his

lips before he could stop them, and together, they sang the chorus.

Beware the maid of the sea,
She's as wicked as wicked can be.
With her siren's voice, she gives men no choice
to fall for a maid as treacherous as she.

Their voices mixed in harmony, their smiles continuing as they sang the simple tune together. Trevik leaned back on his hands then, too, a soothing reverie wrapping up his life, his reality, as if he'd only ever existed with this woman seated beside him.

No one else had ever had such an effect on him. No one else had ever spoken to his soul like this woman seated beside him. He was just like the men in that song—helpless against this woman's pull.

Their eyes connected on and off as they sang, neither of them able to hold the other's gaze until finally, the song ended, their voices seeming to echo past them and out to the sea. The waves responded in hushed movements.

"Ye be a fine singer, Trevik," she said in a voice barely above a whisper.

"Even if I do smell o' pilchards?"

She laughed, looking up to the sky. "I told ye, I don't think ye smell of pilchards."

"Well, what else am I to assume if ye don't tell me otherwise?"

She remained silent.

"Be it another fish? Mackerel? Trout?"

She shook her head, clearly amused. "No, ye don't smell of fish at all."

"Then what be it? Wood? pasties?" He winced. "Onions?"

She laughed again. She studied him in silence, then finally stated, "Lemons."

"Pardon?"

She looked at him. "Lemons. Ye smell of lemons."

"Lemons." He mulled the information over in his mind. He supposed that made sense, seeing as how that was the item mixed in the common soap he purchased. But he'd been using it so often, he didn't really think he smelled of it. "Be that better than pilchards?"

"Oh, yes." Her eyes were upon him. "Far better."

Suddenly, warmth pressed into his finger. A moment of confusion settled around him. Had he lost feeling in his hand? Had the water from the waves somehow splashed upon the rock and warmed without his realization?

Then the truth settled around him. Miss Hollow. It was her warmth, her finger touching his.

His heart stuttered, and their eyes met. Why could he not look away? And more importantly, why was she looking at him in such a way? With…admiration, was it? Appreciation?

Then Trevik realized something for the first time. It was not Miss Hollow who was trapped in his net. He was trapped in hers—her net of lovely words and singing, of shimmering eyes and shining hair. Of beauty, her physical nature, and her very soul.

Yes, he was trapped. But this was a net he didn't want to escape. This was a net he wanted to stay in, comforted by her gaze, her kindness, her goodness.

He knew it was futile, imagining a life with a mermaid, imagining a life with Miss Hollow. She didn't want the only thing he could offer—the life of a fisherman's wife.

And yet he couldn't keep himself from her any longer. His soul craved hers, like roots craved the rain. Like petals craved the sunshine.

Like Miss Hollow craved the sea.

He needed to be near her, to feel her closeness and her warmth for himself, if only for once in his life.

CHAPTER THIRTY-SEVEN

*M*orvoren didn't know what had possessed her to touch Trevik's hand. It was as if they were tethered together by some invisible force, pulling them closer and closer.

Or perhaps it had nothing to do with an outside force and everything to do with her own desires—to feel him close, to touch him.

His eyes caressed her face, and the breath slipped from her lungs as his focus settled on her lips.

Trevik's ability to forgive, to look past her many shortcomings and her tumultuous past, were unmatched. Singing with him had captured her attention, stolen away her senses, and now, she wanted to do nothing more than kiss the man, to share in his affection and feel him close to her.

But she couldn't. She knew her desires to choose a different life would remain the same, and giving in to a kiss would only mislead Trevik, make him think that there was some hope between them, some chance to be together, when there wasn't.

With every ounce of power she had left within her, she tore her gaze away from his and stared down at her lap. "We ought to return to your mother and sister," she mumbled in a whisper.

Trevik watched her for a moment, and her heart constricted. She didn't want to hurt him, but surely kissing him would do so even more.

"Yes," he finally agreed, clearing his throat.

Without hesitation, he stood, retrieving his jacket. The cool wind from the sea wrapped around her, as if Trevik had been the one thing to protect her from it.

Instead of leaving her as he ought to have, Trevik, stood by her side, offering his hand to her. She hesitated before sliding her fingers across his palm, warmth and energy shooting throughout her arms and unsettling her heart.

He helped her stand with a firm grip, his fingers lingering around hers as their eyes caught once again.

Desire swirled in her chest, along with something else— something far more powerful, something she couldn't focus on.

His eyes flashed to her lips again before he looked to the rock they stood upon. She could see the battle within him, his fight between staying and leaving. How she wished she could help him, but she was fighting a battle of her own.

"Trevik," she whispered, "I can't...I don't want..."

His dark eyes met hers. "I know. Ye don't want the life of a fisherman's wife."

Hearing the words from his own lips made her pause. He understood. But then, how could he? *He* was a fisherman. His mother had been a fisherman's wife. He was surrounded by the trade. And still, he understood her plight?

Confusion fused around her thoughts. How could he understand when *she* didn't? For so long, she thought she knew what she wanted, and now, she couldn't make sense of her desires. How could she *not* wish for a life with this man? This perfect, wonderful, patient fisherman.

He gave her a half-smile, though pain flickered in his eyes

as he stepped away from her. "Ye be right. We ought to find me family."

His family. Could she ever be a part of his family? Or was she going to allow her fears to consume her future as they had once consumed her past—and now consumed her present?

"Wait," she whispered as he walked past her.

He stopped, keeping his focus on the sea. She opened her mouth to speak, but nothing escaped. What could she say when confusion bound her tongue?

"Worry not, Morvoren."

He tried to walk away again, but her hand shot out to catch his before he could leave.

"Morvoren?" she whispered. He'd said her name.

He closed his eyes, as if silently chastising himself. "Miss 'Ollow," he corrected.

But it was too late. Her name on his lips solidified her desires.

"I know what ye wish for," he said. "'Tisn't a life with I."

"How can ye know what I wish for, when I don't even know what I want any longer?" she asked.

"I thought ye said…" he began.

"I know what I said. But now, with ye…I hardly know."

Wariness still tinted his dark eyes, but she couldn't blame him. After all, she'd been adamant that everything about his trade repulsed her. Even still, with all of her intolerance, Trevik had helped her, encouraged her, and forgiven her.

And now, as she peered up at him, the truth in his eyes was evident. He *did* feel something for her, just as she felt something for him—something strong and powerful that coursed through her as warmly and thoroughly as the blood in her veins.

"Trevik," she whispered, but she could say nothing more, his eyes delving into her soul.

He drew a step toward her, then another and another until there was only a breath between them.

Still, tethers held her back, worries from their last meeting infiltrating her mind. "What about your crew?"

He shook his head. "It matters not what they think any longer. I be finished takin' their advice for what I want with me own life. I've the right to choose. Just as ye do."

"And…what do ye choose?"

"Ye already know what I choose, sea-maid." A half-smile spread across his lips, and he dropped his jacket haphazardly onto the rock. Slowly, he reached up, caressing her face with his fingers as soft as a whisper.

His caress was so gentle, the love in his eyes so apparent, that Morvoren knew in an instant what, rather, *whom*, he had chosen. Her eyes filled with moisture, a tear sliding down her cheek.

"Are ye all right?" he whispered, brushing the moisture away with a thumb.

She could only nod, raising her chin to better see him. She had never been better, she had never felt such a swelling in her chest, her heart overflowing with love.

His eyes moved between hers, then a moment later, they fell to her lips. Her mouth parted, and her breathing grew shallow as he neared.

He hesitated, his breath on her lips. Was he questioning his decision to draw closer to her? Worrying about what it would mean for their future?

Morvoren couldn't deny that she'd had the same worries, but now all she could think of—all she desired—was Trevik's kiss on her lips.

She reached up, slowly sliding her hands up his waistcoat before settling on the lapels. Curling her fingers around the fabric, she gave the slightest pull toward her.

That was all Trevik needed, for in the next moment, his firm lips pressed against hers.

Warmth wrapped around her limbs, his breath against her cheek as his mouth lingered against hers. A dizziness swam through her mind so greatly, she feared falling from the rock into the waves of the sea. But Trevik held her firmly, securely —yet more tenderly than she'd ever been held, as if she were the most important person in the world.

And she knew in that moment, that to Trevik Honeysett, she was.

He pulled back briefly, only to tip his head farther to the side and continue their kiss, a kiss she returned without hesitation. She moved her hands from his lapels, sliding them up until her fingers became tangled in the soft hair at the nape of his neck, their bodies drawing closer together.

A deep moan sounded in the center of his chest, vibrating against her own. His arms slipped around her waist, his hands pressed against the small of her back as he pulled her in.

Their kiss deepened, and she struggled to maintain hold of reality. This was a fisherman she was kissing, after all.

And yet, she found that she cared less and less about that fact. After all, he was so much more than a simple fisherman. He was her rescuer. Her confidante. Her friend. And somewhere along the way, she'd fallen in love with him.

Her fears slipped away of attaching herself to the trade, of Trevik becoming like Uncle or Father, only now realizing the ridiculousness of such worries. Trevik had more than proven himself to her with how generous he was, how loyal he was.

Could she truly bury her fears once and for all and accept a life she'd said she never wanted and turn it into the life she'd always desired—a life full of love, laughter, and the sea?

As if on cue, Poppy's giggling drifted toward them above the sound of the sea, interrupting the perfect world they'd created between them, and Trevik pulled back.

Instantly, they looked to where the sound of Poppy's laughter had come from, but she was still nowhere in sight.

Morvoren glanced back to Trevik, his eyes already upon her, and she smiled shyly, dipping her head.

"I s'pose we really ought to get back to them now," she murmured.

His hands moved from the small of her back, resting at her hips. "Indeed. If Poppy sees us, all o' Tristwick'll know what we been doin'."

She rested her hands on his chest. "And does it matter now if they know?"

"Not to I."

She searched his eyes for any hint of hesitation, but she could find nothing but sincerity in their depths.

He smiled, standing back to don his jacket before offering his arm to her. She took it, and together, they walked across the rock. The sun had halfway set, in a world of both sky and sea—just how Morvoren felt walking beside Trevik now.

"Thank ye."

She glanced up at him. "For what?"

"For not slappin' I this time."

A bubble of laughter escaped her lips. "So ye admit, then, that ye were kissin' me that day aboard your lugger?"

He gave her a knowing look. "Per'aps I did enjoy it." He straightened. "Once I found out ye'd survived."

She laughed again, and together, they progressed toward Poppy and Mrs. Honeysett.

They moved in silence, a perfect peace Morvoren hadn't known could exist settling around them.

The feel of his kiss still lingered on her mouth, and she pulled her lips in to hide the smile refusing to leave her. He'd been so good to her that evening. Patient and kind. Considerate and forgiving. He'd even shared more about his father.

Her stomach tightened at the thought of that dreadful seiner betraying the elder Mr. Honeysett in such a way. She couldn't believe anyone could be so terrible.

Then again, she could. It sounded exactly like something Uncle would do.

Her heart dropped. No, she was being ridiculous. There was no possible way that he...that Uncle...

An odd ringing occurred in her ears, drowning out the ocean, causing her to forget the feel of Trevik's arm beneath hers, though she still held onto him.

Don't ask him, she begged herself. *Don't ask the question ye don't want to know the answer to.*

And yet, her tongue had always had a mind of its own.

"Trevik," she began, forcing a light tone, though darkness clouded her vision, "when did your father make his agreement with that seiner?"

He gave her an odd look. "Nearly seven years ago."

Her throat tightened. Seven years. That was how long ago...But then, surely it wasn't the same location. "And it was here in Tristwick? Or...or St. Ives?"

"No, not at all."

Relief rushed through her limbs, weakening them to the point that she could hardly take another step.

Then Trevik continued. "The seiner reached out to 'im all the way from Mevagissey. Said 'e was hopin' to expand."

No. No, no, no. Morvoren squeezed her eyes closed, turning her head away from Trevik as bile rose in her throat, a storm wreaking havoc in her heart.

Seven years ago. Uncle had lived in Mevagissey seven years ago, before moving to St. Ives, before clutching Father in his claws.

But it had to be a coincidence. It had to be.

"What..." She could feel his eyes upon her, but couldn't meet his gaze, her chin trembling and eyes blurring. "What was 'is name?"

"Truscott," he said darkly. "James Truscott."

Her uncle's name on Trevik's lips sank deep into her mind, chilling her to her core. And yet, was she truly surprised? Did she ever really think she could escape Uncle?

"Are ye well, Morvoren?"

She forced a smile, grateful for the darkness the sun setting had finally allowed her. "Yes. Just…tired."

He nodded, pulling her in closer, making her heart ache all the more. She didn't know if he believed her, but he allowed her secrets to keep.

Morvoren needed to tell him. She knew that. But how could she find the words to admit that her uncle was the one who'd caused Trevik's father's an early departure from this life?

The words stuck on her tongue, emotion burgeoning painfully in her throat.

Why, why had heaven played such a cruel trick on her again? Why could she have not discovered the truth before… before she'd given her heart away to the one man who'd protect it? The one man who seemed to want her?

The one man who *shouldn't* want her?

CHAPTER THIRTY-EIGHT

*M*orvoren had slipped away from Trevik the moment they'd arrived at the Honeysett's home, sliding into bed and feigning sleep before Poppy had even come in to dress.

It was for the better. Morvoren knew she'd have to tell the family the truth, but the mere thought of looking them in the eye and admitting that her uncle was the man who'd ruined their lives…how could she do such a thing when she could hardly fathom the truth herself?

She prayed that sleep would provide her with the rest she needed to feel better prepared to tackle the issue on the morrow, but instead, she spent a restless night tossing and turning on her tear-soaked pillow.

By morning, the pulsing across her brow and the tightness in her neck could attest to the sleep she hadn't received. She dressed for church services and walked with the Honeysetts to the grey-stoned chapel.

Mrs. Honeysett's and Trevik's watchful eyes continuously shifted toward her as their small party walked across the cliff-side, then shuffled along the wooden bench in the church. She did her best to pretend that all was well, delivering feigned smiles and striving to listen to the sermon, all while ignoring the confusion Trevik must have felt for her odd behavior.

In truth, she didn't know how to behave around him any longer.

Trevik had chosen her last night. Above his crew, above his security, above everything. Deep down, she knew he would forgive her eventually, as would the rest of his family. But Tristwick, the Cardys, would not. Her presence had been divisive enough for the fisherman's crew in the last three weeks, and she couldn't put them through more.

She knew she shouldn't be blamed for Uncle's actions in regard to the Honeysetts. And yet, she still felt the sorrow of what her uncle did as if she had done it herself. And she knew, as much as the Honeysetts would profess otherwise, their hearts would ache each time they peered into Morvoren's eyes, for they would be seeing the niece of the man who'd killed their father.

How could she survive that? After everything she'd already put the family through, after risking their future with the fishermen of Tristwick, after putting herself upon the family and taking advantage of them. She couldn't do it, she couldn't allow that constant reminder to them that she was the connection to their pain—a pain that would never leave.

So *she* would leave.

The sermon stretched on for what seemed like days, Morvoren willing the vicar, Mr. Biddle, to sit down and cease his prattling off scriptures. As much as she dreaded speaking the truth, she knew the longer she waited, the harder speaking would become.

Finally, when Mr. Biddle ended and bade farewell to his congregation, Morvoren followed the Honeysetts from the church.

When she caught sight of Captain Kendricks near the

carriages, however, she held back from the Honeysetts and slipped toward the captain instead.

"Miss Hollow," he greeted with a tip of his hat to her.

"Good mornin', Captain," she greeted, looking over her shoulder.

Mrs. Honeysett and Trevik were speaking with the Bosankos, Poppy with a friend of hers. None of them had yet to realize that she'd slipped away.

"I trust your ankle has fully recovered," the captain said, smiling kindly.

"It has, thank ye. I...I be wonderin', has Mrs. Honeysett spoken to ye about any connections ye might have in Bodmin? Anyone who might be in need of a maid or shop assistant?"

At this point, she'd settle for a job in the workhouses. Anywhere would suffice, so long as she could no longer hurt the Honeysetts.

"Oh, yes. She did mention that. I have a few friends in the navy who have settled there, quite happily. I believe one of them might need maids at an inn he's acquired. I'm not certain about the others, though..."

She nodded. "Do ye know if the work be needed soon?"

She glanced over her shoulder, her heart skipping as Trevik's gaze found hers. Blast. She'd been hoping to do this without notice.

Captain Kendricks winced. "I'm afraid I don't know when he'd need help. I will be sure to ask him."

"Thank ye. I...I'd prefer to depart from Tristwick as soon as possible. I'll be ready the moment he needs me."

The captain narrowed his eyes a fraction. "I'll be sure to let him know. But I...forgive me, I thought my wife might have spoken of it. Did Mrs. Honeysett not mention to you possibly working at Golowduyn during the winter?"

Morvoren swallowed the ache back down in her heart. That was before, when Mrs. Honeysett would have wanted

Morvoren to remain within walking distance. "She did. But things have changed. I think it'll be best for me to work farther away from Tristwick."

Concern creased in his brow. "Are you well, Miss Hollow? Is there anything we can do for you?"

But she was already backing away. "I be fine, thank ye, sir. Give my best to your wife."

Then she spun on her heel and made for the Honeysetts. Trevik's eyes were still on her. Before she could even reach them, Poppy waylaid her, linking an arm through hers and redirecting her to the cliffsides.

"Come, let's walk 'ome together. Mother and Trev always take far too long."

Morvoren sent a fleeting glance toward Trevik, then followed Poppy without the heart to protest. At least Poppy's constant talking would prevent Morvoren's depressing thoughts from continuing.

And yet, she couldn't have been more wrong. Poppy hardly said a word as the two girls traversed the cliffside. Above pointing out a few dolphins hopping in and out of the water in the distant shores, her tongue was as bound as Morvoren's.

Dark storm clouds glowered on the horizon, a furrowed brow to the sea's blue face. A storm would be fitting for Tristwick at that moment. Nothing was going right.

"Morvoren," Poppy said, speaking through her musings, "be somethin' wrong today?"

Yes. Everything was wrong today. "Not at all. Why?"

"I just…ye've been more silent 'an usual, and I just wanted to be sure ye were well."

Morvoren's smile faded. She couldn't keep up the façade any longer. But she also couldn't tell the girl on her own. Poppy would need the support of her family around her.

"I be well. I just…have somethin' to speak with your family about. When we all get home."

To *their* home. Morvoren didn't have a home anymore.

Poppy's face fell. "About your leavin'?"

Morvoren chewed the inside of her lip, giving a simple nod.

With a nod of her own, Poppy faced forward. "I thought, after seein' ye and Trev last night…"

Morvoren swallowed the emotion rising in her throat. What could she say to help the girl understand without giving away one of Morvoren's darkest moments?

"'Tis complicated," she finally settled with.

Poppy didn't respond.

Morvoren longed to help the girl who'd been the sister she'd never had, but any words she had would not be the words Poppy wished to hear, for they were the very words Morvoren wished to say—"I'll stay."

Instead, she looped her arm around Poppy's and drew close to her, willing their proximity to comfort one another since words could not.

They rounded the bend in silence, their mood as sullen as the approaching clouds, as cold as the wind bringing them in.

Then Poppy gasped, stopping in her tracks as her free hand reached up to clutch Morvoren's arm.

"What is it?" Morvoren asked, her eyes swinging about before settling where Poppy had focused her attention.

Tristwick had finally come into view, and on the stretch of beach visible with the low tide, stood Lieutenant Harris.

Morvoren's own heart picked up, feeling for Poppy's plight.

"What 'e be doin' 'ere?" Poppy whispered, though from where they stood, there was no chance of the lieutenant hearing them. "'E ne'er comes to this beach to walk. Only Tregalwen or Golowduyn."

"Have ye spoken with him since he told you he was leavin'?"

Poppy shook her head, her eyes still fixed on him.

"Then," Morvoren began, "could he be here to talk with ye?"

"Oh, no. I…" Poppy's brow lifted the slightest fraction. "Per'aps? But no."

They stood in silence, neither moving. "What do ye want to do, Poppy?"

Poppy merely shook her head in silence. Slowly, Morvoren watched the hope and excitement flee from her eyes, Poppy's shoulders lowering and frown returning. "I'll just go 'ome. 'E can't be 'ere for I. I be too young. Too…silly."

Morvoren's heart twisted, feeling the girl's agony as her own. But how could she allow her dearest friend—her *only* friend—to give up hope?

"Poppy," she said fervently, turning to face her directly, "ye love that man. Ye have since the moment ye saw him, regardless of ye bein' young or not."

Tears sprung to Poppy's eyes, and she struggled to blink them away.

"All that matters now," Morvoren continued, "is makin' the decision that ye won't regret for the rest o' your life. Whether that be goin' down and speakin' with him…or goin' home and ne'er seein' him again."

With a brow tainted with worry, Poppy glanced back down to the man. She wrestled with herself in silence, chewing at her lip before she gave a firm nod. "I…I need to speak to 'im. Even if 'e don't feel the same as I, I want 'im to know."

Morvoren smiled, her chest swelling with pride for the young woman's courage. "Then go, speak with him."

Poppy's eyes widened with excitement, a smile growing on her face. She backed slowly away, pausing with another glance at the lieutenant.

"Go!" Morvoren cried out with a laugh, and Poppy giggled, turning away and skittering down the curved path of the cove.

Morvoren watched her retreat for a moment, smiling to herself before the solitude she'd felt for years crept back around her. Watching Poppy leave was only a fraction of the pain she was going to feel. She'd grown so used to having this family be her own, how was she ever going to leave them? How was she ever going to survive without them?

"Morvoren?"

She jumped, whirling as Trevik walked up behind her, the growing turmoil of the waves below having drowned out any sound of his approach.

"Trevik," she breathed. Should she run straight to his house? Plead illness? Escape Tristwick without telling him anything of what she knew about the connection between her uncle and Trevik's family?

No. She would face her fears with courage—just like Poppy had.

"Where be your mother?" she asked, glancing over his shoulder. Matters would be easier with her there. She wouldn't be as furious as Trevik would be.

"She took the shorter route 'ome," he said. He stopped a few feet away from her, clearly hesitating before speaking again. "Are ye well this mornin'?"

She nodded, strapping a smile as best she could to her lips. "'Course."

He didn't believe her, worry still creased in his brow. "I just thought that ye were upset about…last night."

Morvoren swallowed, wincing at the needles prickling her eyes as tears filled them. She'd hoped to avoid any mention of the previous night. The memory of the joy that had been ripped from her grasp burned too greatly to recall.

She looked at the storm swiftly approaching, light flashing in the dark clouds like a candle flickering in the night sky. "Last night? Oh, that was nothin', surely," she said, if only to convince herself that she'd imagined the connection between them. After all, if it was only her imagination, leaving Trist-wick would then be far easier for them both. "How can I be upset about a simple kiss that meant…meant nothin'?"

When he didn't respond, she dared a glance in his direction. In an instant, she wished she hadn't. Hurt tainted his brown eyes, and his brow lowered.

"'Twas nothin'," he said, repeating her words.

Her lips parted, the breath escaping her lungs and leaving her chest concave. How could she have called their kiss, their affection, his *choosing* her…nothing?

His eyes hardened further as silence continued, and she saw the truth too late. Trevik might have forgiven her for the connection she held with Uncle, but he could never forgive her for what she just said.

He fixed his eyes on the sea. "What were ye speakin' about with Captain Kendricks?"

Did he know? "I was askin' for work…in Bodmin."

"Ye be leavin' then?" he asked, his voice flat.

She nodded. "I…I can't stay. 'Tisn't because of ye. It be—"

"Don't." He shook his head, walking past her to stand at the edge of the cliff overlooking Tristwick. "Don't pander to I just to spare me feelin's."

"I'm not," she said. "It be somethin' else." She drew a deep breath. She needed to tell him the truth about Uncle. He needed to understand.

"What excuse do ye 'ave for I, then?" he asked, though his tone hardly sounded as if he wished for an answer. "That ye 'ave another friend expectin' ye? That ye be too tired to process fish all day?"

Morvoren frowned, forcing herself to not become hurt with his words. "No, that isn't—"

"Do ye just wish for a wealthier 'usband, then?"

"Stop," she said, tears flooding her eyes, "ye know that isn't—"

"Be that Poppy down there?"

She blinked, her head spinning with his swift change in topics.

She leaned to the side to see past his tall figure. Below, Poppy still spoke with the lieutenant on the beach. The waves grew closer toward them as the storm approached.

Another movement from the corner of her eye caught her attention, and she peered up at the opposite side of the cove. A figure cloaked in black stood on the ridge directly above the Honeysett's home, his top hat and walking stick standing out from his silhouette.

Walking stick. That…that was the same man she'd seen before, when the pilchards were brought in. Was it not?

Unease swirled within her. "Trevik, do ye know that—"

"What she be doin'?"

Morvoren hesitated. Trevik was clearly changing topics to avoid her words, but then…

She paused, the man slowly walking away from the cove before he disappeared down the opposite side.

His departure did nothing to settle her nerves.

One problem at a time, she told herself. First the truth, then the questions. She couldn't wait a moment longer to speak with his family altogether. He needed to know now.

"Trevik, last night, when ye were speakin' of—"

"Did ye tell 'er to go down there?"

She paused. Why would he not let her speak? "No. She chose to go."

His sharp eyes were upon her, and Morvoren's chest tightened. Weeks ago, Trevik had warned her to stop encouraging Poppy's love of the lieutenant, to avoid them both getting hurt. Would he think she'd put Poppy up to it? *Had* she?

"And what she be sayin' to 'im?"

Her breath escaped in short bursts, the world around her spiraling so swiftly, she could hardly remain upright. "She… she be sharin' her feelin's with him."

His eyes hardened, his lips thinning as he pulled them in. "Ye encouraged 'er to go down there, didn't ye?"

She opened her mouth, but she couldn't protest his words.

"I told ye," he said. "I told ye not to encourage it."

"She wanted to," she repeated. "She knew she'd regret not speakin' with 'im, so she chose to do so of her own accord."

He turned back to his sister. "She'll regret doin' this," he muttered.

Morvoren moved to stand beside him, Poppy and Lieutenant Harris still facing each other, their expressions impossible to read from the distance. "Ye can't know that, Trevik," she said, forcing a softened tone. She could only imagine how he must be feeling—protective over his younger sister, defensive over Morvoren's thoughtless comments. "Per'aps the lieutenant will stay for her."

Trevik's laugh was bitter, chilling her more thoroughly than the wind. "That man'll go to sea whether Poppy shares 'er feelin's with 'im or not." He looked away. "Life and responsibilities can't be so easily set aside. And we both know that feelin's be as fleetin' as the sunshine."

As if on cue, the clouds covered the sun above, and another chill rushed over her limbs.

"I told ye not to interfere." His voice was taut, as if it would snap at any moment. "She be too young to know love, and too young to know the pain that'll come from it."

Was he still speaking of Poppy? Morvoren wasn't so sure. "She isn't too young to know her own mind, though."

Thunder rumbled nearby, rolling over her words in a deep, throaty moan.

Trevik scoffed again, then fell silent as his eyes focused on the beach. Morvoren followed his gaze, watching as Poppy slowly backed away from the lieutenant, then the girl turned on her heel and fled up the pathway leading toward the houses of Tristwick. The lieutenant called after her, his voice barely above the sound of the rushing waves, but Poppy continued her escape.

Her actions could only signify one thing—rejection.

Trevik's eyes were upon Morvoren's in an instant, condemning and hard. "Ye see? This what comes o' your meddlin'."

Then he swiftly turned and followed after his sister.

Her mouth dropped at his accusation. She tried to hold her tongue, tried not to become defensive at his blaming her, but her exhaustion, her sorrow, and her insecurity melded together like smelting copper, and her indignation soon masked the ache she felt at his words.

"This ain't 'cause of me, Trevik," she said, trailing after him, taking two steps for his one. "I was simply tryin' to help her, unlike what ye've done. Kept her locked away, stoppin' her from flirtin' with anyone."

Trevik didn't respond, simply stormed ahead of her.

"She be sixteen, Trevik," she said. "She doesn't have to get married now, but for heaven's sake, ye ought to allow the poor girl to fall in love if she so desires."

Thunder boomed closer, hollow and deep, and she glanced up to find the sky entirely consumed by the dark clouds that had been on the horizon only moments ago.

"Did ye hear me, Trevik?" she questioned, still trailing behind.

"Yes, I 'eard ye. And I think ye be as daft as me sister."

She pulled back at his slight. She knew he behaved only out of concern for Poppy's well-being, but she couldn't abide his stubborn pride.

"Better to be daft than without any feelin' at all," she bit back.

A flash of light flickered above, then a crackle of thunder resounded around them, followed by a deep rumbling as constant as the waves of the sea. Thick raindrops speckled the ground first, a foreshadowing of the storm to come. Large droplets dotted the pathway and fell against the tip of Morvoren's nose as they neared the cellars.

As they neared the cobbled pathway down to the beach, Lieutenant Harris crossed their path, and he stopped, staring at them both.

Trevik glowered at him. "I told ye not to 'urt 'er, 'Arris," he said. "All those months ago. I warned ye."

The lieutenant opened his mouth, no doubt to defend himself, but Trevik drove forward up the pathway toward his home without a glance back.

Morvoren hesitated but a moment. Trevik had spoken with Lieutenant Harris about Poppy? She eyed the young man, his strong jaw twitching, his eyes reflecting the pain she could only imagine was the same within Poppy's. Did he love her, then? Or was he merely sorry for injuring her?

He turned pleading eyes on Morvoren. "I never meant to hurt her. I...I would never wish..."

Morvoren longed to stay with him, to hear what had happened between him and Poppy, but Trevik was already making headway up the cliffside. She couldn't allow him to confront Poppy alone. The last thing that girl would want is for her unsympathetic brother to chastise her behavior after such a devastating loss.

"I know ye didn't," she said, backing away. "Excuse me."

Then she left his haggard expression and charged forth toward Trevik. She couldn't feel remorse for Lieutenant Harris. At least not yet. She had to ensure Poppy was well. She had to tell the Honeysetts about Uncle. She had to pray that Trevik...that Trevik didn't hate her.

She kept with his pace, though one step behind, passing a few residents of Tristwick who watched them with curious gazes. The rain had ceased its warning by the time they neared the other cottages, now falling down in droves. She spotted Edern Cardy smoking his pipe, ever-watchful at his usual place just outside his door.

"Quite a storm, Trev," the man said ominously above the rain, the waves, and the thunder.

Trevik stormed past him. "It'll pass. 'S'cuse me, Edern."

The old man's spindly eyebrows shot up in surprise, then they scowled once again as he looked to Morvoren.

Typically, she would reserve her kindest of smiles for the man, hoping an extra dose of sugar would help him realize she truly was nothing to worry about. But that morning, she didn't have the patience.

She shook her head, delivered an audible groan, then strode straight past him, arriving at the Honeysetts' door just moments after Trevik.

"Where be Poppy?" Trevik asked, removing his cap.

Morvoren followed him inside, shutting the door behind her as Mrs. Honeysett came out from the kitchen with a sorrowful look.

She glanced warily down the corridor, then continued in a softer voice. "She don't want to talk, Trevik."

Morvoren stood near the doorway, wiping water from her brow. This was not how today was supposed to go. How could she tell the Honeysetts about her uncle if they were all upset with her for only trying to help Poppy?

"What 'appened?" Trevik asked, his back turned to Morvoren. Whether he did so on purpose, she couldn't say.

Rain slapped against the windows in the sitting room, but Mrs. Honeysett spoke all the quieter, wiping her hands dry on a spare cloth. "She told Lieutenant 'Arris 'ow she felt about 'im. 'E thanked 'er, but…that ain't the response ye want after pourin' your 'eart out to another."

Morvoren's heart ached for the girl. Had she truly been the cause of it? Should she have told Poppy to keep her feelings to herself?

Regret mounted before her, an incredible elevation she couldn't hope to surface—especially when Trevik turned to face her. Rainwater beaded down his face, his scowl ever fierce.

"See what ye've done?"

His words sliced through her defenses, rendering her speechless.

"Trevik, what are ye goin' on about?" Mrs. Honeysett asked at once, but Trevik ignored her.

"Ye couldn't leave 'er be, could ye? Ye 'ad to meddle in 'er life, just as ye've meddled in everyone else's 'ere in Tristwick."

Lightning flashed outside, lighting the Honeysetts' home, but a darkness entered Morvoren's soul.

"Trevik," his mother warned, but he didn't stop.

"I was tryin' to help her," Morvoren said, her voice muted as thunder cut her off. Lightning continued flashing out of the window, a constant flicker of brightness in the otherwise muted colors outside. "I only wanted her to have the chance to choose her own life away from—"

"From Tristwick?" he finished for her. Another flash, another clap of thunder. "From fishermen? When are ye goin' to realize that not everyone needs a life away from we? That not everyone be as *prideful* as ye?"

He spat the word out with disgust, and it slid down Morvoren's conscience, tainting her soul. Another blinding light lit the area around them, thunder not hesitating a moment to follow directly after.

Prideful? He'd called *her* prideful? Trevik knew pride hadn't kept Morvoren from respecting fishermen. Her uncle and Father had.

"How could you—"

"Trevik!"

Mrs. Honeysett's exclamation cried out above another clap of thunder, and they turned to face her.

Instead of her eyes upon the two of them, arguing like the children they were claiming not to be, she focused out of the window.

In turn, she and Trevik faced the glass, as well, and Morvoren's heart dropped as smoke billowed up from the cliffside.

"The lugger?" Mrs. Honeysett asked.

But Trevik was already on his way out of the door.

CHAPTER THIRTY-NINE

*T*revik didn't look back to see if he was followed.

He didn't have time—time for his argument with Morvoren, time for Poppy's heartache, time for his *own* heartache. He needed to get to the docks to see if his lugger—their one link to surviving that winter—was going up in flames.

Lightning streaked across the sky, breaking off in crooked lines, like branches of a tree alight with fire. Thunder clapped in succession, and rain blew in sheets with the gusting wind. Still, he ran forward, holding up his hand to ward off the rain pelting his eyes.

"Trevik!"

The shout came from up ahead, and he peered through the rain as Gryffyn ran toward him, waving his arms in the air. "It be the lugger!"

Trevik cursed, catching up to him. "'Ow bad?"

"The mainmast be struck," Gryffyn said between panting breaths. He turned back around, racing down the mud-caked pathway with Trevik. "It still be standin', but I don't know for 'ow much longer."

With no mainmast, the lugger could still sail—albeit much

slower. Still, if anything happened to the other two masts... their winter, their future, would hang precariously in the balance.

As they passed the cellars, more men joined them—including Enyon Penna and the Cardys—their mothers, wives, and sisters straggling behind with a few children in tow. The ocean now covered the thin stretch of beach with crushing waves as dark as the clouds above, reaching close to their feet as they moved down the cobblestones.

"Collect the buckets!" Trevik shouted behind him. "Start an assembly line to douse the fire!"

The group splintered into two, most of the women sprinting to the cellars to collect the buckets. Trevik forged ahead with Gryffyn and the Cardys, the Roskelleys joining alongside them just as they rounded the ridge and the dock came into view.

Trevik's heart wrenched at the sight. Black smoke plumed up from the lugger despite the pouring rain, and fire lapped at the rigging. Just as Gryffyn had said, the mainmast teetered dangerously upright, a large crack visible midway down.

"That mainmast needs securin'," he shouted to his men as they raced forward. "It can't withstand—"

A large gust of wind blasted into him, stealing the words from his lips as salt water sprayed across his face. His footsteps slowed as he was no longer able to see in what direction he ran.

Wiping the moisture from his eyes, he attempted to speak again, pushing back against the wind, but a great cracking split through the air, and his words ended. The lugger tossed back and forth, wave after wave lunging at the bulwark of the *Pilferer* until finally, the half-attached mainmast teetered back too far.

"No!" Trevik shouted.

But it was too late. Neither his word nor his will could stop the post as it fell, crashing into the mizzenmast and over the hull. The rigging snapped and cracked as it broke from mast to mast.

As if the weight of the structure had fallen directly upon his chest, Trevik skittered to a stop, his legs nearly giving way as he could no longer draw in a breath. He knew he needed to move forward, to secure the rest of the lugger, but his feet refused to move.

They couldn't sail with a single mast, nor could they fish without sailing. They could hardly afford the repairs now required, either. So how was he to keep all of Tristwick fed through the winter without a lugger?

He squeezed his eyes closed. The time for worrying was gone. They still had one more mast standing, and he would not allow that to fall, too.

Forcing his feet to move, Trevik propelled forward, his crew right behind him. "We 'ave to stop the blaze," he commanded. "Cut down the riggin', toss anythin' overboard that might catch fire."

His men nodded at once, and together, they forged ahead, waves and wind and rain lashing upon them and the *Pilferer* as they finally boarded the lugger.

Trevik had known a split second of worry over his crew not listening to his commands. After all, the trust between them had been severed. But to his relief, they worked in unison, all in want of the same thing—to ensure the livelihood of the *Pilferer*.

The Roskelleys went straight to work at the foremast, removing the rigging and tossing it overboard to douse the flames in a flash. Trevik and Gryffyn ran about the fallen masts, cutting flaming ropes and flinging them into the waves as well, giving no care to the blazes that burned their hands.

The others removed the valuables from off of the deck—belongings, blankets, smaller hand nets, and spare leads—tossing them down to the assembly line that had formed across the beach.

Soon enough, buckets of water were brought toward the lugger next, each member of Tristwick performing their duty to ensure the security of their future.

Trevik's fingers burned, his lungs weak from the smoke. Soot fell against him as he worked, but he wouldn't stop. Doing so would only allow his thoughts to stray to the woman at the center of the assembly line. The woman who worked alongside as if one of them.

The woman who had broken his heart.

Morvoren quickly swiped at the rain streaming down her face, then accepted the next bucket of water before heaving it to Poppy, who retrieved it with swollen, red eyes. Morvoren couldn't decipher if she cried still for the lieutenant or for the *Pilferer* now.

Mrs. Honeysett delivered the next pail to her, and Morvoren passed it along. She longed to do more for the men, more for the lugger, but as the crew tossed flaming ropes overboard, swaying back and forth on the rocking boat, she knew she would only get in the way.

Lifting another bucket toward Poppy, Morvoren stole a glance at the lugger. She couldn't believe the damage the boat had sustained so swiftly. How was Tristwick to survive the winter?

A few women who were not a part of the assembly line collected the items the men had dropped and carried them to the cellars for safe keeping. As they walked by, Morvoren overheard their conversation.

"Least the nets 'ad been taken out o' the lugger 'fore," one woman said.

"But what good be drift nets with no lugger to shoot 'em?" another responded. "The pilchards'll be long gone 'fore any repairs'll occur."

More words of fear and dismay passed between them, and Morvoren listened until they moved out of earshot. She glanced around her, accepting another bucket as she noted older women standing by, unable to help with the assembly line as they peered up at the lugger, tears in their eyes.

Across the cove, others stood just outside of their homes, hands over their mouths in dismay, the small faces of their children pressed up against the windows as worry creased their young brows.

Another bucket was passed, then another. The wind died down, and the lightning lessened, the flames aboard the lugger no longer visible.

Finally, Morvoren glanced up at Trevik. Soot covered his weary face, and rainwater dripped from his cap. His brown jacket was soaked through due to the downpour and the waves slipping over the lugger.

"Be there nothin' else we can do?" she asked Mrs. Honeysett, accepting another pail.

She merely delivered a sorrowful shake of her head. "Pray, dear. That be all we can do."

Morvoren had never heard the woman so devoid of hope, the knowledge thoroughly crushing her heart.

But if praying was the only thing to be done, then pray, Morvoren would. And she prayed harder than she ever had before.

She prayed for the lugger's deliverance, for the storm to soften and for the funds to be had for the lugger. She prayed for Trevik's softened soul and understanding, for Poppy's broken heart. Then she prayed for her own courage—the courage she needed to leave this family, this community, behind.

Minutes trickled by, and the assembly line ended. A few of the men left the lugger, trudging toward the women with heavy feet and heavy hearts, their faces and clothing soiled from the flames.

"Come," Mrs. Honeysett said. "There'll be many injured who be needin' mendin'. We can see to 'em in't lofts."

Poppy followed her mother, but Morvoren remained behind, her eyes fixed on Trevik where he lingered on the dock, his back turned to her as he faced the *Pilferer*.

He removed his cap, ran both hands through his sopping hair, then dropped his arms limply at his sides.

Morvoren wanted to do nothing more than wrap her arms around his sunken shoulders and tell him that everything would be all right.

Instead, she remained where she was. She didn't have the right to comfort him. Not anymore. Because to him, she wasn't anything any longer.

CHAPTER FORTY

*T*revik stared at the wreckage before him, the weight of Tristwick's future upon his shoulders. The lightning had lessened, though the rain still bled from the clouds.

How could this have happened? How could his life have changed so swiftly? One minute he was arguing with Morvoren about Poppy, and the next, he was watching his life go up in flames.

Before long, Gryffyn left the lugger, coming to stand beside Trevik and peering up at the boat.

"What'll we do, Gryff?" Trevik asked, shaking his head. His hands stung from where he'd gripped the burning rigging.

Gryffyn gripped Trevik's shoulder. "We wait out the storm," he said, his deep voice gruff. "Then we assess the damage and recoup when we can."

"And if we can't afford the repairs? Or the lugger can't be fixed for months?"

A long pause preceded Gryffyn's words. "Then we do what we must to survive. We've 'ad worse winters with little to no pilchards at all. We'll survive again."

Gryffyn's words whispered logic to Trevik's anxious spirit. But then, this winter wasn't supposed to have been a battle.

This winter was supposed to give them time away from their constant struggles, to bless them from the work they'd put in year-round.

"I just don't see 'ow—"

"I warned ye this would 'appen."

Trevik's words ended abruptly as Edern walked toward him, his grandson in tow. Rain poured down from the brims of their caps as Edern stared at Trevik condemningly.

"Go 'ome, Edern," Gryffyn said beside Trevik, crossing his arms over his barreled chest. "Ain't no good'll come from speakin' o' this now."

"No, I'll speak of it when it pleases me," Edern growled back, turning to Trevik again. "Ye shouldn't 'ave given that girl refuge in your 'ome. This storm, the lugger bein' damaged, it be a direct result of 'er presence 'ere, and ye know it."

A weary weight pressed hard against Trevik's shoulders, as if the waves battering the lugger now battered his soul. Morvoren had cut him to his core. Even now, their conversations echoed in his mind, recurring over and over again like the rain pelting his face.

The kiss meant nothin'.

She be leavin' for Bodmin.

She don't like fishermen or their way o' life.

She'd wounded his pride and broken his heart. He'd offered her his world, and she'd turned her back on him, stripping him of his hope and leaving his soul exposed.

Gryffyn's clipped words cut through his thoughts. "Ye can't truly be so daft as to believe that girl be the cause o' all this, Edern."

"Can't I?" Edern challenged. "Then 'ow can ye explain 'er behavior now?"

Trevik drew his attention to Edern, but the man merely tossed his head to the cliffside. Slowly, the four of them peered up to where he motioned.

Standing at the top of the cliffs near Trevik's home, Morvoren peered down over the wreckage. Her chin was level and her footing sure, despite the wind whipping her sodden skirts against her legs and pulling her blonde strands loosened from her chignon behind her with the storm. Her expression was hardly visible from their position near the dock, and yet, from where they stood, Trevik couldn't deny what he saw any longer—a pleased, proud, and scorned mermaid.

"That right there," Edern said, his voice low and threatening, "that be the sight of a sea-maid lordin' o'er 'er work, proud o' what she done to us all. And ye…just…let 'er." He spaced out his words, each one a dagger into Trevik's back. "Ye've forfeited the trust we 'ad in ye, Trevik. Jowan and I will no longer be workin' with ye."

Trevik pulled his gaze from Morvoren, darting at once to the Cardys. He'd feared them doing this from the beginning, but to have Edern actually saying the words stung harsher than he'd ever thought. Would they be the only crew members who'd leave? Or would others soon follow? "Edern, ye can't be serious."

The man didn't respond, Jowan either. He didn't look as sure as his grandfar, but his eyes were wary as he peered up at Morvoren.

"As if ye could find work elsewhere," Gryffyn growled, clearly having none of the Cardys' nonsense.

"We've taken work with the Trenary seiners. Started a few days past."

"What?" Gryffyn barked out. "Ye traitorous—"

"They give fair wages," Edern said without remorse. "Fair wages and more work 'an Trevik can offer we now."

Trevik swallowed his disgust. Surely he could still salvage this. "Edern, ye've worked with me since me father—"

"I 'ave," he interrupted again. "And I would've continued, were we followin' your father. That man 'ad more sense. 'E

323

ne'er would've forfeited the security of 'is men for a sea-maid's song."

Gryffyn lunged toward Edern in an instant with a snarl, but Jowan—still a full head shorter than Gryffyn, but just as thick round the shoulders—stood before his grandfar.

"Ye don't know Trevik's father then at all," Gryffyn said, his fists clenched as he peered over Jowan's head. "Locryn ne'er would've let the maid suffer as ye wished 'er to. Trevik's done 'im proud, and the rest o' the crew, too."

Trevik remained silent through it all, Edern's words once again breaking his spirit.

Edern merely sniffed in derision at Gryffyn's defense of Trevik. "Proud? 'Is father'd be ashamed." Then he walked away, Jowan right behind him as they trekked up the cliffside toward their home.

"Don't listen to 'im, Trevik," Gryffyn advised. "'E be mad, as ye well know."

Trevik tried to nod in agreement, tried not to become too dismayed. After all, what did it matter if the Cardys left if he didn't have a lugger to fish from anyway? But when he cast his eyes up at Morvoren, who still stood standing on the cliffside, his heart hardened.

Edern was right. He'd been right all along. No, Morvoren wasn't a sea-maid, but Trevik never should have allowed her to remain in his home. Not only had he chosen her above his crew, he'd encouraged her to stay, chose her over the Cardys, even though he knew an upheaval would certainly occur.

And how had she repaid him? How had she repaid him for all of it? She still chose to leave. She'd kissed him, ignored him, injured his sister, and now…this, standing above a grief-stricken Tristwick without a care in the world, all while his crew crumbled to pieces because of *her*?

She may not have brought the storm upon them, but she'd brought another type that was even more destructive.

And he'd had enough of it.

CHAPTER FORTY-ONE

orvoren couldn't find that blasted salve anywhere. She'd gone through every space in the Honeysetts' kitchen, and still, it was nowhere to be found.

She knew Trevik and the other men must have burned themselves in the chaos of the fire and storm, and treating them with salve would be the least she could do.

She shuffled aside the plates and bowls in the top shelf of the hutch again, but when her search came up empty, she leaned back with a sigh.

What was the use? No matter what she did, if she found the salve or not, nothing could make up for the blow Tristwick had been dealt that day. Perhaps it was better to keep the knowledge of her uncle for another time, when the news wouldn't be so painful.

Or perhaps—

The front door opened, and she whirled to face who she prayed would be Poppy.

But of course it wasn't.

"Trevik," she breathed.

He closed the door behind him and removed his cap before his eyes finally found hers.

The blood drained from her face. She'd never seen him so…emotionless.

"Are ye well?" she questioned, her voice timid.

"What are ye doin'?" he asked, ignoring her question with his own. He dropped his sopping cap onto the bench nearby without removing his gaze from hers.

"I-I was hopin' to find the salve," she explained, annoyed with her hesitance. "For your burns." Why did she feel like she'd been caught in the act of some heinous crime?

He moved forward in silence, water trailing behind him and puddling across the wooden floor.

She stepped aside as he opened the hutch and instantly produced the salve.

Her cheeks burned. She'd checked that shelf multiple times. How had she not seen it?

"Thank ye," she mumbled, holding out her hands for the salve, but he moved past her, maintaining his hold of it.

"I'll take it down meself," he said. "Ye've done enough already."

Morvoren pulled back, watching as he retraced his steps to the door. "What do ye mean by that?" she asked.

"Ye know what I mean." He picked up his cap and placed it atop his wet hair.

Something swirled within Morvoren's heart. Anger, indignation, misunderstanding. Had he not heard what she'd been meaning to do with the salve? It was for him. For his burns. How could he insinuate…

"As a matter of fact," she said, coming up behind him, "I *don't* know. I was findin' that salve for ye."

He paused with his handle on the door. He spoke over his shoulder, only his profile visible. "Ye promised that me family wouldn't be 'urt by your stayin' 'ere."

Morvoren blinked, shifting her feet with unease. Her wet clothing still clung to her person. "Ye be referrin' to Poppy again? Trevik, I told ye. I didn't mean to."

He shook his head. "It be more 'an Poppy. Ye've wounded me whole family. And all o' Tristwick beside."

She frowned. "All of Tristwick? How do ye figure…" Her words faded away as realization settled in her mind. "The storm. Ye…ye think I caused it?"

His silence spoke more than words ever could.

She stared off to the side in a daze. "Ye can't be serious. Surely ye don't believe that *I* called this storm in. That I set your lugger ablaze."

"No, I don't believe ye called in the storm. But I do believe ye to be the cause of the turmoil within me crew."

Her chest tightened.

"The Cardys 'ave decided to leave the *Pilferer*," he said, turning to face her with hardened eyes. "They signed up to work with a seinin' company."

Morvoren's mouth dropped open. "What?" she breathed. "And they did so 'cause of me?"

He raised his brow, as if to say she should already know.

She shook her head in dismay. "I ne'er intended to…Had I known in the beginnin'—"

"But ye did know. I as good as told ye what'd become o' me crew if ye continued with your games." He shook his head. "'Course they be leavin'. 'Twouldn't be a surprise if more left, too. After all, who would want to work for a drifter who be such a poor judge o' character as to allow the likes of ye in 'is 'ome?"

His pointed gaze pinched her heart. How could he say such things, how could he blame her for the superstitions of his crew? Had he not promised only yesterday to choose her above them all?

Or had he merely said what she'd wanted to hear?

Her muscles tensed. "Is that how ye truly feel?" she asked, her voice hard. "Or how *they* feel?"

He shrugged. "'Appen they be the same."

She shook her head, building the walls back around her

heart to prevent herself from feeling the pain he'd inflicted upon her. She knew he was lashing out because she'd hurt him, too, but tears still sprung to her eyes. "What happened to ye trustin' me, knowin' I'd ne'er do anythin' to hurt any of ye?"

His lips set in a firm line, and he took a step forward, leaning toward her. "What 'appened to ye not carin' whether I be a fisherman or not?"

Her words from the evening before weighed on her chest until she could hardly breathe. Clearly, he assumed her departure, her not wanting to be with him, was because he was a fisherman. "I don't…'T'ain't—"

"Don't give me your lies, Morvoren. Ye've made your desires perfectly clear. Why else would ye still be leavin' after we kissed? After I promised ye that I'd give ye anythin'—" His voice cracked, catching in his throat.

Morvoren's heart broke at the sound. She knew he had feelings for her, but she'd already decided that leaving would be for the benefit of them both—for the benefit of his whole family, even Tristwick. Surely this evening was proof. The departure of his crewmates, the town being pulled apart because of her presence, Poppy being hurt, Trevik in pain.

And yet, she couldn't leave without his knowing the real reason for her departure. "It be somethin' else, Trevik. Somethin' else that's kept me from—"

He waved a passive hand, cutting her off. "It doesn't matter. Either way, ye'll still be leavin', won't ye?"

He peered down at her, his eyes searching hers, as if he was lost at sea, searching for any sign of hope for survival.

She opened her mouth, longing to deny his statement, but she couldn't. "I…I *can't* stay. There be more to it than ye bein' a fisherman though."

He barked out a laugh that chilled her. "No there ain't. It be as simple as that." He moved closer to her until she had to crane her neck to still look into his eyes. "But ye go on ahead and do what ye do best—run away. And ye just keep runnin' away 'til ye find what it is ye want in life. 'Cause we both know, ye ain't goin' to find it with I."

Tears spilled down her cheeks. It wasn't true. None of it was true. She'd been happier with him than she'd ever been before. He was the person she wanted to spend her life with.

But would he still want her after all of this? Knowing the truth about everything?

"Trevik," she said, her chin quivering. "My uncle…"

"Don't." He held up his hand, silencing her once and for all. "I don't want to 'ear any of it." He looked away, as if meeting her gaze would make him weak once again. Straightening to his full height, he continued. "Ye be right. Your leavin' will be for the best. For all of us."

Trevik regretted the words the instant he said them. And when he finally dared a look at Morvoren again, the tears trailing down her cheeks and her quivering chin threatened to undo him.

Take back the words, Trevik. Beg 'er forgiveness. Beg 'er to stay.

But he held strong. She didn't want him—she'd as good as said that again this evening—and no amount of begging would change her mind.

"Do ye really want that?" she asked in a whisper. "Do ye really want me to leave?"

He opened his mouth, ready to say the words again, to tell her directly that his life would be easier without her. He was ready to say goodbye. Ready for one less troublesome person in his life.

So why would the words not come? He peered down at her, the vulnerability in her eyes cutting him as deep as any knife.

"I don't…" he began, but the chance to finish his sentence never came.

The door opened behind him, and they turned as Poppy and Mother filed into the home, their faces ashen.

"Be it the lugger again?" he asked at once, glancing behind them to the door they held open.

Why was he continuously having this fruitless argument with the love of his life—the love who'd never choose him—when his lugger was still in danger?

But as Mother stood to the side, another figure appeared in the doorway, bringing with him the cold darkness Trevik had hoped to never feel again.

There was no mistaking the man's black eyes and long, drooping nose. "Mr. Truscott," Trevik stated, gritting his teeth. Anger surged throughout him as memories of the man before him intermingled with memories of Father. "What do ye think ye be doin' 'ere?"

The man appeared taken aback for a moment, but Trevik knew it was all a ploy to play the innocent fool. He'd done the same with Father seven years before.

What was he doing there? And why now, especially after so long?

"That is a sorry welcome, indeed, for an old friend," came Mr. Truscott's buttery smooth voice.

He took a step within the home, but Trevik moved forward at once to prevent him. "I told ye last time that ye were no longer welcome in our 'ome."

A flicker of annoyance flashed over the man's face, but he straightened, moving back to stand out in the rain, water dripping down from the brim of his top hat.

"I will respect your wishes," he said. "It is, after all, your right and your property to do with it as you wish. But then…" He paused, looking over Trevik's shoulder. "I trust you'll extend me the same courtesy and return to me my own property."

His property? What the devil was the man on about? Trevik had nothing of his, and he was sure of it. He'd sworn to never entangle himself with Mr. Truscott after what he'd done to Father.

But when Trevik caught the man's eyes focused at the back of the room, he slowly looked over his shoulder.

Morvoren stood still, her face white.

"Morvoren?" Trevik questioned, his heart tremoring.

She didn't say a word, yet somehow, he already knew the truth.

"Yes," Mr. Truscott said from the doorway. "My niece."

CHAPTER FORTY-TWO

*M*orvoren couldn't breathe, the ground swaying beneath her feet, her world crumbling around her. Uncle. How had he found her? And *why* had she not told Trevik the truth earlier?

Confusion littered his brow as he glanced between Morvoren and her uncle—the man Trevik only knew as the person who'd destroyed his family.

She'd asked him if he'd truly wished her to leave, and she thought she'd seen hesitance in his eyes. But now she knew what his answer would be.

"Come along, Morvoren," Uncle Truscott said. "It is time to go home."

His smooth voice brought back the memories she'd done so well to stifle. His anger and constant threats, his cruelty and barbaric behavior. Keeping her from food, reading, friends, the sea. She couldn't go back to it all. She couldn't live such a life again.

"Morvoren be your niece?" Mrs. Honeysett questioned, her stunned expression making Morvoren feel even smaller.

"Of course she is," said Uncle with a smirk. "Can you not see the family resemblance?"

Morvoren grimaced at his amiable tone. He knew very well he was not related to her by blood, yet he always knew just what to say to charm those around him into believing that he didn't have a cruel bone in his body. But surely the Honeysetts knew better.

Still, her breathing shallowed as she imagined what they must think of her. Would they assume the worst—that she'd known of the connection between Uncle and the Honeysetts all along?

Their eyes were upon her, questioning, fearing, until she finally found her voice.

"I didn't know," she said, looking at each one of them before settling her eyes intently on Trevik. "I swear I didn't know." Her voice broke, tears flooding her eyes as emotion made it impossible for her to say another word.

Trevik frowned, though she couldn't tell if he believed her words before he turned back to her uncle.

"It would appear that my being here has unsettled the lot of you," Uncle Truscott said with a genial smile. "I take it my niece did not inform you of our connection?"

Silence.

He sniffed. "Unfortunately, this does not surprise me. My niece has always had a penchant for falsehoods."

Morvoren, desperate for the truth to shine past Uncle's darkening lies, took a step forward. "I didn't know of any connection until yesterday." Trevik's eyes darted toward her in question, and she lowered her voice. "When ye said his name, I-I panicked. I feared, if ye knew he was my uncle, ye'd ne'er wish to see me again." She glanced to Mrs. Honeysett and Poppy. "That any of ye would e'er wish to see me again."

"I take offense to your words, niece," Uncle said in mock offense from the door. "To suggest that a relation to me would be considered upsetting to you is beyond hurtful."

She ignored him, still speaking with the family, desperate for them to know the truth. "I was goin' to tell ye, but one thing after another kept happenin'. Church, Poppy, then the lugger."

"Ah, yes," Uncle piped in. "Terrible business, a lugger being destroyed during a storm. We saw the smoke on our way here."

Morvoren did her best to ignore his words, but when they finally registered, she paused. "We?"

He gave her an innocent look, though something lurked behind his dark eyes. "Oh, yes. The thief taker I hired to find you." He gave a short laugh. "You weren't easy to discover, I give you that, dear niece."

Morvoren's stomach sloshed back and forth. The man with the walking stick on the cliff. Of course he'd been sent by Uncle.

"Now," he began again, still in that sweetened tone, though she knew a snake lurked beneath, "I've grown weary of this little cove. Come, Miss Hollow. It is time for you to return home. Your Mr. Foss is waiting for you quite anxiously."

Morvoren started. She'd been so upset about Uncle's connection with the Honeysetts that she'd nearly forgotten about Mr. Foss.

Uncle paused then, observing her head to toe with a curled lip. "Heavens. We'll have to do a great deal to make you presentable for Society again, I daresay. But never you mind. I am up for the task, as usual."

He'd peered at her in that same degrading way countless times before, even if she was dressed for a ball. She'd never received his approval, and she never would. So why would she ever consider going back with him? Especially to Mr. Foss, who didn't care whether she lived or died?

"No, Uncle," she said, acutely aware of the Honeysetts' eyes upon her. "I ain't goin' back with ye."

His smile slowly faded away. "I see you've lost all manners

while here, including your proper tongue. Do stop speaking so heinously and come here at once."

Morvoren could always tell when Uncle's time for games was spent, his voice turning as cold as his eyes.

"Miss Hollow," he said again, taking a step forward.

Trevik's hand immediately shot forth, preventing his entrance into the house. Uncle narrowed his eyes at Trevik, a silent battle taking place between the two before Trevik spoke. "I was smaller when ye saw me last, Truscott. Would ye like to see 'ow I've grown?"

Uncle hesitated, then retreated back with a subtle step. "Still harboring grudges, I see." He clicked his tongue in disappointment. "I thought we'd be able to move past this. But I see my hopes were in vain. Ah, well. I will respect your wishes if you would be so kind as to respect mine and deliver my niece to me. If not, I'll gladly enter…"

Morvoren held her breath, but Trevik didn't move. "This be me 'ome now. I'll not allow ye to terrorize me family or anyone else within these walls."

His family…or anyone else. That was the category Morvoren had fallen into. Not someone he cared about, not even his friend. Simply *anyone else*.

Uncle narrowed his eyes, glancing between Morvoren and Trevik before a smile stretched tightly across his lips. "Oh. Oh, I see now. You've gone and fallen in love with a fisherman and his family." His cruel chuckle echoed unwelcomingly about the walls of the Honeysetts' home. "How amusing. I suppose your dream to be parted from fishermen altogether was not realized after all then, was it, my dear niece?"

Morvoren's chest tightened, and she gave up hope altogether of being able to breathe freely in his presence. "It matters not what happened," she said, hating how quiet her voice sounded compared to his. "All that matters is that I'll not be returnin' with ye this evenin'."

His smile faded once again. "Is that so? And you think that

you'll stay here? That you'll be *wanted* here? After all you've done to deceive these fine folks?" He faced the others. "I assume my niece has spoken of her great dislike for all fishermen? That she said she'd rather die a thousand deaths than to ever live with one again? Surely you do not wish to house such a deceptive girl any longer."

Morvoren cringed. She'd said those words the night she'd left Uncle, referring to Mr. Foss.

What would the Honeysetts think of her? They were sure to throw her out now.

Mrs. Honeysett stepped forward first, her lips in a grim line. Then she came to stand beside Morvoren and wrapped her arms around her. "Yes. We do still wish to 'ouse 'er. And we'll do so for as long as she wishes to be with us. For Morvoren be our family now."

Poppy was quick to join on Morvoren's other side, pumping her head up and down and lacing her arm through Morvoren's.

Their actions were enough to undo all of Morvoren's defenses. Had Uncle not been there, watching her every move, she would have crumbled to the floor in a weeping mess. These women, they were everything she'd ever wished for in a family. Even though they now knew of her connection to Uncle, even though she'd not told them herself, they were still willing to defend her.

But Trevik...

She hesitated, willing herself to keep her eyes off of him. He didn't need to make a stand in regard to her. He was the last person who owed her anything.

Still, he stood by the door, watching Uncle with a dedicated gaze.

"Well," Uncle said with a heavy sigh, "it would appear that you have found some loyalty in these rats."

Morvoren raised a lip, about to speak out in protest for his cruelty, but he pushed on.

"It is a shame, though," he continued, "for now that you've found a family of your own, I fear I'll have to take you from them all the same."

No. No, he was bluffing. He couldn't take her from them. He would never be able to move past Trevik.

"You see," he said, "I was going through my belongings after you left, and I discovered a few missing coins from my possession. I assume you took them?"

Her heart thudded mutely in her ears. She *had* taken them, counting them as payment for all he'd ever done to injure her. But of course they would come back now to haunt her.

When she remained silent, Uncle stared hard at her. "You are aware of what the punishment for thievery is, are you not, Miss Hollow?"

Her throat tightened as if on cue. She was more than aware.

But surely Uncle was jesting. To threaten a hanging for a few coins? That was not an idle warning any longer. "I can give ye back your money, Uncle," she said, her voice quivering.

"All of it?"

She hesitated. "Yes."

"At this moment?"

He was calling her bluff. She bit her cheek. "Half of it now. Half of it later."

Uncle sucked in a breath, as if truly disappointed, but Morvoren knew it was all part of the act. "Shame. If it was all of it—"

"We'll pay the other 'alf."

Trevik's deep voice cut through Uncle's like a ray of sunshine, and Morvoren's heart stumbled to the floor, rolling straight toward Trevik. But he wouldn't pick it up. He'd already done enough.

"Do you know how much she took?" Uncle asked.

"Don't matter," Trevik returned.

Morvoren ducked her head, humbled at his willingness to help her, even after everything.

Uncle's eyes shimmered. "Hmm yes. You do have an admirer, Miss Hollow. So your trickery strikes again."

No one responded. All ears remained on Uncle to see how he'd respond to their offer to pay Morvoren's debt.

She wasn't surprised when he slowly shook his head. "I think my niece would learn her lesson better if she paid the debt in full herself."

Morvoren raised her chin, refusing to allow him to see her cower, though her insides churned.

Mrs. Honeysett made a sound of disgust. "Ye wouldn't do such a thing to your own niece, your own flesh and blood, send 'er to the gallows for a few shillin's?"

Uncle tugged at his coat sleeves and peered up through the rain still pouring down around him. "The thing is, this young woman isn't my flesh and blood at all. Her mother was the sister of my dearly beloved." He raised his brow. "Truth be told, Miss Hollow has been a thorn in my paw from the moment she arrived under my care."

"Then let 'er be with us," Mrs. Honeysett said, her arm around Morvoren tightening.

Her embrace simultaneously strengthened and weakened Morvoren.

"Oh, I'd never consider such a thing," Uncle said. "I fed her, I clothed her, I educated her. And now…" His eyes returned to Morvoren's, dark and greedy. "Now I'll receive my payment for all the years of torment." His smile disappeared. "Now, Miss Hollow. You will return to St. Ives with me and marry Mr. Foss, or I'll press charges against you for thieving."

Morvoren knew if he threatened such a thing, he'd make good on his promise.

"We'll not allow such a thing to 'appen," Mrs. Honeysett said. She turned, pressing her hands to Morvoren's cheeks and speaking in lowered tones. "Ye don't listen to 'im. Ye'll stay with us. We'll keep ye safe."

Morvoren's breathing grew ragged, though she tried to listen to the woman's words.

Uncle always receives what he wants.

He laughed from the door. "As if you can stop the law, Mrs. Honeysett. I can only imagine what the constable would charge you all with, if you refuse to give me back my ward." He appeared thoughtful for a moment. "Although, I suppose it doesn't matter if one of you gets sent to gaol, as you've no lugger to fish with anyway."

Morvoren turned disgusted eyes on him. "Don't threaten them," she said. "Not after what ye've already done to them."

"You mean the elder Mr. Honeysett? Oh, that man practically carried himself to gaol. Couldn't keep his promises. But then what can you expect from a drifter—"

Trevik's fist landed squarely in Uncle's jaw, ending his words and sending him flying backward. He fell onto his back on the muddy pathway, rain pelting his face as his hat tumbled a few paces away.

Morvoren gasped, and Mrs. Honeysett clasped her arms around Morvoren all the tighter as she cried out. "Trevik, no!"

But Trevik was advancing once more on the man, his fists balled as he stood over him, grabbing him by the jacket and hauling him to his feet.

"Say one more word about me father, and ye'll find yourself at the bottom o' the sea," Trevik said through clenched teeth.

Uncle sputtered, rain falling across his lips. "Unhand me, you-you worthless boy, or I'll have you in gaol, too."

"Trevik, let 'im go," Mrs. Honeysett said from the doorway, the three women rushing forward.

Trevik kept hold of the man's lapels before pushing him away, and Uncle stumbled before righting himself.

He straightened his jacket smartly, then reached for his top hat which he promptly replaced atop his head. "Now," he said, facing Morvoren, "you will come with me, or I'll have you thrown in gaol—and your precious fisherman, too."

Morvoren's heart dropped. Had Uncle planned this from the start—provoking Trevik to an act of violence so Uncle would have his way?

She shook her head, tears falling freely down her cheeks. There was no other way. She loved Trevik, more than life itself. And she couldn't injure him and his family further than she already had.

This was no longer about fearing if the Honeysetts wouldn't wish for her to live there—for they'd already forgiven her. This was about her desire to have Tristwick and the Honeysetts thrive by keeping Trevik with them.

More than anything, how could she ever allow Trevik to be sent away by Uncle—just as the elder Mr. Honeysett had been—and then die because of it?

Morvoren had been unable to help them years ago, but she could help them now.

Silence reverberated between their small group, the waves rushing below the cliffside, soft thunder rumbling in the distance.

Then she took a step forward.

"No," Mrs. Honeysett said, seeming to know Morvoren's thoughts before she said a word. "Ye can't go with 'im. We'll find a way."

But Morvoren shook her head. "I'll go with ye, Uncle."

The satisfaction on his face—blood trickling from his nose and his lip beginning to swell—was enough for Morvoren to wish to strike him, as well, but she simply continued speaking.

"I'll go with ye only if ye promise—in writin'—that ye'll leave the Honeysetts alone. And…and that ye make the repairs to their lugger."

Uncle barked out a laugh. "I'm afraid you have no bargaining chips to make that happen, my dear niece."

She raised her chin. "Once I become engaged to Mr. Foss," she paused, swallowing the disgust rising in her throat, "you'll not mention a word of my thievin', for fear of it tarnishin' your relationship with my future father-in-law—your future business partner."

His smile faded, his eyes narrowing.

"Without that over my head, nothin' will stop me from makin' Mr. Foss ever regret takin' me for his wife." She raised her chin, forcing her voice to remain steady. "Then I'll do whate'er it takes to ruin the merger 'tween your two companies."

The look of hatred in his eyes appeared once again, and like an old friend, she welcomed it. This could only mean that she'd struck a nerve within him.

"But," she continued, "if ye agree to the arrangements I've set, I'll return with ye. I'll change my accent, my behavior. I'll encourage the union 'tween the two companies and ne'er make ye regret another thing. And I'll…I'll be an obedient wife to Mr. Foss."

Her eyes flickered to Trevik's, and his heavy frown wore at her heart.

This is the only way you'll be safe and your family protected, she thought, willing him to read her mind.

"No, Morvoren," Mrs. Honeysett whispered again from behind, but Morvoren kept her gaze steady on her uncle's.

Finally, he jerked his head to the side, as if cracking his neck in irritation. "Very well. You have an agreement." He turned to Trevik. "Meet me at the Golden Arms this evening. I'll send for my man of business, and we shall sign the papers before we set off for St. Ives."

Trevik didn't respond. Poppy sniffled behind her, but Morvoren nodded. "I'll retrieve my things."

She made her way into her room—Poppy's room—and gathered her few belongings, taking one last sweeping glance before she returned to the sitting room with her portmanteau.

Uncle still waited outside in the pouring rain, wiping his bloody nose with his handkerchief, but the Honeysetts had converged within the house, awaiting Morvoren.

"Ye can't go with 'im, Morvoren," Poppy whispered, tears streaming down her face.

Morvoren took her hands in hers. "I don't want to leave, especially ye. But I can't see your family be injured on account of me or my uncle any longer." She reached forward, embracing her tightly. "I'll try to write to ye."

She released her, then moved to Mrs. Honeysett. "We can fight this," Mrs. Honeysett said softly. "Ye don't 'ave to go."

But Morvoren knew Mrs. Honeysett understood her plight. "I thank ye for all ye did for me. I'll ne'er forget your kindness."

"Come, Miss Hollow," Uncle called from the doorway. "I've grown weary of being in this rain."

Morvoren humbly followed her uncle's voice, pausing in the doorway where Trevik stood guard. She looked up at him, and his brown eyes found hers in an instant.

"I be sorry for everythin'," she whispered. "And I 'ope ye can forgive me one day."

Trevik's jaw twitched as he clenched his teeth, but he said nothing in return.

She longed to wait, to force something from his lips, but Uncle wrapped his long fingers around her arm and pulled her out into the rain.

She followed him down the pathway, past the Cardys', where Edern stood outside, watching with a curious gaze. He needn't worry about Morvoren any longer. She'd never be back to Tristwick. She'd never see him or the Honeysetts again.

At the thought, she looked over her shoulder, not caring if she tripped on the trail as Uncle led her swiftly to where his carriage awaited.

The Honeysetts stood outside their home, Mrs. Honeysett

and Poppy embracing with silent cries. Trevik stood a few paces in front of them, as if he'd followed after Morvoren. Their eyes connected, and despite the distance, she could see the ache in his gaze, the longing for her to stay.

And that was enough for her.

She faced forward again at Uncle's tugging, and she obediently followed, though she knew she was walking toward a future she'd never wanted—a future she should have known she couldn't escape.

CHAPTER FORTY-THREE

*T*revik made his way to the Golden Arms that evening with a heavy heart. He didn't usually travel across land at night, the lugger being his normal place of residence.

But that life seemed to be in his distant past now.

He entered the small inn, looking around for a moment before spotting Mr. Truscott—the filth of the earth—occupying a table at the corner of the inn, taking a drink of brandy.

Another man sat beside him, but Morvoren was nowhere to be found. Not that Trevik expected her uncle to allow them to see each other.

It was better this way, though. Trevik didn't know if he could bear seeing her without taking her in his arms, throwing Mr. Truscott flat on his back once more, and warning the man to never lay his hands on the love of his life again.

It had taken everything within him not to do the very same hours before, but Mr. Truscott had delivered too many threats, and Trevik had had to concoct a plan if he had any hope of helping Morvoren's situation.

As Trevik approached, Mr. Truscott waved him over to the

table, motioning for him to take a seat across from him. "This is Mr. Oates. He will be overseeing the signing of the agreement to ensure all is in order."

Trevik couldn't be more grateful for the rush Mr. Truscott seemed to be in. He was ready to be finished with the whole business himself.

Mr. Truscott pushed forth a piece of paper, sprawling script across the length of it. "As you can see, my niece has already signed at the bottom, agreeing to her part of the arrangement."

Trevik looked at the document, scanning the words. Ever since Mr. Truscott had taken advantage of Father, Trevik had made it a point to ensure he was learned enough in the ways of contracts and business arrangements. He was grateful for that now, for Mr. Truscott seemed to wish to confuse Trevik with his wording, what with how loquacious the document was.

Finally, he reached the end, Morvoren's scripted signature at the bottom imprinting itself on Trevik's heart just as it had the paper.

He'd been shocked when he'd discovered her to be Mr. Truscott's niece. But not once did he blame her for not saying so. After everything they'd been through, after how harshly Trevik had spoken with her, how could she have entrusted him with such knowledge?

How he wished that she had. Instead, he was stupid enough to believe that she was leaving for Bodmin because she didn't love him, because she didn't want to accept a life of a fisherman's wife, not because of her connection with her uncle.

How foolish he'd been. How foolish they'd both been. If they would've just shared their feelings, not given in to the hurt they'd caused each other, they might have been together still.

"As you can see," Mr. Truscott said, bringing Trevik back

to his dismal reality, "you will receive the materials for your lugger in but a few weeks, and I will forgive Miss Hollow of her debt. In exchange, my niece has agreed to be a dutiful wife to Mr. Foss." He paused, leaning forward just a fraction. "In all matters."

Trevik fisted his hands beneath the table, refusing to give in to the man's goading this time.

"Might I suggest you sign swiftly?" Mr. Truscott continued. "I am every bit as anxious to be done with this business as I am certain you are."

Mr. Oates offered the pen and jar of ink to Trevik, but he merely stared at it. "Thank ye, but that'll not be necessary at the moment."

Mr. Truscott's severe scowl appeared instantly. "What do you mean, Honeysett?"

"I will not be signing that agreement."

Mr. Truscott's eyes darkened, as they had while looking at his niece. What devil had possessed this man to behave so cruelly to his own family?

"Did ye truly think I'd sign this after what ye did to me father?"

Mr. Truscott's nostrils flared, but he drew a deep breath and placed a calm smile on his face. "Mr. Oates, will you excuse us for a moment?"

"Certainly," the man mumbled, and he looked almost relieved to leave the tension-ridden table to enjoy a drink at the bar by himself.

Once they were alone, Mr. Truscott took a sip of his brandy. "You cannot leave the past to die, can you?"

"Clearly ye can't either in regard to your niece."

His smile turned grim. "You can't imagine the half of my trials with a niece like her. Since the moment she stepped over my threshold, she has caused me nothing but grief. I'm certain you can attest to the amount of trouble she is, no matter your feelings for her."

Trevik would have smiled in a different situation. How often had he called Morvoren trouble? How often had he lost patience with her, cried out with annoyance due to her behavior? But then, those things that drove him mad were also the things he loved most about her. Her passion, her honesty, her loyalty to those she loved.

"So tell me, Mr. Honeysett," Mr. Truscott continued, "why will you not sign the agreement?"

Trevik leaned back in his chair, forcing a look of ease as opposed to his insides roiling. "I've another proposition for ye."

"Do go on."

"We can amend what ye 'ave now, drop the requirement to repair me lugger, so long as ye add in that ye won't charge me for assaultin' ye, and…that ye've been paid back in full what Morvoren owes ye."

Trevik was never going to accept the man's funds for repairing the *Pilferer*. But feigning to accept the agreement before now allowed him to ensure Morvoren wouldn't be beholden to her uncle forever. At least, so he hoped.

Mr. Truscott raised a brow, pressing a hand to his swollen lip. "You're asking me to lie? After all, I've not been paid—"

Trevik dropped a coin purse onto the table, the pile landing with a thunk. "Take what she owes ye."

Mr. Truscott stared with a smirk. "You are aware that Miss Hollow has already signed the agreement. Even if we make a new contract between the two of us, the other still stands. She will marry Mr. Foss."

Trevik was more than aware. The very thought of Morvoren marrying anyone other than himself—especially Mr. Foss, of all people…he could hardly stomach it.

He'd wracked his brain for another solution, but Mr. Truscott was right. Morvoren had already made the agreement. And if Trevik knew one thing about that woman, it was that once she set her mind to something, she couldn't be persuaded to do otherwise.

"I be well aware, sir," he said.

"And you are willing to let your lugger remain broken, only to ensure I do not condemn Morvoren?"

Trevik nodded.

"But why would I condemn her, if she's already promised to marry Mr. Foss?"

"Why would ye, indeed," Trevik countered with a pointed look.

If he knew one thing about Mr. Truscott, it was that the man would hold anything over Morvoren's head to get her to do as he wished. But Trevik couldn't bear the thought of Morvoren living such a life.

"So what say ye?" Trevik asked, growing impatient with the man's silence.

"You must have fallen for her siren's song hard, boy," Mr. Truscott said. "I understand it well, for my wife held the same appeal—beauty behind trouble." His eyes took on a faraway look, but he blinked it away before nodding. "Very well. I accept your proposition."

He waved Mr. Oates back over, and the man reluctantly left his drink to join them at the table. Trevik watched in silence as he drafted a new contract. He forced himself to remain calm, attempting to convince himself that this was better than not doing anything to help her, but as each moment ticked by, and as each new word was written, he grew more and more unsettled.

How could he let Morvoren go through with this? Surely there was something else—anything else he could do to rescue her from a life with such men as Mr. Foss and Mr. Truscott.

Mr. Truscott signed the agreement first, then he slid it toward Trevik.

He read over the words multiple times, struggling to focus. His eyes blurred as he imagined what her life would be like now—changing her accent again, doing whatever her uncle asked of her, being controlled by Mr. Foss, never being allowed to swim in the sea.

How could he willingly allow her to make such a sacrifice for him? For it *was* for Trevik. His lugger, his family, his community, his freedom.

The pen he held hovered above the paper, ink threatening to drip from the tip. Feeling broken and more humbled than he cared to admit, he looked to Mr. Truscott and spoke with a soft voice. "Please. Ain't there anythin' I can offer ye to allow Morvoren to choose 'er own life?"

It was as if Mr. Truscott had been expecting Trevik to crumble to pieces. "Now that you mention it," he said with a slow smile, "I have been hoping to make an arrangement concerning the oil from the fish runoff."

Trevik couldn't shift the weight on his chest as the man continued.

"I will allow Morvoren to remain with you, if you deliver to me the oil you expend weekly. You take ten percent, I take ninety."

Trevik scoffed. That was hardly a fair arrangement. "Be reasonable," he growled.

But Mr. Truscott raised his hands in retreat. "I am being *more* than reasonable. As I said, I've expended a great deal of time, energy, and my hard-earned wealth to improve my niece to the point where she would be worth marrying. I expect to make all of that in return tenfold." He smiled. "So, what say you to my arrangement?"

Trevik held his tongue. He knew what the man was doing, touting his control over the situation because he knew Trevik was desperate.

But Trevik could never make such a deal. He couldn't remove so much of the oil when all of Tristwick relied on it to give them light throughout the winter.

Nor could he trust the man to make an honest agreement

with him—at least not another one. More amendments would be added, indecipherable clauses would be included, and Trevik would find himself in the same situation as Father. He couldn't do that to Mother and Poppy. They needed him.

"Mr. Honeysett?" Mr. Truscott pressed, but Trevik was already shaking his head.

Silently, he signed the three copies of the agreement before him, one for him, one for Mr. Truscott, and one for Mr. Oates. It was bad enough that Trevik was making *this* deal with the devil. But knowing it was in Morvoren's benefit—and that he had a copy of the contract clear as day for himself, as well—it was a sacrifice he was more than willing to make.

The paper was slipped from his grasp the moment the pen left the paper, and Mr. Oates rolled up the document and secured it in his bag before standing.

Mr. Truscott stood with his own copy of the agreement, gulping down the last of his drink. "Pleasure doing business with you, Mr. Honeysett. Although, you'll excuse me if I wish our paths never cross again."

Trevik sniffed. At least he and the man could agree on one thing.

He walked past him. "Now, I'm off to write yet another agreement with my niece. Good day."

He walked away without a glance back. Trevik remained at the table, rubbing his eyes with his forefinger and thumb, wracking his brain for anything that might help him save Morvoren from a life of misery.

But with the document signed, what could he do?

He dropped his hand, his shoulders sinking forward as he stared at the agreements before him. He'd just signed away the security of his lugger being fixed to ensure Morvoren was safe. And yet, she still had to marry a cad—and she still had to interact with her uncle.

So what had it all been for?

How he wished he could pull her from the room she was

locked away in upstairs and take her back to Tristwick to marry her himself.

But it was too late. She would live the rest of her life just out of Trevik's reach, forever alone, forever unhappy.

And it was all his fault.

CHAPTER FORTY-FOUR

$\mathcal{M}$orvoren stared out of her bedroom window, eying the sea she could only catch a fraction of.

One week had passed since she'd seen the Cornish seas in all their glory from atop Tristwick's cliffs. Since arriving in St. Ives, Uncle had kept her indoors, attempting to reteach her all of the manners and elegance he'd said she'd lost while with the Honeysetts.

She'd done her best to speak properly, to smile at his friends, to curtsy, eat, speak, and dance in a manner befitting a proper young lady. She would show Uncle that she could keep her end of the bargain because he'd kept his—repairing Trevik's lugger and leaving the Honeysetts alone.

Though she felt peace knowing she'd done all she could to help the family her uncle had injured, it did not stop her tears at night. Nor did it stop her from standing atop the bench near her window to catch a glimpse of the sea whenever she could.

She'd always loved the view, just as she'd always loved the sea. But now, eying the sliver of the lilting, turquoise water meant more to her. Now, it reminded her of Trevik.

The door opened behind her, and her lady's maid

appeared. "The Fosses are 'ere to call, miss. Your uncle bids ye to come down."

"Thank ye," Morvoren said, but she quickly shook her head. Hearing the maid's words always brought back memories of her time in Tristwick. "Thank *you*. I will be right there."

Morvoren left the safety of her room behind and walked down the stairs of Uncle's townhome, rallying her courage and fortitude for what lay ahead.

Her time in Tristwick had seemed like an utter dream compared to the way she was living now. But it wasn't time to dwell on such a thing. She was already dawdling, and Uncle despised it when she did so.

Would her betrothed, too?

After a week of dinners, balls, card parties, and more, Morvoren still had not spoken more than a few conversations with the man. He was still more interested in the women standing near to him during card games or the ones eager to share a moment in the gardens with him during balls.

Morvoren tried not to let it bother her. After all, Uncle had told her she'd experience such infidelity no matter whom she married. She might have believed him once. But after knowing Trevik…

She swallowed the emotion rising in her throat as she reached the landing of the stairs. This was her decision. Her choice had allowed Trevik and his family the security they so desperately deserved.

Besides, she shouldn't be dwelling on such things when she had a wedding to plan. The banns would be read for the first time in two days, officially announcing their engagement, and from that point forward, she would be Mr. Foss's.

She allowed herself one final shudder before she straightened her spine, raised her chin, and walked into the drawing room.

Uncle and the Fosses stood in the center of the room. The

curtains had been opened, allowing the bright early afternoon sunshine to fill the room to its capacity. The walls were a soft, light blue, the wooden floors immaculately polished, and grand cushion-backed chairs were placed comfortably about the spacious room.

It was opulent, yes. And neat and beautiful and striking. Yet Morvoren found herself longing for something simpler. Floors scuffed with the marks of hard-working boots. Uncomfortable wooden benches that held the weight of an entire family. Dark walls that surrounded a room like a warm embrace.

"At last," Uncle said, spotting her first. "A veritable angel adorned in white, come to grace us with her presence."

Morvoren glided through the doorway just as Uncle wished her to, pausing as he came up to greet her.

Just as she wished for a different room, how she wished for a different man to greet her.

Uncle reached forward, feigning a kiss to her cheek, whispering in her ear instead. "You have kept them waiting for far too long. You had better make up for your poor behavior."

She lowered her head in submission, then moved farther into the room to greet her betrothed and future father-in-law.

"Miss Hollow," the elder Mr. Andrew Foss greeted with a bow. "You look lovely today."

Morvoren nodded her gratitude. In the limited time she'd spent with the Fosses, she'd learned that the father was far more respectable than his son, if not a little vain. At least he had the decency to converse with Morvoren.

"Does she not look a portrait, son?"

The younger Mr. Richard Foss smiled, his eyebrows pulling in as if to accentuate his words. "You are from Heaven itself, Miss Hollow."

He bowed low, but when he straightened, his eyes sought the doorway instead. Morvoren glanced over her shoulder, seeing a maid flitter swiftly by.

She didn't know what was more upsetting, the fact that the man was making eyes at someone else with his betrothed in the room—or being relieved that he wasn't looking at her with that same leering gaze.

She wasn't surprised with his wandering eyes. After all, he'd have Morvoren soon enough upon their marriage. Until then, why would he not spend his time with other women who were easier to obtain?

She moved farther into the room, taking the seat nearest to the fire, though they all shuffled a few steps closer to her as she settled.

"We have been looking forward to this day for quite some time," Uncle said. "To share an intimate moment with our closest friends—well, our family. Have we not been eagerly awaiting them, niece?"

Morvoren nodded, as numb as she usually was during such events as these. "Yes, Uncle," she responded dutifully with her placid smile.

"As have we," the elder Mr. Foss agreed. "It will be good to speak about...matters."

Was it just Morvoren, or had he hesitated?

She brushed the matter aside as Uncle continued, puffing the man up by complimenting one thing after another that Morvoren didn't care about.

She smoothed out her white skirts and readjusted her pearls. Uncle wouldn't take the necklace back as he had all her other jewelry. These were a gift from the Fosses for the betrothal. Uncle had made her wear them to make a better impression.

"Anything to distract from that awful skin you've destroyed over the last few weeks," he'd said. *"And do something with that hair."*

Her lady's maid had spent hours on it that morning. Morvoren hadn't missed wearing her hair in such a style. Yes, it was elegant, with piles of curls twirled into a graceful style.

But the pins dug too deeply into her scalp and seemed to weigh her head down to the floor.

Or perhaps that was simply her mood doing so.

Footsteps thumped toward her, and she glanced up to see Mr. Richard Foss standing directly before her. The tips of his yellow teeth peeked out from his lips as he spoke. "My father said you attended the Larings' ball last evening. I'm sorry to have missed you. Had I known, I would have been certain to save you a dance."

She forced her typical smile and bowed her head. "Yes, I was there. But there were so many people, it is no wonder I was lost in the crowds."

If only that were true. Morvoren had witnessed the man in the card room, drinking and flirting with women all evening. If Trevik were there, he'd be sure to teach the man a lesson he'd not soon forget, no doubt laying him flat out as he'd done to Uncle.

But Trevik wasn't there. She'd chosen Mr. Foss instead. Yes, for Trevik and his family's lives. But then…what was to become of *her* life? Could she truly give up her worth, her value, and her freedom to marry a man who held even less respect for her than Uncle did?

"Don't they look handsome together?" Uncle said, his voice crawling up her skin like an unreachable itch. "My niece and your son."

Mr. Andrew Foss nodded in silence, though he shifted in place uncomfortably.

Morvoren tried not to stare—*"Staring is what heathens do, Miss Hollow"*—but the man's uncharacteristic discomfort stuck out to her like a rock tumbling in the waves.

Uncle seemed unaware, of course, focusing entirely on himself. "Well, shall we commence with the discussions?"

Morvoren nodded, but the elder Mr. Foss paused, remaining where he stood.

"If you have but a moment to spare, Mr. Truscott?"

"Of course, sir. Of course." Uncle instantly glanced to Morvoren, sizing her up as if attempting to decipher if she was the one whom Mr. Foss disapproved of. "What do you wish to discuss, Mr. Foss?"

The younger Mr. Foss moved from Morvoren's side and stood before the window, staring out of the glass with his hands clasped behind his back.

Was he avoiding his own unease, or did he care less about what his father had to say than he cared about Morvoren?

She didn't think she'd like to know the answer to that question.

"Well," Mr. Andrew Foss began, his surprisingly thick hair standing rigid, not a strand out of place, "I am sorry to say, but it is a delicate matter. One in regard to your niece."

Morvoren's heart stopped. Her? A delicate matter? A torrent of possibilities flooded her mind with what the man could be referring to, but she froze when Uncle's eyes focused on her.

"My niece?" he asked, feigning surprise. His stare penetrated Morvoren's confidence. He was threatening her, that much was clear. But to what end? How could she stop what Mr. Foss had already heard?

"I'm afraid so," Mr. Foss continued. "Now, I am not one for gossip. I cannot abide by it. But my source was notably concerned. You see, only just last night, I heard that Miss Hollow's time in Sennen did not actually occur."

Uncle pulled back, sending another glance to Morvoren. She read his look in an instant, pulling on her best impression of innocence.

"Wherever did you hear such a thing?" Uncle laughed. "Of course she was in Sennen. Were you not, niece?"

Morvoren nodded. "I was." How she hated lying to people day in and day out to ensure Uncle's cover for Morvoren's departure remained valid. According to him, Morvoren had spent three weeks in Sennen with a trusted friend under the constant supervision of a chaperone.

Mr. Foss still appeared hesitant, though he'd stop shuffling his feet. "I have it on good authority that my source was telling the truth," he continued. "Furthermore, I was told that Miss Hollow was not with friends, but instead living unchaperoned with a lower drifter's family, under the same roof as an unmarried male."

Uncle's face reddened, and he sputtered, unable to conjure a single word, but Morvoren hardly noticed.

She was too overcome with shock, tears welling in her eyes. For the last two weeks, the Honeysetts had existed purely in her own memory. Uncle refused to speak a word about them while swearing Morvoren to silence, too. But now, to have her time with the family—her time with Trevik—brought to the forefront of her attention by someone other than herself, the memories rushed back unwavering, as powerful as a broken dam.

Being caught in Trevik's net in the sea. Being welcomed into his home. Her friendship with Poppy and Mrs. Honeysett. Trevik's kiss.

She'd given them up for their own safety. But that did nothing to stop the ache from returning full force into her heart.

Uncle's continued sputtering brought her back to the present, though her longing to see Trevik again remained the same.

"And just who is this source who has spread such fanciful rumors about my dear niece?" Uncle blurted out. He didn't have to hide his anger, no doubt furious that the truth of Morvoren's attempted escape was beginning to make its rounds through Society.

Morvoren couldn't help but wonder the same.

"My source is my own," Mr. Foss said, all hesitation gone.

Uncle was clearly revealing more than he intended as his

anger rushed forward. "Well, this is simply preposterous. What reason have we to lie about such a thing?"

"To save our business arrangement." Mr. Foss glanced to Morvoren. "And to save your niece's reputation."

Morvoren swallowed. He knew. There was no denying it any longer. But then, what did that mean for her?

"Well, I don't have to save either," Uncle said a little too vigorously. "For my niece *was* in Sennen."

Mr. Foss shifted his jaw back and forth, as if tasting Uncle's words. He must have decided he didn't like them, for he turned to study Morvoren instead. "And what do you have to say about all of this, Miss Hollow? Were you in Sennen, or were you not?"

CHAPTER FORTY-FIVE

*M*orvoren could hardly breathe. She glanced to Uncle, whose stare made her want to crawl back to her room and lock the door behind her.

"My dear Morvoren," Uncle said—using her given name for the first time in her memory, "do tell Mr. Foss where you were." His pointed gaze told her that he expected her to lie.

But…she couldn't. Not anymore. Not with her memories of the Honeysetts forefront in her mind. Lying had been the very thing to make her teeter too close to the point of the cliff, and keeping secrets to herself had sent her over the edge.

With a deep breath and knowing all of the implications that would come from telling the truth, she stood from her chair and faced Mr. Foss directly.

"I was in Sennen, Mr. Foss," she stated simply. "But—"

"Morvoren," Uncle interrupted sharply.

"I suggest that you let her speak, Truscott," Mr. Foss said with a look of warning.

Uncle's eyes widened to the point of hysteria, and even Mr. Richard Foss turned to watch how the drama unfolded, as he became apparently aware that something of interest to him was occurring.

But Morvoren didn't care who watched. The game was up, the contract was finished. She had been instructed to never do anything that would jeopardize her relationship with her future in-laws, but then…wouldn't lying do that? Let Uncle have her head. Let him press charges, threaten her, injure her. Let him starve her, for all she cared.

She was done being his pawn. She would not let another family—even one like the Fosses—become entangled with him without their full knowledge of Uncle's many flaws.

"I was in Sennen," she began again, her voice soft yet confident, "but only for a few hours. The rest of my time was spent in a small fishing hamlet with a family of drifters. And one of them was, indeed, an unmarried male."

Mr. Foss didn't appear surprised, though the veins in Uncle's forehead bulged bright blue against his reddened skin.

Mr. Richard Foss stepped forward from the window with a frown. "What can you mean by this behavior?" he asked. "Living in such a way when you knew you were to marry me?"

Morvoren had done her best to hide her disgust of Mr. Foss for a fortnight. She'd turned a blind eye to his repulsive behavior and pretended she could live with such a man as her husband. But now, he had the audacity to call out her own actions while knowing full-well what he himself had done?

She huffed out a cold laugh. "This coming from the man who left the ball last evening with a woman under each arm —again?"

His eyes widened, and he looked away, no doubt to hide his blush. His father's lip twitched.

Before Morvoren could decipher if he was hiding a smile or not, Uncle stepped toward her, gripping her arm.

"You must be ill, niece," he said through gritted teeth. "Why else would you be speaking such nonsense? Come, you must rest."

He tried to pull her toward the door, but she wrenched her

arm free. "No, Uncle. The truth is out. Ain't no reason to hide it now."

She felt the beginnings of her accent starting to blossom within her, stretching out its petals that had lain dormant for too long as they reached toward the sun.

"The truth? You can hardly know the truth if you are not well," Uncle said, attempting again to reach toward her, but she sidestepped him.

"I would listen to your niece if I were you, Mr. Truscott," the elder Mr. Foss said. "End the charade before you make a further fool of yourself." He motioned to his son. "Richard, shall we?"

The father and son moved to the door, Mr. Richard Foss glancing at Morvoren with a wary gaze, unsure if she'd reveal something else she knew about him.

"So...I won't be marrying Miss Hollow, then?"

Mr. Foss glanced back with a look of impatience. "No, son. You will not."

A lightness filled Morvoren, a jittery feeling overcoming each of her limbs as the words settled happily within her mind.

He was not going to marry her? She would not have to marry *him*?

Uncle rushed forward, attempting to prevent their departure. "But Mr. Foss, we have not even discussed the future of our companies."

"As it happens, sir, I think it best if we do not merge our companies after all."

"But-but, do not act so rashly, Mr. Foss. These plans have been in the works for months now."

"Yes, they have," Mr. Foss responded calmly, the perfect juxtaposition to Uncle's pulsing veins and spitting words. "And truth be told, I've been having misgivings about the entire matter since we began."

Mr. Foss left the room, his son a step behind him as Uncle

trailed after them. Morvoren scurried to the door as their conversation continued, anxious to hear their words. She paused in the doorway, watching as the Fosses were brought their coats and hats.

"I understand your hesitance in allowing your son to marry my niece now," Uncle said. "She is a little worse for wear at times, but I assure you, she can behave."

Mr. Foss shook his head as he opened the door himself. His son walked out first with a fleeting glance at Morvoren, who emerged slowly toward the entryway where they all stood, but the elder Mr. Foss lingered behind.

With his hat in his hand, he shook his head. "I have far less qualms about my son marrying Miss Hollow than I have regarding my business being associated with yours. After all, she spoke the truth." He paused, promptly placing his hat on his head. "*You* did not."

Then with a nod in Uncle's and Morvoren's directions, he left the house without a glance back.

The moment they left, the happiness that had filled Morvoren's heart slipped away, for Uncle turned on her, all feigned politeness gone as his sneer turned vicious.

"You," he said, "you were the cause of this, weren't you? You were the one to spread word about your time with those forsaken drifters."

Morvoren pulled in her remaining strength and shook her head fiercely. "Don't ye dare blame me for this. I've done nothin' but what ye've wanted me to do for days, Uncle. I held true to my word, just as I do now."

He shook his head, and she wasn't even sure if he'd heard her. "You think you have won, but you haven't. I'll just find another man for you to marry, another company to merge with my own. That contract is still binding, and you'll do as I say, regardless of the man I choose for you."

Before, Morvoren would have humbly accepted his words. But now, having been reminded how freedom felt beneath her wings, she would never go back to the way things were.

She raised her chin and made her way up the stairs in silence, Uncle calling behind her.

"Yes, that's right. You had better go to your room. And don't expect to be let out until I've found for you another husband to benefit the family!"

Morvoren didn't respond, merely continued up the steps at a slow pace before reaching her room and leaving the door ajar. At the same steady pace she'd kept before, she moved straight to her wardrobe, retrieving her reticule and her mother's shawl before wrapping the warm fabric around her shoulders.

Then she made her way straight from her chambers and headed back toward the stairs.

She felt strange, as if she were floating above the ground as she moved.

Before when she left Uncle's, she'd been rushed and frightened, sneaking out in the dead of night. Now she was calm, collected, and sure. When once she'd stolen a few of Uncle's pennies to make her way by stagecoach, now she left without tuppence to her name.

She continued down the steps, her mind and body strong as one, even as Uncle's voice called up from the main floor.

"Did you lock her door?"

Her heart lurched. He thought she was a maid, coming down from barricading Morvoren in her room. But she'd never allow that to occur again.

"No, she didn't," Morvoren stated firmly.

Uncle's footsteps thumped angrily forward, his eyes red as he stared up at her. "I thought I told you to stay there," he spat out.

"Ye did."

"Then what are you doing?"

"Leavin'."

He barked out a cruel laugh. "No, you are not."

"Yes, I be. And ye can't stop me."

"You will cease speaking in such an improper manner, Miss Hollow," he growled, reaching for her arm. He squeezed her tightly and drew her near to him, anger alight in his eyes. "And you will return to your room, or I'll alert the authorities."

Morvoren had expected this. She'd prepared for this. She'd meant to respond coolly, to let him know just how greatly she didn't care what he did any longer. But a spark of anger lit within her. Anger at herself for allowing this man to injure her for so many years and anger at Uncle for doing the injuring.

"Then report me, Uncle," she bit back through clenched teeth. "I'd rather die by hangin' than spend another moment in your presence."

She tried to step past him, but he blocked her way. "If you leave now, I'll see that the Honeysett's lugger is never fixed."

She sniffed with derision. "Ye can't threaten that. The contract was signed. The lugger has to be completed by now."

His eyes flickered away from hers, and her heart thudded in her ears. "Uncle…"

He withdrew his hold of her, and she knew the truth at once. "Ye ne'er fixed it, did ye?"

He squared his shoulders and faced her again. "No, I didn't. But before you go on and accuse me of not fulfilling my end of the bargain, you'll be interested to discover that Mr. Honeysett refused my help in funding the lugger's repairs."

She narrowed her eyes, trying to discern fact from fiction as he continued, a satisfied smile spreading across his lips. "Apparently, he didn't want any of your help after you lied to him and damaged his family."

No. No, Morvoren refused to believe such words. "Ye lie."

"Do I?" he asked, pushing forward. "Or do you know,

deep down, that I speak the truth? None of them want you. They never wanted you."

Tears pricked her eyes, but she refused to let them flow freely. Uncle always did this, twisted the truth with his words. But she would not listen to him any longer.

With swift footing, she darted around him and made for the door, heaving it open as she forced her breathing to continue.

Uncle didn't try to stop her this time, his voice calling from inside his home. "Even if you arrive in Tristwick before the constable reaches you, they will never take you back." He bared his teeth, growling his words. "You were a burden to them just as you've always been a burden to me."

Morvoren stared down at the paved steps leading away from Uncle's townhome. Then his arm gripped hers from behind, whirling her around to face him.

"I'll be glad to be rid of you," he spat out. "You've been nothing but a plague upon my house from the moment you arrived. Just like your mother was to my good name."

Morvoren stared up at him, pride welling in her heart at the mention of her mother. "Ye are the only one who can take the blame for tarnishing the Truscott name, Uncle. And ye deserve to bear it alone."

Then she raised her head and slowly descended the steps to her freedom, to her future. To the sea.

CHAPTER FORTY-SIX

$\mathcal{M}$orvoren reached the long stretch of sand a quarter of an hour later. She walked past strangers and familiar faces with her head held high, standing at the edge of the sand, her slippers peeking out from the bottom of her white gown.

She didn't realize until then that she hadn't changed into her walking boots. If by some miracle Uncle didn't send the constable after her, she'd have a wretched time walking anywhere in these slippers.

But no matter. Uncle would press charges. And she would not be spending her final moments of freedom dwelling on footwear, of all things.

She raised her sights instead to the sea. Though not Tristwick, the view from St. Ives was beautiful in its own right. The stretch of the deep blue waves extended far beyond the bay, sparkling in the early afternoon sunshine. She drew in a long breath of the salty air blowing back the curls at her temples.

Couples meandered across the beach toward the water, and ladies skittered from shop to shop behind Morvoren, their arms full of their latest purchases.

Morvoren hardly noticed them. It was just her and the sea

in this perfect moment of tranquility. Indeed, the only thing to improve upon this perfection would be if—

"Morvoren?"

Her heart skipped about her chest. The constable wouldn't use her given name. Nor would Uncle.

"Morvoren!"

The breath rushed from her lungs. It couldn't be him. It would be too wonderful, too perfect.

And yet, when she finally turned around, she could no longer deny the truth standing before her eyes.

With his brow raised high and his warm brown eyes caressing her face, Trevik stood before her, his chest rising and falling as if breathless.

"Trevik?" she whispered, tears billowing in her eyes. "What...what are ye doin' here?"

Worry creased his brow as he took in the sight of her, then his eyes softened. "We've come to take ye back to Tristwick."

We? She glanced over his shoulder, only then noting Gryffyn Bosanko and Captain Kendricks standing behind him, small smiles on each of the grown men's faces.

"I brought 'em with me," Trevik said with a motion toward his friends. "'Appen your Uncle needed persuadin' to let ye go."

She shook her head, unable to process what was occurring. He'd come to rescue her? To bring her back to Tristwick? Hope flowered in her heart, but she quickly pressed it down. They may have been able to intimidate Uncle into allowing her freedom, but they couldn't do the same for any constable sent her way.

"What are ye doin' out 'ere alone?"

"Waitin' to be sent to gaol."

He gave a short laugh, but she shook her head. Perhaps he didn't understand what she'd said. "I left Uncle," she explained, attempting to make sense of her own words as Trevik slowly closed the distance between them. "Mr. Foss severed their business relationship and ended the engagement 'tween me and 'is son after 'e found out 'bout me time in Tristwick."

Trevik didn't respond, merely took another slow step toward her.

"I broke the contract with Uncle," she said, her eyes flickering to the growing smile on his lips. Was he truly not comprehending the danger she was still under? "That means there be nothin' stoppin' him from pressin' charges."

Trevik nodded. So he did understand. But then…why was his grin shining brighter than the sun above?

"Trevik, what be goin' on?" she asked, glancing back at the other two men, who still watched the exchange with half-averted eyes.

"Do ye not wonder 'ow Mr. Foss came to know 'bout your time with us?"

She narrowed her eyes. "He said he heard from a source…" Her words trailed off as Trevik's dark eyes shone. "It was ye?"

His eyes traced her features. "'Twas Mother's idea. The three o' we came 'ere and spoke with Mr. Foss last night, caught 'im leavin' some sort o' party. Captain Kendricks came to use 'is weight as a respected officer, and Gryff…well, 'e came to use 'is other sort o' weight."

He smiled, though his expression swiftly turned contrite. "We didn't know 'ow else to free ye. I couldn't stomach the idea of ruinin' your reputation, spreadin' round where ye were. I know 'ow important that be for women. It took Mother a week to convince I to go about the plan at all." He seemed to pull back for a moment as if to shield himself. "Are ye angry?"

"Angry?" she blurted out with a half-sob, half-laugh. "How could I be angry? Ye saved me from livin' a life with a…" She shook her head, unable to come up with a word strong enough for a man the likes of Mr. Foss—a word that wasn't a curse, that is. "No, I ain't be angry, Trevik. I can't thank ye enough. But…but I fear 'twas in vain. The constable—"

"Will not be comin'," Trevik interrupted. He shook his head with disgust. "I assume your uncle didn't tell ye 'bout the agreement I made with 'im meself?"

"What agreement?"

"I refused the repairs for the lugger in exchange for another contract, one detailin' that 'e'd forgive ye for the debt and me for strikin' 'im. I 'ave the document meself." His brow raised. "That man don't 'ave any power over ye any longer."

A moment passed as she tried to process his words. That was what Uncle had left out of his explanation. That was why he hadn't mended the lugger. Of course he wouldn't share with her the truth, because he wanted to keep her under his control forever. That was why he'd allowed her to leave. That was why a constable had not yet found her—because there would be no constable.

She brought a hand to cover her mouth, tears slipping down her cheeks. "Ye mean, I be free?"

His own eyes glistened. "Yes, Morvoren. Ye be free. Ye can do whate'er ye wish to do from now on."

The words reached her ears like a lovely tune.

Without hesitation, she leapt forward, closing the distance between her and Trevik and wrapping her arms around his neck. He instantly responded, encircling her in his strong embrace and nuzzling his nose into her neck.

"Thank ye," she whispered, "for everythin'."

He didn't respond, merely drawing her closer.

They stood in their silent embrace a moment longer before Morvoren opened her eyes and peered over Trevik's shoulder just as Mr. Bosanko and Captain Kendricks pulled their eyes away from them.

She smiled, taking a step back from Trevik, who glanced over his shoulder at his friends.

He cleared his throat awkwardly and looked away. "So…

now ye be free, ye must decide what ye wish to do." He looked anywhere but her eyes—the sea, the men behind him, the large buildings across St. Ives. "We be prepared to be your chaperones all the way to Bodmin, if ye wish. Or we can 'elp ye find the Prouts. Or…or ye can come back with us to Tristwick…"

Morvoren beamed at his subtle hinting. "Tristwick," she said softly. "I want to be in Tristwick."

Finally, he met her gaze. "Ye be certain?"

She nodded. "If ye be certain that I won't be the cause of any more trouble."

He chuckled. "I doubt that ye could e'er not be trouble, Morvoren Hollow."

Despite herself, she joined in with a smile of her own.

He offered his arm to her, and she took it with pleasure.

"Told ye she'd want to come back," Mr. Bosanko said as they approached. "Glad to see ye again, Miss 'Ollow."

"I'm glad to see ye, too."

The four of them moved forward to where Captain Kendricks's wagon awaited them. Out of habit, Morvoren glanced anxiously over her shoulder. Then she faced forward again with a smile. She needn't worry about Uncle or anyone else following her or finding her ever again.

For with Trevik beside her, she knew she was finally safe.

CHAPTER FORTY-SEVEN

revik had never before experienced a longer ride
home in his entire life. He knew he'd had to bring
the other men along in order to succeed in his plan to help
Morvoren home, but at this point, he was counting down the
minutes until they arrived in Tristwick. As much as he liked
Gryffyn and Captain Kendricks, he'd prefer proposing
without an audience.

Throughout their journey, he and Morvoren sat in the
back of the wagon, informing one another about all that had
occurred to the both of them since they'd parted.

Trevik shared the news of the Cardys working for the seiners, though they remained in Tristwick. "We've managed to
hire a few men in their absence, some miners from Wheal
Favour," he explained.

"Will the Cardys be so greatly upset that they've been
replaced?" She looked away. "Or with my returnin'?"

Trevik shook his head. "It 'ardly matters. Edern saw ye
bein' carted away by your uncle. That be more 'an enough
evidence for 'im to know ye ain't no sea-maid, what with ye
havin' family on land. I 'spect 'e and Jowan'll come 'round
eventually. If not, they can leave Tristwick if they wish to."

Trevik then went on to explain the good fortune that had come to them while making the repairs to the lugger. "Me father had a friend in the lumber business who 'elped 'im out years before," he said. "We made the same arrangement. 'E fixed the deck in exchange for oil from the fish throughout the winter. A fair trade."

"And the masts?" she asked.

"Captain Kendricks and Lieutenant 'Arris used their connections in the navy to bring about a swift mendin' to those, as well," Trevik explained.

The two men had ridden to Penzance themselves, being shuffled from place to place before finding the parts and the men to fix it. They'd worked tirelessly for days until the masts had been mended—something Trevik would be indebted to them for forever.

"But how could ye afford the repairs to both masts?"

Trevik swallowed his pride, as he'd done when Captain Kendricks had first offered his solution. Lowering his voice, he explained. "The masts had to be purchased outright, so the captain agreed to fund them personally. I'll be payin' 'im back in increments as me wages come in from fishin'."

Morvoren shook her head in awe—the same Trevik had done when the repairs had been finished only the day before. They'd lost a week of fishing—thousands upon thousands of fish—but the future did not look so bleak after all.

"So I assume the lieutenant has already set sail?" Morvoren asked in a soft voice, averting her gaze.

He looked away in shame. He couldn't believe the last time they'd spoken had been in an argument. How he regretted his behavior that Sunday.

"Yes," he said, seated across from her in the wagon, their legs occasionally bouncing against each other as the wheels hit the divots in the road. "'E left a few days ago."

"And how be Poppy?"

"Better." After Morvoren left, he'd apologized profusely to

his sister for her heartache, explaining how he only wished to protect her. She'd forgiven him, as she always did. But Trevik still needed to apologize to Morvoren for the accusations. "I… I know we argued 'bout this 'fore ye left. And I can't tell ye 'ow much I've come to regret…"

His words trailed off as she shook her head. "There's no need to apologize. We both were speakin' out o' love for Poppy. And out o' fear for the future."

He nodded. "Still, I be sorry for blamin' 'er pain on ye."

She gave a little nod, forgiveness filling her eyes as she smiled at him.

The wagon rolled on, and Trevik listened next as Morvoren detailed the last week of her life. It had taken everything within him not to return straight to St. Ives and remove the living from Mr. Truscott for what he'd done to his family and Morvoren, but never again would he risk not being with this woman for the rest of his life.

They arrived in Tristwick just as the sun began to pull its light toward the sea. Morvoren and Trevik thanked the captain profusely as he dropped them off, then did the same to Gryffyn before he walked toward his home.

When the two were finally alone, they entered the Honeysetts' house, but Trevik remained in the doorway. Morvoren glanced back to him with a curious look. "Where be the others?"

"They be workin' late at Golowduyn today," he explained, "to 'elp in the captain's absence."

She nodded, and as her warm eyes roved about the room, Trevik's eyes remained on her.

He'd never seen a more stunning woman in all his life. Morvoren had always been beautiful to him, but that evening, dressed in white, with perfect curls, long white gloves stretched the length of her delicate arms, and pearls strung about her neck…a sudden and unfamiliar wave of insecurity rushed over him.

She stood out, dressed in such a way and standing in the midst of his humble home. She could have been a lady, a lady in fine clothing with friends in high places. Yet she'd chosen to come back to Tristwick, to be poor and inconsequential to Society.

But why?

"Trevik?"

His name on her lips pulled him from his anxious thoughts, and he blinked, still staring at her.

"Are ye well?" she asked softly.

He nodded, taking a step back. He couldn't do this now. He needed to catch his breath before he fell over. Losing consciousness while proposing would hardly help the case of a poor fisherman.

"I'll be 'eaded out on the *Pilferer* soon," he explained in a rush. "Feel free to make yourself at 'ome. Poppy set up the bed already in 'er room."

Her eyes brightened. "She did?"

"Mother told 'er to wait, but Poppy knew ye'd return."

She shook her head with a little laugh. "I've missed 'er." Then her eyes settled on his. "I've missed ye all."

His love for the woman standing before him overflowed from his heart, filling every inch of him until he could no longer draw in a breath.

"Right," he said, looking away. "I s'pose I'd best be off, then. I'll be seein' ye tomorrow."

Tomorrow? What was he doing?

Morvoren nodded in silence. Did he imagine the disappointment in her eyes? Still, he turned away, leaving her behind and heading to his crew and the awaiting lugger. Every step he took seemed to berate his decision.

Cow-ard. Cow-ard. Cow-ard.

His men glanced up in surprise as he reached them, the boat swathed in orange light from the setting sun.

"What are ye doin' 'ere, Trev?" Gryffyn asked.

Trevik looked from his men to the boat. "Am I not allowed to fish on me own lugger?"

"No," Gryffyn said pointedly, folding his arms and blocking his progression toward the boat, "not when you're s'posed to be up there instead."

He tipped his head toward the cliffside, and Trevik looked up. His heart jumped when he spotted Morvoren standing at the edge overlooking the sea, her white dress billowing behind her.

She was utter perfection.

"I'll ask ye again," Gryffyn said quieter that time, "what are ye doin' down 'ere?"

"I...I don't know."

A few chuckles sounded aboard the lugger and around the deck.

"Ye be daft, Trev," Gryffyn said.

"Not even I be that stupid," cried young Charlie from the top of the lugger, eliciting more laughs.

Still, Trevik scowled. "I just...I mean, look at 'er, Gryff. She be standin' there all perfect, and 'ere I be, as plain as a...a fisherman."

"A fisherman she came back for."

"'Appen she came back for me mother and sister."

Gryffyn laughed then, raising his voice. "Ye 'ear that men? 'E thinks she came back for 'is mother and sister!"

Laughs and jeers sounded again, and Trevik fought a smile of his own, attempting to shove Gryffyn aside, but the burly man didn't budge a foot.

"Go on," Trevik said. "We've got fish to catch."

"Not tonight, ye don't. It'll be extra work for the lot o' we, but we'll manage without ye for a night." He narrowed his eyes. "Now, ye've been pinin' after that girl for weeks, Trev, and we be sick o' hearin' about it. Go speak with 'er." Then his expression softened. "'Tain't every day ye find a woman who loves ye the same as ye love 'er."

The weight from Trevik's chest lifted, hope spreading light upon the darkness within him. "Ye...ye think so?"

Gryffyn nodded. "Now go on up there 'fore Poppy returns, or ye'll ne'er get to speak with Miss 'Ollow."

The men laughed again, and Trevik stared up at Morvoren, his heart skipping a beat as her eyes seemed to find his.

Gryffyn was right. Morvoren felt for Trevik just as he felt for her. And every moment he wasted down there by the dock was a moment wasted that could have been spent with Morvoren.

What the devil was he doing?

With a determined stride, he turned on his heel and left for the pathway, his crew whooping behind him as he ran away.

"Don't destroy me lugger, Gryff!" he called over his shoulder.

Gryffyn responded, but Trevik didn't hear what he said, only one thought—one woman—on his mind.

CHAPTER FORTY-EIGHT

$\mathcal{M}$orvoren's heart stuttered as Trevik left his crew behind and darted up the pathway toward her, bobbing in and out of sight as he passed by cottage after cottage.

Butterflies erupted in her stomach, and she whirled around to face the sea again. The sun had slipped behind the clouds, lighting them with a dusty mixture of orange, brown, and white as the cool, turquoise sea whispered of the quick approach of winter.

She watched the waves lilting toward the shores, trying to mimic their peace, but her hands clenched together. Had Trevik simply forgotten something at his house? Was that why he hadn't spoken with her yet?

When his footsteps shuffled behind her, her heart leapt to her throat, and she was no longer able to breathe.

"Morvoren?"

She turned toward him, not having to feign surprise, for his actions still rattled her—the way he'd left her so abruptly in his home, now running back toward her for...for what?

"Trevik." She felt the need to curtsy. She'd obviously spent too long living at Uncle's. "Did ye forget somethin'?"

He stood a few paces away from her, his chest rising and falling in the creamy light the sun cast upon them. "No, I didn't," he replied, his eyes fixed on her. "In fact, I been thinkin' 'bout this for a long time."

Her breath caught in her throat. "Thinkin' 'bout what?" she managed.

He stared, his mouth open as he breathed heavily from his run up the cliffside. He shook his head, then in the next moment, he was holding her in his arms.

His hands slipped around her waist and settled at the small of her back, pulling her close to him as his lips found hers. She responded without hesitation, sliding her arms around his neck and breathing in the lemon scent she'd so desperately missed.

The ocean roared beneath them, the wind blew in her ears, and yet she could think of nothing else, she could *feel* nothing else, but Trevik and his arms wrapped around her as he shared his love for her.

After a moment, he pulled back, resting his forehead against hers as he softly shook his head.

"I be done waitin'," he whispered. "And I be done regrettin' things I ought to 'ave said long ago."

With that, he pulled back, moving her hair from her brow and staring deep into her eyes. "I love ye, Morvoren 'Ollow. I know I ain't be no fancy gent. I'll not be able to afford dresses for ye as pretty as this one or provide ye with any number o' fine things. Bein' married to a fisherman 'tain't an easy life, as ye be more 'an aware." He swallowed, shaking his head as he did so. "But if ye can find it in your 'eart to do so, I can promise ye a life full o' love and laughter." He paused with a tip of his head and a raised shoulder. "With just a bit o' pilchard smell along the way."

Morvoren laughed, moving to stand on the tips of her toes to draw him closer, her arms wrapped around his neck. "I don't need an easy life, Trevik. Nor do I want one. All I want —all I need—is a life with ye."

He blinked swiftly, but not before she caught the glistening in his eyes. "Be that a yes, then?"

She smiled. "That be a yes."

Then his lips pressed against hers once again.

She didn't know how much time passed as Trevik held her in his arms, but when a squeal on the wind caught her attention, she pulled back and peered across the cliffside to where Poppy ran toward them, flapping her arms in the air like a seaweed in the water.

Mrs. Honeysett followed swiftly behind, shaking her head in amusement at her daughter's behavior.

"She's been dyin' to see ye," Trevik said, taking Morvoren's hand in his and pulling her toward them. "They both 'ave."

Morvoren couldn't deny that she felt the very same. When Poppy reached them, she jumped toward Morvoren, swinging her arms around her. "Oh, I be that 'appy to see ye again! And I saw ye two kissin'! Does that mean ye'll be stayin'?"

Morvoren pulled back, laughing through her tears of joy. "Yes, I'll be stayin' 'ere, Poppy."

Mrs. Honeysett reached them then, wrapping Morvoren up in a long, tight embrace. "Welcome 'ome, dear."

She kissed Morvoren softly on the cheek, then released her hold of her, allowing Trevik to take his place at Morvoren's side.

Together, the four of them walked toward the edge of the cliff, staring at the final rays of light splayed out across the sea. The *Pilferer* drifted out upon the waves, its sails matching the soothing colors of the balmy sunset.

"Ye missed the lugger," Morvoren said, wrapping her arm around Trevik's back.

"I know. But I be more 'an 'appy to stay 'ome with ye tonight."

He pressed a kiss to the top of her head, and she leaned into him, taking a deep breath of the air around her.

Home. That was where she was. And that was where she would always remain.

EPILOGUE

*M*orvoren took Trevik's offered hand and followed him as they left their home and set off toward the beach. The warmth of the May sun incessantly pressed down upon them, but Morvoren couldn't be happier about the heat. It would make swimming in the sea all the more enjoyable.

They walked hand-in-hand down the pathway, their easy smiles continuing as they passed by the Cardys' home where Edern stood just outside.

"Headed out for a walk?" he asked, straight-lipped.

The tension between them tightened, as it always did when the Honeysetts and the Cardys spoke.

"Indeed," Trevik responded. "'Ave to take advantage o' this sunshine while we can."

The man nodded in silence, then his eyes settled on Morvoren. It had taken a great deal of time—eight months, in fact—for Edern to finally come around to the idea of Morvoren staying in Tristwick. Only in the last few weeks had he begun to finally acknowledge her in a way that didn't just involve scowls.

"Mrs. 'Oneysett," he finally greeted, tipping his cap to her. Then he turned away.

Morvoren smiled, knowing such an action had taken a great deal of pride-swallowing for the man. Poppy still hadn't forgiven Edern for his foolish behavior, but Morvoren couldn't fault the old man's superstitious ways. At least, not to a large degree.

Once they were past Edern, Morvoren glanced up slyly at her husband. "Why didn't ye tell 'im where we were really goin'?"

Trevik smirked. "'Cause I didn't wish for 'im to think ye still be a mermaid, causin' yet another disaster on me 'ands."

Morvoren laughed. "Wise man."

They continued along the pathway, passing by a few other families before the Bosankos stopped them.

"Enjoyin' your day, ye two?" Mr. Bosanko said, Charlie beside him, tossing rocks down the cliffside into the water.

"Absolutely," Trevik said.

Morvoren made to stop and speak more with the man, but Trevik pulled her along. Mr. Bosanko gave her a knowing look, then returned his attention to his son.

"A bit anxious, are ye?" Morvoren asked, peering up at Trevik.

He shrugged. "To 'ave ye alone for a moment? I s'pose."

She smiled up at him, her heart swirling with love for the man. They'd been married for a little over half a year, and still, warmth overcame her each time she thought of how greatly her life had improved—all thanks to Trevik.

She couldn't blame him for his anxiousness, however. Living with Poppy and Mrs. Honeysett—and having Trevik's schedule of fishing at night—made it extremely difficult for the two of them to receive any time together alone, but they'd found certain ways to work around it.

Namely, heading to the sea every spare moment they received.

"If one more person tries to stop us, I'll ignore 'em," Trevik said as they neared the cellars.

She smiled again, flattered that he so greatly wished to spend time with her.

She gave a contented sigh as they continued forward, resting her head on the side of his arm as they ambled toward the cobbled pathway down to the beach. "The mackerel 'ave been fine this year, 'aven't they?" she asked.

Trevik instantly shook his head. "No. No talk o' fish or work."

"Then what be we allowed to speak of? Your mother? Poppy?"

"Heaven forbid. No. Poppy ain't—"

"Morvoren!"

Trevik groaned. "I swear she knows the second we be alone together."

Morvoren patted his arm, then turned around to face Poppy, who sprinted toward them, waving a paper in her hand.

"Morvoren, I've somethin' to show ye!"

"Come, maybe she 'asn't seen us," Trevik said, tugging Morvoren forward.

She laughed. "She can 'ear ye right now!"

"I most certainly can," Poppy said with a condemning look at Trevik. Then her face brightened again as she looked at Morvoren. "I need to show ye somethin'."

The paper she'd waved in the air before was now held behind her back, and Morvoren narrowed her eyes. "What is it?"

Poppy hesitated, glancing at Trevik.

He grunted. "Oh, so I don't get to be privy to what ye 'ave to say?"

Morvoren reached up, placing a quick peck to his cheek, then urging him down the pathway. "Ye continue on. I'll be just a moment."

His grumbling continued as he moved forward, and Morvoren smiled before facing Poppy. "Now, tell me. What has gotten ye so excited?"

Poppy drew a deep breath, then pulled the paper—a correspondence—to her chest.

"It be from Lieutenant 'Arris," she whispered in a soft squeal. "'E's written to I!"

Morvoren's lips parted in surprise. "Well what did 'e say?"

She waited, as if for dramatic effect, then finally, she blurted out her response. "'E's asked me to wait for 'im!"

"What?" Morvoren breathed.

Poppy pumped her head up and down. "'E explained everythin'. That day I shared me feelin's with 'im on the beach?" Morvoren nodded before Poppy continued. "'E said 'e was afraid o' hurtin' I. But 'e says right 'ere…" She paused, finding the line before reading it aloud to Morvoren. "'I could not share my feelin's for ye, but when ye turn a year or two older, I 'ope to be able to tell ye just exactly 'ow I feel for ye. Wait for me, if ye wish to. For I'll be thinkin' of ye each day until I return.'"

She stopped, holding the letter to her chest and staring up at the sky with an airy sigh. "Ye see? And now I be seventeen, so I just be one step closer to sharin' 'is love."

Morvoren smiled, shaking her head. Months ago, she'd given Poppy the advice to behave in a way that she'd never have regrets. And now, it seemed Poppy was doing just that.

"I be that 'appy for ye, Popp," Morvoren said. "Now to wait 'til his ship returns."

"Oh, I know. I can' 'ardly fathom waitin' a day longer. I just…" Her words trailed off as she stared down at the letter again, clearly becoming distracted by his words.

"Poppy?"

She looked up in surprise, then a sheepish grin took hold of her features. "I be sorry. I just can't concentrate on anythin' right now." She glanced beyond Morvoren's shoulder.

"Oh, me brother be waitin' for ye still. Can we talk about it later?" She backed away, squealing again. "Oh, I just be so 'appy!"

Then she bounded back to the house, as if she were a four-year-old skipping to a tune instead of the grown young woman she was growing into.

Morvoren watched her for a moment, shaking her head in amusement before moving to catch up with her husband. Together, they continued down the pathway to the beach. The sea thrift were once again in blossom across the cliffside, waves of their small pink flowers quivering in the wind.

"What be all that about?" Trevik asked once she reached his side.

"Oh, nothin' really. Just Lieutenant Harris writin' to Poppy."

His brows lowered. "And what did 'e 'ave to say for 'imself?"

Morvoren knew Poppy wouldn't care if she shared the news with Trevik. In fact, she often told Morvoren to talk to her brother about matters she knew would upset him.

So with a certain degree of delicacy, she responded. "'E as good as shared the fact that 'e 'as feelin's for 'er, too."

They neared the water, but instead of Trevik admiring the beach, he looked down at Morvoren with a frown. "I don't like that."

She laughed. "Why not?"

"'Cause 'e be tied to the sea, that be why. Men can't easily leave such a thing behind…or women, for that matter."

She let him stew for a moment, his silence continuing until they neared the small rowboat they'd secured near the top of the beach.

"Come now, Trev," she said as his scowl remained. "Don't let this ruin our outin' together."

His frown grew. She smiled, holding his face between her hands and kissing him soundly. When she tried to pull back, his hand snaked through her hair and held her securely in place until she laughed, and their lips broke apart.

"It worked," she said. "Ye ain't frownin' any longer."

He smiled, leaning forward to kiss her again, but she swooped out of the way. "First, we need to get this boat into the water."

He sighed. "Ye know just what to do to get your way."

"What else do ye expect from a siren?" She winked, then she helped him heave the boat into the water.

Their conversation centered around their plans for the summer as they hopped into the rowboat and paddled out to the sea, then they both fell silent once they were surrounded by nothing but water, the land far behind them.

"Are ye ready?" she asked.

Trevik nodded, securing the oars and dropping the small anchor into the water before they both undressed—Morvoren to her shift and Trevik to his trousers. Then together, they jumped into the calm, steady sea.

Long ago, when Morvoren had been a child, she'd made a promise to herself that if she were to ever marry, she'd only do so if she could find a husband who'd allow her to still swim in the sea.

Well, not only had she found herself a husband who allowed it—she'd found one who encouraged it, one who joined her every moment he could. And she couldn't be more grateful.

She still couldn't believe how perfect her life had been since leaving St. Ives and her uncle behind. Despite her best fears, Uncle had remained away from Tristwick, and the last word she'd heard of him was that he'd taken his company back to Mevagissey—much to Morvoren's relief.

Now, she rarely thought of the man, and only ever in passing. Instead, her thoughts were filled with fish, family, Trevik, and the sea.

And what could be better than that?

Trevik watched his wife bob up and down in the water, grateful for the chance he had to spend these moments with her. Any time with Morvoren was time well spent, even though he always found it extremely difficult to be motivated to work afterwards.

He was only grateful she'd been so patient with him and his schedule. He'd suggested finding a new home for the both of them in Tristwick, but Morvoren had immediately protested.

"I can't leave me family now I finally have one," she'd said days before their wedding.

Though Trevik liked to complain about the lack of privacy, he was still grateful for the friendships Morvoren had forged with his family—now her family. It did his heart good to know that she wasn't alone any longer.

He also couldn't believe how well she'd taken to the life of a fisherman's wife. She pulled her weight and more at the cellars, and still, she had a smile on her face—proving to be a strength to him and his entire family. A strength he wasn't sure how they'd ever lived without.

"What are ye thinkin' about?" Morvoren asked, coming out of the water again and brushing her hair back from her brow as they slowly made their way back to the boat.

"Merely 'ow 'appy I be. And 'ow I 'ope ye be just as 'appy as I."

When they reached the boat, he held on one-handed as she wrapped her arms around his neck, fingers stroking the width of his bare shoulders.

"Ye know I'm happy, Trev. How could I not be, swimmin' in the sea with the love o' me life?"

He pulled her in for a kiss, then leaned back with narrowed eyes. "So ye'll still love me even if I end up smellin' like a fish?"

"If ye keep takin' these swims with me, ye'll smell like the sea instead."

"So that be why ye always bring me out 'ere."

She shook her head, her nose brushing past his. "No, I bring ye out 'ere so we can kiss without Poppy interruptin'."

He chuckled. "I can't complain 'bout that."

Then he took her lips with his again.

Before the two had joined in marriage, neither was sure what their future held—their story unfinished. But there, in the waves of Tristwick, with their hearts intertwined, their ending had finally been written.

And it was a glorious ending filled with the promise of a happy tomorrow. For what else could be expected of a fisherman and the mermaid he'd rescued from his net?

THE END

AUTHOR'S NOTE

I started my research for *In the Waves of Tristwick* a few years ago, and even still, I know I'm only skimming the surface of what there is to know about fishing in Cornwall in the 19th century. Below, I've outlined a few of the subjects I spent most of my time on while writing this book. I hope some of it will interest you, too!

For those of you who have not yet read one of my author's notes before, buckle up. I get long-winded when it comes to anything Cornish.

SEINERS vs DRIFTERS

Ever since I wrote about the Honeysetts in Behind the Light of Golowduyn, I knew I wanted to write their story, particularly a fisherman's story. I had no idea about the feud between the seining companies and the independent drifters (sometimes referred to as "drivers" or "drovers") until I began my research. At first, I waffled between which path to place Trevik on, but after only a few hours, I knew there could be no other life for Trevik but being a drifter.

Unlike all of Tristwick's beliefs, seiners weren't all terrible people, just like all drifters weren't good people. But it is true that the seining companies did receive special treatment with some of the laws during that time. This was because seiners were believed to be better for Cornwall because they brought in more fish than drifters could. However, as Trevik was apt to point out early on, years later, Cornwall would begin to see that the drifters' year-round fishing was far better for Cornwall's commerce than the seiners' seasonal schedule.

In 1818, the seiners far outnumbered drifters in Mevagissey— forty-four to six. Forty years later, however, there were only two seining companies left and more than sixty drifters.

The story Trevik mentioned in the beginning with Sir Percival St. John being served writs for fishing too close to the shore was, in actuality, true. Although I changed his name from St. Aubyn, and the incident took place more than a few years before the Regency Era.

What happened to Trevik's father was also based on history, at least in part. Many people were against fishing on the sabbath, so much so that they really did create a barricade around a boat, preventing it from bringing in the catch made on Sunday. Talk about being held accountable by an entire society!

FISHING

Fishing was one of the most difficult things I had to research for this book. Not only did it take weeks to try to figure out what kind of boat Trevik would use (a lugger, a gig, a driver?), I also had to figure out what fish was caught during which time of the year, how they caught said fish, how long the net was, how they tied and preserved the net, how many men would be aboard the lugger, how they rolled in the net, how they brought the fish in for processing, when the net was kept in the lugger and when it was brought into the cellars—and this was probably only half of what was required.

One of the first things I needed an answer to was why the drifters fished at night. Most research books didn't touch on this, as it seemed to be common knowledge for everyone else but myself. I eventually found a couple answers though. One, the pilchards moved lower to the seabed during the daytime, so the drifters' nets couldn't reach the pilchards at such depths. And two, the fish could see the nets drifting during the day, so they would avoid the nets altogether.

Once I finally found that answer, I moved on to the multiple practices of fishing aboard a three-masted lugger. I wanted to include everything I learned in the story, but my word count just wouldn't permit it. One of the things I had to omit was the fact that, on top of fishing for pilchards, the drifters also fished for hakes at the same time. Hakes can measure up to twelve pounds and have terrifying, sharp teeth. (Seriously, look them up. Stuff of nightmares, they are.) So the men had to use special hooks and fresh pilchards for bait. With his size of crew, Trevik would have brought up around six hundred hake and six thousand pilchards in one night. That's a whole lot of fish!

As mentioned in the story, with the return of peace to England, the fish—though fewer in catch than other years— brought in higher prices since the ports were opened. A hogshead of pilchards is about three thousand fish, depending on the size and type. During times of peace, a hogshead fetched one hundred and eight shillings, but in other years, the price could drop as low as thirty shillings.

CELLARS

As mentioned in the story, cellars were run in different ways, with attitudes, temperatures, work, and other factors contributing to the overall feel and mood. It was true, though, that the women would pass around a bottle of brandy to share, using it to keep up their energy throughout their long days.

In the east of Cornwall, the cellars were called Pilchard Palaces. Since Mr. Truscott started his fishing company in Mevagissey (which is slightly more east), this allowed Morvoren and her uncle the ability to use the very name in the west.

The work in the cellars was difficult, as we saw with Morvoren's first day. As mentioned, the train oil, or pilchard oil, that came from the pressed fish, was used for many different things, including lighting lamps, curing leather, removing rust from iron, and yes, even water-proofing decks. It could even be boiled together with other ingredients to be used as paint. From one hogshead of pilchards, the women could gather as much as two gallons of oil.

Many companies did end up selling their fish and oil abroad to other countries like Italy, but it took a great deal of money to hire someone to ship the pilchards across the sea. For Trevik, as well as many others, it made more financial sense for them to keep the fish or sell them closer to home.

MERMAIDS

From the moment I started reading about fishermen, I knew I wanted to add in a mermaid to the story. I'm just incredibly pleased that a mermaid became integral to the plot.

In my research, I found a large number of sea-maid stories from around Cornwall. The first one, the Mermaid of Zennor, is about a young man who fell in love with a mermaid after she sang in church. I was able to include this in *In the Waves of Tristwick* a couple of times, once with Trevik being completely captured by Morvoren's singing, and another by naming Morvoren's friend after the mermaid Zennor.

I also found facts to pull from the Mermaid of Lamorna—who would sing on the cliffsides and watch a storm roll in seven days later—and the Mermaid of Padstow, who was thought to have cursed a town with a sandbar after being left for dead by the man she'd rejected. I had so much fun finding different ways to include these in my story, even if they're all a little bit gruesome.

Another fun fact: the modern Cornish name Morvoren literally means sea maiden.

LANGUAGE

I did my best to write the Cornish dialect and accent, but one never realizes how difficult it is to write in an accent until one actually does it! Morvoren's was particularly difficult, as hers wasn't as strong as Trevik's. However, once she was around Trevik and his family, her accent came back much thicker. This is the same for my husband—his English accent is always present, but it sounds much stronger when he's around other British people.

I was also able to add in a few words I've read from a few sources as being unique to Cornwall, including Cornish piskies (not pixies), *palchy* (unhealthy), *docy* (charming), *gawky* (stupid person), and *mimsey* (minnow). Did you catch all of those in the story?

Another thing I was able to add in was the short prayer that was thought to have been said before meals in fishermen's homes. The beginning says, "Lord, make us able to eat what's on the table." And at the end of the meal, the following words were said: "The Lord be praised and our stomachs be aised."

Finally, I will say here, as it's a question I get asked frequently, Tristwick is not a real location, though I based it off of St. Isaac, Boscastle, and a few other coves I love. I make up all the names of the titles in my books (except *lowena*) to make them as unique as possible. Each location name I've created is usually combined with one or more Cornish words. *Trist* means sad in Cornish, whereas *wick* is simply similar to a few other Cornish location names. I chose *trist*, or sadness, because that is how Morvoren's story began. And when she least expected it, joy came after all the sorrow. Isn't that how it always is?

SONGS

Songs have always been important in Cornwall, even in the 19th century. I did a lot of research by reading songs written hundreds of years ago (and then some), in order to write my own. I was going to use authentic songs from the period, but I thought it would be fun to try to write my own. And it was!

The song that Trevik sings when Morvoren first finds him in the cellars tying the nets is the same song that I wrote for On the Shores of Tregalwen—Hannah and Thomas Causey's story. I loved being able to bring *Tykki Duw* (or butterfly) back in!

MISCELLANEOUS

Some soaps in the Regency Era did have lemon added to them. I looked at my options and chose lemon as the best option for Trevik. After all, what woman wouldn't want a man who smelled of lemons? In this day and age, it means that he's just been cleaning, right??

Finally, I always like to add in a bit of my own experience into each of my stories. When I was in Cornwall, we visited the beautiful Porthgwarra. I was hoping to see the crystal blue water there, but we arrived at low tide, so the beach and half the cobblestones were covered in thick seaweed—just like Poppy mentioned happening in Tristwick. And yes, it really did stink terribly!

CONCLUSION

Thank you so much for reading my story! I really hope you enjoyed it. If you did, consider writing a review here. I read every single one of my reviews wherever I can find them, as it helps me feel connected to those who love my books!

Feel free to also sign up for my newsletter here to never miss the latest news about my upcoming novels.

Lastly, my favorite places to be are Instagram and Facebook, so if you aren't following me yet, please do! I love to connect with readers as I share more about my stories.

I can't wait to virtually meet you!

Deborah

ACKNOWLEDGMENTS

Well. Well, well, well. I truly never thought I'd see the day where I'd finally be writing the acknowledgments to this book. I won't go into detail about how difficult writing this story has been for me. I will say though, that writing isn't easy. In fact, it's insanely difficult. It's a blessing and a curse—a trial as we slog through the words and a miracle when we finally write "The End." I truly couldn't live without writing, but sometimes I wonder how I actually survive from story to story. I'm only grateful that I do!

That being said, I couldn't do it without the support of so many friends and family members.

First, all you lovely bookstagrammers, book reviewers, and readers—you are one of the main reasons I write! Hearing your kind words about my stories, listening to you be as excited about my characters as I am—it's really a dream come true. First, Marilee (@marilee.loves.to.read), Lauren (@the-bookscript), Kristin (@herliterarytravels), Lindy (@read-inglindy), and Steph (@ink_and_page) thank you all so much for your support and kind words! They always buoy me up! Mandy (@probablybookinit), you've supported my Cornish Romance series for a looong time and I couldn't be more grateful for it. Tasha (@the_clean_read_book_club), thank you for binge-reading my books and for being such a force for goodness in the clean romance world! And finally, Ashlee (@bookswithnopictures), I hope you'll forgive me for my copious use of the word "core." Although, you basically asked for it…

Next, I need to thank my beta readers who push me to not be so dang lazy in my edits and who point out where and how I can improve my stories and my writing—Kasey Stockton (for giving me all the encouragement I could ever need, and then some), Arlem Hawks (for helping me see exactly where my work needs improvement and not being afraid to say it), Joanna Barker (for having the same sense of humor as me), and Martha Keyes (for always having my back with historical facts and grammar choices). Thank you all for being willing and able to read my work!

Thank you to Martha Keyes for giving me the single word of encouragement I needed to put Morvoren in her shift in the sea. You also backed me up on several historical details in this novel, none of which I can now remember, so…thanks, I guess?

A special thanks goes to my editors, Jenny and Emily. I'm so grateful to have had your support over the years. Thank you for helping my books to shine!

Thank you to my critique group, Jess Heileman, Martha Keyes, and Kasey Stockton. You ladies are the best of the best. I'm so blessed to have you all on this crazy writing journey.

I need to give a special shoutout to Kasey Stockton. How many times have you saved me from spiraling down into an endless abyss of darkness? I'm so grateful for you.

Thank you to my family who have been there for me through the trial this year has been. Your support and love has meant the world to me. Mom, Dad, Joanna, Patrick, John, and Hayley, thank you for always listening to me as I blabber on and on about things that make zero sense to you and still pretending that you know what I'm saying. Mom Joanna, Jen, and Chloe, thank you for always reading my stories and being the best supporters in the world!

I am so grateful to my Heavenly Father who has blessed me with the desire to write and share these stories with the world. My main desire and goal with my books is to spread His light and joy to this world, and I'm blessed that I have the opportunity to do that.

Thank you to my children for teaching me patience and long-suffering. (Haha.) Really though, you are my greatest joys and delights. I love being your mother.

Finally, as always, thank you to my husband, my British boy, my favie. This book was a slog to get through—for us both. No one knows but you and I the work that went into it, the tears, the heartache, the grief, the joy, the pain, the excitement. Thanks for not only sticking with me through it all, but for holding me up when I could no longer stand. I love you.

ABOUT THE AUTHOR

 Deborah M. Hathaway graduated from Utah State University with a BA in Creative Writing. As a young girl, she devoured Jane Austen's novels while watching and re-watching every adaptation of Pride & Prejudice she could, entirely captured by all things Regency and romance.

Throughout her early life, she wrote many short stories, poems, and essays, but it was not until after her marriage that she was finally able to complete her first romance novel, attributing the completion to her courtship with, and love of, her charming, English husband. Deborah finds her inspiration for her novels in her everyday experiences with her husband and children and during her travels to the United Kingdom, where she draws on the beauty of the country in such places as Ireland, Scotland, and her beloved Cornwall.

Made in United States
North Haven, CT
15 April 2022

18298194R00250